PRAISE FOR TAMARA THORNE & ALISTAIR CROSS

"*Mother* is about as disturbing as one can get. Thorne and Cross are seriously twisted individuals who know how to horrify and entertain at the same time."

— FANG-FREAKIN-TASTIC BOOK REVIEWS

"A great combination of strong characters that remind me of my V.C. Andrews characters, wonderful creepy twists, and a plot that will recall Mommie Dearest in an original take that shocks and delights at the same time. This is a full blown psychological thriller worth the investment of time and money."

— ANDREW NEIDERMAN, AUTHOR OF THE DEVIL'S ADVOCATE AND THE V.C. ANDREWS NOVELS

"*Mother* is a thriller in the truest sense of the word. What begins with a walk through a nice neighborhood in a nice town quickly becomes a chilling and unnerving descent into madness that is harder and harder to escape. Because I wear a fitness tracker I have scientific proof that the finale is a wild ride. Although I was curled up on the couch reading, *Mother* caused my heart rate to go up ten points! I'll never look at a neighborhood block party the same way."

— QL PEARCE, BESTSELLING AUTHOR OF SCARY STORIES FOR SLEEP-OVERS

Thorne and Cross bring the goods with THE CLIFFHOUSE HAUNTING, a clockwork mechanism of gothic chills designed to grab the reader by the scruff and never let go until the terrifying conclusion. Atmospheric, sexy, brooding, and brutal, the book manages to be simultaneously romantic and hardboiled. Highly recommended!

— JAY BONANSINGA, NEW YORK TIMES BESTSELLING AUTHOR OF THE WALKING DEAD BOOK SERIES

"In *The Ghosts of Ravencrest*, Tamara Thorne and Alistair Cross have created a world that is dark, opulent, and smoldering with the promise of scares and seduction. You'll be able to feel the slide of the satin sheets, taste the fizz of champagne, and hear the footsteps on the stairs."

— SYLVIA SHULTS, AUTHOR OF HUNTING DEMONS

In this classic-style gothic, young Belinda Moorland takes a job as governess for the children of Eric Manning, whose family mansion, Ravencrest, was reassembled stone by stone after crossing over from England. Now stalked by a bevy of quirky, shady characters ... the sinister estate and its naughty nightside hijinks take center stage in this expert tale of multi-generational evil - and love. *The Ghosts of Ravencrest* will chill you and make you hot and bothered at the same time. There's nothing like a stay in a California town created by Thorne and Cross.

— W.D. GAGLIANI, AUTHOR OF THE NICK LUPO SERIES

Alistair Cross' new novel THE CRIMSON CORSET ... is taut and elegantly written taking us into the realms where the erotic and the horrific meet. Reminiscent of the work of Sheridan Le Fanu (CARMILLA, UNCLE SILAS) in its hothouse, almost Victorian intensity, it tells a multi-leveled story of misalliance and mixed motives. The language is darkly lyrical, and the tale is compelling. Read it; you'll be glad you did."

— CHELSEA QUINN YARBRO, AUTHOR OF THE SAINT-GERMAIN CYCLE

"Tamara Thorne is the new wave of horror - her novels are fascinating rides into the heart of terror and mayhem."

— DOUGLAS CLEGG, NEW YORK TIMES BESTSELLING AUTHOR

Tamara Thorne has become one of those must-read horror writers. From her strong characters to her unique use of the supernatural, anything she writes entertains as much as it chills.

— HORROR WORLD

Think Mario Puzo meets Anne Rice ... Balance is what Thorne does best ... (*Candle Bay*) is a love story. A mob story. A family drama. A wise combination of creepy, thrilling, titillating, and good old vampire fun."

— MICHAEL SCHUTZ, DARKNESS DWELLS RADIO

FANG MEETS FANG

The vampires of Candle Bay and Crimson Cove come together for the Biting Man Festival in Eternity, California, to celebrate a centuries-old tradition that quickly turns murderous as they're faced with old enemies, uncontrolled bloodlust, and the unpredictable antics of a self-proclaimed vampire slayer who is hellbent on destroying them all.

> With Darling Girls, Thorne & Cross have united their brutal and sexy vampire sagas, conjuring a riot of vibrant characters all charging toward a clever, chilling conclusion of bloody mayhem and carnage."
>
> — MICHAEL SCHUTZ, AUTHOR OF EDGING

BOOKS BY THORNE & CROSS

The Vampires of Crimson Series

The Crimson Corset - Book 1

The Silver Dagger - Book 2

COMING SOON: The Black Wasp - Book 3

Darling Girls - Featuring the Vampires of Crimson Cove and Candle Bay

BOOKS By THORNE & CROSS

Darling Girls

Mother

The Cliffhouse Haunting

THE RAVENCREST SAGA

The Ghosts of Ravencrest - Book 1

The Witches of Ravencrest - Book 2

Exorcism - Book 3

Shadowland - Book 4 - Coming Soon

Non-Fiction

Five Nights In a Haunted Cabin

Books by Alistair Cross

The Angel Alejandro

Sleep, Savannah, Sleep

The Book of Strange Persuasions

Books by Tamara Thorne

Haunted

Moonfall

Candle Bay

Eternity

Thunder Road

The Sorority

The Forgotten

Bad Things

DARLING GIRLS

The Vampires of Candle Bay and Crimson Cove

TAMARA THORNE & ALISTAIR CROSS

ROCKFORD PUBLIC LIBRARY

Darling Girls © 2018 Tamara Thorne & Alistair Cross

All Rights Reserved

Glass Apple Press

First edition April, 2018

This book is for your personal device only. No part may be reproduced or transmitted in any form or by any means, graphic, electronic, or mechanical, including photocopying, recording, taping, or by any information storage or retrieval system, without written permission from the authors.

This book is a work of fiction. Names, characters, places and incidents either are products of the authors' imaginations or are used fictitiously. Any resemblance to actual persons, living or dead, events, or locales is entirely coincidental. All rights reserved.

Cover Design by Mike Rivera

❈ Created with Vellum

*Darling Girls is dedicated, with love,
to Johnnie Venezia,
for always being there.*

ACKNOWLEDGMENTS

Thanks to Q.L. Pearce for friendship and insights; Berlin Malcom at BAM Literature for all her hard work; Mike Rivera for his great art; Libba Campbell, the best editor in the world; and, of course, the Man in the Dark Hat, for the beautiful music, the great caviar, and the dark, dark night.

AUTHORS' NOTE

Dear Reader,

Since we began collaborating, we have always combined our worlds, freely using each other's characters and locations from singular works. We've enjoyed watching our fictional universe grow, and that's how the concept for **Darling Girls** was born. We've both previously written novels about vampires - **Candle Bay** (Thorne), and **The Crimson Corset** (Cross) - so it was only natural for our vampires to mingle. And that's what they do in **Darling Girls**.

Darling Girls takes place at the Biting Man Festival in the mysterious little California town of **Eternity** - where Tamara's novel of the same name is set. It's a new story about both vampire clans and includes many other characters we've met before in the Thorne & Cross universe. We like to think of **Darling Girls** as a companion, not a sequel, to the earlier novels.

With that in mind, here's all the history you need to know about the vampires of Candle Bay and Crimson Cove - and the books that precede **Darling Girls**:

Candle Bay - Shrouded in fog on a hillside high above an isolated California coastal town, The Candle Bay Hotel & Spa has been restored to its former glory by the mysterious Darling Family. Once again, it's filled with happy vacationers, but its seemingly all-American hosts hide a chilling, age-old family secret.

Assistant concierge Amanda Pearce is not only mesmerized by the picturesque hotel, but also by her handsome new boss, Stephen Darling, and a mysterious guest named Julian Valentyn. But the suspicious activities within the hotel - violent deaths, missing bodies, blood splattered on walls - fill her with terror and trepidation. Little does Amanda know that the Darlings are vampires and that a murderous vampiric vendetta has begun - and she's caught in the middle. As the bloody feud unfolds and her feelings for Stephen deepen, Amanda must face the greatest decision of her life: to die, or join the forever undead.

The Crimson Corset takes place in a tourist town just north of Candle Bay. In Crimson Cove, California, the night is no one's friend, for after sunset, the vampires of the village awaken to satisfy their wanton appetites. On one edge of town is The Crimson Corset, a notorious nightclub run by undead proprietor, Gretchen VanTreese, where patrons can slake their darkest thirsts. At the other end is Eudemonia, a health spa and retreat, owned and managed by Michael Ward - also undead. He, unlike Gretchen, believes in the peaceful coexistence of humans and vampires.

New to Crimson Cove is Cade Colter - a young man with a rare genetic trait that will break the uneasy centuries-old truce between Gretchen's side and Michael's. As Gretchen's plans are stymied by Michael and his Loyals, she realizes she's going to have to take a more cunning course if she wants to get her hands on - and her fangs into - Cade. So, she begins laying a sophisticated trap ... a trap that puts everyone around Cade in mortal danger.

Welcome to our world ... and happy reading,
Thorne & Cross
February 1, 2018

THE PLAYERS

THE PLAYERS
　　**Repeat Offenders (characters who have made appearances in other Thorne & Cross novels)

The Darlings
　　**STEPHEN DARLING, hotelier
　　**NATASHA DARLING, hotelier
　　**IVY DARLING, their sister
　　**LUCY DARLING, their sister
　　**IVOR DARLING, their brother
　　**ORI DARLING, their uncle
　　DAISY DARLING, their cousin

From Crimson Cove
　　**MICHAEL WARD, owner of Eudemonia
　　**WINTER, security
　　**CHYNNA, security
　　**ARNOLD (ARNIE) HOSS

In Candle Bay

**JULIAN VALENTYN/KELIU, proprietor of Valentyn Vineyards
**AMANDA PEARCE/TALAI, Stephen Darling's fiancee
LOIS TRINSKY, real-estate agent
NEIL TRINSKY, vampire hunter
ERIN WOODHOUSE, student
**EDDIE FORTUNE, radio deejay
NORMAN KEELER, prostitute
**FELIX FARQUHAR, Julian's assistant
BRUNO, Julian's guard
RANDY PETERS, owner of the Petting Zoo
KRISTOPHE, bouncer at the Petting Zoo
BOBBY BLACK, coffee shop owner
JIM BOTTOMS, night morgue attendant
**NETTIE GRUBEN, works at the Candle Bay Hotel and Spa

In Eternity
**ZACH TULLY, sheriff
**HARLAN KING, Mayor, banker
CURTIS PENROSE, shopkeeper
**ELVIS PRESLEY, shop owner
BILL KISSEL, owner of Bill's Pickles
FLOURNOY GREBBLE, employed at Kissel's Pickles
**MARTHA ANN and ELMER DIMPLES, owners of Dimples' Boarding House
KARL and KORA KOHLKOPF, attendees of Biting Man
**TIM HAPSCOMB, deputy
DIEGO VILLANUEVA/TUPA, temple priest
BELA LUGOSI, actor

Plastic Taffy
**RAMON, lead singer
**DAVY, guitar
**PAUL, guitar
**MICK, drummer

V-SEC (VAMPIRE SECURITY)
MARILYN BAKER
CECIL TREVOR
MATTHEW MOON

Pets
RENFIELD (RENNY), the Trinsky's Jack Russell Terrier
PRISCILLA, Elvis' Yorkie

Honorable Mentions

**THE TREASURE, Julian's father, King of Blood
  **KATE MCPHERSON-TULLY, Zach Tull's wife
  **JOSH MCPHERSON-TULLY, Zach Tully's son
SALLY STARKEY, desk Sergeant
ROY, gas station attendant in San Miguel
JOHN HENRY HOLLIDAY, doctor
CONNIE, police dispatcher
TOM BLACK, deputy
MILO, priest
CORNELIUS, priest
GALEN, priest
LUCIUS, priest
GORDON RENQUIST, Search & Rescue
TOMMY, Search & Rescue
WILLY WILKENS, Eternity resident
ARLEY MORDRED, Eternity resident
CREIGHTON DAVIES. Eternity resident
**GRETCHEN VANTREESE, from Crimson Cove
**JAZMINKA, from Crimson Cove
**SCYTHE, from Crimson Cove
**EMERIC, from Crimson Cove
HARRY DONALDSON, hotelier
**ABSINTHE, Chynna's tiger
**HYACINTHE, Chynna's tiger
ED WOOD

HOBART, Norman's college roommate
BOB TROTTER, jogger
**DILLY, head of Security under Ivor for at Candle Bay
OPAL MILLER, deceased local
ERNIE, daytime morgue attendant in Candle Bay
TINA, Neil's younger sister, attorney,
JACOB, Neil's younger brother,
**PHIL KATZ, from Eternity
**JINXY, Julian's former assistant
MISS FINCH, school teacher
**JIM MORRISON, from Eternity
**JEREMIAH JOHNSON, from Eternity
**AMBROSE BIERCE, former Mayor of Eternity
**AMELIA EARHART, postmistress of Eternity
**JACK THE RIPPER, from Eternity
BALDY, a boarder at Dimples
THE VALKYRIE, HUSBAND, STACEY, MARCY, diners at Bobby's Coffee Shop
**JACKSON COOP, Resident Eternity
CLARKE, unsuspecting driver

PROLOGUE

Ten Years Ago:

Two nights had passed since the Trueborn, Julian Valentyn, had subdued his father - the self-proclaimed "Treasure" - and returned him to his prison in the catacombs beneath the Candle Bay Hotel & Spa. Julian had yet to reappear and Amanda wondered if he ever would. While she hoped he would be successful in removing his father, the king of all vampires, from the world, she worried about what would happen when Julian returned. Would he leave her alone? *Is it too much to hope for?* She looked up at Stephen Darling, standing beside her on the balcony, and hoped he would be able to protect her from the Trueborn's desires.

Stephen smiled. "It's a beautiful night."

Amanda gazed at the sky. Stars twinkled between wisps of misty fog. "Yes, it is."

"I didn't think you would accept my invitation." Stephen spoke lightly, but she knew there was much more to what he said. He was referring to more than just the invitation to his suite.

"I've done a lot of thinking, Stephen."

"Indeed? About what?"

"You. Us. What you are, what I am."

He turned to her, placing a hand lightly on the swell of her hip. "And?"

She tingled at the touch, raising her face to brush his lips with hers. "I want you to kiss me."

He took her in his arms. She basked in his scent and his taste as their lips came together.

Bliss.

"Stephen," she murmured between kisses, "I love you."

His eyes were black pools shot with golden embers that seemed to glow in the dark. "I love you, Amanda." He bent to kiss her again.

"Ouch!"

"I'm so sorry." He pulled back, his hand over his mouth. "I didn't mean to hurt you."

Amanda tongued the dot of blood from her lower lip. "It's okay."

"No, it's not. I can't kiss you again until that infernal elixir is out of my system. My self-control is compromised."

Amanda pressed a finger to her bleeding lip, gathering droplets of blood on the tip. He stared at it and she felt him tremble. Her own body quivered with desire, with a need so powerful that she shivered. The ache inside of her sharpened and she pressed close to him.

Feeling his hard desire pushing against her, she put her hand to his mouth, urging him to taste the crimson drops that clung to her fingertip.

"No," he whispered. "I cannot."

"Taste me." She heard the desperation in her own words and didn't care. "Taste me. Taste my blood." Her fingers pressed harder against his lips.

He shook, nostrils flaring, eyes glinting amber as he took one finger into his mouth, sucking it, laving it with his tongue until she ground herself against him in her need.

Stephen licked the blood drops from her other fingers and he seemed to grow bigger, stronger, harder as he put his arms around her.

They kissed again, long and deep, their bodies twining together.

Amanda groaned.

A growl sounded from deep in Stephen's throat.

He broke the kiss. Amanda's hands clutched Stephen's hips, urging him closer, closer. She threw her head back and Stephen buried his face in her neck. "Do it," she whispered. Her hands were in his hair now. "Do it."

"No. I ... can't ..."

She felt the warmth of his tongue, the graze of fang.

"Yes. Do it. I want you to."

When the pain came, it was even more delicious, more gratifying, and more orgasmic than she'd ever dreamed.

1
PRESENT DAY: FITS AND STARTS

"This is *not* acceptable!" Amanda Darling threw the crystal wine glass against the wall. She glared at the hostess who'd set the goblet on the table in Satyrelli's, the posh mezzanine restaurant in the Candle Bay Hotel & Spa. "Do *not* get your ridiculous fat thumbprints on this glassware, you useless peon. This will come out of your paycheck!"

"But–" The girl looked near tears.

Amanda opened her mouth again.

Stephen sighed, glad the last customer had departed as he stared at the splinters of crystal littering the floor. "Amanda, darling, calm down."

"I will *not* calm down, Stephen! I have told them and told them and *told* them that there mustn't be smudges on the goddamned crystal! It's as if they go around pressing their dirty thumbs against every surface imaginable, just to spite *me*!"

"Now, now, Amanda, darling. You–"

"*Stop* calling me darling, Stephen. I never know if you're using a term of endearment, or using what should be my legal last name, just to taunt me! It's maddening!"

Stephen Darling stared at his fiancée, exasperated. He'd long ago given up asking himself where the girl he'd once loved had gone. He knew the answer to that: Vampirism did not suit Amanda. In fact, it had ruined her. *And it's my fault.* Now, he simply did what he could to keep her contained. But there were times - times like now - when he wanted to reach across the table and break that delicate neck he used to nuzzle. He gritted his teeth and managed a smile. "It's fine," he said to the hostess. "It's not coming out of your check. Don't worry about it."

"The hell it isn't!" Amanda's face purpled. If there was anything she hated more than being defied, it was being defied in front of an audience.

But Stephen took perverse joy in it. "Be silent." He spoke in the tone that warned Amanda that one more word was going to be the end of them.

Huffing, she sank into her seat and crossed her arms.

"Now, then." Stephen turned his head to the hostess, but kept his eyes firmly fixed on Amanda. "Leave us, and don't worry about the glass."

"Yes, sir, thank you." The girl practically ran to the kitchen.

Stephen planted a tight smile on his lips and spoke in dulcet tones. "If you ever, and I mean *ever*, cause another scene like that, you will not set foot in this restaurant, or this hotel, again. We will be finished."

She rolled her eyes. "Don't pretend you can threaten me! I'm more powerful than you and all your brothers and sisters, Stephen! We both know that."

"But *darling*, you have yet to obtain my hand in *vampiric* marriage." He paused. "So, until then, you really have no power at all, now, do you?"

Amanda's blue eyes - which used to melt his knees - now flashed red, and she patted her breast, as if trying to calm her heart. Stephen's fangs tingled with the need to tear into that porcelain flesh.

"None of this is yours, *darling*." He spat the words. "You'd be wise to remember that. Using 'Darling' as your surname is merely a convenience. Until we are married under vampiric law, you own nothing."

Her eyes softened. "Let's not quarrel, Stephen. You know how it upsets me when we quarrel." She touched his hand and when Stephen recoiled, her eyes filled with crocodile tears.

He knew just where to hit her - the threat of never marrying her had always worked - but he knew eventually he'd have to either make good on those threats, or go through with something he no longer wished to do. Guilt wasn't a good foundation for marriage, but the Biting Man Festival was fast approaching and he would have to decide soon.

Amanda dabbed at her eyes with a napkin. "You're so cruel to me, Stephen. Why are you so cruel?"

"Be silent." Stephen's lack of concern for her wounded feelings was apparently more than she could take. She threw her napkin on the table, shoved her chair back, and stood. "I'm going to change my clothes and go for a walk. Not that *you* care!"

A busboy turned to stare.

"Perhaps you should take some sustenance before you go, Amanda."

"Fuck off, Stephen Darling!"

More heads swiveled as Amanda flung her silver fur stole over her shoulder and stalked from the restaurant, head high, chin up, shoulders back. Though only five-foot-four, she cast a very long shadow. *Especially in those Ferragamo stilettos she purchased without checking the budget.*

Stephen was glad his sister, Natasha, hadn't witnessed the debacle. While it was true that Amanda was extremely powerful for a new vampire, that didn't stop Natasha from putting her in her place. But Natasha did it with far less tact than Stephen, which was a mixed blessing.

Stephen vowed Natasha wouldn't hear about this latest tantrum. She was up the coast in Crimson Cove, on a vacation at the luxurious health spa Eudemonia, where she was picking up some meditation tips from her old friend, Michael Ward.

Stephen wished he was with them right now. He needed some peace of his own.

∽

MICHAEL LIGHTLY DINGED the edge of a singing bowl, signaling the end of the session. "Did that help?"

Natasha sighed. "My shoulders are still as stiff as old bones." She rubbed one. "The yoga helps a bit, but I've got to master meditation - either that or I'll need to kill my brother's fiancée." She paused. "Now, *that* would relax me ..."

Michael chuckled. "It takes practice, but I've no doubt you can do it." He looked around the cozy room. Located underground in the heart of the Eudemonia spa building, all external sounds were cut off. The only noise was the soft babble of a gentle waterfall on one stone wall. Tropical plants grew nearby, hanging from the ceiling and thriving in huge terracotta and blue enameled pots on inlaid tile that edged the gleaming oak floor. Cushions - zabutons, zafus, and bolsters in rich blacks, browns, and tans, littered the floor. It was the next best thing to being outdoors. Ores and natural minerals were rich in the earth of Crimson Cove, but the richest were here at Eudemonia. The ores gave great balance and helped keep certain appetites under control. Appetites for bloodlust and rage. And Natasha Darling carried a lot of rage. He could see it in the set of her shoulders, the knots of her muscles. He could smell it, too - a musky, smoky scent that emanated from her pores.

Natasha sighed. "This is such a beautiful room. It's imbued with a sense of peace I've rarely felt. But it's as if I'm only sensing the tip of it. I envy you your serenity, Michael."

If she only knew the truth of it. Around Natasha, his tranquility was but a mask; she, like no one else, brought out the carnality of his nature. He cleared his throat. "Why don't we try a more natural approach?"

Natasha looked up at him. "How do you mean?"

Snared in that gaze, Michael was captivated again by the woman's unrelenting beauty. He shook the inappropriate thoughts away, as he had so many times. He took a seat on a zabuton beside her. "Why don't you tell me what's bothering you? There's plenty of time to practice technique, but perhaps for now, it might help to simply get your problems off your chest."

She didn't hesitate. "Michael, there's so much. As you well know, it's difficult running a hotel."

"Indeed. It is often a trial." He watched her roll her neck, working out stiffness. "Would it help if I massaged your shoulders?" The very words disturbed his inner calm in a way that both pleased and unnerved him.

"If you don't mind, that would be lovely." She locked her eyes - so dark they appeared black in the candlelight - on his and he quickly banished the emotion they elicited and regretted his celibacy for the first time in years.

He slid his zabuton behind her and steepled his fingers, willing energy and heat into his cool hands. Natasha, without a word, removed her thin black sweater then pulled her hair out of the way.

Controlling his breathing, he laid his hands on her shoulders and her breath quickened under his touch. He tried not to think about it. "Take a slow deep breath, Natasha. Fill your belly. Now release. Exhale until there is nothing left. Yes, that's right. Again."

Her skin, pale porcelain cut only by the black straps of her bra, was as he remembered from so long ago. He found himself breathing with her.

"Your hands are unnaturally warm," she murmured. "It's nice to feel such a touch."

He exhaled. "I can teach you the technique. It's a variation on what humans refer to as Reiki. It's a way of centering energy." He began kneading her shoulders, slowly, gently. "It feels as if your muscles are made of steel."

"They're always this way." She sighed. "You wouldn't think vampires would have such problems."

He chuckled as he pushed his fingers into the stiff muscles and kneaded. Listening to her groan of pleasure, he remembered other times he had touched her, so long ago. And pushed those thoughts away. "Tell me what's going on."

"Did you ever meet my brother's fiancée, Amanda Pearce? She's called herself Amanda Darling for quite some time now."

"The blonde with the pinched face?"

"The very one." Natasha's muscles stiffened.

"I only met her once, briefly, when Winter and I came down for Julian's party. I suppose it's been a decade since then."

"About that," Natasha said. "Julian wanted to celebrate the return of his father to imprisonment. It was a year after the whole incident. I was against it because Julian was responsible for our brief addiction to his elixir - and that led to Stephen's lack of control. He never would have turned Amanda if not for Julian's trickery."

"Your shoulders are stiffening again. Take a very deep breath. Hold. Exhale." He continued the massage. At that very same party, Natasha had told him the story of the Trueborn's miraculous elixir - how it allowed them to stay up and alert during the day, even endure sunlight, how it fed their appetites ... and almost ruined them with its addictive properties. "Another breath."

"So she'd only been turned for about a year when you met her." Natasha said. "She had yet to become the trial she is today."

"She grew into it?"

Natasha nodded. "I was never terribly fond of her but Stevie was smitten. So was Julian."

"Julian? Seriously?"

"Yes. He told us all sorts of stories - evidently, he knew her in his homeland, Euloa, millennia ago. He loved her and first tried to turn her in that incarnation. She killed herself before Transition. Later, she was reborn again in Euloa while his father still ruled, and that time, she was murdered by the paternal hand. After that, over the centuries every time she reincarnated and Julian found her, she took her own life."

"May I ask you something about Julian?"

"Anything."

"I knew he left Candle Bay to establish Valentyn Vineyards and the Chantrieri Winery, but he came with you to Crimson Cove last year to help with our problem with Gretchen VanTreese. May I assume you're no longer enemies?"

"We have quite a cordial relationship these days - and a mutual interest in keeping his father - the so-called 'Treasure' - from escaping the catacombs under the hotel." She paused. "You know Julian's taken the addictive qualities out of the elixir, don't you? He calls it Lixir and markets it worldwide. It's quite useful now."

"It is and while we do have a supply of Lixir and occasionally use it to heal bite marks rapidly, none of us have ingested it. It doesn't seem natural to me to do so."

"I understand - I rarely touch it myself. And I still don't utterly trust Julian, but I do feel sorry for him. He was crushed when Amanda rejected him in favor of my brother, a mere human vampire." She gave him a sardonic smile. "So was I."

Michael nodded. "So what happened this time?" He worked on a knot near her spine. "She's been vampiric over a decade but hasn't killed herself. Why? That sounds rather out of character."

"This time, she likes it. Perhaps because she chose Stevie over Julian, I don't know. But, Michael ..."

"What?"

"She's strong. Too strong. It's frightening how strong she is."

"How can that be? She's nothing but a baby vamp."

Natasha shook her head. "I don't know. I really don't. But I worry about it. She's become surer of herself, more uncompromising. Stevie tries to keep her in line, but she becomes more difficult to control with each passing year."

"This must be very frustrating for you, Natasha."

Her laugh was harsh. "That's an understatement. And now the Biting Man Festival is coming up. Several years ago, Stevie promised her they would marry at this festival. You know, do the whole traditional vampiric ceremony."

"And he's going through with it?"

"I don't know. He feels guilty for turning her. I think it's possible he'll marry her, but I hope not. Once he does, she becomes a real Darling. Legally one of us." She paused. "I love my brother - you know that - and I would do anything for him, but ... this. I dearly hope he finds the courage to end this travesty."

Michael heard fury rising behind her voice and spoke mildly. "Do you think she wants to take possession of your hotel?"

"I ... yes. How did you know?"

"Greed is at the core of everything negative in this world."

Natasha turned to look at him, her dark eyes troubled. "She'll want control of the hotel, our other business interests, and our entire family. That's why I can't relax. If she gets the chance to make that happen, we're in for a world of grief."

Michael studied her. "Why don't you talk to Stephen as a family? You can't stand back and allow him to destroy what you have. It doesn't sound like he really wants to marry her - your support may help him break the engagement."

"You're right, but one of the reasons our family has gotten along so well all these centuries is that we - Uncle Ori, Stevie, Ivor, and I - respect each other's personal decisions even when we disagree with them. Even the twins abide by that rule. We try never to tell one another what to do."

"Hopefully, Stephen will come to his senses on his own. If not, I advise you to forgo your rule and speak with him about it - all of you, if necessary. Your family's happiness is at stake. As is your business and your fortune."

"And that brings us back to why I'm here. I intend to have a serious talk with Stevie before the festival, but I'm afraid I'll lose my temper. So, Michael, teach me how to remain calm so that I can do this right." Her smile was razor-thin.

"I'll do my best. For that matter, I am willing to help you talk with Stephen and your family - to act as what your Uncle Ori would call *consigliere*."

Natasha laughed. "I may take you up on that. Uncle Ori would certainly approve."

He watched her stretch and forced his thoughts to remain pure. "So, are *you* going to Biting Man?"

"I have so many duties at the hotel ..."

"It would do you good to get away. To see old friends. And old enemies. Remember our run-in with the Kohlkopf clan?"

"That family of clowns?" Natasha laughed. "*They're* going to be there?"

"So I've heard."

"It would be worth going just to see what they're up to these days." She pulled her sweater back over her head, smoothed her glossy dark hair with her fingers. "The twins are going. It's all they can talk about. And of course, Amanda assumes she and Stephen are going. I think he's looking for a way out of it. I hope."

"By telling Amanda he won't marry her?"

Natasha nodded. "He hates confrontation and, believe me, it's going to get ugly when - if - he tells her no."

"All the more reason for you to speak with your brother. It sounds as if he wants out - you can help him with that." He stretched. "Your going to Biting Man might help keep the Amanda problem in check, as well."

"That's a very good point. Are you going?"

"My people are trying to talk me into it. Winter is attending. He's hell-bent on taking me along, as is Chynna. I'm just not sure I should leave. You know, after what happened at the Crimson Corset ..."

"It's been months, Michael. I think if Gretchen's cronies were going to come back, they would have by now." She paused. "I know you lost some good people. Is that why you're hesitant to leave? Are you short on guards?"

Michael sighed. "It isn't that. It's just ..."

"Are you worried Gretchen's lieutenants will come back?"

Jazminka and Scythe, two of Gretchen's finest and deadliest, had disappeared without a trace. Still, that wasn't what worried him. "It's Emeric," he said. "There's been no sign of him since that night. Gretchen's goons, we can handle. But Emeric ..."

"You don't think he'll come back for the gifted young human Gretchen was after, do you?"

"Doubtful. I suspect Emeric has bigger fish to fry."

Natasha chuckled.

"What is it?"

"Look at us," she said. "We're making the same argument. We both want to go, and are trying to talk ourselves out of it for reasons that - let's be honest - aren't terribly valid."

Michael nodded, though he wasn't sure he agreed. It had been many decades since he'd attended a Biting Man, and thought that this - the big centennial celebration - might be worth the trip. "Let's make a deal. I'll go if you go, and we'll make a pact to leave these burdens behind us. It's not as if they won't be waiting for us when we get back. What do you say? Deal?"

"Deal." She touched his hand, and a thrill shot through him. "I'm glad you *can* leave your burdens here. Amanda - my biggest burden - is looking to get married *at* the festival. Your point about my going to keep an eye on things is very well taken."

"If it comes to it, perhaps we can find a way to put an end to your problem." He raised an eyebrow.

"An idea worth considering." She smiled. "Ah, Michael. I miss the old days when life was easier and you weren't celibate. *That* was truly relaxing."

"Indeed." He smiled and kissed her forehead. "Indeed."

2
BUMPS IN THE NIGHT

Coastal Eddie Fortune stared at the blond woman - barely more than a girl - as she strolled toward the KNDL van. He was parked on the boardwalk near the entrance to the amphitheater where Plastic Taffy - more of a middle-aged man band than a boy band now - was playing. And his number one fan, Neil Trinsky, wouldn't leave him alone.

Neil, whose Axe Body Spray overpowered the scents of hot dogs, popcorn, and cotton candy wafting from the midway, stared at Eddie with the intensity of a Mormon on a mission as he waited for a reply. "It's like a really big deal this year, right?" He bit into a huge dill pickle he'd bought on the boardwalk.

"Not sure what you're talking about," Eddie lied. There was something familiar about the young woman dressed in black. He hoped she'd come over. She might distract Neil the Vampire Hunter from his quest to obtain knowledge Eddie didn't possess.

"Did they threaten you?" Neil bent close. Although he was handsome, the mixture of breath freshener and the pickle vinegar was nauseating.

"Did who threaten me?"

"The Vampire Council! I know you know all about Biting Man."

"Neil, Biting Man is nothing but a pun - and a bad one - on Burning Man."

"But you said-"

"Neil, I say a lot of things on the radio. I'm an entertainer. You'd be wise to remember that." The girl was only twenty feet away and suddenly, Eddie made the connection. She was from the Candle Bay Hotel. *Amanda*. He'd last seen her right here on a very foggy night over a decade ago. *She hasn't changed a bit.*

"You lied about the Vampire Council?"

Eddie had made up the Vampire Council to cover up more important things, like the location of Biting Man. He ignored Neil and waved. "Amanda!"

Her head swiveled and she stared at him then veered his way, a red smile on her lips. She walked up to his table and fiddled with a KNDL decal as she stared at Neil, nose wrinkling.

Neil withered a little and continued to stink. "H-hi."

"Go home and wash that cheap canned cologne off before you even *think* about talking to me."

Eddie hid a grin. "Neil, I'll see you around, okay?"

Neil's eyes narrowed as he looked from Eddie to Amanda's breasts. "See you, Eddie." He licked his lips, winked, then turned and sauntered back toward the midway.

"Coastal Eddie," Amanda said. "You're a lot grayer than the last time I saw you. Stressful life?"

"Occasionally," he said. "But I'm getting up there - I'm supposed to have gray hair. You, however, look as young as you did a decade ago. You must be thirty by now. What's your secret?"

Amanda laughed. "Wouldn't you like to know?"

"I remember that night you came by - I was set up right here and the same band was playing."

"A girl asked you to sign her breast."

"That happens so often, I can't say I remember it. But I recall that it was very foggy. You'd told me you'd just started working at the hotel. I was worried about you."

"That was a waste of worry."

Her voice was so icy that he stiffened. "I'm glad you survived." He spoke slowly. She was beautiful, dressed in clingy black pants, and a scoop-necked tank that revealed the tops of small, perfect breasts under a studded leather jacket. Her blond hair floated in the ocean breeze, gossamer silk. In the distance behind her, the lights of the Ferris wheel twinkled and roller coaster cars whooshed on the rails. The old carousel began turning and the calliope wheezed to life, playing a portion of Saint-Saëns' *Danse Macabre*. It felt like an omen as he studied her skin, so pale it was nearly translucent, her eyes, so blue and piercing.

"Are you still working at the hotel?"

"I am." She picked up a KNDL-embossed pen.

"It's all free swag. Take whatever you like while you can. When the concert lets out it'll disappear in a heartbeat."

She laughed and put the tip of the pen to her lips, watching him.

He didn't take the bait. "You must have worked your way up from concierge by now."

She raised an eyebrow. "You could say that."

"Day manager?"

"I hooked up with Stephen Darling. I'm part of the family." She bent closer, giving him an eyeful of cleavage and slick red lips. "I would've thought you'd have figured that out by now."

"That you hooked up with Stephen?"

"No, that I'm one of the people you warned me about." She reached out and ran a finger down his cheek then tugged his short salt and pepper goatee. "Or are you getting senile in your old age?" Her blue eyes flashed red for an instant, like a Siamese cat hunting in the dark.

He gripped the vial of holy water he'd taken from his watch pocket. "I've given up all that conspiracy stuff." He glanced around but they were alone. Too alone for his peace of mind.

"Don't lie, Eddie. I listen to the radio. You not only haven't given up, you're syndicated. Everybody hears you, not just the peasants in Candle Bay."

He shrugged. "Guess I forgot."

"I love your Vampire Council stories. They'd make a good superhero movie."

"My, what big ears you have."

She bent and kissed his forehead then stared at him with those hypnotic eyes. "I'm hungry. Think there's anything good to eat around here?"

Keeping his hand under the table, he twisted the cap off the vial, hoping he wouldn't have to find out if holy water worked on the Darling clan. He'd heard it did on the Crimson Cove vampires, but that didn't necessarily mean the Darlings could be repelled by it. *Especially this one.* Amanda gave off something that the other Darlings didn't. While they were obviously - to him anyway - vampires, they were controlled and civil, never showing their vampiric nature. He was afraid of being hypnotized by them, but was pretty sure there was no reason to worry about being bitten - the Darlings wouldn't have lasted here for decades as hoteliers if they indulged in such behavior. But in Amanda he sensed something darker, something dangerous and uncontrolled.

"The boardwalk concessions are in the other direction, back toward the rides," Eddie told her. "There's nothing much beyond my van. Just darkness and the beach." He tensed as she ran her hand over his cheek. In the distance, Plastic Taffy stopped playing and the crowd went wild. He glanced at his watch. "The concert is about to let out. I'd hit that hot dog stand before it gets crowded if I were you." He began to raise the holy water.

She looked toward the amphitheater and shrugged, reached out and tugged his beard once more, then sauntered off into the darkness.

Eddie exhaled. His hands were shaking and a few drops of holy water slopped on the table as he put the cap back on. On KNDL, *Hotel California*, the live version, was ending. He pulled on his headset.

"The stars and moon are brilliant tonight, my friends. They stand out in the darkness, beacons to lead you to safety. Jack-the-Ripper-fog is expected to return tomorrow night, dear listeners, so follow the beacons while you can." He shivered, bathed in déjà vu.

"It's the dead of night here at the amphitheater by the Candle Bay Midway. The coaster is riding the rails, the Octopus is flailing passengers from its arms, and the Plastic Taffy concert is letting out. Stay tuned for interviews with Paul, Davy, Mick, and Ramon. We'll find out how they've been doing and what they're up to. But first, how about some good old-fashioned *Radar Love?*"

The music started and Eddie glanced toward the amphitheater. The lights were up and people were streaming out. He'd never been so happy to see a crowd.

∼

Stephen Darling stood on the balcony, clothed in night and thin, misty fog. Years ago, when he'd proposed to Amanda, he'd never anticipated what she would become. *Never.*

He'd been a fool, a smitten fool, so in love he couldn't think straight. Of course, Julian's elixir had fogged his brain, but the effects had been temporary, lasting only a few weeks. After that it was all on him.

The first year or two with Amanda had been heavenly. They were truly in love and doted on one another, sharing bottles of AB Negative on their weekly anniversaries, taking long walks on the beach in the moonlit darkness. They'd been the best years he'd had in a very long while.

A foghorn sounded out on Candle Point, low and mournful. He could just make out the flashing beacon on the lighthouse, something the fog rarely allowed. Amanda had been an adept, fitting into vampire culture with an ease and serenity that amazed him. And she'd learned the tricks of "invisibility" and hypnosis faster than he'd ever seen a baby vamp learn. Her physical strength astounded him - it was as if she'd been a vampire for a century or more. He'd wanted to ask Julian Valentyn if he knew why this might be, but didn't dare: He knew Julian was heartbroken that his long-lost love had rejected him, and that meant he might be angry as well. The Trueborn had left the premises quickly after Amanda had chosen Stephen, and when he did visit, he studiously avoided them both.

Things had been good for a while, then Amanda's personality gradually changed. Vampirism and Amanda's DNA just didn't mix. *Or perhaps mixed too well.* He'd heard it happened occasionally. He thought of the taste of her blood, which was unlike anything else he'd ever experienced. *Perhaps that has something to do with it.*

The decision to turn Amanda was something Stephen had had to live with for more than a decade. If he married her, he'd live with it the rest of his life - and a very long life it would be. *Perhaps marrying her is the right thing to do,* said one half of him. It seemed reasonable. Someone needed to take care of her - she wasn't fit for society and he felt responsible. But the other half of him rebelled against the idea - was repulsed by it, in fact. He couldn't imagine an eternity with Amanda. *That is the very definition of Hell. It would be better to be dead.*

He sighed and stared out into the night knowing, in the deepest recesses of his heart, what he must do, for his sake as well as his family's: He needed to let go of his guilt. He needed to let go of Amanda. It wasn't fair to her that he kept her hanging onto the hope of marriage. He didn't love her. *And she doesn't love me. She's using me for her own purposes.* Not only that, he was letting his family down. He knew none of them approved, but even Natasha tried not to interfere.

Nothing good could come of marrying Amanda, and he knew it. But how to tell her? How to send her away without infuriating her and igniting her need for vengeance? That was the part that set his stomach spinning, his head aching. He knew she wouldn't take it well - that there would be drama. Drama and disaster, two things the Darlings scrupulously avoided. It was how they'd survived for so many centuries.

He stared out into the night, wondering where she was and what she was doing. The possibilities chilled him.

~

THOUGH THE RAVAGES of his addiction were beginning to show themselves in the gauntness of his face, the dark hollows under his eyes, and the sallow color of his skin, Norman Keeler still looked good enough to make plenty of money. The surfer-look attracted johns like nothing else.

Not so long ago, he'd been a student at Cal Poly SLO, an engineering student who hated his classes. They weren't like high school;

there was no one-on-one with instructors, just big lecture halls and labs and he couldn't concentrate - it was all too big and boring.

His grades began to fall along with his interest in graduating, then his fate was sealed at a party one night when Hobart, his roommate, brought him a taste of heroin. Then another. Soon, he was skipping classes to work a second part-time job at a burger joint to cover his burgeoning habit. When his addiction hit two hundred dollars a day, he quit school and turned his first trick - a guy Hobart had met at The Petting Zoo in Candle Bay.

It turned out Norman was good at blow jobs - he didn't love it, but that didn't matter, because heroin was a demanding mistress and he did love her. He became a regular at The Petting Zoo, and picked up tricks for many months before he got ousted for a lack of discretion. Since then, he had found customers of a different sort on the street.

Sometimes it was the street the Petting Zoo was on, but the bar's bouncer, Kristophe, sent him such dirty looks when he passed by that he withered under his gaze.

The boardwalk was better. He could always find a few customers there and tonight had been a good one - Plastic Taffy always attracted a lot of closeted men, his primary customers now. They couldn't admit what they liked to their wives and friends, but Norman always knew what they wanted. They didn't have to tell him.

He'd just serviced his last john of the night in the amphitheater lavatory. The guy had a bad toupee and worse breath, but a big wad of cash. He'd paid so well for a BJ and a prostate tickle that Norman wouldn't need to work tomorrow.

He walked past Coastal Eddie's van and headed down the sidewalk toward the North Pier, knowing that, sometimes, Plastic Taffy went out there to drink after the show. Norman decided that tonight, he'd see if he could run into them, maybe share a beer if he was lucky. He loved their music and wanted to tell them so.

Occasionally, patches of fog obscured his view, but it wasn't a bad walk. It was quiet - hardly anyone ever wandered a half mile from the midway. He tasted salt spray on his tongue and breathed in the scent of the sea, filling his lungs, feeling alive. He could just see the white foam tipping the crashing waves across the beach and nearly took off his shoes to get his feet wet.

But the pier loomed so he took the steps up and stood on the wooden planks, leaning on the railing, watching the waves, wondering if he should go home, get some help, and maybe go back to school for something more interesting than the math and physics of engineering. Low in the sky, the half-moon encouraged him.

But the very thought of going home made him want another hit.

That's when he heard something - *clack clack clack* - behind the waves. He turned toward the boardwalk and peered into the night.

A girl in high heels - *clack clack clack* - was approaching. She passed under a sodium lamp and he could see her tight pants, her white cleavage, her blond hair. Her red lips. He hadn't been with a girl in a long time. *Too long.* He wondered if she was looking to hook up. A woman would be a welcome change.

He watched her approach, saw her see him. He didn't want to scare her, so he waved.

She waved back.

And smiled.

∽

THE BOY-WHORE'S body went limp, the blood ceased to flow, and Amanda withdrew her fangs. The young male hadn't been very filling, though the faint hint of heroin in his blood was a kick. She looked at him, at the skateboard sticking out of his knapsack, at his skin-tight jeans, his loose blue tank top and sandals. His eyes were watery green, his hair a blond shock of surfer-boy bangs swooping across his forehead. He was handsome for a drug addict. She preferred cleaner blood most of the time, but now and then an addict's blood was just what she craved. Like tonight.

She grinned. *Stephen would never approve! That son of a bitch!* She couldn't get her mind off him, even with a belly full of fresh blood. *His threats are getting old.* But what could she do? If he didn't marry her, she would have nothing. She had a backup plan, of course - she always had a backup plan - but she preferred not to use it. *And it might be difficult to execute.* The best thing that could happen was for Stephen Darling to stop being such an utter child and just marry her. *Like he promised he would! Prick!*

She kicked the corpse that lay crumpled at her feet, enjoying the dull sound of her toe connecting with dead meat. She kicked again, again, and again, aiming for the chest. When she heard the sigh of the last bit of air escape, she shoved the body over the pier where it splashed into the water.

She decided to head home. *I'll give Stephen a long deep kiss - and let him taste the dead surfer boy on my lips.* She knew Stephen blamed himself for her behavior, and she enjoyed rubbing his nose in it. *He's such a bleeding heart. Such a ... weakling.*

Amanda left the dark pier at the north end of Candle Bay just as a van pulled up. She stood in the shadows as doors opened and raucous male voices, half-drunk, echoed among the patches of low fog. "Man, I hate this bubble-gum shit," one voice slurred. "And we gotta do it again tomorrow," another bemoaned.

It's them. She moved closer to see the van. It was yellow, coated in a wrap showing guitars and drums and musical notes. In the middle of it all, in pink day-glow letters, were the words, "Plastic Taffy."

Amanda reached into her push up bra and adjusted herself for maximum impact then stepped out of the shadows and strutted toward the band. They were tossing empty beer cans at a dead seagull.

"Hello, boys!" she called. "Miss me?"

They faced her, and one by one, grinned.

"Hey!" said Ramon, the lead singer. "It's the kinky chick." He nudged Mick, the drummer.

"You come back to give us some more of those sweet kisses of yours?" asked Davy.

Amanda smirked. "I know what you boys like."

"You can give me one of your hickies any time, lady," said Paul, sliding the van door open and gesturing to Amanda.

She climbed in, a smile on her lips. This would be bite number three for each of them - and that meant good times. Now, she just needed to get through the sex. Luckily, even with all four of them, it wouldn't last long.

3

THE SMELL OF SUCCESS

Lois Trinsky looked at the dirty clothes strewn across her son's room and sighed. The stink of the place curdled her stomach. She held her breath and began gathering things up - dirty shirts, socks, and underwear, all hosed down in bad cologne. And she didn't even know where to begin dealing with the rest of the mess.

As far as she knew, there was nothing that could effectively remove the globs of chewing gum from the carpet, and nothing but a new paint job would cover the places on the walls where he'd obviously been finger painting in what looked like ... *blood?* She didn't even want to think about that. She kept her eyes lowered, ignoring the stacks of moldy dishes and the sea of comic books, many of which were stuck to the floor by some mysterious adhesive.

Lois toed a half-eaten dill pickle. She didn't know where Neil had gotten his slothful ways. *Did I neglect him? Maybe it's because I was so busy working all those years. Or maybe if he'd had a father to guide him, he'd be a little more ... balanced.* But Lois didn't think it was any of those things. Not really. Her other two children were fine: Tina, 28, was an attorney and Jacob, 23, was working on his doctorate - and they grew up in the same house. The simple truth was this: Neil was born without ambition or drive. The filth he lived in was just a symptom of his character. His idea of success was scoring tickets to Comic Con. *Well, at least he keeps his body clean.* He'd always been impeccable – if not obsessive – about that.

She'd tried for many years to get to the root of her son's problems and show him a more constructive way of life – Neil had been in therapy at least a dozen times and with each psychiatrist, hypnotherapist, family counselor, psychologist, herbal treatment specialist, and even several sessions of good old-fashioned wilderness therapy, he'd only grown to resent her more. And then there were the myriad diagnoses and pills that followed. Prozac when he was diagnosed as depressed. Xanax when one doctor diagnosed him with generalized anxiety disorder. Ritalin, more than once, when she was told her son had ADHD. Lithium and Topamax on the multiple occasions he was diagnosed as bipolar back when being bipolar was all the rage. She'd even tried getting him involved in church functions once – a mistake she hadn't made twice. Exposure to spirituality seemed only to infuriate her son.

And she'd long ago given up involving him in sports of any kind – he simply wasn't interested. Thinking perhaps she'd been gifted with one of those misunderstood musical geniuses she'd heard so much about, she'd gotten him piano lessons. Those didn't take, so she bought him a guitar and lessons. Trumpet, clarinet, and even drums – Neil wasn't the least interested in any of them. Baseball bats, soccer balls, volleyballs, tennis rackets ... they were all promptly ignored and shoved aside.

There were only two things Lois had ever bought for her son that he'd taken any interest in: exercise equipment and his computer. He used both every day, all day in fact, like some kind of religious practice. Aside from those, there was only one other thing Neil had any interest in besides girls: vampires.

The vampire obsession began when he was about twelve. Unlike his previous fixation with all things *Star Wars*, his preoccupation with the undead had never died. Even now, his walls were a hodgepodge of posters featuring the creatures in various states of defeat: vampires with stakes in their hearts, vampires bursting into flames at the sight of silver crosses, vampires who'd been beheaded, vampires melting and smoldering as they were drenched in what Lois assumed was holy water. The ceiling was reserved for posters of Sarah Michelle Gellar as *Buffy the Vampire Slayer*. She had long been his one true love.

Sex, vampires, weights, television, comic books, and his computer. Beyond those, Lois' son was a non-entity, and this filled her with sadness and, she hated to admit, shame. She couldn't help thinking he had some potential - that one day, he'd find something that called to him, something worthwhile that would fulfill him and make him into a productive member of society. But at thirty-two years of age, the possibility of that happening was pretty slim.

And she knew she did him no favors cleaning up after him. She'd tried to stop, really she had. She'd told herself over and over that if she didn't clean up after him, he'd eventually be forced to take care of it himself. The trouble was, that wasn't true. It had been nearly six weeks since she'd touched his laundry, made his bed, or tidied his room, and now it had gotten so bad that the smells - rotting food, sweaty bed sheets, soiled clothes, and Neil's reprehensible body spray - had begun creeping upstairs and into the rest of the house.

Resigned, Lois had struck a deal with her son: If he'd just go scrub off all that cologne, she would start cleaning his room. He'd agreed and pried himself away from his computer, and here she was. Again.

Lois sighed and left her son's bedroom, making her way toward the washing machine where she'd begin the first of what would undoubtedly be a dozen loads of laundry. Again.

∽

NEIL TRINSKY RUBBED Axe Body Wash - *Dark Temptation* - over his perfect torso and six-pack abs. Hot water spat in his face as he scrubbed down. It felt great.

Mom had toughened up about cleaning his room since he'd turned thirty - that was when he'd promised to move out of his basement apartment - which was really just his old room but, well ...

"She needs me," he sang to the tune of Olivia Neutron-Bomb's *I*

Honestly Love You. "She honestly ne-eeeds me. She can't do anything without me ..."

And it was true. "Who takes the trash out?" he asked the shower. "I do! Who mows the lawn? I do!" He cleaned his pits and shaved them. He didn't need body hair - it only trapped the funk. And it stopped the dog from trying to yank out the sweaty pit pubes. Renfield always went nuts for Neil's pits. "God, dogs are gross. Renfield, you out there?"

The chunky Jack Russell terrier whimpered from his station on Neil's discarded clothing behind the bathroom door. Neil peeked out of the shower - as expected, Renfield was nose-deep in his shirt's well-perfumed pits. "Gross! You're fucking gross!" If there was a God - *Yeah, right,* Neil thought - he couldn't figure out why He'd created dogs. *Except to irritate me!* But Neil knew that, as surely as there was no Tooth Fairy or Santa Claus, there was no God either.

Neil poured shampoo into his wavy black hair. It was pretty long now and the girls he'd met online liked it that way. He kept it in a ponytail when he wasn't on Skype, but when he wanted to impress the ladies, he let it flow over his shoulders so he looked like a guy from a romance novel. He'd even considered ordering a kilt and having some pictures taken so he could really wow the women of the internet. "I've got the legs for it," he sang to the shower head. "Oh, baby, have I got the legs for it. And the cutest little tush in town!" He shook it and grabbed the hand-held shower head and pulled it down like a microphone, letting out a shriek worthy of David Lee Roth in his prime. "Yeah, baby, I have GOT THE GOODS!" Another shriek.

Renfield whimpered. Mom knocked on the door. "Is everything all right, Neil?"

He doo-bee-dooed into the water then shrieked again, "Oh, baby! Everything's all right! It's outta-sight!"

Mom left, but Renfield started howling.

"Shut up, dog!" he ordered.

Renfield howled louder.

Mom was back. Of course. "Neil, what are you doing to that dog in there?"

I'm fucking him up the ass! "Nothing, Mom. He just doesn't appreciate good music when he hears it." Neil shut off the faucet and carefully left the shower head hanging in the water over the drain that was clogged with the body hair he'd shaved off. He smiled. *What would she do without me to give purpose to her life?*

Stepping out, he opened the bathroom door for Renfield then wrapped one towel around his luxurious locks and another around his chiseled body. He used a third towel to wipe condensation off the mirrors then dropped all three on the floor and started posing, admiring the tight, lean definition of his core, the chiseled look of his biceps and triceps. The strong cleft chin and arched eyebrows that all the girls commented on. A couple of them said he looked like Ian Somerhalder. He hated the actor because he prostituted himself by playing a disgusting dirty bloodsucker on *The Vampire Diaries*, but he had to admit that Somerhalder was almost as good-looking as him. *Almost.*

Neil flexed his pecs. The light was perfect. He looked around for his phone to snap a selfie, but he'd left it downstairs in his room. He considered calling Mom to bring it to him, but he'd seen enough of *her* for one day. With all the things he did to keep her life full and save her from Empty Nest Syndrome - a term he'd picked up from one of the many family therapists he'd totally mind-fucked - Neil would have thought the woman would appreciate him more. But she didn't. "Nag, nag, nag, nag, *nag!*"

For now, all he wanted to do was twenty minutes of cardio, a half-hour of triceps, and maybe some preacher curls - his biceps looked like they could use a little pump. And then, after dinner - Mom loved making him dinner - he'd return to his room, turn off the lamp and watch *Buffy the Vampire Slayer* while rubbing one out, until it was time to meet up with a chickie who called herself BellaVampira6969 on Skype. After that, he'd return to his true task: researching the vampires of Candle Bay, Crimson Cove, and beyond. Something was up in the vampire world. He could feel it, even if that little bitch Coastal Eddie wouldn't tell him anything.

Leaving the towels and his clothes on the floor for Mom, he padded downstairs and, as the dog watched, dressed in his black jockstrap and tucked a tiny vial of holy water into the pouch. "Never leave home without it," he crooned. Then he put on some music, and climbed on the treadmill, singing along with Alice Cooper's anthem about school being out forever. "Yeah!" he punctuated the song with his best Van Halen screech every now and then. Renfield hated that. But that was Renfield's problem.

4

SO LONG, AND THANKS FOR ALL THE BLOOD

The Darling twins, Juicy Lucy and Poison Ivy, had gotten into their secret stash of Lixir and had been semi-awake all day. With sunset still over an hour away, they were now bored out of their skulls. "I wish I was asleep," Lucy told her sister.

"I know, right?" Ivy said. They lay on their big black bed in their suite, where the radio, set to KNDL-FM, played *New Kid in Town*. The girls were restless but unwilling to leave their quarters: big brother Stephen was being even stricter than Natasha about proper behavior. "Stevie can be such a nag," Ivy said.

"Yeah, I wonder what's eating him."

"Not Amanda!" Ivy cackled and Lucy cracked up.

"She sure came in late last night," Lucy said. "Around dawn."

"No wonder Stevie was such a twatsicle," Ivy remarked. "She's driving him nuts."

"Yeah, she's a bitch."

"Bitch supreme with cheese! I can't stand this song." Just as Ivy reached for the remote, the boring tune ended and Coastal Eddie's deep syrupy voice came on.

"The body found under the north pier in Candle Bay this morning has been positively identified as Norman Keeler, nineteen. Keeler was known to be a local prostitute."

Lucy giggled. "Small loss."

"Shhh. Listen," Ivy said.

"The young man was assaulted sometime last night by a person or persons unknown," Eddie reported. "While the CBPD isn't talking, Bob Trotter, who found the body, said, and I quote, 'I was jogging this morning and saw an arm sticking out of a pile of seaweed near the pier. I got closer and it was this guy - a young, blond guy - and he was so dead that he was as white as fish bellies. And something had torn his throat out. Are there wolves in Candle Bay? Because that's what it looked like.'

"No, Bob, there are no wolves in Candle Bay, unless they are of the shapeshifting variety." Eddie paused. "And I'm happy to tell you, guys and gals, friends and neighbors, that as far as your Uncle Eddie knows, werewolves have yet to move into our tiny town ... They're afraid of our vampires."

"Werewolves!" Lucy shrieked out a giggle and Ivy grinned and reached for her, pushing her fingers under Lucy's red tank to tickle her ribs. "Stop it!"

"No, I'm a werewolf and I'm going to eat you all up!" Ivy threw her leg over her sister and loomed above her. She attacked Lucy's armpits - she had always been the ticklish one.

Lucy flailed and laughed, tears streaming. "Stop it!"

Instead, Ivy pulled Lucy's shirt up and began motorboating with a vengeance.

Soon, Lucy's giggles softened and she reached up and unclasped her sister's bra. "Two can play this game!"

"I dare you."

She took the dare.

∽

"I UNDERSTAND that you returned shortly before dawn." Arms folded, Stephen held his temper, speaking with exaggerated calm.

"That would only be news if I'd come in shortly *after* dawn," Amanda said, filing her nails.

Stephen had called Amanda to his office moments after his brother, Ivor, the hotel security chief, told him about the body with its throat torn out that had been found near North Pier. With every word, his heart sank. There were no Rogues in Candle Bay; the Darlings prided themselves on keeping the town pristine and safe both for themselves and for the humans who lived there. Now as he, Ivor, and Amanda sat in his office, Stephen had no doubt who was responsible for the killing.

He was about to say so when Orion Darling buzzed. Stephen punched a control and the door slid open. He and Ivor stood, Amanda didn't - she didn't even bother to look up at the nominal head of the Darling clan.

"Thank you for coming on such short notice, Uncle."

Ori, a DeNiro type who dressed as impeccably as the fictional godfathers he adored, nodded and came to stand behind the desk next to his nephew. "A body," he said.

"Yes," said Ivor. "Dilly filled you in?"

"She did. And she asked me to tell you the security department meeting starts in twenty minutes. In your office."

"I'll be there."

Ori stared at Amanda, who ignored him. "A youth found under the pier." He shook his head in sadness. "The occasional junkie up in the graveyards is understandable, if not agreeable. However, a young man whose throat has been ripped out by a vampire is *not* acceptable. Look at me, young lady."

Amanda looked up from beneath her perfect blond brows, boredom filling her eyes.

"You were chosen by my beloved nephew here and because of this and the fact that - as far as I know - this is the first time such a thing has happened - I will not banish you for the offense. I will, however, banish you if it occurs again." He looked at Stephen. "Is this acceptable to you, Nephew?"

Stephen nodded. "I would understand if banishment occurred now."

"I didn't do it," Amanda said, glaring at Stephen. "Don't accuse me of something without proof."

"Of course you did it, *darling*," Stephen said. "Dilly saw the blood on your clothing when you came in."

"And I've just had Housekeeping check your room," Ivor added. "They confirmed what Dilly saw."

Amanda shrugged. "I cut myself."

"Show us," Stephen said.

"I used Lixir on it. It's already healed."

"Look, Amanda." Stephen was hard-pressed now to keep his cool. "We *know* you did it."

"Bullshit."

"Language, Amanda," Ori admonished. "Your fiancé is jumping to conclusions but he has little choice. Nor do we, unless you explain. Please tell us where you went last night. We wish to hear everything about your evening."

"Since when is a Darling considered guilty until proven innocent?" Outraged, Amanda stood up. "How dare you question me!"

Ori spread his hands and smiled thinly. "Even though you are not, at this point, a family member, you have only to tell us the truth concerning your whereabouts last night and we will apologize for accusing you."

Amanda turned her glare on Stephen. "He spoke harshly to me in front of the help in Satyrelli's and I was angry, so as he can tell you, I went for a walk."

"Where?" Stephen asked.

"I went to the cemetery hills and wandered until nearly dawn." Her eyes went soft and filled with tears. "I was trying to sort things out. I was upset."

"Did you feed?" Ori asked.

She shook her head. "At Stephen's suggestion, I had half a bottle of blood before I left. My appetite was sated." Her lower lip stuck out like a small child's.

"Is the bottle in the refrigerator in our suite?" Stephen asked. While they did not sleep together anymore, they did continue to share his two-bedroom apartment.

She didn't blink. "No. I finished the last half of an open bottle."

"Where's the bottle?" Ivor asked.

"I left it in the empties bin, of course."

Ori cleared his throat. "Amanda, I dare say that blood wouldn't boil in your mouth."

She let a crocodile tear roll down her cheek. "Why would you say that, Uncle? That's cruel."

"Tell us about the rest of your night, Amanda." Stephen was working hard to keep his anger hidden.

"There's really nothing to tell." She gave Stephen another manufactured tear. "You were angry with me and I was upset. I wandered several cemeteries and rested under the giant oak by St. Ignatius' statue for hours. I watched the moon cross the sky."

"Through the fog?" Stephen prodded.

"There was only a little ground fog last night. The moon and stars were beautiful. You know that. Don't try to trick me, Stephen." Anger bubbled into her voice then vanished as if it had never been there. "With the first glimpse of dawn, I came home to sleep."

Ori folded his hands. "You are an intelligent young vampire, Amanda, so you will understand when I tell you that without witnesses to verify your story, we cannot fully trust it. Tonight, we must insist that you remain indoors so that-"

"Indoors?" Amanda spat. "Indoors? What am I, a prisoner? Just because you think you should accuse me of something I didn't even know about until tonight? Really? I'm your nephew's fiancée! Doesn't that earn me some respect?"

"Amanda," Ivor said, his deep voice still as deep water. "Your remaining indoors under our watch will give us time to find the true culprit. It will absolve you." He looked at his watch. "I must go to my meeting. We will be patrolling the grounds in force tonight - and a few of us will be going down to the boardwalk as well. We cannot allow any more bloodshed."

Stephen looked at Amanda as Ivor spoke. He saw spite and hatred under her manufactured tears. "We all have work to attend to. Amanda, perhaps you should start going over the week's receipts. I'll be by regularly to see if you need anything."

"That's so thoughtful of you, Stephen," she spat. She walked to the door and glanced back at him when he didn't buzz her out. "Well?"

He waited until Ori and Ivor joined her at the door then buzzed them all out at once. As soon as they were gone, he pulled a flask of rum-infused B Negative from his drawer and took a long pull. *Could she be innocent?* He wanted to believe her, but he was no fool. Not anymore.

~

GOOD GOD ALMIGHTY, *my throat hurts!*

This was the first conscious thought that Norman Keeler had. He was aware of that agonizing pain before he knew where - or even who - he was. Because the very cords of his throat had been shredded and torn out, it had taken nearly twenty-four hours for him to be reborn, and once he was, he was assailed by a hunger so deep, so painfully acute, that his agonized throat became an afterthought.

He was hungry. No, *starving*. There was a deep need within him - a greedy one that consumed him and needled into his very blood and bones. It was like a heroin craving - but it wasn't heroin he was jonesing for. It was ... something else ...

And he was cold. Very cold. He opened his eyes.

And saw nothing.

Then he remembered the strange woman on the pier - her pale face, her jutted breasts, her ... her *teeth!* He recalled those tiny ivory daggers in her mouth, so like little blades, sinking deep into the flesh of his throat. He touched the skin there. It was smooth, but the pain remained. *Am I dead? What the hell is going-*

Whistling. Playful, light-hearted whistling. It came from somewhere beyond ... well, wherever the hell he was. Norman felt around, finding the smooth walls of his tomb slick and cool to the touch. He gasped for breath - feeling like he'd forgotten to breathe - and detected the scents of chemicals - and something else. A very faint something that was rotting, like a bowl of spoiled fruit in a faraway room. But mostly, he just smelled disinfectant and other things, foreign chemical things.

He slowed his breathing and listened to the whistling, trying to determine where it came from. It was, he realized, a particularly be-boppy rendition of *Luck Be a Lady Tonight*. It stopped and Norman heard a decidedly male voice - he couldn't make out the words - then a slight tapping, as if someone were patting a hard surface from somewhere outside. Then the man's words were clear: *'Hard luck, man. Guess you won't be slurpin' the sausage anymore.'* The man chuckled.

What the hell? What the unholy hell! Panic seized him and Norman began to scream, pounding at the walls of his cold, black tomb.

~

Jim Bottoms loved working nights in the morgue. It was quiet, serene, and he could do just about whatever he wanted except when a body was brought in. When that happened, he had to hide his box of Twinkies and his German porn magazines - *Ach, Fräulein! Vhat amazing boobies you haf!* Helga was his current favorite, a buxom blond-braided beauty posed in a green Oktoberfest dress with beer, garter belt, stockings, and no panties. Or blouse. He'd had to leave her waiting on his desk to make the rounds, but he promised her he'd come back soon. Come being the key word. He couldn't wait to splash her up proper with his own brand of Jim Bottoms' baby-gravy. "Get out the Kleenex, Helga, you big pink apple strudel you, I'll be back soon to taste your pie."

He left his office and entered the morgue, whistling Sinatra. The tables were empty - Jim liked a clean room and always put all his guests away at night. It helped keep the smell down, too.

He patted one of the compartments of the body fridge. "How you doing tonight, Mrs. Miller? Comfy in there?" Mrs. Miller, bless her soul, had come in last night, not long before the poor guy who'd had his throat torn out. Mrs. Miller - Opal to her friends - had slipped off her stool and broken her neck while watering her plants. She died instantly, or at least painlessly. "Good job, Mrs. Miller."

He resumed whistling, thinking about the poor guy in the middle cabinet. Jim felt bad for the throatless surfer. He was paper-white from blood loss and wrinkled from the water and his neck looked like special effects from *The Walking Dead*. His boss told him the guy had been a he-whore.

Jim, whistling about lady luck, approached the boy's compartment and patted the door. "Hard luck, man. Guess you won't be slurpin' the sausage anymore." He chuckled.

Craving another Twinkie even though they were going straight to his derriere, he turned to head back to the office.

That's when the screaming began. Startled, Jim stumbled back, slipped, and landed on his prodigious ass.

"What the hell?" somebody yelled from inside one of the compartments.

"No!" Jim scooted back, grappling to stand up.

"Get me out of here!"

"Holy fuck and a half!" Jim grabbed for the desk phone as the screaming continued. It had to be the he-whore because it sure as hell wasn't Mrs. Miller.

He dropped the phone as realization struck. "You bastard! I'm onto you." This was just the kind of sick joke that old Ernie, the daytime morgue attendant, liked to pull.

"Let me out of here!"

"Not on your life, Ernie."

"I'm cold! Let me out!" Ernie started screaming again and pounding on the walls.

Jim considered. It *was* cold in those boxes. Maybe Ernie accidentally locked himself in.

"Let me out!" The screams and pounding grew louder.

Jim approached the fridge and realized Ernie had gone all out, moving the he-whore and taking his spot so that he could really give him a scare. Jim stood there, calmly listening to the screaming, the pleas for freedom. "Ernie, can you hear me?"

"Let me OUT!"

"I might." Jim smiled to himself. "Do you promise never to do this again?"

"LET ME OUT!"

"Promise!"

"I PROMISE! FUCKING LET ME OUT!"

"Okay, okay, you act like *I* put you in there. You've only yourself to blame." He pulled the drawer open.

And screamed.

A face full of sharp teeth - a face that was *not* Ernie's - shrieked and then tore Jim's throat out.

∽

"YOU DON'T NEED A PINT A NIGHT," Michael told Natasha Darling.

"I don't know how you do it." She looked around at the other vampires of Eudemonia. Each sat in a tall chair in the private dining room, where they'd gathered for a few glasses of a nice A Neg Romanian, a fine classic vintage.

"It's all about the meditations," said Winter. Next to him, his mentally challenged sidekick, Arnie, nodded enthusiastically.

"And the ores," added Michael. "We each partake of only a couple of pints per week, and are quite satisfied."

Natasha sighed. "Perhaps one day I'll be able to show the same kind of restraint." She glanced meaningfully at her nearly empty glass of Romanian.

"It takes practice," said Chynna, her pale skin and silky blond hair reminding Natasha of a porcelain doll. Chynna, however, was no delicate doll. Natasha had admired her warrior skills when she and her family had last come to Crimson Cove to assist Michael's group in a battle against Gretchen VanTreese. With or without the aid of her well-trained white tigers, Chynna was a force to be reckoned with.

Winter chuckled. "Lots and lots of practice. But you can do it. Maybe not quite to the extent that we do - you don't have the same amount of calming ores in your ground in Candle Bay."

Arnie nodded. "Papa Winter says you can do it!"

Natasha smiled, almost believing them.

5

REMEMBER! VAMPYRS ARE PEOPLE TO!

B*iting Man Festival.* Neil Trinsky, hunched over the glow of his computer, typed the words into Argonaut, his favorite search engine for exploring the Deep Web. He'd given up Googling the things he wanted to know because they weren't in public databases. But everything was in the Deep Web if you knew where to look. "Come on, baby, show me!"

Suddenly a list of URLs appeared on the screen. He clicked one that read *Biting Man Centennial* and began reading.

WHAT VAMPYRS DONT WANT YOU TO NOW!!!

VAMPYRES HAVE BEEN MEETING *in secret for many eras. Ever since the first caveman was turned into a Creature of the Night, vampyrs have craved the company of other vampyrs.*

REMEMBER! VAMPYRS ARE PEOPLE TO!

Vampyrs must have affectation, not just blood, to survive the many long nites of the eras they span. So they invented they're own festival eons ago, back when the Greek Gods ruled the world. Today the festival is called BITING MAN and it happens every year in sacred places like STONEHENGE IN ENGLAND, THE PIRAMIDS OF EGYPT AND ICEHOUSE MOUNTAIN!

"This is crap," Neil said, continuing to skim. "They don't meet in Stonehenge! That's ridiculous. There's not enough shade!"

He went back to the Argonaut list and tried another link. "*Biting Man Festival Rumored to be Imminent in Northern California*," he read, after logging into the Very Vampiric People Channel. "That's more like it."

"*Biting Man is the name of a celebration that is supposed to be the vampiric version of the Christmas holiday where they celebrate the birth of the first vampire.*" So far, it was ringing true. "*We here at VVP have donned our deerstalkers and have been investigating, but there's very little information to be had. Iconic conspiracy deejay, Coastal Eddie Fortune, has recently mentioned a Vampire Council and VVP believes that it is at the heart of Biting Man.*

"*We asked Mr. Fortune if this was true, but he didn't answer. We believe it IS true, but that Mr. Fortune fears for his life and doesn't want to comment. In the past Mr. Fortune, who is very, very reliable, has mentioned that there is a Biting Man held in California almost every year. We have researched this and connected Mr. Fortune's statement to things he's said about Icehouse Mountain in NorCal. British Isle Vampires are said to hold Biting Man at Stonehenge and while we don't know for sure that it's true, Icehouse Mountain has its own set of ancient standing stones that they call Little Stonehenge. Not only that, but there are rumors that Icehouse Mountain is hollow and that an ancient civilization built a city inside. (This is common knowledge as is the fact that the Count St. Germain has been seen on the mountain many times over the decades. The local Amerindians consider him a great shaman as they believe only the most powerful shamans can visit the sacred city within the mountain.)*

"*While Mr. Fortune won't answer any questions, we believe he may be a friend to vampires and that he knows, via the Vampire Council, that Biting Man will be held at Icehouse Mountain. And we have deduced that this big celebration must be held in summer because there's too much snow most of the year.*

"*If anyone knows more, please email us.*"

"I'm going to the source, you little bitches, and I'm not stupid enough to tell *you* queers anything!" Coastal Eddie would be outside the amphitheater again tonight and Neil was going to make sure Eddie told him all he knew.

Neil stood, stretched, and opened the door. Renfield wagged his tail, but Neil ignored him. "Mommmmmm!" he yelled. "When's dinner?"

"Twenty minutes." Her soft voice floated down the stairs.

"What are you making?" he yelled.

"Veggie burgers, your favorite!"

"They're *not* my favorite!" Neil rolled his eyes; the woman had no concept of healthy eating. "Are they *organic*, at least? And preservative free?" No way was he allowing all those chemicals into the temple that was his body.

"Of course, Neil."

"Fine. Hurry. I need to go out!"

"Where?"

Nosy little bitch! "The boardwalk. I have to see Coastal Eddie! It's important. Hurry!" He sighed and unzipped his fly. Sometimes you just had to rub one out to relieve the stress.

∼

ENOUGH WAS ENOUGH.

Stephen Darling had gone downstairs to check on Amanda. She wasn't in the back offices going over the books. Instead, she sat at the far end of the vast lobby, next to an attractive young man who didn't appear comfortable - probably because she was leaning too close to him, her hand repeatedly touching his knee as she laughed and giggled, making enough noise to draw stares.

As Stephen approached, he heard the young man say, "I don't know, ma'am. I've never really done that before."

"Amanda." Stephen stood stock-still. "Come with me. We must speak."

The man, a twenty-something guy in a business suit, looked grateful until Amanda waved Stephen away. "Not now, *darling*," she said. "I'm engaging our guest with friendly conversation like you asked me to."

"Now." Stephen's voice went flint-hard.

The guy in the suit cleared his throat, and with obvious reluctance, Amanda rose.

"You're such a buzzkill, Stevie," she said.

Stephen took her arm, digging in a little too hard as he escorted her into the relative privacy of a back office and shut the door.

Inside, he shoved her into a chair.

Amanda giggled. "Stevie. What's gotten into you? You're being so *rough* with me." Another giggle. "I like it when you're assertive." She opened her legs.

"Shut your legs and listen to me."

Her eyes went wide and her knees slowly closed.

"We're done. I've had enough."

Shock chased the arrogance from her face. "What do you mean, '*done*'?"

"You know what I mean. It's over."

She made a move to stand. "But-"

He pushed her back down. "But nothing." He ground his molars together, speaking with forced calm. "I've endured all I'm willing and able to endure, Amanda. You simply aren't the same woman I once loved. You've become belligerent, arrogant, and worst of all, sloppy. Sloppy as a woman, and sloppy as a vampire. We can't afford it, I can't tolerate it, and I will *not* subject my family to it any longer."

Her chin quivered and her eyes welled, mock-sadness filling them.

"Oh, knock it off, Amanda. Your tears are impotent. I've seen more than enough of them. I'm immune."

As quickly as they'd appeared, her glistening tears dried and thunderclouds of anger flashed red in her eyes. But she didn't move.

"Do you hear me, Amanda? Are you listening?"

She remained eerily still.

"Amanda!" He shook her shoulder.

The moment he touched her, a scream exploded from her throat - a scream that could have shattered glass. "Don't touch me!" She threw herself from the chair, crashed to the floor, and writhed like a madwoman. "Get off me! Get off me!" She smacked her own face, pulled her hair, and ripped at her blouse as she staggered to her feet. "*Help!* Someone *help!*"

Stephen stepped back. Way back. "Jesus Christ, Amanda! What's wrong with-"

"Someone! Help! *Help!*" Grabbing a vase of flowers from the desk, she threw it against the wall, and shrieked. "He's beating me!"

He was astonished, trembling, unsure of what to do. The door burst open. Ivor stepped inside, closed and locked it just as she threw herself at Stephen. They toppled to the floor and rolled, broken glass biting into his hands and face.

Amanda rolled on top and head-butted him, smacking her forehead right into his face. Pain shot, splintered, and hot blood gushed from his nose. Using all of his strength, he bucked her off, gained the advantage and wrapped one hand tightly around her throat. Her screams came to an abrupt halt.

"Do you need help?" Ivor asked with icy calm.

"Not yet." Stephen raised his head and spoke into Amanda's ear. "Listen to me." He squeezed harder as she struggled. "No one else is coming, and even if they do, they won't believe a word out of your lying mouth." She made a gagging sound, but her eyes showed that she was listening. "No one wants you here. I'm the only reason my family tolerates you - and the moment I stop making excuses for you is the moment everyone stops acting as if they can tolerate you."

Tears slipped from the corners of her eyes as her face turned a bruised shade of purple.

"Here's what you're going to do, Amanda. You're going to get up and walk out of this office. Quietly. If any guests are in the lobby, you're going to smile as if nothing's wrong. You're going to go upstairs and get your things. Again, you're going to do this quietly. Pack what you need, then leave this hotel. Quietly." He eased his grip. "And don't you ever come back, Amanda. If you do, I'll make sure it's the last thing you do on this earth."

He let her suck in a little air. "Am I understood?"

Her eyes frantically searched his face. Within them, he saw fury, panic, then, finally, what looked like resignation.

"Am I *perfectly* understood?"

She nodded – as much as was possible.

"Good." He removed his hand and her face immediately regained its natural pallor.

She stood, looked around wildly, and opened her mouth.

Stephen held his hand up. "Not one more word." He moved to a chair and dabbed his bleeding nose with a tissue. "Not one more. Ivor, would you be so kind as to accompany my *ex*-fiancée?"

"With pleasure. And I will remain with her until she's off the property."

Without a word, Amanda turned, head down, and went to the door, Ivor behind her.

"And Amanda, darling?"

She turned.

"If you so much as touch anything that doesn't belong to you on your way out, I'll have your hands permanently removed."

She hurried from the room.

Slowly, the feeling began returning to Stephen's limbs. He hadn't been upset like this in centuries and was surprised by his own aggression. Surprised, but not sorry, he thought as he dabbed Lixir on his wounds. *It's been a long time coming...*

∼

"It's chilly out tonight." Lois Trinsky tried to hand Neil his heavy corduroy jacket with the lamb's wool lining.

"Jesus, Mom, I wouldn't be caught dead in that thing." He pulled his black leather jacket off the coat rack and shrugged into it.

Lois knew better than to bother arguing. Once Neil made up his mind, he never changed it. *He's a lot like his dad.* His father had been insufferable and opinionated and she'd had to hide her pleasure when he ran out on the family. Not that Neil was that bad, but she wished he'd find his own place; she needed some peace.

"When will you be home?"

"None of your business." He shoved past her, half-kicking Renfield out of the way as he opened the door. The dog whimpered and Neil threw him a dirty look.

"As long as you live here, it *is* my business," Lois said. It was a boring litany that she had repeated so many times over the years that she didn't know why she bothered. *Respect. That's why I bother.* "If I hear noises at two in the morning and don't know it's you, you're likely to get shot."

"Mom, you should give me your gun. It's not safe for you to have."

She laughed. She hadn't meant to, but it simply escaped, amused and full-bodied. Giving Neil a gun was the last thing she'd ever do. *Talk about unsafe!*

He was glaring at her, nostrils flared, cold eyes hard, and lips thin. "Don't you laugh at me! Don't you *ever* laugh at me!"

"Sorry, honey. I didn't mean to laugh." Even as she said the words, she felt a tiny thrill of fear run down her spine. Her son sometimes frightened her. She forced a smile. "Say hello to Coastal Eddie for me."

"What? Why? You don't know him! You don't know anything!" His eyes narrowed. "Do you?"

Lois Trinsky had spent the last fifteen years hiding her feelings from her son, keeping the peace, trying to get along. She was mistress of her emotions and even when she wanted to reach out and slap Neil's face, she refused. "No, sorry, Neil." She forced a smile. "I'm just interested. Are you going to see him about vampires again?"

"Yeah, and he'd better tell me what I want to know about the Vampire Council this time." With that, he was out the door and on his Vespa, heading toward the boardwalk in the foggy, foggy night.

~

"Little asshole!" Amanda screamed at the Vespa that shot right into her path. She downshifted, her red Miata growling at the douchebag who'd cut her off. The guy shot her the finger and she started to punch the gas then caught herself. She didn't need any dents in her precious M-5. "You deserve death, you little shit."

The guy kept going toward the boardwalk, while Amanda turned east and headed for the onramp to the 101, driving slowly until the fog thinned near the highway. On the ramp, she saw a hitchhiker and slammed on the brakes, staring. It was Surfer Boy, the guy she'd drunk at North Pier the previous night. *But how can that be?* Had some other vamp bitten him twice more? She'd sucked the guy dry, though, and he should have been dead.

The man came running at the Miata, desperation and yearning on his face. It was him, all right. She didn't know how or why, but he had turned. He yelled something that sounded like "I love you!" She sped up and flew past him.

Once she was northbound, she pushed the guy out of her mind and laid hard on the accelerator, wondering if she was so strong she could turn a human with one bite. *I'm special!* Smiling, she punched on the radio and thought about how surprised Julian Valentyn would be when she showed up. He had no idea he was her backup plan.

∼

NORMAN KEELER HAD BEEN CLOSE, so close. He'd smelled *her* - his Maker - on the wind and followed that scent to the freeway. Not only that, he could read her thoughts after a fashion. They weren't clear, not exactly, but they were hers, he was sure of it. Though he didn't know her reasons for it, he knew that she'd planned to get on the freeway and drive north. So that's where he headed. It was the only thing that mattered - getting to her.

Since waking in the morgue, finding *her* had been the only thing that mattered. Well, that, and blood. Lots and lots of blood. It was as if his addiction to heroin had been replaced by those two things - finding blood and finding *her*.

He'd stood on the freeway onramp, watching, his knapsack full of the necessities - a skateboard, a few toiletries, and nothing else. Finally, a red sports car had appeared. *It's her!* He'd rushed at her car as it sped by, proclaiming his love. But she hadn't batted an eye. She'd simply swerved out of his path, punched the gas, and kept going.

Norman stood in the middle of the road, watching her taillights. He wasn't discouraged, not at all. He'd found her once and he'd find her again. Smiling, he turned and stuck his thumb out. He had to follow her, had to know her. She was all that mattered.

∼

"What are you smiling about?" Michael asked as Natasha rejoined him at their table outside Eudemonia's acclaimed restaurant, Suspire. The human clientele was all indoors, which made their patio table - hidden among potted flowers and ferns - private enough to share a bottle of AB Neg without fear of being seen.

Natasha sat down as Michael topped off her goblet. "My brother finally did it."

Michael raised his eyebrows.

"He kicked Amanda out and broke the engagement. He told her never to return."

"Do you expect repercussions?"

Natasha, truly relaxed for the first time in a decade, raised her glass. "Not yet. I'm sure there will be, but the guards have been ordered not to let her back in."

Michael raised his glass. "A toast then. To Stephen."

"To Stevie."

They drank.

"Where do you think she's going to go?"

Natasha smiled. "I'd bet just about anything she's headed to Mill Valley."

"Why there?"

"Julian."

Michael raised his brows. "I see. Should you warn him?"

She chuckled. "No. I think he can handle her." She paused. "You know, this means we can go straight to Eternity without making a trip back to Candle Bay."

"Wonderful, but don't you need to pack?"

"I believe I have everything I need with me." She watched Michael as he sipped from his goblet. His long black hair was pulled back into a low ponytail; it looked silver where the moonlight touched it. He was beautiful. She loved being with him though, truthfully, she did miss the passionate part of him. When the time was right, she'd ask him when - and *why* - he'd chosen such a path. *"Love and sex are complications I do not need,"* was all he'd ever said. But Natasha knew there was more to it.

He glanced at her and there was something in that deep amber gaze that told Natasha he missed her, too.

This is going to be a very long trip if we do nothing more than cast longing glances at each other, she thought.

He chuckled, as if he'd read her mind. He just always seemed to *know* somehow.

"Do you want to ride up with the others?" he asked.

She looked him straight in the eye. "How would you feel about us traveling alone? It would give us time to talk about business - and old times."

"That sounds perfect." Michael smiled. "What about your sisters?"

She didn't want to think about them, but she had to. "The twins ... I don't know. I guess they can drive up on their own."

"Why don't you have them come here and then they can join Winter, Chynna, and Arnie in our van? There's plenty of room. That might be easier for everyone."

"Lucy and Ivy can be quite a handful."

"Chynna won't let them disturb the peace, be assured of that. She can turn tigers into pussycats. She likes a challenge."

"Let's do that then," Natasha said. They clinked glasses, sat back, and enjoyed the scent of night blooming jasmine as the stars twinkled overhead.

6
BUGGY WHIPPED

Up in the Candle Bay amphitheater, Plastic Taffy was sounding more like Metal Grating tonight. The concert had barely begun, but it was nothing like the usual good-times-and-rainbows Plastic Taffy. Their guitars crunched, the drums hammered, and the lead singer, Ramon, wailed and screeched like Axl Rose with a chest cold ... riding a goat.

Listening from the KNDL van on the boardwalk, Coastal Eddie barely recognized their classic pop-tunes-turned-bad-metal. *What have they been snorting?* He wondered what the audience thought and wished he were home listening to a real album side of Guns 'N Roses. This was torture.

Through the thickening fog, Eddie spotted a familiar figure making its determined way toward him. He sighed, closed his eyes, and counted calmly to ten as Neil Trinsky, World's Greatest Vampire Hunter, approached.

"Eddie."

"What is it, Neil?"

Neil stood, hands fisted at his sides, even the one holding the ever-present dill pickle. Amber lamplight danced in the cracks of his well-worn leather jacket. "I know where the festival is, Eddie."

"I don't know what you're talking about."

"You know - *Biting* Man." He said this with such superior snobbery that Eddie couldn't stop his eyes from rolling.

"I told you, kid. There's no such thi-"

"Bullshit! I call bullshit, Eddie!" He moved closer, jabbing the pickle at Eddie's nose. His cheap cologne, which had been trailing him like a loyal dog, had gone missing. "It's in Eternity."

Eddie hoped the guy hadn't seen his eyes widen. Quickly, he tried to compose himself. "No," he said. "Biting Man is a myth. It doesn't exist. I've already told you that the Vampire Council-"

"Bullshit! Man, it's all over your face like sperm on a whore's ass! It's in Eternity, and I'm going!" He laughed. "Sperm on a whore's ass, man. Sperm on a whore's ass!" Satisfied with himself, he crunched into the pickle and chewed smugly.

Eddie cringed.

"And if you don't tell me all about it, I'm going to totally out you!"

"Out me?"

"Yeah. When I get there, I'll tell the Vampire Council it was you who told me where to find them!"

Eddie stared at the kid. Would he actually try to walk into Biting Man looking for the fictional Vampire Council? With the dill pickle corked in his mouth like a pacifier, he certainly *appeared* capable of such stupidity. "Look, Neil, believe me when I tell you, you're wrong."

"Then why do you look so nervous?"

"Quit trying to gaslight me. It won't work."

"You're scared because you know I'll do it. Now tell me what day Biting Man starts! Tell me, or I really will tell the Vampire Council that you sent me to kill them all!" Neil flexed a fist.

"You mean the internet didn't give you all the information you needed?" Eddie tried to appear casual and tried even harder to hide his amusement. And his unease.

"Tell me." Neil's jaw clenched, his shoulders tensed - he looked like a panther preparing to pounce, and Eddie wondered just how much damage the guy was capable of doing. Though Neil was only about five-foot-eight, stupidity was more dangerous than size.

Holding Neil's gaze, Eddie squared his shoulders, rose and stepped back from the table. "There's nothing to tell, Neil. I know nothing about so-called vampires. Like I said, I'm an entertainer. I'm just amusing the audience when I talk about these things. No one takes me seriously."

Neil blew out a breath and Eddie recoiled.

So that's where the stink's been hiding! It smelled like cinnamon Pucker-Buttons and Sen-Sen had collided in his mouth.

Neil raised a sticky-looking palm. "Okay, okay. I just have one more question. How do you kill a *real* vampire?"

Eddie coughed, shrugged, and stared into the fog-filled night. "I don't have a clue, Neil. I've never killed one."

Trinsky jabbed the pickle stump at Eddie's nose. "If you're lying, you'll regret it, you little bitch!" He turned and stalked into the darkness.

Asshole. Still, Eddie felt uneasy. Neil had been his own personal Annie Wilkes for the last fifteen years, growing weirder as time passed. He'd been only an annoyance for most of that time, but in the last few years, he'd gotten pushy and ballsy and mean. *All those questions about vampires.* Eddie actually knew a little about Biting Man - he was fairly sure it was happening soon in Eternity, and he knew it was going to be big this year; it would draw hundreds if not thousands of vamps from across the country. Though he wasn't worried about vampires coming after him, he had no intention of crashing the party. No. But he *was* worried that Neil Trinsky might. These days, the guy gave off an especially aggressive - and unbalanced - vibe.

Eddie wished he'd brought his tech along tonight because he suddenly didn't like being alone out here even though he'd peacefully broadcast from this very spot at least a hundred times before.

Plastic Taffy ended something he couldn't identify, something that had no place in heavy metal, and the crowd didn't cheer. That didn't stop the band though - they launched right into a dreadful metal version of Air Supply's *I'm All Outta Love.* It was sacrilege.

∽

Troubled, Lois Trinsky fed Renfield and tried to watch the evening news, but she couldn't concentrate; her mind was on her son. Things had never been easy with him. It hadn't been so bad when Jacob and Tina still lived at home. In fact, it wasn't so bad even after Tina moved out, but once Jacob left for college five years ago, things with Neil had become nearly unbearable.

He consumed her. He consumed her time, her income, her energy, and gave nothing back. He wouldn't get a job - he claimed no one was hiring. Evidently, no one had been hiring for at least a decade. She'd tried over and over to make her firstborn fledgling leave the nest, but every time, he'd cry and act so devastated that she'd given up.

But after tonight's juvenile performance, she knew she had to take action. *He's killing me. I have no life of my own.* She couldn't even date; she'd been asked out regularly over the years but she was always sorry when she accepted because once Neil found out, he'd object. Vehemently. *"All they want is your body,"* he'd say. *"You're acting like a slut,"* he'd say. He'd even managed to threaten a few of her suitors. One guy she really liked and went out with several times - a real estate agent like herself - brought her a letter Neil had sent him. It was as ugly as it came, accusing him of rape, calling him a homosexual, and threatening to turn him in to the police if he didn't leave his mother alone. And so, the poor man had done just that and she'd never heard another word from him.

She hated that she'd come to resent her own son.

Renfield jumped on the couch and nestled next to her. He whimpered when she scratched behind his ear - there was a sore spot. *Again.* She'd found a few tender spots on him recently, and this raised red flags. *Is Neil hurting the dog? Is the cycle beginning again?* She didn't dare say anything for fear he'd do worse.

"This is no way to live, is it, Renny?" She rose and carried the terrier into the kitchen and gave him a slice of ham from the fridge. His tail began wagging immediately. Renny was one of the reasons she'd been afraid to kick her son out of the house - she was afraid he'd take the dog with him. *So board him for a few days, say he ran away. No more excuses. You've got to make Neil leave the nest.*

But she worried that it was a bad idea. After putting the chain guard on the front door - in case Neil returned unexpectedly - Lois went down to the basement, hoping to find out what her son was up to now. She tried the door. Neil, in his arrogance, had left it unlocked.

Stepping inside his dimly lit room, her heart sped up and tripped over a few beats. *He'll be furious if he catches me snooping.* But Lois felt compelled. Steeling herself, she took a deep breath, her nose twitching at the sickly-sweet smell of dirty laundry and Axe Body Spray. It was much better than before she'd cleaned, but the odors seemed to be part of the fabric of the room; you couldn't scrub them out. She passed his weight machine, avoiding the crusty-looking jock strap hanging from it, and crossed into the alcove where he kept his computer.

She touched the mouse and the screen lit up, startling her. She saw writing on a yellow legal pad next to it. Without touching anything, she bent to read.

"Coastal Eddie knows lots more than he's Admitting. He KNOWS all about the Biting Man Festival. I know he does, but he won't tell me Anything, that little bitch!!! He says the Super Secret Vampire Council won't allow it but I Believe he's been Threatened and can't talk because they'll Kill him.

"Or else he's an Insider. That would mean the Vampires have taken him into their Confidence. Maybe he wants to be a Vampire and wants them to make him One of Their Own. But no matter what, I Must make him Confess the TRUTH, even if I have to Kill him!! I will Stop at Nothing until I get The Truth! The World as we Know it Depends on ME to find out! I'm a Man on a Mission - a very Important mission. Important enough that if They ever Update the Bible, My name will be in it. I'd be bigger News than that alleged Lord Almighty!"

Again, Lois desperately regretted exposing her son to the church. Panic buzzed through her. *He's delusional! Is he developing a God complex?* She'd hoped the bad cycle wouldn't return, but it obviously had. Not only that, there was malevolence in his words. Neil had flirted on and off with violence since childhood, but she hadn't seen any recent signs. *I've been blind.* Now, she clearly recognized the old patterns of anger, frustration, paranoia, and the sense of grandeur that had always preceded his previous swings toward darkness.

Another thought struck: *And it's my fault.*

Years of therapy had warned her against wandering down the dark alleyway of self-blame, and logically, she knew she wasn't responsible. Jacob and Tina had turned out great, after all. In fact, they were socially upstanding citizens. *So, where did I go wrong with Neil?* She sighed. *No. I didn't cause this. It's just who he is, like it or not.* The important thing, she decided, was to make sure no one got hurt.

She left his room, shrugged into her coat, and headed to the amphitheater.

She knew Neil would beat her to Coastal Eddie, but she would still warn the man to be careful. It was the least she could do.

∼

AMANDA PULLED the red Miata off the highway just past San Miguel to fill up the tank at a dinky run-down gas station that, judging by the dull red ball in the sky, had once been a 76. Now it was called EAT-GAS-HERE and had an equally run-down cafe next to it that looked permanently closed in the patchy fog. But when she ran over the strippy thing, the bell dinged and as she got out of the car, a young moron with the biggest Adam's apple she'd ever seen came out of the dimly-lit station. He led with his lower body whipped forward so it looked like his torso and head were eternally trying to catch up to his legs.

"Help you, miss?" His nametag read, *Roy*.

She played her eyes from the top of his dishwater-colored hair to his dirty sneakers, and back again. He straightened up as she did - he obviously liked being eyed like a piece of meat. "You poor guy," she cooed, giving him a winning red smile. "You're stuck out here all by yourself?"

He gulped a laugh and she thought he was about to say "Golly gee," but it came out, "Golly, yes. It gets pretty lonely out here, miss. Would you like me to fill your tank?"

There was no guile or double meaning on his part, so Amanda licked her lips and gave him her best fuck-me smile. "I'd love it if you filled me up," she told him. "I want the best you've got."

"Yes, miss." Roy blushed as he lifted the nozzle and took it to the Miata.

She stood close to him. Out on the highway an occasional car whooshed by but there was no one else on the access road. He put the nozzle into the gas tank. "I like the way you do that," she purred.

"Do what?" He gulped, his eyes playing over her body, coming to rest on the pale cleavage peeking out from under her black leather jacket.

"The way you put your nozzle in my tank." She let her tongue touch her upper lip. "I bet you know how to treat a woman right."

The gawky guy turned red and smiled.

Amanda removed her jacket so he could see her breasts in their full glory under the scoop-necked top. "Warm out tonight."

"Uh, yeah. I'm pretty warm." Roy kept his gaze super-glued to her torso. When the tank was full, he replaced the nozzle. "Can I do anything else for you tonight, miss?"

"Check my tires and radiator?"

"Sure."

"And my oil? I'll bet you're great with a dipstick."

"Uh, ye-yes."

She watched him service her car. He finally pulled the dipstick out, pronounced her oil clean and full, then fumbled around, trying to get the stick back into its slot.

"You're having trouble finding my hole." Amanda slithered up next to him and placed her hands over his. "Let me help you." She looked up at him, making sure his main view was of her cleavage. "You're trembling. No wonder you're having trouble." She slowly glided the dipstick home. "There now, isn't that nice?"

"Ye-yes, miss." His boner was against her thigh and he knew it and tried to pull back.

She hugged herself to him and rubbed against it. "You're hung like an ox," she said. *And you're twice as stupid.*

"Uh, thanks." He trembled, despite the boner.

"What do you say we have a little fun, Roy?"

"What do you mean?"

He wasn't much more than a kid and his nervousness only increased her appetite. "You know what I mean, don't you?"

"I, uh..."

"Are you a virgin, Roy? Have you ever been with a girl?"

"Uh, sure."

She knew he was lying. "You're adorable. Why don't you unzip your pants?"

"Really?"

"Really."

"Right here?"

"There's no one around, Roy. It's sexier out in the open."

He didn't ask twice. The zipper came down.

She slowly tugged his pants down around his ankles, crouching before him like a hungry cat. His cock was impressive in girth and length, shining whitish-pink in the dull fluorescent light. She touched it with one cool hand and a drop of dew glistened, then dripped onto her palm. She made herself smile as she looked up at him. "You're very big." She let her voice go dark and husky.

"Th-thanks." His breath quivered and his Adam's apple bobbed.

"Look at me."

He looked down.

"Whatever happens, I want you to hold perfectly still."

The pupils of his baby-shit-brown eyes grew huge and she knew he'd gotten the message.

"Yes miss. I'll hold still."

Amanda smiled, then opened her mouth. She took him deep, and only when her lips touched the hair-matted base of his cock did she extend her fangs. She heard him suck a sharp breath through his teeth as the skin broke.

"Golly!"

She sucked his warm, coppery blood into her mouth, moaning as she drank from him.

He stood stone-still despite the sweet pain he must have felt.

She continued suckling from him, gnawing at the flesh a little when the blood slowed. His prick withered and went limp in her mouth, resting on her tongue like a cold dead lizard. Once she'd taken as much blood as the bite was willing to give, she spat him out, his dick flopping lifelessly from her mouth. He moaned his pleasure despite the impotence.

"You like that?" she asked.

"Mm-hmm."

Amanda took his balls in her palm, lifted them and used her tongue to probe at the tender flesh in the hollow of his thighs. She located his femoral artery, she bit down, hard.

The gas station attendant didn't move a muscle.

And Amanda didn't stop until his heart did.

She stared down at Roy's apparently lifeless body and thought about the guy whose throat she'd ripped out under the pier - *Surfer Boy* - and how he showed up on the onramp tonight. That was impossible unless he'd been bitten twice before and Amanda doubted that. The Darlings had told her it took three bites to turn a human. Even Julian - *a Trueborn!* - preferred to convert humans through three successive bites. *But not me. I'm special. I'm more special than Julian!*

Amanda toed Roy's body, then kicked it, hard. "You're dead," she muttered, and almost walked away. Almost. Surfer Boy should have stayed dead, too. *I ripped his throat out for Christ's sake!* But she knew for certain now that she was different from the Darlings. After all, she was as good at vampiric tricks now as it took most of them a century to become, Stephen had told her so. And he'd also said that there were several species of vampires. She wondered if any of them could turn a human in one bite. *I must be a different species ... a better species, stronger, more powerful.*

She grinned down at the dead man. "And I don't need *you* coming after me like that little puppy dog, Surfer Boy." She crouched over him and tore into his throat with her fangs, shredding the meat, severing cords, and ripping out flesh and muscle, biting deeper, deeper, until she reached the ridges of bone at the back of this neck. When she got to that, she put both hands on his head and twisted it off. No vampire could survive being beheaded.

Finished, she felt satisfied. No ... exhilarated. She smiled and wiped her mouth.

7

NEIL THE VAMPIRE SLAYER

Coastal Eddie Fortune didn't feel blood dripping from his ears, but figured it was due to the numbness that was setting in: Plastic Taffy had lost its little mind. It was all he could do to not inform his listeners that the aging boy band was having a midlife crisis and needed to be taken to the Caledonia Sanitarium for a good long rest. The atrocities committed in the name of heavy metal were the kind that inspired disaster movies and serial killers. They had just finished doing something unspeakable to Ozzy's *Mr. Crowley* and now, if he was guessing right, they were combining their sugar-popping sounds with Slayer's *Raining Blood*, and no one who heard it would ever sleep well again.

He groaned and briefly wondered once more what the boys were shooting up, then his thoughts returned to Neil Trinsky, who had stalked back into the busy midway after making his round of ridiculous threats.

Eddie wondered if the Darlings knew about Neil. Would he have the nerve to bother them? Maybe go snooping in an attempt to find out more about Biting Man or the fictional Vampire Council?

He wished he'd never made that shit up. It'd been amusing at the time - but it had only excited Neil all the more.

"Excuse me. Are you Mr. Fortune?"

Eddie glanced up at an attractive mature woman with a dark blond bob. She wore neat navy pants, a tan sweater, and a coordinating scarf around her neck. He hadn't even seen her approach. "Yes, ma'am. That's me."

Her eyes darted uncertainly. She wasn't beautiful - Eddie might have called her cute if she hadn't looked so tired - but there was something in the set of her large brown eyes, the taut line of her mouth, and the pixie nose that charmed him. She was a little younger than he was, maybe in her mid-fifties, give or take a few years.

"I ... um ... my name is Lois, and ... I ..." She fidgeted with her scarf, becoming more adorable by the moment, then she sighed and held her hand out. "Let's start over. I'm Lois. Lois Trinsky."

Eddie took her hand and paused, suddenly nervous. *Trinsky?*

"I believe you know my son, Neil?"

What the hell is going on here? "Well, I've, uh, made his acquaintance a few times." *Try about a hundred!*

Lois studied him. "I don't quite know how to say this, Mr. Fortune, but I believe my son may ... cause some problems for you."

Eddie cocked a brow. "Go on."

"He's never been a very ... stable boy, er, man, and he's obsessed with vampires. And well, now he seems to think you have something to do with them, and when he told me he was coming to see you tonight, I thought I ought to warn you." She was rambling now, toying vigorously with her scarf. "The thing is, he was doing pretty well for a while. I thought he'd outgrown some of the, uh, some of his problems. But I'm afraid ... I'm afraid he's, uh ... relapsing. Again."

"Ms. Trinsky-"

"Please, call me Lois."

"Lois. I'm Eddie. Are you saying you believe your son is a danger to me?"

"I don't know." Her voice splintered and her hands shook.

"Why don't you sit down, Lois?" He patted the chair next to him.

She sat, collected herself, and sighed. "I'm sorry. I just don't know what to do. I shouldn't have come." She cringed as Plastic Taffy hit an especially loud and sour note.

"No, I'm glad you came. Has Neil ever …" Eddie cleared his throat.

"Ever what?"

"Hurt anyone?"

She shook her head. "Nothing serious, not that I know of, but he was always getting in fights when he was little. He got sent home from school a lot." She blinked her wide brown eyes at him. "I think he's hurt animals, though I never caught him at it. He's not very nice to our dog. It worries me."

Eddie bit his lip, listening closely as Lois began telling him the story of her very troubled son. Neil was every bit as unbalanced as Eddie had figured. The only surprise was that a loser like Neil had come from such a nice, normal woman.

"So that's it," Lois said after telling him about Neil's refusal to leave the nest. "I'm at a loss. Tonight he said he was going to 'make' you tell him about something - something about a vampire council?"

"He was here and he did try to get me to tell him about it, but Lois, I made up the vampire council story to try to convince him not to poke his nose in places it doesn't belong. But it only made him more determined to snoop. Has he mentioned Biting Man?"

"No, who's that?"

"It's a what." He chuckled, thinking he liked Lois Trinsky. "It's something he read about on the internet. He had to dig pretty deep to find it, too. It's a sort of holiday for vampires and he wants to attend."

"Boy, it takes all kinds, doesn't it?" Lois shook her head. "My dentist told me that young people come around wanting him to give them pointed caps for their eye teeth."

"I've seen plenty of those," Eddie told her. "Crazy stuff."

"But, Eddie, the thing is, Neil isn't interested in vampires in the usual way." She paused. "He doesn't want to *be* a vampire; in fact, he seems completely disgusted by them. He wants to be like Buffy."

"He wants to kill." Eddie watched the color drain from her face.

"But why?"

"Who knows?"

"Can I ask you a question, Eddie?"

"Shoot."

Her hands twisted together on the table. "I don't want you to think I'm crazy."

He smiled. "You've listened to my show, haven't you?"

She nodded.

"Then you know I won't think you're crazy."

She didn't return his smile. "Are they ... *real*? Vampires, I mean. Not kids dressing up or having their teeth sharpened but ... *real* vampires. Do they exist?"

Eddie saw a woman capable of handling the truth. Before he had time to talk himself out of it, he said, "Yes. They're real, Lois. They're real. And they're here in Candle Bay, and many other places as well."

Lois glanced back at the darkness beyond the KNDL van, down at the ocean, up the path to the amphitheater, then scanned the midway before her eyes returned to his. "Here? Really? Like the *Lost Boys* on the Santa Cruz boardwalk?"

"No, not like that at all," Eddie told her. "They keep to themselves - they're respectable - and if a rogue vamp comes around with murder in his or her eye, they take care of the problem. In that way, they actually protect people." He thought of Amanda last night - and the dead male prostitute found this morning - and wondered if they'd be doing anything about her. He was virtually certain the boy was her kill. He studied Lois. "You don't look very surprised."

Her laugh lacked humor. "I've listened to you for a long time, Eddie, and I'm pretty sure I know when you're not bullshitting your audience. Plus, I've seen some of the websites Neil looks at on the Deep Web." She was silent a moment. "I think there are a lot of things in this world kept hidden from the public. I only wonder how Neil found out about all of this."

Eddie felt a pang of guilt, and wondered if his radio show was doing the world a disservice. "Lois, he's been listening to me at least half his life and-"

"It's not your fault. He's always fixated on things. First it was the Cookie Monster - imagine a three-year-old yelling "Die! Die! Die!" at the Cookie Monster! Then he fixated on *Star Wars* for a few years, but when his hormones kicked in, he switched to *Buffy the Vampire Slayer*.

He discovered her before he found you." She pulled her sweater closer. "Only now I guess he's after *real* vampires."

Eddie gave her a thin smile. "When someone searches long and hard, they'll always find what they're looking for."

She nodded and started to rise. "I guess so."

Eddie touched her hand. He didn't want to lose track of Lois. "Would you like to go out for coffee later? We could hang out until the concert's over then go to Bobby's Coffee."

"I wish I could, but I've got to get home." She glanced around again, anxiety edging her mouth. "I don't want to get home after Neil. I don't want him to know I was with you. He can be very possessive. It wouldn't be good for either of us."

Eddie wanted to pop the kid in his chops, but instead, he took Lois' hand and rose with her. "How about coffee tomorrow?"

She looked at him, surprised, then a smile lit her face and despite the lousy lighting, he saw her blush. "I'd like that. Do you eat lunch?"

He grinned. "Yes, I do. Where?"

"Bobby's Coffee? Tomorrow at noon?"

"I'll be there."

∽

NEIL WAS PRETTY SURE the girl riding the Ferris wheel with him was a vampire. He fingered the flask of holy water in his pocket then touched the ash stake hidden inside his leather jacket as their chair rose another notch. The wheel was still being filled.

He'd spotted her in line, alone. She was a slim, big-busted redhead with a tattoo of a bat with bloody fangs on her bare glitter-dusted shoulder. Her complexion was pale, her coral-painted lips and charcoal-shadowed eyes standing out like beacons meant to guide him to her. He popped a cinnamon Pucker-Button then walked right up, smiling like they were old friends, ignoring the people behind her in line.

"Hey," he'd said.

She blinked hazel eyes at him. "Hey." Then she reached out and tugged his wrist. "I thought you'd never get here. I thought I had to ride alone!" She raised her voice for the benefit of the others in line.

"Sorry I'm late." He moved closer, impressed with the girl's improv skills.

They stood in line for almost ten minutes. The glitter on her skin dazzled the eye, her hair smelled like peaches, and her gaze kept taking him in, all of him, flickering up and down his body as if he were the last piece of cake at a birthday party. She wanted to devour him; he sensed it. She wanted to drink his blood.

But he had to be sure and once they were locked into the swaying seat on the big wheel, he wasted no time. "What's your name?"

"Erin." She gave him a coy grin. "Erin Woodhouse. What's yours?"

"I'm Neil." He edged closer to her, but not so close he'd risk getting glitter all over himself. "What's a pretty girl like you doing here all alone?"

She giggled. "I'm here with a friend, but she's afraid of heights."

Neil looked down at the people below. How anyone could be afraid of heights was beyond him. *Pussies, that's what they are. Little bitch pussies.* "Her loss, my gain." He flashed a winning smile.

She giggled again.

Neil had had enough foreplay. As the wheel went up another notch, he reached into his pocket and withdrew the flask. After taking a swig, he held it out to her.

"What is it?"

"Tequila." He tried not to let his eyes betray him. If she were a vampire - and he was sure she was - the holy water would burn its way down her gullet and leave her dead in her seat. He wasn't sure what he'd do in that case; thinking ahead only clouded his judgment. It was best to just go with your gut and act fast.

She hesitated, then said, "Why not?" She took the flask and swigged it.

Neil watched her, eyes wide, waiting.

Liquid exploded from Erin's mouth. "Ugh! This is salt water!"

No smoke rose from her lips, no skin melted. Neil's heart sank in disappointment.

"What's wrong with you?" Erin's finely-arched brows drew into a scowl. "Why'd you give me that? Are you trying to roofie me?"

"No! It's holy water. I was worried you might be a vampire."

She blinked at him as they reached the apex in the ride and the wheel came to a temporary stop. "A vampire?" she asked. "Are you serious?"

He offered another quick shrug. "I like to make sure I'm in good company when I go on a ride with a girl." His eyes settled on her boobs.

Erin cleared her throat. "You realize they aren't real, don't you?"

"Your tits?"

Her jaw dropped. "Fuck you. I'm talking about vampires. *They're not real.*"

"That's what they say." Neil dragged his eyes up to her face. It took some effort.

"You're a strange guy, Neil. So tell me, did I pass your test?" The wheel began turning.

"I guess so." He glanced at her shoulder. "So why the bat tat?"

"Oh, that? I'm a vampire fan, like you."

He scowled. Bat-Tat Girl was *nothing* like him.

"I have a blog solely devoted to vampires." Her eyes lit up. "I review TV shows, novels, comic books, and movies and I have a hundred and fifty thousand followers! I even go to vampire cons when they come around." She paused for air. "What about you? Are you an Anne Rice kind of guy, or a Bela Lugosi type?"

"Neither." He stifled a yawn. Bat-Tat had a nice rack, but that was the only thing interesting about her now.

"I can never choose a favorite, either. I like them all! But the one I got this tattoo in honor of is Lestat!" She paused. "I was a kid with a crush. It's my only ink."

Lestat? Fucking Lestat? He swallowed a groan and fought against the rage that bubbled within him. *She's worse than a* real *vampire!* For a moment, he considered staking her just for having bad taste. "Nice," he said instead. "That's real nice."

"I've seen all the movies and read all the books-"

"Speaking of nice," said Neil, utterly bored. "You have some great tits. I like them real."

Her mouth turned into an O of shock.

"Just calling 'em like I see 'em." He let his eyes rove her body. "And you should let me see 'em."

"Who the hell do you think you are?" She stiffened, and the seat rocked as she half-stood and looked around in search of an escape. There was none, of course.

She's all mine till the end of the ride!

He smiled and stretched an arm across the back of the seat, widening his knees. "Chop, chop, Bat-Tat. The ride's almost over and God's not looking."

Her eyes told a thousand stories at once. Stories of shock, disgust, rage, and hatred. Beneath that, however, he saw the glint of lust. Like most women, she wanted him, but had to act coy. It was just part of being female, he guessed. Maybe they taught it in school. He didn't know, and he didn't care; he was only sure of one thing: Underneath the frigid exterior, they were sluts, every last one of them. *Including Mom.*

"Come on," he said, watching her with heavy-lidded eyes. "No one will see but me. We're all alone up here. *All* alone."

She spoke through gritted teeth. "Go to hell, you pervert."

Neil shrugged. "Can't win 'em all."

They were silent for a few moments. For Bat-Tat, he could tell it was awkward and tense, but for Neil, it was good times. He enjoyed making people uncomfortable, and he *loved* it when they were truly offended. He closed his eyes, soaking up the night, the cool summer breeze ... and the little bitch's prickly vibes of disgust.

But he was bored again and decided to give it one more try. "Hey," he said. "Wanna see *my* tattoo? It's Buffy." He'd impressed his fair share of women with the design - Sarah Michelle Gellar rising triumphantly from his well-coiffed black bush, her hand ready to hold a stake - but not just *any* stake. His *erect* stake. It was a gorgeous piece of art. "Buffy says she'd like to shake your hand." He chuckled.

"Fuck off." She crossed her arms and wouldn't look at him.

"Suit yourself."

She did, and when the ride ended, Bat-Tat left her seat and hurried away, glittering into the night. She was playing hard to get. Neil decided to shadow her, at least until he spotted a real vampire. It was a nice view if nothing else.

∼

Eddie Fortune, grateful the music had finally ended, popped three ibuprofen, washed them down with soda water, and nodded, smiled, and handed out autographs, signing everything from KNDL bumper stickers to napkins and breasts - and even the magnificent glitter-covered ass of a beautiful redhead with a bat tattoo on her shoulder. It was a typical night outside the amphitheater.

Finally, the crowd dwindled to a trickle, then stopped about the time the amphitheater lights shut down. After promising his listeners a new interview with Plastic Taffy, Eddie signed off, packed up the last scraps of KNDL swag, folded the table and chairs, and stowed them in the van. His cell rang. It was Ramon asking him to meet the band at North Pier to record the interview. Eddie started to protest but Ramon said please and claimed the guys wanted to do it there because it was quiet and peaceful. Eddie agreed. The sound quality wouldn't be so hot, but then Plastic Taffy wasn't sounding so hot either.

As he drove down the access road to the pier something ate at him; he wasn't sure what. Maybe it was because the north pier was where they found the boy-prostitute's body less than twenty-four hours ago. Or maybe it was Neil's visit that put him on edge. Plastic Taffy usually wanted to meet at the station, but their request wasn't all that odd - that wasn't it. Once, they'd insisted on being interviewed in the amphitheater lavatory.

He pulled into the empty parking lot at North Pier and a moment later the garish faux-psychedelic Plastic Taffy van parked next to him. The four men piled out, rowdy as ever, but none were carrying beer bottles, and that was a little weird, too. With a sigh, Eddie climbed out, opened the KNDL van's side door to set up to record, then nodded to the musicians, who were watching him as if he were a bikini-clad beach babe. "Hey guys. New threads?" He didn't ask about the eyeliner and black lipstick.

They giggled, even chortled, at his remark. "You like?" Davy turned in a circle to show off his black and red leather vest and pants. The hair on his chest was tinged with gray and Eddie wondered why he didn't shave like his bandmates. *That's weird, too.* This was definitely not the Plastic Taffy he'd come to know and loathe. This was worse. All wore black leather pants and vests. Ramon's was purple with silver hippie fringe, Paul's was gold and black, and Mick's was solid black.

"All right," said Eddie, finishing a sound check. "We'll just do the fast version, okay, guys?"

They nodded and formed a close half-circle around him.

"Good evening, babes and dudes, this is Coastal Eddie, KNDL-FM, and I've got a special treat for you. I'm here by the fog-covered pier on the mighty Pacific with a band whose work has spanned decades. Looking at them now, I'd venture to say they've made some changes to their brand recently."

A couple of them chuckled. Ramon moved close enough that Eddie found himself edging away. It wasn't the brutal scent of musky aftershave that bothered him as much as the strange twinkle in the lead singer's eye.

"That's right, ladies and gentlemen, I'm here with Plastic Taffy, the Central Coast's own performers of such hits at *Leaving the Girl, Girl Don't Leave Me,* and *Hey Girl, You Got My Number.* Tonight, they played a slightly different gig at the Candle Bay Amphitheater, and we're going to find out what this night in the life of Plastic Taffy looks like behind the scenes. Ramon, when you and Paul formed this band so long ago, did you ever imagine you'd still be playing to large audiences all these years later?" He held the mic out to Ramon, who closed the distance with an oddly even step.

"Well, Eddie, that was a long time ago, but I think we all knew we didn't want to be one-hit wonders, so yeah. I think we knew it would last."

Davy swept in, licked his black-painted lips, and spoke in a low, but booming voice. "There's a new Plastic Taffy in town, folks, and you're going to love us!" He gave Eddie a slow unnerving wink. "Do you like trying new things, Eddie?"

"Speaking of new things," said Eddie, who was having a hard time maintaining his slow mellow patter. "I couldn't help noticing the very ... *dramatic* change in your appearance ... and your music. Would you like to tell us why you decided a change was in order?"

Paul giggled, and Ramon and Davy both swiveled their heads to look at him. "It was my idea," said Davy.

Mick retreated to the back of the van and appeared to be taking a leak.

Eddie suppressed a groan. *Better not piss on the van, pal.*

"Times are changing, man," said Davy. "And we, like the times, need to change."

Yeah, you just reached 1985. Profound, man. "And how did you choose your new image?"

Three sets of eyes moved to Mick, who turned, tucking his pecker in a little too late to keep it from Eddie's line of sight. "My idea," called Mick, jaunting back toward the microphone.

Eddie almost dry-heaved when the drummer took the mic in his unwashed hands and pulled it to his lips, practically giving it head. "Rock on, Candle Bay!" He made devil horns in the air - despite the fact no one was looking.

This is just embarrassing, thought Eddie. "So, Davy decides a change is in order, Mick chooses the new threads. What do Paul and Ramon contribute to this transformation?"

Mick moved close to the mic. Eddie thought he was going to speak, but he didn't. He appeared to be trying to smell Eddie's neck.

Before Eddie could slap him away, Ramon said, "I wrote some new songs, and Paul revised some of the cover tunes we did tonight."

"That's fasci-"

"I have a question for you, Mr. Fortune," said Mick.

"Uh, shoot." Eddie pushed the mic toward him.

"What kind of cologne are you wearing? You smell delicious." Mick grinned and Eddie thought he saw a quick flash of teeth that were a little too long - but it was gone as quick as it had come.

"It's all me," said Eddie. "Now about these new songs of yours. Does this mean your fans can expect a new album?"

"Albums are dead, man," said Davy. "Dead as disco and the Doors. But the fans can expect several new tunes that can be downloaded in the coming months."

"And," said Mick, his eyes on Eddie's mouth, "we shot some new music videos earlier this year that'll be available to watch on YouTube with the release of the new material."

Eddie opened his mouth, freezing when Mick's hand shot toward his face. He touched Eddie's lips with icy fingers, his eyes fixed on his mouth.

"Take it easy, man," Davy told Mick.

Mick gripped Eddie's jaw, his hand an iron vise.

"What's going on?" Eddie slowly shut the mic off.

"Come on, Mick." Ramon put a hand on the drummer's shoulder, but Mick wouldn't be moved.

"I want him." Mick's hands were cadaver-cold.

Realization dawned - *Vampires! They're goddamned vampires ... hungry ones!* Eddie told himself to be calm as he slipped his hand into his watch pocket to touch his vial of holy water. "Look guys," he said. "This has been good times and all, but I really need to wrap it up." He thought fast. "I'm expected to check in with my parole officer in ten minutes, and if I'm even thirty seconds late, he'll come looking for me." Eddie swallowed. "He knows where I am." The lie came quick and easy.

"You hear that, man?" said Davy. "He's got a cop coming to check on him." He moved to Mick's other side and he and Ramon pulled the drummer back several feet.

Mick's nostrils flared. "But I want him." The cords stood out in his neck as he fought against the restraint of his bandmates. "I want him!"

Eddie hurled himself into the van and slammed the sliding door shut.

"I want him!" The van rocked as Mick charged it like a furious bull.

Eddie shot to the front seat and slammed the locks down.

"I want him!" Another hard hit that was sure to leave a dent.

"Jesus Christ." Eddie stared out the passenger-side window as the saner members of the undead boy-band tackled their drummer.

Paul straddled him and beat his head against the ground, yelling, "Get hold of yourself, Mick!"

Mick looked wildly around, and slowly came to his senses. The other three helped him to his feet.

"Sorry about that, man," called Davy, smiling. "Maybe another time?"

Eddie peeled out leaving Plastic Taffy staring after him.

This was bad. This was very, very bad. With all the doting fan girls the band had acquired over the years, sustenance would come all too easily to them. And that meant a shit storm of drama. "Jesus Christ." Swallowing, Eddie sped toward the Candle Bay Hotel.

8

THE DIRTY UNDEAD

Stephen Darling looked up to see a tall slim man in jeans and a Grateful Dead T-shirt hurrying toward the front desk. *That can't be Eddie Fortune. Can it?* The man had aged, his tanned face seamed, his ponytail and goatee more salt than pepper.

"Mr. Darling?" the deejay said, looking Stephen straight in the eye.

"Mr. Fortune. It's been a very long time."

"And *you* haven't aged a day." Anxiety edged Eddie's joke.

"What are you doing here? I believe we banned you at least twenty years ago."

"Thirty," Eddie said. "I was a young idiot. Sorry about trying to organize a protest against your hotel."

Stephen nodded. "You only embarrassed yourself." He allowed a trace of a smile to cross his lips. Eddie Fortune and a small group of fans - and one newspaper reporter - had shown up one fall evening bearing signs protesting vampire-owned hotels. The news article had brought the hotel extra business - and a lot of requests for vampire-themed rooms. Those had inspired some redecorating and their dungeon and Dracula rooms were never empty. "I must thank you for the publicity."

"Yeah, my pleasure. Again, sorry about that. We need to talk." His eyes shot from one side of the lobby to the other. "Now."

Stephen nodded. The deejay smelled faintly of fear and the look in his eyes betrayed a tinge of shock. "Very well. How serious is this talk going to be?"

"Deadly."

"We'll go to my office, then." Stephen came around the desk and led Eddie Fortune to the mezzanine and back to the hall of offices. Eddie had googly-eyes the entire time. Just as Stephen buzzed his door open, Uncle Ori appeared and raised his eyebrows. "Uncle, I believe you've heard of our local radio personality, Eddie Fortune?"

"Indeed." He turned dark eyes on Eddie. "I am surprised my nephew has brought you here." He moved closer, anger sparking red in his eyes.

"There's trouble," Eddie said. "Or I wouldn't be here."

"Let's go inside." Stephen ushered the pair into his office, to the two chairs before his desk. "Sit, please." Eddie did so immediately and after brief hesitation, Ori sat beside him. Stephen folded his hands on the desktop.

"What kind of trouble?" Ori asked before Stephen could speak.

"Someone is making vampires," Eddie announced.

"What?" Stephen asked.

"Someone turned the local rock band into bloodsuckers." Eddie paused, worry on his face. "Uh, excuse me. I didn't mean to be rude."

"That's all right, go on." Stephen and Ori listened while Eddie told them about his run-in with Plastic Taffy.

"You're certain they've been turned?" Ori asked.

Stephen saw no anger in his uncle's eyes now. *Lucky for Eddie.* Ori could be very impetuous - that was one of the reasons he rarely interacted with hotel guests.

"I saw fangs. One of them tried to bite my neck."

"I don't blame him." Ori smugly folded his hands.

"Uncle, please." Stephen turned back to Eddie. "*Tried?*"

"The others dragged him off me. I came straight to you." Eddie shook his head. "I didn't know what else to do."

"You did the right thing," Stephen told him.

"Yes," Ori agreed.

"We need to talk turkey," Eddie said. "Can we do that?"

Stephen eyed Ori. "We guarantee no harm will come to you, don't we Uncle?"

Ori adjusted the pin on his red silk tie then grunted. "Speak freely, Mr. Fortune."

"I think you call them Rogues," Eddie began. "Vampires that are not part of your circle?"

"We do."

"There's one in Candle Bay and I think I may know who it is." He paused. "And it's probably going to piss you off."

"Try me," Stephen said. "Remember, we've guaranteed your safety."

"Last night while I was broadcasting by the amphitheater, a woman named Amanda approached me. She claimed to be one of you." He paused. "Ring any bells?"

Stephen nodded. "Go on."

"She seemed agitated. Hungry, maybe. After we spoke she walked toward North Pier."

"And?"

"This morning the body of a male prostitute was found under that pier. His throat was torn out. It's all over the news-"

"We are aware of this." Ori spoke softly. "Your point?"

"The mood she was in, the agitation she gave off ..." Eddie locked eyes with Stephen Darling. "I believe Amanda is responsible for his death."

Stephen nodded. "And the band?"

"The band has a habit of going to North Pier after their performances. They like to drink beer out there, let off a little steam, you know?"

"Yes. And?" Stephen prompted.

"I have no proof, only a hunch. I think Amanda may have turned the band, too. Maybe there-"

"I believe your instincts are correct." Stephen sighed. "And I am very sorry to say so. We will deal with the situation and until we inform you otherwise, I suggest you remain cautious, Mr. Fortune. Is there anything else?"

"Uh ... no, that's it."

"Very well." Stephen could tell the man wanted to say more – probably ask questions – but he rose and escorted Eddie into the mezzanine and out the front door. "Where are you parked?"

Eddie pointed. "Halfway down that row."

"I will see you to your vehicle." Stephen walked so briskly that Eddie had to trot a few steps to catch up.

"Making sure I don't come back inside?"

Stephen didn't reply until they reached the KNDL van. "No, Mr. Fortune. I'm making sure you arrive at your vehicle intact."

The deejay looked shocked as he pulled his keys from his pocket. "Well, thanks. I appreciate it."

"Mr. Fortune, take my card." Stephen scribbled on its back and handed it to Eddie. "Call me on my personal phone any time after twilight. The second number belongs to our security head. Call her during the day. I will inform her of the situation."

Eddie took the card, relief on his face. "Man, I was half afraid I wouldn't come out of that hotel alive."

"I've heard your show, Mr. Fortune. You're quite entertaining and you've really never done anything to threaten us – not for thirty years, anyway." He gave a small, tight smile. "We do not harm humans. As business owners, we have an interest in protecting the citizens of Candle Bay from any of our kind who ... *stray*."

Eddie met his eyes. "So I've heard and, after so many years, I know it's a fact." He paused. "Amanda Pearce. I met her when she first arrived in town. She seemed very nice. Back then."

"She was." Stephen didn't try to hide the regret in his voice. "Unfortunately that has changed. We believe she has left town, but she may return. Do be cautious, Mr. Fortune."

Eddie nodded. "What about Plastic Taffy? What will you do?"

"We will bring them in tonight and have a *very* serious talk with them. What happens next will be up to them. Thank you for bringing this to my attention. You've no doubt saved lives tonight. Keep your eyes open and let me know immediately if you witness anything else. Above all, watch your back."

∽

NEIL TRINSKY GREW bored with Bat-Tat Girl when he saw her getting her butt signed by that little bitch, Coastal Eddie. After that, he'd continued his hunt, but hadn't found a single vampire at the boardwalk. After a pointless ninety minutes he left, slowly cruising his Vespa through the foggy town. He wound the little bike through the graveyards on Cemetery Hill - most of the Central Coast was buried in one of them - but all were securely gated and locked. Finally, he'd come to the Candle Bay Hotel and cruised the lot, wondering if he should go in and see if any filthy bloodsuckers wanted to be staked.

But he'd never gone inside because he'd spotted Coastal Eddie's van parked smack dab in the middle of the lot, surrounded by SUVs and cars bearing AAA stickers, stick-figure family decals, and bumper stickers bragging about honor students and boy scouts. He couldn't believe his eyes.

"You little bitch." He stood in the shadow cast by a black Ford Escape plastered with liberal bumper stickers about feeding families instead of banks. *Stupid treacle.*

He peered around the Escape at the KNDL van, two slots away. *He's friends with vampires? I knew it!*

The lobby door opened, casting warm amber light out from beneath the porte-cochere. Two men exited and even at this distance he recognized Coastal Eddie's ambling stride. Peering around the SUV, he watched the two come closer and soon recognized the man in the dark suit as one of the Darlings. *Stephen Darling.* Their voices were lost to the breeze.

When they arrived at the van, he strained to hear them. Even after daring to slip one car closer in the shadows, he still couldn't make out the words - they spoke too softly, trading secrets, no doubt. *Eddie's a dirty vampire lover! He's probably getting himself invited to Biting Man! Maybe he wants to be turned before he gets any fucking older. Little bitch!*

Just before the van's engine roared to life, he heard the vampire tell Eddie to report back to him and to watch his back.

They're talking about me!

Neil hid until the van pulled past, then got on his Vespa. Tonight, he would finally find out where the reclusive Coastal Eddie lived. And how he was involved with the dirty undead.

9

THE PETTING ZOO

"That little shit is following me!" Eddie told the smiling Buddha on his dashboard.

He'd become aware of the bike riding his ass right after he'd turned out of the hotel lot, but it hadn't registered until he arrived at KNDL and exchanged the station van for his own custom Chevy Express. As soon as he pulled out of the lot, he saw the tiny motorbike take up behind him and realized it was the same one that had followed him earlier. For one horrible moment he thought maybe Mick the drummer was after him, looking for blood, but when Eddie hit the gas, the bike couldn't keep up. That's when he knew it had to be Neil Trinsky on his Vespa.

Thank the gods the damned psychopath doesn't have a real bike!

Neil had tried to wheedle out of him where he lived many times over the years but Eddie had never caught him following him before. It might have been funny if the guy hadn't behaved like such a maniac tonight. Eddie slowed and let him almost catch up, then sped up again. He kept the game up as he headed back into town - he didn't want Neil to have the faintest clue where his little house in the hills was. "I've got an idea," he told the Buddha as he drove toward South Pier where most of Candle Bay's nightlife was located.

Driving across Ocean Avenue - Candle Bay's version of Main Street, U.S.A. - he saw that the boardwalk had closed for the night even though it wasn't yet one a.m. That was the way of Candle Bay, a town full of little white clapboard businesses and homes, a town he thought of as a place Lovecraft could have invented, locked up tight against monsters the inhabitants knew surrounded them. It was fitting. It was apt. He glanced in the mirror and didn't see Neil for a moment - he was too close to see. *What an idiot. The fearless vampire hunter needs to learn some discretion.*

Reaching South Pier, he passed several taverns before pulling up to The Petting Zoo. His old pal Randy Peters (nee Peterson) ran the Zoo with such aplomb that gay men came from as far south as Devilswood and north from Caledonia. "Neil, the boys at the Zoo are going to love you!" Eddie chuckled. The dashboard Buddha bobbed happily.

Inside the tavern, he headed straight to the bar. "Hey, Randy!"

Randy was wiping out a glass. "Hey, Edds, how they hanging?"

"Swinging pretty low these days."

"I know what you mean, Edds, I know what you mean." Randy was getting pretty gray himself. He inspected the glass and set it under the bar. "Want anything?"

"How about a Killian's?"

Randy opened a chilled bottle and handed it over. "Glass?"

"No, it's okay." Eddie took a long pull then leaned forward. "I've got a crazy fan following me. He should be walking in any second now. He's a straight shooter. I need to get rid of him so I can go home."

"Want me to have Kristophe run interference?"

Eddie followed Randy's gaze to the six-foot-six bodybuilder who spent his nights at the Zoo. He wasn't an official bouncer - just a close buddy of Randy's who kept an eye on the patrons. "That'd be great."

Randy put two fingers in his mouth and gave a sharp whistle.

Kristophe, in jeans so tight it was surprising he didn't squeak when he walked, made his way to the bar. The sleeves of his white T-shirt had been ripped clean off, exposing skull-crushing guns, and he could have cracked walnuts between his pecs. Eddie chuckled. Neil was in for a treat.

~

Coastal Eddie really is a queer? Neil couldn't believe his eyes when the deejay pulled into the lot of The Petting Zoo. Uneasy, Neil parked the Vespa and sat a moment, deliberating. *What if someone sees me and thinks I'm a queer, too?* But his only other option was to sit outside and wait until Eddie reemerged. *And who knows how long he'll be in there?* And what if Eddie was meeting another vampire? *A queer one!* It made perfect sense to Neil that vampires would hang out in gay bars - *Look at Edward Cullen for Christ's sake!* - and he decided he'd better just go in and get it over with.

The place was full and for Neil, that was a blessing. He walked in quietly, slipping through the crowd and taking a seat at a booth at the far end of the room. Eddie was talking to the bartender, his back to Neil. There were two platforms in the center of the room, and on each of them, a half-naked man danced. Men - sweaty and drunk, all of them - crowded around the platforms and tossed bills at the dancers while, overhead, Cher demanded to know if anyone believed in life after love.

The whole thing was sickening. Neil wished there was a God so He could smite them all, just like He did the dirty queers in Sodom and Gomorrah.

"Hey, handsome," said a bow-tied, greasy-chested waiter. "What can I get you?"

Neil couldn't even look at him. "Sparkling water."

The waiter left and Neil watched Eddie. The bartender didn't look like a vampire, but if Neil had learned anything, it's that those dirty bloodsuckers were sneaky bastards - you could never really tell.

The man who returned with Neil's drink was not the waiter. "It's on me." The guy spoke in a deep rusty voice. He set the glass in front of Neil then took a seat across from him. "I'm Kristophe, what's your name?"

"Uh, Neil. Thanks." He nodded at the water.

The guy, who must have weighed two-fifty - all muscle - held out his hand. "Nice to meet you, Neil."

The handshake was strong enough to break bones.

Kristophe's nose looked like it had been broken at least three times and his hair was a military-precise crewcut. Despite the tight jeans, it was obvious to Neil this guy wasn't gay, and that was a great relief. Probably, he was a bouncer and was on break and, recognizing the only other straight dude in the place, came over for a reprieve from all the gayness. "I haven't seen you around here before. You new to town? Visiting?"

"I'm local. I've never been here before. I came tonight because I'm soaking up atmosphere for a blog I'm writing - it's about Candle Bay culture." The lie was brilliant, if he did say so himself.

"A blogger? Hey, I blog too, bro. What's your URL?"

Neil's hands fidgeted under the table. "Uh, I haven't unveiled it yet. Soon. For now, it's top secret." He smiled.

Kristophe nodded. "Are you on Facebook?"

"Uh, sure." Neil, barely listening, turned his head as Eddie twisted to glance around the room.

"Sweet, let's connect."

The next thing Neil knew, the guy was sitting beside him. He had his phone out and opened to Facebook. He smelled like sweat and Drakkar Noir. "What's your last name? I'll send you a request."

Neil told him and tried to inch closer to the wall; it was futile, there was no place to go. He was trapped.

"Sent," said Kristophe.

"I'll confirm when I get home." Another lie.

"You sure got a pretty little mouth." The guy grinned.

Terror spread through Neil like brushfire just as a meaty hand landed on his thigh and squeezed.

"Oh, I, uh, look dude ... I'm not into that. I mean, I'm not quee- homosexual. Not that there's anything wrong with that, but-"

The guy tossed his head back and laughed, the cords of muscle in his neck standing out.

Shit. At five-foot-eight, Neil knew he couldn't take the guy. *This was a very bad idea.*

"How do you know you're not gay?" Kristophe's eyes twinkled.

Neil couldn't believe he'd missed how totally queer the guy was.

"Have you ever tried it? You might like it."

The hand moved higher and Neil tensed. "Well, no, but-"

"Then you don't *know*, do you?"

Neil's mouth worked silently.

"Would you like to dance?" He gave Neil's thigh another hard squeeze.

"No!" It came out as a squeak. "I mean, no thanks. I'm just here to observe the place, you know?"

Kristophe laughed again, released Neil's thigh, and crossed enormous arms over his massive chest. "Whatever you say."

"No, really, I'm not gay." He glanced at the bar. Eddie was still there.

Kristophe leaned close - he moved fast for a big guy - and said, "I think I can change your mind about that." He made a purring sound, and Neil swallowed hard as the guy's hot wet tongue darted into his ear. *Please, dear God, even though you don't exist - please, get me out of here!* Neil flinched away, his shoulder rising to meet his ear.

"Sorry," said Kristophe. "Too soon?"

"It's okay, dude. I'm just not into -" At the bar, Eddie was getting to his feet. "Look I really need to g-"

"All I'm saying," said the bodybuilder, "is that you ought to at least give something a *try* before you say you don't like it. Didn't your mom used to make you at least *taste* your vegetables?"

What the hell is this guy talking about? Neil craned his neck, trying to see past the man, who'd moved so close he took up his entire view. "I really need-"

"And," Kristophe plowed on, "didn't you sometimes find that you *did* like your vegetables, after all?" His hand squeezed Neil's thigh again. "Just a little taste and if you don't like it, you don't have to eat it. Just like Mama always said."

Neil saw Coastal Eddie's empty barstool and thought he spotted a gray ponytail in the crowd, heading toward the doors. "Let me out, dude, I have to go."

"Aren't you at least going to taste your drink?"

"No, I need to leave. Something came up."

The muscle man grinned. "Besides me?"

"Uh, yeah. I have to go *now!*"

The guy remained motionless. "So, will I get to see you again?"

"Sure. I'll friend you on Facebook, like you said." *Damn it! Move!* Eddie was nowhere to be seen.

"All right." Kristophe slowly - very slowly - slid out of the booth. "We'll talk then and set something up."

"Sure." The guy was a psycho. "Whatever you say, dude."

At last, Kristophe was on his feet.

Neil shot out of the booth - only to find himself crushed in the man's iron embrace, powerless to do anything about it. "What the-"

"It sure was nice meeting you, Neil." Kristophe stroked the back of Neil's head as if he were a puppy.

"Uh, yeah, sure." He didn't want to piss the guy off; he could break ribs with one little squeeze. Neil managed to get an arm up and give the man an awkward back-pat.

"So nice to meet you," Kristophe repeated, still stroking his head.

"You too. I gotta go." Neil's voice strained from lack of oxygen.

"I'll see you on Facebook."

Neil almost shrieked when he felt the man's hand on his ass - his palm taking hold of an entire cheek and giving it a hard squeeze and a little shake.

Kristophe chuckled. "Firm. You work out?"

"Uh, yeah."

"Sweet. I want to see your equipment sometime."

Neil squeaked and, at last, the guy let go.

Kristophe winked then batted his lashes. His hearty laughter chasing Neil as he ran, pushing his way through the crowd and into the parking lot.

Eddie's van was long gone.

"Shit!" Neil stomped his foot. "Shit, shit, shit!" He could still smell the bodybuilder's aftershave, still feel the weight of his palm on his ass. He felt a little sick and hoped like hell that being a homo wasn't contagious.

Discouraged, he got on the Vespa and headed home for a long hot shower.

10

TRAVELIN' VAMPS

It had taken hours for Norman Keeler to hitch a ride, and that only took him ten miles up the coast to Caledonia, an artist colony renowned for its beauty and fine restaurants.

It was Norman's fault that the ride got shortened. Clarke, the guy who picked him up, was going all the way to San Jose and said he'd take him along, but when they stopped in Caledonia for gas, Clarke wanted to get something to eat. Norman was hungry, but not for food - he didn't know what he hungered for until Clarke opened his rare roast beef sandwich to squirt on horseradish. That's when Norman saw the bloody meat and knew exactly what he wanted. Not the meat - but the blood.

Returning to the car, he'd taken the backseat, saying he needed a nap. The parking lot was deserted - they'd been the sandwich shop's last customers of the night - and as soon as Clarke started the car, Norman grabbed him by the neck and pulled him into the back seat. Shocked at his own strength, Norman drank his first meal. It had been messy, but delicious. Now Clarke was sprawled in a bloody heap on the floor of the back seat.

Norman hit the road, driving Clark's Ford Flex north, on the scent of his maker.

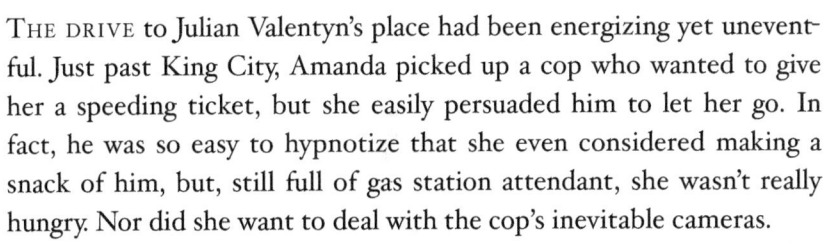

THE DRIVE to Julian Valentyn's place had been energizing yet uneventful. Just past King City, Amanda picked up a cop who wanted to give her a speeding ticket, but she easily persuaded him to let her go. In fact, he was so easy to hypnotize that she even considered making a snack of him, but, still full of gas station attendant, she wasn't really hungry. Nor did she want to deal with the cop's inevitable cameras.

That had been her last stop, however brief, and now she arrived in Mill Valley, at the southernmost tip of Wine Country, just a dozen miles above San Francisco. She and Stephen had visited the beautiful and bucolic little town once when they were first together, staying in a cabin in the woods outside one of the wineries. They'd slept all day and roamed all night, almost as if it were their honeymoon.

But it wasn't a honeymoon! And it never will be! At the last moment, Amanda saw the sign announcing Valentyn Vineyards and in her anger, careened off the highway too fast, spraying gravel before the red Miata grabbed the asphalt on Valentyn Vineyards Road. She slowed. Grapevines grew on either side of the narrow thoroughfare as far as the eye could see. Finally, she arrived at a massive white wrought iron gate that said "Valentyn Vineyards" in ornate script across its top. Iron grape vines and leaves twined between the bars. The gate was locked and a small sign said it would open at 9 a.m.

"Well, that won't fucking do at all!"

Amanda pulled the Miata off the road, parked by the fence, and grabbed her handbag and overnight case. She easily tossed both items over the gate then began climbing, using the ornate curves of iron as footholds. A moment later, she threw her leather-clad legs over the top and shimmied down. "You really ought to consider razor wire, Julian."

She glanced at the sky; she had plenty of time before dawn, and in any case, she'd been using a lot of Lixir, so she could stand some sun. Even though he'd taken the teeth out of the potion - it was no longer addictive or as strong a stimulant as the stuff Stephen had in him back when he turned her - it still would let her deal with sunlight just fine. Stephen hated that she used the drug regularly. *Fuck you, Stephen, you dickless prick!* She started walking.

11

JULIAN VALENTYN

Julian Valentyn, relaxing in his favorite Curule chair, had been going over Valentyn Vineyards' and Chantrieri Winery's accounting figures for the last month and was pleased with the results. His business, nearly a decade old now, was officially in the black. For that matter, it had been in the black from the first year thanks to the veinery hidden within the massive building, but the IRS would never know about that. The Batflower Veinery had taken a bite out of Slater Brothers' business in its very first year of operation. The vineyard and winery were merely pleasant covers for his true business – supplying vampires all over the world with the best bottled blood money could buy. And his specialty bottles – the popular ones that blended fine alcoholic spirits with blood as well as the expensive Lixir-infused bloods that allowed vampires to deal with sunlight and eat small amounts of human food – had made him richer many times over.

Julian stood, intending to visit the greenhouses, but the bank of security cameras caught his eye. Someone was walking up the road leading to the winery and eventually up the hill to his house. He stood there, watching the lone figure. As it drew nearer to the camera, he could see that it was pulling a case behind it. Glancing at the gate monitor, he saw a small car parked just outside.

He punched a number on his cell, activating a walkie-talkie app.

His man picked up instantly. "Yes, Master Julian?"

"Felix," he said, still watching the figure on the screen; it was clearly female. "We have a visitor who is on foot, halfway to the winery. Would you be so kind as to drive the cart down and fetch her? Bring her to the house."

"Of course. Will handcuffs be required, Master?"

"Carry them, but don't use them unless you sense danger. And if she is vampire, let me know immediately."

"Very well, Master."

Julian hung up. He still missed Jinxy, dead over a decade now. If he'd turned him, he would still be here. Felix Farquhar somehow reminded him of his long-lost assistant, though his appearance was far more genteel, as were his manners. Julian admittedly enjoyed being called 'Master' - he always had - but Felix took it to new heights, saying it with such love and devotion that it was sometimes embarrassing. Julian had no doubt that Felix yearned to be a vampire and was doing everything he could to convince Julian to turn him. *And I may do just that. Eventually.*

∾

FELIX RECOGNIZED her before she spoke: She was the woman in the charcoal drawing Julian kept on the easel. Idling the cart, he raised the cell, took a photo, and pressed send before nodding at her.

"Good morning, madam." He watched her approach. "Do you have business here?"

The blonde stared hard at him and he knew she was vampire. He quickly opened the two-way speaker on the cell and said "vamp," under his breath so that only Julian would hear.

"I'm here for Julian Valentyn. Where is he?" She stared hard into his eyes, her irises going black as she tried to hypnotize him.

He glanced away, refusing to be influenced. "I have instructions to bring you to him." Felix studied her, goosebumps trailing down his spine. He sensed danger pouring from her, and fervently wished Master Julian had turned him. He felt unprepared, despite the fact that he carried holy water and a revolver loaded with silver bullets. His cell flashed a message from Julian: *Caution and kid gloves. I will meet you on the veranda.*

"Let me help you with your bags." Felix left the cart, quickly brushed his hands over his immaculate charcoal suit, then stowed the woman's suitcase and smaller bag in the rear, before escorting her to the passenger door where he offered his arm. She took it, pressing her fingers painfully into him as she climbed into the cart.

Seated, she pressed a fingernail into his wrist, drawing blood. "Look at me," she said. But he wouldn't, nor would he show her his pain.

Trying to catch his eyes, failing, she slowly released him and licked her bloody fingertip. "What's your name?" she asked as he took the driver's seat.

"Felix."

"The cat?"

"Farquhar."

She laughed. "What kind of name is that?"

"I believe it originated in Scotland, ma'am."

"Figures. Home of haggis. Do you like haggis, Felix?"

"I've never had it, but I doubt I'd like it." He began driving.

"Most food from the British Isles is pretty bad, but I like blood sausage, myself." She twirled a lock of pale gold hair around her finger. "Do you like blood sausage, Felix? Or spotted dick?"

"No, madam. I prefer to sink my teeth into melons. The juicier the better."

Her laughter rang like wind chimes. "I like you, Felix."

"Thank you, ma'am." He forced a smile as they passed the winery and began the climb to the house.

"Do you like *me*, Felix?"

He kept his eyes on the road. "Of course, madam."

"How long have you worked for Julian?"

"Several years."

"Kinky."

He glanced at her, wondering what, if anything, she meant, but she stared straight ahead, so he remained silent. The woman gave off danger like a skunk gave off stink.

∽

She hadn't changed, of course. Julian Valentyn watched as Felix parked the cart in front of the wide veranda. Amanda got out and looked at him, her lips full and quivering.

Despite himself, Julian's heart began to pound and his mouth went dry. *Stop it, you're reacting like a human!*

"Julian!" Amanda ran toward him and when she threw herself into his arms, he resisted the urge to hold her.

"Oh, how I've missed you!" She was weeping.

"Amanda." Julian tried to keep a steady voice. "It's been a very long time."

"Too long!" She buried her face in his chest, her body quaking with sobs.

At last, he raised a hand to her back, patted it.

"I was wrong. I was wrong, Julian. I love you. It's always been you." She looked into his eyes. "How I wish you had been the one to turn me."

How he had ached to hear those words ... but as she said them now, Julian found himself going on alert. Why the change of heart? He couldn't escape the feeling she was manipulating him, but despite that suspicion, he breathed in the scent of her hair - strawberries and cream - and let his hand stroke her back, relishing the feel of her body against his.

Felix, carrying her bags, came up the stairs, eyes averted, and disappeared into the shadows of the veranda.

"Let me stay with you, darling. Please?"

Julian took her shoulders and held her at arm's length. "Why are you here, Amanda? Has something happened?"

Her face crumpled. "It's Stephen. He ... he beat me after he read my private journal and found out how much I've always loved you! Oh, it was awful, Julian! I've left him." She broke into fresh sobs. "I can't bear to think of it." She swayed a bit, as though she might faint.

Or that's what she wishes me to believe. Her story didn't ring true, yet he'd never known Amanda to lie. She'd been so sweet and gentle, so naive, when last they met. *But it's been a very long time since then; since she was human.*

"Why don't we go inside and talk about it?"

"Yes." She sniffed, wiped her eyes, and allowed Julian to lead her into the house.

As they entered, he glanced at Felix, but his man looked away.

∼

SHE WAS LYING. Felix could practically taste the bitter tang of her lies and wondered if Master Julian had detected it as well.

Felix would say nothing - it wasn't his place. But this woman ... she was dangerous.

12

GOOD ROAD KARMA

Norman Keeler was having a hell of a time. The Flex blew a tire a dozen miles north of San Simeon and he had to change it on the side of the skinny highway. He'd never changed a tire before and was clumsy and very aware of the bloody corpse in the back seat. Not only that, he was terrified a cop or a tow truck driver or some stupid good Samaritan would stop and try to help and, sure enough, when he was about to tighten the lug nuts on the spare, a tow truck driver pulled over - a big beefy red-faced guy in overalls. Norman wondered how he took a leak in those things.

"Need some help?"

Norman shielded his eyes against the truck's glaring headlights. "No, sir, I'm almost done. But thank you."

"Welcome, son. I'll just sit here while you finish up - that way, you don't have to work in the dark."

"Thanks." He figured that if he said no, it might arouse suspicion. Norman tried not to think about Clarke's body. He'd hunted for something to cover it with, but the car yielded nothing more than an empty water bottle and a ChapStick. He bent to tighten the nuts and suddenly the trucker was right beside him. "Why don't you let me do that? You're having a hell of a time and I can have you back on the road in two minutes. No charge."

"Well, okay. Thanks." Norman handed the lug wrench to the guy and stood by the passenger window trying to block the view.

Not three minutes passed before the trucker put the lug wrench, the blown tire, and the jack in the back of the Flex. "There you are, good as new."

"You didn't have to do that. Thanks again." Norman stared at the man's red face and found himself thinking about all the blood under the skin that gave the guy the rosy glow. *Stop it! Don't think about blood!* He didn't know what was going on with him, but he was acting like a goddamned vampire or something. *I'm freaking out of my mind!*

"Don't think a thing about it. It's good road karma, you know?"

Norman nodded, noticing the throb in the trucker's jugular. "I'll see you around." He turned and got into the Flex, then glanced in the rearview, saw the trucker hoisting himself into his big tow truck, and sighed. Both relieved and confused, he put the key in the ignition.

"Hey, buddy!" The trucker was back, tapping on the window.

Norman controlled his shaking hands, turned the car on, and rolled down the window a few inches. "Yes?"

The trucker proffered a bottle of water. "Thought you could use this. You look thirsty."

"Thanks. I'm - I am." He rolled the window further down and accepted the water.

"Where you headed tonight?"

"San Jose."

"Good. Remember, you're driving on a temporary spare. Get the real tire fixed first thing tomorrow." The trucker glanced at his watch. "Jesus, it'll be light in two hours."

Norman tried a smile. "I'll do that. Thanks."

The trucker slapped the top of the car. "See you- Hey, wait a minute."

Norman glanced up, saw the trucker staring into the back seat, and put the Flex in gear.

"Hey!"

Norman tore out, heading onto Highway 1, the trucker's yelp as he ran over his toes, following him.

"Goddamn it!" He glanced in his rearview. There were no headlights behind him yet; the trucker hadn't pulled out - no doubt he was doing the hotfoot and calling the cops. Norman had to ditch the car - and the corpse - pronto. He hit the gas and headed toward Big Sur and the tall, steep cliffs.

As he drove, he found himself becoming more and more uneasy. *What if I really am a vampire?* That was nonsense. Or was it? He touched his gums and his teeth felt normal, but when he'd bitten into Clarke's neck, he'd thought he had fangs. And if he wasn't a vampire, why did he crave blood?

Shit, what happens when the sun comes up? What happens if they catch me and put me in jail and the sun comes up and I burn up?

Norman sped, taking curves too fast, aware of the ocean far below on one side and mountains hugging the narrow highway on the other. He needed to ditch the car and find a safe dark place, just in case.

A moment later, he saw a turn-out on the ocean-side of the highway and stomped the brakes, skidding across the road. Grabbing the knapsack that contained his skateboard, he parked and shut off the lights then moved to the cliff where, far below, waves broke and the seafoam glowed in the light of the moon. The drop was almost straight down.

In the distance, he saw headlights approaching. *Cops!* He returned to the car and put his shoulder to the open door, trying to shove it toward the cliff. Even as he pushed, he knew he wasn't strong enough to do it, but he had to try.

The car moved and he nearly stopped pushing because it startled him. He was a wiry little guy, not a muscle man, but he was a lot stronger than he thought. He began pushing again, recalling how easily he'd pulled Clarke into the backseat.

Maybe I'm a vampire and I've got super-powers!

The car went over the cliff. He heard it tumbling down and finally, it hit the rocks below. Norman breathed relief, turned and watched the highway. The headlights were getting close. He looked back over the side of the cliff. He was a pretty good free-climber and there were undoubtedly caves or at least outcroppings that might shield him from the sun if necessary.

Norman began his descent.

13
MORNING WOOD

It had been a very long night for Stephen Darling, but now dawn was only twenty minutes away. He tapped his fingers on the desk as he waited for Natasha to come to the phone at Eudemonia.

She dispensed with hellos. "Stevie? What's wrong? What has she done now?"

"Amanda? Nothing as far as I know. She hasn't returned to the hotel."

"She uses Lixir like it's lifeblood. She may return during the day. You've alerted Dilly and her crew?"

"Of course, Tasha."

"You aren't considering taking her back?"

Despite himself, he chuckled. "Stop worrying, sister dear. It's not about Amanda. Not directly, anyway."

"What's going on?"

Quickly, he told her about the body found under the pier and assured her it had been taken care of and would not affect them. "But Amanda has left us another problem, Tasha."

"Tell me." Her impatience was palpable.

"Plastic Taffy."

"That local band?"

"Yes-"

"What about them?"

"Amanda turned them."

"What?"

"She turned them. All four of them."

"What happened? Have they killed any humans?"

"No, I don't think so. The deejay Coastal Eddie-"

"What about him? He didn't say anything on the air, did he?"

"Tasha, Tasha, you really need to concentrate on those meditation lessons. Let me speak."

She sighed. "Sorry. I'm putting you on speaker so Michael can hear, too. Hang on."

He waited while his sister told Michael Ward about the band. A moment later, Michael greeted him, sounding much calmer than Natasha. "Hello, Stephen."

"Hello, Michael, it's good to hear your voice."

Tasha broke in. "Stevie, it's almost bedtime. Tell him."

"Evidently Amanda turned the band and they tried to attack Coastal Eddie while he was interviewing them after the show."

"Coastal Eddie," Natasha spat. "He's such a worm."

"No, Tasha, he's not. He immediately came to the hotel and told me about his run-in with them. If he hadn't, I doubt we'd even know it happened until they did damage."

Michael spoke up. "Coastal Eddie does have his good points."

Natasha said something that Stephen couldn't hear, then asked, "Has Ivor already taken care of them?"

"Destroyed them, you mean? No. We brought them in, sat them down and explained the facts of their new condition to them."

"You should have exterminated them, Stevie. You're too softhearted. We can't have them in town. We can't trust them."

"Nor can we allow them in Crimson Cove," Michael added.

"Of course not." Stephen didn't hide his annoyance. "That's why Ori and I decided to send them up to Eternity. To Biting Man."

"You *what?*"

In the background, Michael laughed.

"You heard me, Tasha. We put the fear of the stake into them, fed them, gave them some supplies and told them they could either die now or head up to Biting Man where, if they're polite, they'll be taught the ways of the vampire. They are not to return to Candle Bay. Or Crimson Cove." He paused. "We've locked them in their van for the day. I've already made arrangements with the Kohlkophs to meet them in Eternity."

"The Kohlkophs? You've got to be joking."

"They're in charge of entertainment."

Natasha laughed. "Seriously? I wonder how those dolts managed that."

"They have their ways."

"Well, I hope you know what you're doing," said Natasha. "What if the band makes a run for it and goes into hiding?"

"They won't." Stephen almost regretted his decision. Almost. He began tap dancing, something he'd done since their human days when his sister got edgy. "They're on the verge of a musical breakthrough and are eager to be in the spotlight. And, they wouldn't be hard to find if they went Rogue."

"Sending them up there is preferable to exterminating them," Michael said. "They'll have a chance to assimilate into our culture and learn things that only other vampires can teach them."

"And if they don't fit in, they can be dealt with up there," Natasha added.

"Exactly."

"This will be interesting, if nothing else," she allowed.

"Indeed," Michael said. "We will watch for them on the road."

"Ivor will put them on the highway as soon as the sun sets tonight."

"Then we'll be on the road, too," Natasha promised.

∼

NEIL TRINSKY HAD SET his alarm for five a.m., wanting to leave for Eternity before sunrise - before his nosy mother could interfere with his plans. *By the time she realizes I'm gone, I'll be halfway there.* He scowled as he thought of her.

Pushing down his irrepressible morning wood, he rifled through the laundry basket in search of clean underwear. Mom had failed to put away his clothes. *Lazy little bitch.* He shoved shirts, pants, socks, and underwear into a large suitcase.

Once he'd packed it full, he went up to the bathroom for toiletries, Renfield close at his heels, wagging his tail and looking at his master with dull questions in his stupid eyes. Neil grabbed his toiletries and threw them in his old black backpack. A few sticky Pucker-Buttons that must have been rattling around in there for at least five years came rolling out. He sniffed them. *Lemon-Lime, my favorite flavor!* Plucking hair and lint off, he popped them in his mouth. He liked them because they looked like little sphincters. Again, he urged his morning erection down. It showed no signs of withering and he considered rubbing one out.

"Neil? What are you doing?"

He gasped, felt one of the Pucker-Buttons hit the back of his throat and lodge itself in his windpipe. He doubled over, gagging, trying to get breath as his mother fluttered around him in her robe, wringing her hands uselessly. At last she gave him a hard *THWACK!* on the back. The Pucker-Button shot onto the floor in a puddle of stringy saliva.

"Goddamnit, Mom!"

"Are you okay, honey? I didn't mean to scare you." She stepped back, her hand clutching her robe.

"I almost fucking *died*! I'm just fucking *fine*, Mom! What does it *look* like?" He glanced down at the slobbery Pucker-Button on the bathroom floor. "I really wanted that Pucker-Button, Mom. Thanks a lot!" He was amused at her face - she hated all that swearing, but it was hard to get her to say so.

"Where are you going?"

This was the exact conversation he'd wanted to avoid. "Out." He zipped the suitcase and headed back down to his room, Renfield underfoot, his mom at his back. "Why can't I just have some goddamn peace around here?" he shouted.

"Where are you going, Neil?"

Neil sighed, deciding there really wasn't any reason to lie. "To Eternity."

"*Eternity?* What on earth for?"

"I'm going to find out about Biting Man once and for all. Coastal Eddie thinks he's outsmarted me, but he's got another think coming." He clipped his backpack to the suitcase.

Mom took a slow deep breath. "Neil, I don't know if it's safe for you to go. Coastal Eddie said–" she paused, looking nervous. "I heard him on the radio, and he said–"

"Since *when* do you listen to Coastal Eddie, Mom?" He felt a surge of jealousy. *Does she want to fuck Coastal Eddie? Why else would she be listening to his show?* "You know he's a queer, don't you?"

Mom's eyes went wide.

"He is. I followed him and he ended up going to The Petting Zoo. *The Petting Zoo, Mom!* Gay!" he shrieked. "He's gay! Gay, gay, gay, gay, *GAY!*"

"It doesn't matter, Neil, what matters is–"

"I saw him kissing another guy! With the tongue! Then they went in the bathroom where people cut holes in the stalls and poke their peckers through to get blow jobs!"

"Neil! Enough!"

"So if you like Coastal Eddie so much, why don't you just think of *that* before you throw yourself at him like a ... like a slut!"

She smacked him. Hard.

His head rocked back and the suitcase slipped from his hand.

He almost started to cry, but decided he didn't have time. "Anyway," he said, as if she hadn't just abused her own child, "I need your car."

"You are not taking my car, Neil."

"I have to! The Vespa won't make it!"

"Absolutely not." She crossed her arms and stared him down. "If you want to go to Eternity in search of vampires, I won't stop you, but you are *not* taking *my* car." Her voice was steely, but something in her eyes told him she was worried. It wasn't about the car. She didn't want him to go. *But why? Because she can't function without me, that's why!*

"You'll be sorry if you make me have to take it without your permission, Mom."

"And you'll be sorry if I call the police."

He knew she wouldn't do it.

"You can't stop me." He glanced past her and she caught his cue, chasing him upstairs.

They ran toward the kitchen, toward the keys. The dog gave chase.

Neil tore after her, kicking Renfield out of the way, but was too late. She'd swiped the keyring and held it in her fist.

"Give it to me!" Neil gripped her wrist, squeezing and shaking and screaming. "GIVE IT!"

She tried to turn away, but digging his fingers into her fist, he pried her hand open and snatched the keys. She looked at him, defeated, out of breath. "Neil, please. Don't do this. I'm begging you."

"I'm going, Mom."

"Please don't take my car." She rubbed her wrist. It looked red and puffy.

"What do you care anyway? You hit me! You're a … child abuser!"

"You're no child, Neil. You're thirty-two years old and you're *stealing* my car. How am I supposed to do my job?"

"Rent a car, you child abuser!" He stomped down the stairs, grabbed his luggage and dragged it back up.

His mom stood at the door, eyes anxious, mouth working, but she didn't try to stop him. She didn't dare. He'd raise a fist to her if he had to and she knew it. *Fucking coward!* "If you'd buy me my *own* car, like you did for Tina when she graduated her precious college, we wouldn't even be having this fight!"

"Neil, there's something you should know." She touched his arm and he flinched away.

"You can just sit here and listen to your precious *Coastal Eddie* while I'm gone! You can fantasize about having *sex* with him while you diddle yourself, for all I care!" He reached past her and grabbed a jar of dill pickles off the counter. Then he shot out the door, threw his suitcase in the backseat, and gave her the bird as he peeled out.

14

MEANWHILE, IN ETERNITY

In all his years as the Sheriff of Eternity County, Zach Tully had seen a lot of things he never would have thought possible back when he worked as a detective out of Rampart Division in Los Angeles. Eternity was not your normal resort town. Cut off from the world in winter, it thrummed with tourists from late spring to early fall. It was a town unlike any other, one that appealed not only to skiers and other relatively normal sorts, but to crystal packers, Bigfoot hunters, UFO nuts, and just about every other flavor of crazy that Tully could imagine.

When he'd first arrived in the little town - the only one in the tiny county - Tully had felt like he was lost in a house of mirrors. Nothing was ever what it seemed. Eternity was full of colorful characters, but none were the Mayberryesque ones he'd expected. No, instead of Gomer Pyle repairing cars, he got Jack the Ripper on a rampage, and instead of Floyd the Barber, he got Harlan King, proprietor of the King's Tart, telling him stories of his adventures in a war that had taken place long before he was born. And instead of Ellie the pharmacist, he had Amelia Earhart for a postmistress, Ambrose Bierce as mayor, and a healthy-looking Elvis running the local natural foods store. At least he had quickly found his own decidedly normal Thelma

Lou in Kate McPherson, marrying her and adopting her son, Josh, within months of arriving in town. They were the best things that had ever happened to him. Smiling to himself as he parked his cruiser and began his morning stroll around Main Street, he said a silent rest in peace to Ambrose, the Ripper's final victim, over a decade past.

No, Eternity was not the bucolic Mayberry of mid-century television, but he'd become accustomed to its peculiar face, its casual idiosyncrasies, its perplexing sense of humor, and its even more puzzling ideas about justice and law enforcement. Eternity, with all its warts and weirdness, had become his own personal Mayberry and it suited him just fine. Most of the time, at least.

As always, he smelled fresh-baked bread and cinnamon rolls before he reached the King's Tart. Nodding to the geezers on the bench outside the bakery as they laid odds in their never-ending death pool, he pushed the glass door open, setting off the familiar tinkle of tiny bells.

"That you, Zach Tully?" Harlan called from the kitchen.

"It's me." Tully seated himself at one of the small white tables next to the picture window. He peered across the narrow street at Eternity's famous town square, which was really a huge oblong that held a park with gardens, a pond, playgrounds at both ends, and a band shell used twice weekly this time of year. In winter, there was ice skating on the pond. Around the square most of the same businesses that were there when he'd arrived years ago still lined Eternity's quaint Main Street. He glanced to the east, seeing Icehouse Mountain's dark morning shadows looming over the far end of town.

"You're looking positively pensive." Harlan whisked through the batwing doors from the kitchen and came around the counter carrying a tray. He placed a cinnamon roll, its icing still flowing like lava, in front of Tully, then added a cup of strong black coffee, a tiny pitcher of cream, and a napkin.

"You're a mind reader," Tully said.

"And you're a creature of habit." Harlan seated himself across from Tully and sipped his own coffee, his baker's whites adding to his pleasantly plump, cherry-cheeked appearance. His blond hair spilled out from beneath his baker's hat, looking just the same as it had when

Tully had arrived in Eternity. It was the same as his face – not a new wrinkle to be seen. In the years since he'd taken over as sheriff, Tully himself had sprouted some gray at the temples and a few new seams and crinkles on his face. Meanwhile, Harlan, Amelia, Elvis and a number of others who claimed to have arrived through the prehistoric "Little Stonehenge" on Icehouse Mountain, hadn't aged a day. Eternity really was as weird as it claimed to be.

As Tully bit into the hot cinnamon roll, the bakery door opened and Curtis Penrose came in, his short legs somehow leading the rest of his body. Tully groaned.

"Sheriff!" Curtis squawked in his nasal voice.

Tully kept eating until the man, who looked like a balding Sonny Bono, planted himself in front of the table. Harlan made to stand up and Tully gestured at him to stay. Nothing, not even Curtis Penrose, the most annoying shopkeeper on Main Street, was going to ruin his morning coffee and roll.

"Sheriff! It happened again."

"Somebody broke into your candy machine, Curtis?"

"Yes."

"Just now?"

"During the night!" Curtis' froggy eyes did a slow blink.

"Curtis, every time this happens I tell you to put that machine inside your shop at night. It doesn't weigh anything; you can do it."

"But–"

"Frankly," Harlan said, "It's amazing they don't steal the entire machine."

"I chain it down," Curtis said. "I shouldn't have to take it inside at night. Your department should keep it safe, Sheriff. That's what our taxes pay you to do."

Tully poured most of the cream into his coffee, staving off an ulcer he imagined he should have by now as he silently counted to ten. "We have to protect the entire town, Curtis. Our first priority is to keep *people* safe. You have to take some responsibility for your vending machine. Frankly, leaving it outside at night makes it a very attractive nuisance."

Curtis wouldn't meet his eyes. "I want to file a report."

"That's the right thing to do. I think you should go down to the station and file it right now."

"You're here. Can't you take my report?"

"I'm not on duty."

"You're wearing a uniform."

"Just go to the station and tell Sergeant Starkey what happened. She'll take your report."

With a snort, Curtis Penrose nodded and left the shop.

"He'll never learn," Harlan said.

"No, he won't. But I do like a town where the worst crime this week is ripping off a vending machine."

"True, that." Harlan sipped coffee. "I hope it stays nice and quiet. Likely, it won't."

"Do you know something I don't, Harlan?"

"I suspect I do. Have you ever heard of Biting Man?"

"You mean Burning Man?"

"*Biting* Man."

"What's that?"

"It's a festival. I don't think there's even been a little one up here in your short time with us. A few little meetups in the mountain, maybe, but nothing like what's coming." Harlan smiled. "The last time there was a Biting Man this big up here was a century ago."

"What the hell are you talking about, Harlan?"

"It was quite something, let me tell you." Harlan smiled again, his face that of a cherub, his British roots all but gone from his voice.

"Okay, I give. What's Biting Man?"

"It's a vampiric festival. They hold it in the mountain every so often. Kind of a big family reunion."

Tully put up a hand. "Wait a minute. Vampiric as in vampire?"

"What else would I mean?"

Tully had long ago accepted the weirdness of Eternity, had accepted people like Harlan and Elvis and Amelia as the real deal. He'd even accepted the bigfoot rumors - hell, he'd seen the skins. But vampires? "Harlan, you're pulling my leg."

The baker laughed. "Wish I were. Those goddamn vampires can be a real pain in the neck."

15

LUNCHTIME EAVESDROPPING

Erin Woodhouse, wearing not a speck of body glitter, her bat tattoo discreetly hidden by her brown and tan Bobby's Coffee Shop uniform, did a double-take when she saw Coastal Eddie Fortune walk in with a nice-looking woman. He'd been here before, but right now she was worried that he'd recognize her as the girl who'd had him autograph her ass. Bobby Black, her boss, was a Christian, a born-again kind of guy, and he might fire her if he found out.

"Got a customer, Erin," he called from the kitchen.

"I'm on it." The hostess had called in sick, so Erin was pulling double duty. Swallowing, she snatched two menus, then approached Eddie and his friend.

"Two for lunch?" She put on her brightest, most wholesome smile. She could almost feel Eddie's signature burning on her butt cheek. *Please don't recognize me!* She'd only done it because she was pretty sure the creep from the Ferris wheel was following her and she'd wanted it to look like she was hooking up with other people. *That was one idiotic move.*

"Yes," Eddie said, eyeing her.

"Great, follow me." *He knows who I am!* She couldn't afford to lose her job - she had tuition to pay at the end of the month. *Please don't out me in front of my boss!* If Bobby Black found out about the autograph on her ass ... about the tattoo ...

"There's a booth by the window," the lady said. "Could we have that one?"

Erin scanned the crowded diner. "Sure. Right this way." She led them over and handed them menus when they were seated. Eddie still looked hard at her. "Today's soup is pea and our special is the reuben sandwich." She spoke too fast, trying to get away before Eddie could say anything. "Can I start you with something to drink? Coffee? Tea? Soda?"

"Coffee, black," said Eddie's friend, who looked vaguely familiar. She knew how to dress. Her makeup, though light, was perfect for her mature skin and her dark blond bob suited her features. But, honestly, she didn't really look like Eddie's type.

"How about a root beer?" Eddie said. Then he winked at her and turned back to the lady. "Have you eaten here before, Lois? The food's great."

"I have and I agree."

"I'll be right back with your drinks." Erin hurried off.

∼

"I RARELY MEET strange men in coffee shops." Lois Trinsky smiled at Eddie as she unfolded her napkin, but she looked tired, stressed out. Far more so than the night before.

Eddie laughed. "I'm glad you made an exception."

Lois looked over her menu, and Eddie noticed a puffy reddish mark on her wrist that was turning black and blue. "What happened?"

Her cheeks pinked and she looked flustered. "Neil."

Eddie raised his brows. "Your son did that?"

"We had a little battle over my car keys. He won." For a moment, she looked like she wasn't going to continue, then she sighed and said, "He's going to Eternity."

Oh shit. "For ... Biting Man?"

She nodded. "That's what he says."

"And he took your car?"

Another nod.

The waitress, whose ass Eddie was sure he'd signed the night before, returned with their drinks. "Can I get you anything to eat?"

Eddie looked at Lois and she said, "Pea soup."

"We both want the pea soup," said Eddie. "Lots of saltines."

The waitress smiled. "It'll be right up. Just wave if you need anything else." And she was off, making her way toward a large group who'd just entered.

"Lois," said Eddie. "I don't think Neil's going to Eternity is a good idea. Biting Man is nothing to mess with."

"I tried to stop him." She glanced at her wrist. "I was afraid he was going to break it, so I gave up." She shook her head. "Vampires. Who knew?"

The waitress was seating a group at the table next to theirs, her back to Eddie and Lois, pen poised over a pad as she scribbled down orders. Eddie's eyes flickered over her backside. *Yep. That's definitely the ass I signed.*

"I still can't believe vampires truly exist." Lois spoke a little too loudly and Eddie put a finger to his lips.

"Believe it. And if he goes up there nosing around, he's liable to get himself hurt ... or worse." Privately, Eddie didn't think that would be such a bad thing. Neil was trouble, had always been trouble, and as he looked at Lois' swollen wrist, he knew that the boy - the man - was capable of violence. He wanted to punch Neil's lights out.

"Did you report the car stolen?"

"I threatened to, but he's my son, and ..." She trailed off.

"I understand."

"I'm thinking of renting a car and following him up to Eternity, to Biting Man." She looked at Eddie. "I don't know what I'll do when I get there. I just might steal my own car back and leave him stranded. It would serve him right."

"Lois, I know he's your son, but he's dangerous." Eddie looked pointedly at her wrist.

She nodded and when she looked at him, her eyes were full. "I know. I'm afraid of him - he's mean to our dog, too - and I've wanted him out of my house for a long time, but he's ... he's a fixture." One tear tried to roll down her cheek but she wiped it away and smiled thinly. "He's like black mold. You get it in your house and it's a real bitch to get rid of."

Eddie laughed and Lois joined him. He liked the sound. "Look, Lois, you can't go up there alone."

"Why not?" Her chuckles died and she arched an eyebrow. "Because I'm a woman?"

"Your son is dangerous, you're alone, and you don't know much about vampires."

"Eddie." She reached across the table and briefly touched his hand. "I'm a big girl. I can handle myself. And I know plenty about vampires from years of listening to Neil. I've even looked at a lot of those Argonaut pages on his computer."

"Listen, Lois. I can take a few days off. How about we drive up together?"

A myriad of expressions crossed her face, from surprise to happiness to fear. "I'd like that, but it would only make things worse."

"How could our traveling together make things worse?"

"Neil's jealous. His father took off when he was little, but every time he sees me in the company of a man, he overreacts. I'm a real estate agent and if he sees me with a male client in my car, he assumes I'm having a torrid affair." Her cheeks pinked. "This morning, I said I'd listened to you on the radio and he went ballistic, saying horrible things about me and you. Merely because I mentioned *hearing* you."

"Lois, you're his prisoner. You know that, don't you?"

Unable to speak, she twisted her napkin and stared at her coffee. Finally, she nodded. Eddie took her hand. "Look, if he's going to think you and I are having a torrid affair, I think the least we can do is travel to Eternity together and get your car back. We can give him something to worry about." He smiled.

"You don't need–"

"Yeah, I do."

She looked up, wiping away tears. "Why?"

"I want to. And I have old friends in Eternity I'd love for you to meet." He smiled. "Not to mention, I have a new van and I need to break it in. Will any of those reasons do?"

She stared at him then slowly let a smile break through. "Yes. Just so you're not offering to go to protect me. I'm a–"

"Grown woman," Eddie finished. He squeezed her fingers. "You don't need protecting. I can see that. But you *do* need a ride and a vampire expert, right?"

The smile touched her eyes now and she squeezed his fingers back. "I have a little dog I can't leave alone."

"I love dogs. Bring him." Eddie meant it.

"When can we leave?"

"I'll prerecord tonight's show. How about I pick you up at your place about six?"

"I'll be ready." She gave him her address.

∽

"And don't forget, I want my bacon extra, extra, *extra* well done," said the Valkyrie at the head of the table. She was obviously the matriarch and had a brood of children ranging from nearly twenty years old to no more than two.

"Got it," said Erin. "Extra, extra, *extra* well done."

The Valkyrie, who did not need bacon, well done or otherwise, gave Erin a nod of satisfaction and turned to her husband, a docile man with bloodhound eye bags. He lowered his head to look at the menu, developing an alarming double chin that bulged over his collar. As he hemmed and hawed over the menu, Erin heard something behind her that pricked up her ears: *"Vampires. I still can't believe it."* It was Coastal Eddie's lady friend. Erin strained to hear.

The husband finally decided what he wanted and Erin began writing, but she was barely listening. She was immersed in the conversation behind her. They spoke in hushed tones, but she'd managed to pick up a few more words: Eternity. As in the town, she was sure.

"–with no pickles. I *hate* pickles," said Husband.

"Oh! I'll have the same!" shouted an impatient, pimply pubescent son. Erin wrote *X2* next to Husband's order.

"And what do you want, Stacey?" asked the Valkyrie, nudging a placid-faced tweenage girl.

Erin took orders, one child at a time, all the while listening to the couple at the next table.

"I'm thinking of renting a car and following him up there ... I'm going after him ..."

At last, Erin reached the final member of the hungry family. She smiled at a toddler in a blue onesie who sat in a booster seat, glowering. "And what would you like, little man?" The child burst into noisy tears.

The Valkyrie's jaw dropped and she pulled the toddler to her massive bosom. "Little *Marcy* will have the corndog and fries, thank you. *She* would like a chocolate milk to drink."

Shit. Erin gave the Valkyrie an apologetic smile and wrote the order. *Like it's my fault your daughter looks like a boy!*

"I want a corn dog, too!" cried a slightly older child whose gender was certainly male - not that Erin would comment on it.

"Listen, Lois, why don't we drive up together?"

So they were planning a trip to Eternity. In search of vampires. *Going there would be great for my thesis!* She'd have to find a way to get there. *But* where *in Eternity?* It wasn't a large town, but obviously, the event would be a discreet one.

"Did you get all that, young lady?" asked the Valkyrie.

Erin repeated the orders and the Valkyrie approved.

Smiling, she took off to retrieve the pea soup for Lois and Eddie.

16

FIFTY SHADES OF YELLOW

"You shouldn't indulge in so much Lixir," Julian Valentyn told Amanda. It was midday yet she was wide awake, more awake than the Trueborn, who wanted nothing more than to retire to his bedchamber and rest until dusk. He felt logy with the noontime sun.

"Why not?" Amanda reclined on his yellow Grecian chaise longue where she was reading *Fifty Shades of Grey*. "I'm living with you, after all."

"Amanda, you showed up here hours ago. You are not 'living with me' by any stretch of the imagination."

"You could be my Mr. Grey," she purred.

"I do not know who that is, Amanda."

"It's a man who indulges in all sorts of carnal pleasures. Would you like to suck my toes, Julian?"

"No, thank you."

"Spank me?"

"No, that does not appeal."

"Would you like to bite me?"

Julian was intrigued, despite himself. Ever since she'd arrived, Amanda had been acting as if she were in heat, so much so that he had surreptitiously examined her bottle and was surprised to find that it was the non-addictive Lixir which did not affect human vampires' sexuality in a significant way and merely kept the daytime "sleep of the dead" at bay. There was no physical addiction or rampant hedonism to be had, but Amanda certainly behaved as if there were. It had to be something else, something to do with her own physiology. It was the only thing that made sense. There was one condition that would cause this, but it was so rare that he'd only seen it a few times in his thousands of years of life. *It would explain so much.*

He shut off the nonsensical thought and spoke. "Biting you is appealing but inappropriate. You and Stephen Darling are a couple. I have heard that the two of you have plans to marry. Perhaps at Biting Man? Is this not true?"

"Stephen doesn't love me anymore. He called off our wedding." Crocodile tears filled her eyes as she sighed and tried to look sad. It was poor acting at best. Still, the old pull was there; he could not deny it, though he could certainly ignore it. He yawned, desiring nothing more than a long afternoon nap, but would not leave Amanda awake and unsupervised within his home. Felix had gone into town for filters, tubing, and bungs, and to examine the latest shipment of barrels and to place an order; Julian had no other human house servants who were knowledgeable of his vampiric ways. He would wait for Felix.

"Yellow," Amanda said. "Why yellow?"

"I don't understand."

"This couch is yellow. A lot of your upholstery is yellow. And your house. It's yellow and white on the outside, like a goddamn house in *Better Homes and Gardens*. This room is painted pale yellow. That seems kind of silly for a vampire."

He studied her. "You would have me paint it black? Or red, perhaps?"

"Sure. Maybe purple. You know, something that makes a statement."

"Yellow does make a statement, Amanda."

She rolled her eyes. "It says you're effeminate."

Julian laughed heartily. "That's your perception, not mine." He looked her over, taking in the stilettos, the black leather, the tank that revealed the curves of her petite, perfect breasts, the flowing blond hair, the makeup that masked the sweet innocence of her face. She was dressed far too much like those impish Darling twins, Lucy and Ivy. He enjoyed *their* show, but Amanda was not meant for such base costumery. From the very first time he met her in Euloa, a simple human servant called Talai, she'd been perfect in her beauty and in her refusal to become a vampire. But Amanda wasn't the only thing that had changed. His own history had also been rewritten by the Dead Agains, vampiric religious fanatics determined to cast all history through the mirror of Christianity. *They call me the Prince of Blood instead of the Prince of Trueborns now.*

But that was of little concern to Julian. He was more worried about Amanda. The first time he'd tried to turn her, she killed herself in the morning sun after he'd administered the third bite. The second time, still in the ancient homeland, his father had killed her. There had been other times throughout the centuries, the millennia, when he had found her. Always, no matter her skin and hair color, she was easily recognized by the set of her eyes and lips, the slope of her nose and cheekbones. She had the tranquil beauty the Greeks attributed to Aphrodite; in fact, he was fairly sure that she, herself, had inspired some of the most famous art involving the goddess of love.

More often than not, he did not find her, yet he always felt it when she reincarnated, and if she came as a female, he searched for her. When she was a priestess in Machu Picchu she had very nearly let him turn her, but in the end, she had killed herself rather than become a creature of the night. Julian had discovered the bloodberry and its powers by then, but he would have given it all up to have her. But he could not - would not - force her. She had to choose him - and now, he thought, she evidently had. *Why am I not happier?*

"What's so great about yellow, anyway?"

"The color of sunlight?" he asked. "One wants what one cannot have. It is true of all living creatures, I think. It's certainly true of the human and the human hybrid vampire. And of the Trueborn as well."

"It's just silly." She twirled a strand of hair around her finger.

"You're young," he told her.

She radiated irritation.

"You have not even given yourself a chance to truly miss the sunlight since you indulge too much in Lixir."

"Why too much?" She sat up, her eyes sparking. "Is it too much because it's expensive? Or because you say so?" She batted her lashes. "I wouldn't have to use so much if you'd give me some real elixir."

"A vampire does not flourish if she overindulges in hedonism." He sat back, folded his long-fingered hands in his lap and watched her from beneath nearly closed lids. "It is certainly true that young vampires indulge themselves - just as young humans do. Perhaps you ought to consider that."

"Yeah, so?" She looked bored.

"You were very young in human years when Stephen turned you. Perhaps that is another reason why your hedonism overwhelms you. I do hope you will survive it."

She bristled; he could see that his words hurt her, but she had to hear the truth.

Then she was on her feet, hands on hips, glaring. "How *dare* you talk to me that way! Do you have any *idea* how strong I am? How powerful? Stephen told me I'm special! He's never seen a vampire mature into power so rapidly." She stalked toward him. "You love me, Julian. You've always loved me. I thought a Trueborn like you would simply kill Stephen and take me for your own. You disappoint me."

He stood so fast and crossed to her in such a blur that he saw shock on her face as he gripped her arms. It satisfied him. "Are you capable of considering your actions, Amanda?"

"Let go. You're hurting me."

"I doubt that, my dear. I sincerely doubt that." So close, he could smell her scent; a scent that she carried throughout her lives just as she carried the tranquil beauty of Aphrodite, though it was broken now by the cosmetics and the anger in her face. "You're spoiled."

"Spoiled? You bastard! What do you think I am?"

She tried to twist out of his grasp; he was surprised at her strength, though he had no trouble retaining his grip. "I think you are a spoiled child."

"Don't talk to me that way. Don't you dare!" She eyed him. "You've always wanted me and I'm here to give myself to you. I want to *marry* you."

Julian stared down at her. "You chose Stephen over me and I chose to respect your wishes. I have not heard from you in more than a decade, but now you've had an argument with Stephen and you've come to ... to what? Make him jealous? To try to stir trouble between us? I won't have it, Amanda. I am at peace with the Darling family and I fully intend to maintain that peace."

"Fuck you!" she screamed. "Fuck you!" Her eyes blazed red.

He stared down at her, willing himself to appear taller, broader, and he could see in her eyes that it was working. She struggled less and averted her gaze. This creature was not his Talai. This was a banshee and except for that faint attractive scent that he so loved, he was surprised - and quite pleased in an odd way - that he was no longer so attracted to her.

But it was sad. The human Amanda had been a smart, lovely young woman, just as she had been as Talai as well as her other incarnations. Perhaps, he thought, she somehow knew she was not meant to be a vampire, that she was one of those rare humans who simply did not take to it. *Or could it be true? Could she be ... Incendarius?* He would research the question this very night.

She pushed her head into his chest and began sobbing. It was an act, but he sensed that it was nearly heartfelt. "Julian," she cried. "Julian. I was such a fool! You're right. I was so young when Stephen turned me. I didn't know what I was doing! It's you I love. I always have. I only wish it had been you who turned me."

17

GIRLS JUST HAVE TO HAVE PLANS

Erin Woodhouse took a deep breath and knocked on the door of the small office at the back of Bobby's Coffee.

"Come in." Bobby sat at his desk, making out next week's schedule.

She was just in time. "Before you get too far on that, I need to talk to you."

He glanced up and she could see concern in his pale eyes. He gestured at a chair.

Erin sat, hands in her lap. "I've received an opportunity that I'm not in a position to turn down, and-"

"Whatever they're paying you, I'll add twenty-five cents."

Well, this is awkward. "It's not a job, exactly. It's a ... I'm going on a trip. I've been struggling with my master's thesis and this is a perfect opportunity for me to kick it out."

"Great, I understand," said Bobby. "Education is important. How long will you be gone?"

"That's the thing. I don't know. Probably just a few days, but ..."

He studied her. "Where are you going?"

She couldn't answer too many questions. "Up north," she said. "In the state. But I honestly couldn't tell you exactly when I'll be back. It just ... depends."

"Are you trying to quit, or asking for vacation time?"

She didn't love her job at Bobby's, but she didn't hate it either. "I guess that's up to you. If you're okay with giving me an indeterminate amount of time off, I'd be happy to come back. But if that's not acceptable - and I understand if it's not - then I guess I'm turning in my resignation."

Bobby looked at the schedule, at her, and back at the schedule. "Ballpark figure?"

Erin shifted in her seat. "It could be anywhere from a couple of days to a few weeks. I wish I could be more specific, but I just don't know."

He considered. "Why don't we take it as it comes? As soon as you have an idea when you're coming back, let me know. I'd like to keep your position open, but we can't really afford to leave it open for too long. When are you leaving?"

"Tonight."

"That soon, huh?"

Erin gave him a weak smile. "I have to go tonight because I have a ride."

"So, I guess this is goodbye. For now, anyway."

"I'm afraid so."

"If you don't mind me asking, what's your thesis about?"

Erin hadn't anticipated this question and the truth - vampire culture through history - seemed too close to home. "Uh, it's the uh, the worship and ritual traditions of historical and contemporary religious faiths."

Bobby nodded, looking as impressed with her answer as she was. "Heavy stuff. Well, I'm sure we can work something out when you come back." He grinned. "I didn't know you were a Christian."

Me, neither! "Thanks."

Leaving his office, she felt flattered, but a little disappointed that she hadn't been officially let go. She hurried home to pack a bag of essentials and work on her game plan. She already had one - a very loose one. A daring one.

"Do you think this makes my butt look big?" Juicy Lucy asked her sister.

Sprawled on the bed, Poison Ivy watched Lucy pirouette in front of the cheval glass. She couldn't even see the G-string. "Gigantic. Huge. The full moon has nothing on your ass."

"Screw you." Lucy laughed. "Seriously, do you think it works as a swimsuit?"

"At a nude beach, sure." Ivy giggled.

"Then it's perfect!"

"Quit trying everything on and keep packing," said Ivy. "We're leaving tonight!" She pulled a bikini out of her drawer and eyed it. *It's so nice being in the sun again, even if it's only for a few minutes at a time.* She sighed, hoping she never lived to see the day when Julian Valentyn quit making the Lixir that allowed them to enjoy some of the benefits of the living. It wasn't as much fun as the original elixir - that was a trip and a half - but it was still great. "I wish Julian's place was closer. I want to see him. He's so much fun. Maybe we could stay with him a couple of nights. I bet he'd like that."

"Yeah," said Lucy. "But it's going to be great seeing Eudemonia too, right?" She twirled in her G-string once more. "I can't wait to swim in the pool."

"Why? We swim in our pool all the time!"

Lucy gave a final twirl. "Ours is indoors. Theirs is outside, under the stars. I haven't been in one of those in, like, forever."

"It'll be a blast."

～

THERE WERE three parts to Erin Woodhouse's Plan A. It was a simple plan, nothing she'd needed to write down, but now that she was here, she worried she might panic and forget. The sun was down, and that worked in her favor. She'd opted for black pants and shoes, a black jacket, and a black knit cap. She felt like a cat burglar and it excited her way more than it should have.

At the coffee shop, she'd overheard Lois giving Eddie her address. Erin had committed it to memory and now waited in her car, watching from the other side of the street, going over the plan, unable to do anything else until Eddie showed up.

Plan B, following his van, was the answer if Plan A didn't work out. She crossed her fingers that Plan A would work and waited, watching.

Lois' house was a nice little neo-Victorian two-story nestled into a cozy cul-de-sac in the hills on the other side of town from Erin's apartment building. Once she graduated and got a decent job, this was the kind of place she'd like to own. Maybe something a little bigger, depending on whom she married and how many kids they decided on. She was hoping for lots of children.

Inside the house, several lights burned and Erin saw the occasional shadow pass by a window. More than once, she saw Lois peering out the curtains, and felt an irrational impulse to duck. But there was no way she could be seen.

A single black gym bag sat on the passenger seat. She'd packed only the essentials and a few changes of clothes. If she ended up in Eternity for more than a few days, she'd need to find a laundromat. *Or just come home.* That was an option, too. She'd brought plenty of money to pay for a ride back, but she didn't think she'd be leaving early. *I'll stay as long as I need to.* Deep in her gut, she knew this was going to give her everything she needed - and more - to write a mind-blowing thesis.

Headlights sliced through the darkness and Erin ducked lower in her seat.

Sure enough, it was Coastal Eddie's van. He killed the engine and headed to the front door. As he knocked, Erin's heart pounded - but when Lois let him in, she realized that Plan A was underway, and time was critical. She grabbed her gym bag, locked up her car, and darted toward the van. Sweat broke out on her forehead as she peered around, making sure she was unseen. *I can't believe I'm doing this!*

The coast was clear. Erin pressed herself flat against the side of the van, checking the side door. It was locked. *Damn!* The passenger door was locked as well. *Double damn!* She crouched, keeping to the shadows, and hurried to the driver's side. *Bingo.*

Quietly, she hopped in, closing the door with care. She moved to the pitch black back of the van, and brought her cell phone out. Deep within, where no one would see any light, she tapped the screen and used it as a flashlight. Several large shapes loomed.

The van was tricked out nicely, but not as full of junk as she'd hoped. Her saving grace though, was the radio station equipment near the rear. "Thank you, sweet Jesus," she whispered, though she didn't think Jesus cared to lend much assistance to the breaking-and-entering of those who didn't even think of him on his birthday.

Behind the radio equipment, Erin found a large blanket. Quickly, she hid her bag beneath it, then killed the light from her phone, and lay flat on the van floor between the side wall and the equipment, where you'd have to *really* look to see her.

She quickly called a friend to pick up her car then prepared herself for a very long - and uncomfortable - wait.

Plan A was a success. *But it's all so ... stalkery!* Again, she had that cat-burglar feeling and couldn't resist a smile.

18
ON THE ROAD

Stephen Darling, along with his brother, Ivor, had just given the Plastic Taffy musicians a case of cheap hemoglobin - BO Negative - the Jägermeister of bottled blood. It had been in their regular shipment from Slater Brothers and when informed of the error, the company told them to keep it at no charge. The newly-turned vamps wouldn't mind the blended blood's poor taste and repulsive nose - they were like human children who happily filled up on canned spaghetti and hot dogs rather than touch a filet mignon. The baby vamps, still locked in their van, had split a bottle among them. Ivor handed them the directions to Eternity and the phone number of the Kohlkophs, who had agreed to set them up with a paying gig and to usher them into vampiric culture.

Stephen and Ivor watched the van leave the lot. "I hope they survive," Ivor said.

"Yes. They didn't ask to be turned." Stephen hoped they would find a new profession soon. Vampires in the spotlight rarely lasted long. Usually, they were quickly assassinated by their own kind for being too conspicuous.

Reentering the hotel, Stephen called Natasha and told her the band was on its way and should be passing by Crimson Cove in a little over two hours. He'd made a similar call earlier, when he was still groggy with sleep, leaving word that the Lixered-up twins had left Candle Bay for Eudemonia before sunset. Natasha said she and Michael would be watching for them on the road, as would Chynna and Winter, at least if the twins showed up in a timely manner. They were planning to arrive in Eternity days ahead of the main event. Natasha was certain that Amanda would show up there as well, and intended to keep an eye on her. Stephen hoped that was all she would have to do.

Now, standing in the lobby, enjoying the babble of water behind the musician playing Spanish guitar, everything felt right with the world, peaceful and calm.

"Mr. Darling? Sir?" Nettie Gruben waved at him from behind the lobby desk.

"Yes, Nettie?"

"There's a call for you from a Mr. Julian Valentyn?"

"For me? Are you certain he isn't calling for my sister?"

"He was very specific, sir. He's on line two."

"Very well, tell him I'll be with him momentarily."

Stephen ignored the buzz of displeasure coursing through him as he walked briskly across the lobby and took the escalator to his office. He was glad his uncle didn't appear.

Seated behind his desk, Stephen cleared his throat and pressed the button. "Good evening, Julian."

"Stephen. I trust you are well."

"I am."

Julian didn't sound as arrogant as he'd expected. "How can I help you?"

"I believe you are missing something?"

"Missing?" *Oh, no...*

"Your intended is here. She arrived before dawn."

"I apologize. She's very upset with me."

"So I gathered. You've officially parted ways?"

"We have. I allowed the relationship to go on for far too long because I, uh," - *didn't want to incur her wrath* - "didn't want to hurt her feelings."

"She is quite ... upset."

Julian was choosing his words carefully. Diplomatically. Stephen couldn't read the Trueborn. "She was upset when she left. It's my fault. I should have told her it was over long before now, but ... it was very difficult."

"Indeed. I surmised that. I have determined that she is probably Incendarius."

"What?"

"Incendarius. It is a term used for the rare human who becomes more than a simple vampire hybrid upon turning. It's an unusual condition and I have little doubt she is the first you've dealt with."

"I thought Incendarius was a myth." Stephen paused. "I've been around very difficult vampires, vampires with outrageous tempers."

"Yes, but these were probably humans who already possessed that nature," Julian explained. "Or did they seem to be something more? Like my newly-arrived visitor?"

Stephen considered. "The former, I believe. I don't know for certain. None were especially difficult to ... subdue."

"But our friend is, is she not?"

"Yes. She's far stronger than a typical newly-turned vampire, far more apt. Her invisibility skills are as good as mine. It's quite disturbing. And her personality has changed. I have never seen that before in a newborn."

"Then she is Incendarius." Julian paused. "You will not be able to control her for long. It's good that she came to me."

"Julian, can you control her?"

"I am a Trueborn."

"Yes, but can you control her?"

"Of course." Valentyn sounded less sure of himself than usual.

"And you've taken her in?"

"So I've been informed." He spoke cautiously. "At least, for the time being. I will see if I can counteract the problem and access her original soul ... assuming it is still there, which is unlikely. However, if it is, I shall return our friend to you."

"You are a gentleman," Stephen said. "But I must respectfully decline."

There was a long pause. "I understand."

Stephen thought he heard a degree of pleasure creep into the Trueborn's voice. *He's welcome to her.* "I wish you the best of luck."

"Thank you. I shall need it. This is a condition so rare that I've seen it only a handful of times."

"What happened with the other Incendarius you've met?"

"They end up with plenty of blood on their hands before being killed themselves."

Stephen's stomach tightened. "Julian?"

"Yes?"

"I want to apologize for taking her. I shouldn't have done that."

"You were chosen. While you should not have done it, it is not your fault."

~

IT GOT dark early in the mountains surrounding Eudemonia and no human guests were nearby. Chynna trusted Emmeline to take good care of Absinthe and Hyacinthe, but leaving the tigers behind felt somehow traitorous. Perhaps it was the way they'd looked at her - Absinthe with his green eyes, Hyacinthe with her baby blues - when she'd bent to tell them goodbye. She knew they understood her. They always did.

"I think that's about it." Winter hefted a final bag into the back of the white van. "Do you have everything packed?"

Chynna, who hadn't realized her eyes were welling, wiped them quickly. She was hoping he hadn't noticed, but no such luck.

Winter gave her a sad look, slung a heavy arm over her shoulder and gave her a little squeeze. "The cats will be all right."

"I know. It's just that I hate leaving them." She looked into his face. "I'll miss them. It's silly, but I will."

He grinned, showing teeth as white as his short, flat-cropped hair. He smelled of soap and woodsy aftershave. It comforted her. "You know," he said. "I don't think I've ever seen you get teary over anything except those cats."

She laughed. "I try not to cry. It's not good for my image as a badass."

Winter chuckled and gave her another quick squeeze. "You'll always be a badass to me, tears or no tears."

"Wait for us!"

Chynna looked up to see two identical young women hurrying toward them, both carrying what must have been a dozen bags and suitcases. *The Darling twins.* Each wore a two-piece bathing suit, one was red, the other nothing more than a black string and a bra that looked like Band-Aids. Both had a skimpy sarong tied around their tiny waists. "Hurry," Chynna called. "It's time to leave."

"Sorry," said the one in black. "We went for a quick swim when we got here!"

The one in red giggled.

They were petite, both with porcelain skin, obsidian-black tumbles of hair, and tight, youthful bodies with all the right curves in all the right places.

"I'm Ivy," said the one in red as she tossed her bags in the van. "And this is Lucy."

"Hi!" Lucy only had eyes for Winter. She let go of her bags and they thunked to the ground. Her eyes lingered over the bulk of muscles beneath Winter's white t-shirt. "I hope you don't mind that we're riding with you."

It was the first time Chynna had ever seen a *woman* talk to a *man's* chest.

Lucy batted her eyes at him, and Chynna refrained from rolling hers.

"I'm Winter." His hand swallowed Lucy's whole.

"I know who you are, silly. I've heard *all* about you."

"All good, I hope."

Lucy giggled and tried to look coy. "The best."

The handshake involved no shaking at all and seemed to go on and on as the van creaked and rocked while the other sister hefted their bags - there must have been a hundred and fifty of them - and suitcases inside.

Chynna cleared her throat.

"Oh," said Winter, nodding at Chynna. "And this is ... uh ..."

"I'm Chynna." She stepped in, took Lucy's hand and firmly shook it. "Nice to meet you."

Lucy gave a little bow, low enough that Chynna worried the girl's breasts might burst out of their minimum-security prison like escaped convicts. "Enchanté," she said, giggling and jiggling.

Winter's spell was broken when Ivy grunted and dropped a bag. "Let me get that for you." He took an armload of cases and placed them inside, while Ivy and Lucy watched his muscles bunch and bulge.

Chynna noticed he was doing a little extra flexing for them.

He slammed the back of the van shut. "I think that about does it."

Ivy giggled. "This is so exciting, don't you think? I just *love* road trips!"

Her sister's head and breasts bobbed enthusiastically. "Me too! I hope we'll be able to do some *sightseeing*." She looked Winter up and down.

Ivy sidled up beside him. "You poor guy. I hope you can handle us!"

Lucy slid to his other side. "You'll be the only guy in the group!" More giggling and jiggling from both.

"Actually," said Winter, "my pal, Arnie, is coming, too. We can't forget about Arnie."

The twins giggled. "I guess that's a good thing," said Ivy. "I don't know how you'd handle both of us all by yourself!"

Chynna could have sworn he puffed his chest when he purred, "Oh, I'm sure I could handle you both just fine."

The giggles were already setting her teeth on edge and Chynna began to dread the night-long drive to Eternity.

Just then, Arnie came running toward them, arm waving, carrying a single suitcase. "Papa Winter! Wait for me!"

"And here's the man now." Winter headed toward his friend and took his luggage. "Calm down, buddy. We aren't going anywhere without you."

Arnie was visibly relieved.

Chynna watched the twins look Arnie up and down.

Winter slid the side door open, deposited the suitcase, and said, "Ladies, meet Arnie Hoss. He's been with me a long time."

Even now, Chynna saw the sadness in Winter's eyes when he spoke of Arnie. Winter had been a stevedore working on the Hudson back in 1801 in Sleepy Hollow, New York, when he'd been turned. He hadn't understood what had happened to him, and his turning Arnie, a simple-minded but gentle soul, had been accidental. Chynna didn't think Winter had ever forgiven himself.

Arnie blushed in the presence of the Darling twins, looked at his feet, and nudged the ground with his toe.

"Oh, my," said Ivy. "We get to travel with *two* handsome men!"

"All the way to Eternity!" breathed Lucy.

Arnie's blush deepened.

"You hear that, Arnie?" asked Winter. "You're going to have these ladies fighting over you the whole way."

Arnie smiled, head down, cheeks blazing.

"Choose me." Ivy looped her arm through his.

"No, me!" Lucy took his other arm.

Winter laughed and slapped Arnie on the back. "I just can't take you anywhere, can I?"

"No," said Arnie, shaking his head. "I guess you can't."

Chynna was touched by the twin's efforts to include Arnie. *At least they're not all bad.*

"All right," said Winter. "I think that about does it." He looked at Arnie. "You brought your toothbrush?"

Arnie nodded.

"Toothpaste and dental floss?"

Another red-faced nod.

"Plenty of socks? Clean undies?"

At this, Arnie shot Winter a mortified look. "Yes, Papa Winter, *all* of it."

"Okay then. Let's get a move on."

Winter got behind the wheel and Chynna took shotgun. Arnie sat in back, bookended by nearly-naked twins.

As they drove, Chynna noticed that Winter kept glancing in the rearview. She could tell he didn't quite trust the twins with Arnie, and it touched her that he was such a diligent guardian. She hoped the Darling twins, who were already giggling and teasing, were careful of Arnie's feelings. Despite his boyish good looks - he reminded Chynna of a 1970s teen heartthrob - mentally he was slow and had all the vulnerabilities of a youthful mind.

But she knew Winter would make sure nothing happened to Arnie. It was one of the things she admired - adored, actually - about him.

Chynna looked back at the twins. They were being kind and gentle, asking polite questions rather than sticking their breasts in his face. It was clear that they respected his disability.

Suddenly, Arnie lost all interest in the girls. "I want Tim McGraw!"

Winter glanced in the rearview. "Sorry, buddy, we didn't bring it."

"Yes, sir, Papa Winter. It's in the box."

Winter sighed and gave Chynna a long-suffering look.

She smiled and pulled the Tim McGraw cassette from the glove box and popped it into the outdated but still functioning tape deck. She fast-forwarded, and found *Indian Outlaw*. It wasn't Tim McGraw himself that Arnie loved so much as it was that one song. She knew they'd be listening to it over and over, the whole way there, but it beat listening to the giggling, jiggling twins.

The twanging guitars began and Arnie bounced in his seat, clapping and beaming, and soon, all three backseat passengers were singing along in nauseatingly discordant voices. *Yes,* thought Chynna, *it's going to be a very long ride.*

∽

NORMAN KEELER CAME AWAKE in a tiny cave partway down the cliff. He remembered climbing into the bird-shit streaked little grotto not long before dawn, driven to hurry by some new instinct to avoid the sun. His last thought before he lost consciousness was that he really *was* a vampire. With super-powers.

And losing consciousness was the right term. He'd been awake, and then he was gone, as simple as that. Now he looked out at the twinkling stars in the early evening sky and then the ocean below. The Ford Flex was crumpled into the rocks and it was pure luck it hadn't been spotted yet - at least there were no signs anyone had been there.

Suddenly hungry, Norman brushed dried bird crap off his clothing and peered up the cliff. Everything was quiet, not a soul in sight. He'd climbed down perhaps thirty feet. Looking up was slightly dizzying but wouldn't be too much of a challenge to climb - he'd spent his teen years free-climbing at Joshua Tree National Monument and that was harder, if not taller.

He began climbing, concentrating on hand and foot holds, and moved steadily despite the night. It seemed easier to see in the dark now and he felt stronger and more agile than he had any right to be. In fact, he was enjoying himself.

He reached the top, looked around, and pulled himself onto the dirt, next to the broken guardrail. His stomach growled and he remembered the taste of Clarke's blood. He needed more. He began walking up Pacific Coast Highway, toward the forests of Big Sur State Park.

19

POPPIN FRESH AND THE FANG-BOY

Neil Trinsky's ass was as numb as toast by the time he pulled off on the exit for Eternity. His mother's pearly white Altima, while better for a trip into the mountains than his Vespa, was a P.O.S. when it came to sex appeal. *Little bitch car!* The Altima reeked of middle age and menopause, of rich assholes who wanted to buy beach houses, of wine-tasting parties and upper middle class security. There was nothing dangerous about the Altima. Nothing sexy, except for the sticky love stains he'd left on the passenger seat during his after-lunch stroke session. He always liked a little self-love after lunch. He remembered Bat-Tat Girl and wished she was here to suck him off now.

But I'm not here to pick up girls. I'm here to kill vampires! He touched the love stain; it was still moist. Yes, for killing dirty bloodsuckers, this car, with its nice, roomy trunk, was perfect.

Eternity Road narrowed and wound through tall pines and firs that threw dusky shadows dark enough to trigger the car's headlights. He turned them off, not wanting to look like a pussy, and continued on, finally seeing a smattering of cabins as the road began a slow descent toward town. Soon, cabins dotted the landscape, half of them looking occupied. *Empty cabins would make great hiding places for scum-sucking dirty vampires…*

He rounded a curve and all at once, the town came into view. It was as insipid as a Norman Rockwell painting, with a gigantic park in the middle of the little downtown. Tiny cars circled the road and he imagined every store sold skis.

Probably all the restaurants are malt shops. I hope they have decent health food here.

He doubted it, but he kept driving and eventually found himself in forested neighborhoods full of bigger cabins where, no doubt, the town hicks all lived. *They probably eat deer and bear meat every night. Fucking toothless hillbillies.*

He cruised past a log cabin-style sheriff's office and then saw a sign that read "Historic Downtown Eternity Next Right," beside a little stone church with a big-ass bell in its steeple. He flipped it the bird as he passed then followed the road until he found himself on Main, the one-way street that circled the park. Lights were on in a lot of the shops and restaurants and he cruised the entire circle, his windows open so he could scent the air and get to know his base of operations. It smelled like donuts and pine trees.

The shops looked like they belonged in the 1960s. There was a bar called Shalimar's that actually had red upholstered doors. It looked so outdated that they probably allowed smoking inside. Neil wouldn't be risking *his* lungs to find out. Next door to that was the Eternal Beauty Salon, Icehouse Burgers - *Can You Eat Our 2 Lb Hamburger In A Half Hour? It's Free If You Can!* - the Mom & Pop Market, Icehouse Liquor, two video stores, and an outdated movie theater that was playing a double feature: *Gaslight* and Bela Lugosi in *Dracula*.

"Idiots," Neil muttered as he drove on, stomach growling. "There's got to be *something* healthy to eat around here." As he spoke, he saw two men, one in a Smokey the Bear hat, the other dressed in white, standing outside a brightly lit shop called The King's Tart. "Fucking queers," he spat, and then realized it was a bakery - the guy in white had an apron on and the guy in the hat was wearing a sheriff's uniform. He pulled over, rolled down the window, and put on his best smile. "Sirs?" he called. "Sirs? Can you help me?"

Both men approached and he was amazed that the cop - a Rick-

Grimes-looking motherfucker if Neil had ever seen one – wasn't chowing down on a donut. "How can we help you?"

"I was wondering if there are any vegetarian restaurants in town?" *And where the butcher and candlestick maker are.* He suppressed a chuckle.

Poppin Fresh, the baker, rubbed his chin. "Not that I know of, but plenty of places have vegetarian dishes. You might try Strider's Steakhouse across the way. They have a full line of excellent salads."

"A steakhouse? Sorry, smelling meat gives me PTSD."

The men cocked their heads quizzically. It was obvious they had no concept of animal cruelty. "Do you have any health food stores?"

"Sure," said Poppin Fresh. "Keep going another block and you'll see the True Grace All-Natural Market."

"Thanks."

"You're welcome. Here for the convention, are you?"

"Uh, yeah." *Does he mean Biting Man?* "See ya."

∽

"PTSD?" asked Harlan.

"Post Traumatic Stress Disorder."

Harlan frowned. "Oh, shell shock. I wonder what the poor kid went through."

"I'm guessing he's just a hyperactive activist – one of those people who can't see someone eating a BLT without starting a protest. Screams at you for wearing a leather belt, that sort of thing." Tully dug the keys out of his pocket. "Why did you ask him if he's here for a convention?"

"Just to see what he'd say. I expect we're going to see more like him. The vampire lovers, fang-boys and girls, I mean. No matter how small the festival, a few fanatics always manage to sniff out the vamps."

"Harlan, I thought you were pulling my leg this morning."

"God's truth, Zach."

Tully shook his head.

"Oh, ye of little faith. You've seen things up here that no one would believe and you're still questioning me?" Harlan's eyes darkened and dug straight into Tully's. "You need to take this seriously, Sheriff."

"So you're saying that guy was a vampire groupie, Mayor King?"

"Yes, that's the definition of fang-boy."

"A vegetarian vampire groupie?"

"Takes all kinds." The baker chuckled.

"So tell me, Harlan. How do you spot a vampire? Carry a mirror to see if he has a reflection?"

Harlan snorted. "Bosh, no. They all have reflections. Some of them don't like holy water. And as far as I know, the only ones who hate garlic hated garlic when they were human."

"Okay. So I should just keep my eye out for neck-biters?" As Tully spoke, he watched the white Altima pull over a block down at Elvis' market. He hadn't much liked that guy's smile.

"Do you think we'd put up with vampires if they went around biting our citizens?" Harlan laughed. "They generally mind their manners better than regular folks. They patronize everything but the restaurants. They have money. The hotels that knowingly take them in will be full-to-bursting in the next few days and the ones who don't know about them will do pretty well, too." He paused. "Of course, as I mentioned earlier, we haven't had a big Biting Man like this in a century, so I'd keep my deputies on alert if I were you." He nodded toward the Altima. "It's the groupies who make the most trouble."

20

HIT THE ROAD, VAMPS

In the back of Coastal Eddie's van, Erin Woodhouse lay sweating beneath the blanket. A few hours had passed and the excitement had worn off as the miles rolled by, but occasionally, she couldn't help thinking: *I did it! They have no idea I'm here!* She was proud of her stealthy skills but she was also nervous. Getting into the van undetected had seemed the most important thing, but now that she'd pulled it off, she'd begun to worry, especially about the dog Lois had in a pet taxi up front. *What happens when she lets the dog out? It'll find me. How will I explain myself?* Thoughts of police being called, of charges pressed, of being hauled off to jail, played out in her mind.

There was only one good possible outcome, she decided, and that was *not* to get caught. She'd wait it out until they arrived in Eternity and cross those bridges as she came to them.

They had the heater going and it was stifling under the blanket. She wished they'd crack a window or something, but she sucked it up, glad she didn't have to pee - that would be way worse. She concentrated on the buzzy feel of the road beneath her, listening to the conversation between Lois and Eddie, hoping for any information that might be useful to her once they arrived.

Just thinking of it got her excited. *'The Vampire Underground'* would make a great title for my thesis. Or *'Biting Man: Under the Fang.'* She shook her head. Too cheesy. The title would come to her in due time. The thesis would be awesome, regardless. *It will be open-ended,* she thought. *Leave the readers questioning the existence of vampires instead of trying to force them to believe.* They were fictional, she knew that, but if she did her job well, she could raise serious doubt in the minds of her readers.

∼

"Neil stole my Discover Card," Lois told Eddie after going through her wallet for the third time.

Eddie kept his eyes on the interstate. "Report it."

"I suppose I should, but he never has much cash and I'd hate to have him ditch my car somewhere to hitchhike."

"Good point," Eddie said. "Eternity is a small place. I think we'll be able to find your car there or we can ask the sheriff for help. Interesting guy."

Lois looked at him. "You know the sheriff of Eternity? What happened, did you get arrested?"

Eddie grinned. "I talked to him a couple times after he got rid of Jack the Ripper."

"Um-hmm. Stop pulling my leg."

"I'm not. Eternity is one weird place. Have you ever read about it?"

"No. I've heard of it - I know it has some crazy stories about UFOs and Bigfoot attached to it."

Eddie laughed. "That's just for starters. Ever hear of Little Stonehenge?"

"Isn't it sort of like the Mystery Spot in the Santa Cruz Mountains?"

"Oh, it's a lot more than that." Eddie cleared his throat. "Little Stonehenge - or 'the Circle' as the locals call it - is a bona fide prehistoric site. It has standing stones similar to those at Stonehenge, and they've been there for thousands of years. It's something of a tourist attraction, but it's so much more than tourists realize."

"I'd love to see it."

"We can do that. It's a very peculiar place. Weird vibes."

Lois laughed. "How so?"

"It *feels* strange, you'll see. But the story is that it's some kind of time portal. People appear in the Circle on occasion. It's happened as far back as anyone in Eternity knows, or so they say. There used to be a Bigfoot expert up there, Jackson Coop. I interviewed him from time to time. He said he arrived there from an unmarked vortice in Oak Creek Canyon in Sedona, Arizona. One minute he was panning gold, the next minute he was standing in the middle of Little Stonehenge. He stayed, just like a lot of others. They say that once you travel through a vortex, aging stops."

"You don't seriously believe that, do you?" Lois chuckled. "And you said 'used to be.' If he stopped aging, what happened to him?"

"Just because you stop aging doesn't mean you can't die. The Ripper got him."

"Jack the Ripper?" Lois gave him a look that said she thought she was traveling with a lunatic.

"That's what they say." He gave her an apologetic smile. "I only *report* the news, ma'am."

"But do you believe it?"

"It's far-fetched," he hedged.

"So this sheriff, he killed Jack the Ripper?"

"That's what I hear. I talked to him about it but he denied all knowledge. No surprise there."

"So, Eddie ... Did the sheriff come through Little Stonehenge, too?"

"No, he was a police detective in Los Angeles who wanted a change of scenery."

"Glad to hear it."

Eddie nodded. "Eternity's previous sheriff was murdered in the Circle, so Tully was hired to take his place. There was a series of murders he had to deal with - nasty ones. Creatively gory. Jack the Ripper was allegedly behind them. And Tully allegedly got his man." He paused. "Jack fell into a crevasse, so the body has never been recovered and his true identity remains a mystery to all but Tully and a few of the Lifers."

"Lifers?"

"Townies who claim to have arrived through the Circle. Ambrose Bierce, Amelia Earhart, and Elvis Presley are among the celebrity Lifers."

"Eddie, how much of this do you believe?"

"I keep an open mind. And Lois, I want to remind you that you're pretty open-minded yourself, at least on the subject of vampires." He put on his signal and pulled off I-5, lured by the yellow and red glow of a Denny's sign. "Hungry?"

"Starving."

∽

THEY PASSED the turn-off for Mill Valley, which meant they still had a long way to go. As he drove, Winter wasn't thinking much about the twins in the backseat even though they made eyes at him each time he glanced in the mirror. He wasn't thinking about Biting Man, either.

He was thinking of Michael Ward. Specifically, he was thinking of Michael and Natasha. Winter knew they had a history together and it was obvious the two still had a thing for each other. And Natasha Darling was not only decent, she was intelligent, self-reliant, and - as an added bonus - about as hot as a Tabasco-soaked jalapeno on the fourth of July.

Winter knew Michael's reasons for his celibacy, but that was his story to tell. It seemed such a waste. He couldn't help thinking that Michael was missing out on the chance of a lifetime with Natasha Darling, and decided that - even though it was none of his business - he ought to have a talk with his boss and do a little persuading. *He needs a good time more than anyone I know.*

Indian Outlaw ended. Again. And Chynna rewound it. Again. She looked like she'd had enough of Tim McGraw for several lifetimes - *God knows I have* - but she was a good sport.

Winter grinned at her and leaned close. "It still beats the pants off *Achy Breaky Heart.*"

Chynna pulled a face. "You make a good point."

Winter chuckled. He knew she remembered well the days when *that* had been Arnie's theme song and was sure Chynna had been just as glad as he to see it fall from favor. When he'd learned that old Billy Ray had spawned that dreadful Miley Cyrus, the poor guy just couldn't get past it. Chynna turned and looked back at Arnie and the twins, none of whom had lost any enthusiasm; all continued singing and bouncing.

I wonder how Arnie will fit in. Winter knew that turning a human created a lifelong bond and therefore, vampires generally turned only those they wanted to spend their immortality with - which usually meant they chose someone beloved.

While he'd come to love Arnie, Winter would not have willingly turned him; he hadn't known that he himself was a vampire when it happened. Arnie had just been in the wrong place at the wrong time, and now, for the rest of his many, many nights, the simple fellow would remain a perpetual man-child who could never really survive on his own. They'd been lucky to join Michael and his group; not all vampires were as accepting.

And there was another problem, too.

Arnie, with his simple mind, had never completely mastered the art of self-control. Keeping him clear of humans was imperative during this trip. Bringing him along was a bit of a risk, but Winter hadn't the heart to leave him behind. Arnie deserved to experience some of what vampiric life offered as much as the rest of them did.

"What are you thinking?" asked Chynna.

"What?"

"You look pretty intense."

He smiled. "I'm just wondering whether or not those damned Catholics will ever consider making Sinead O'Connor a saint." He smirked.

"Huh?"

"I'm kidding. What I'm thinking is that this will be Arnie's first Biting Man Festival. I'm just hoping that ... you know ..."

"He'll be fine. I'll help you make sure of it." She touched his hand.

"I know," said Winter. "I'm just a little worried that ... some of the others might not appreciate the, uh, situation." Though Winter had turned Arnold Hoss in 1801, vampire culture hadn't changed much, and it was considered bad form to turn anyone incapable of fending for themselves. Children, the handicapped, and the like, were off-limits.

"It was an accident," said Chynna. "And you take damned good care of him." Her lips curved into a wicked smile. "And if anyone has anything to say about it, they can answer to me."

Winter laughed. He'd seen Chynna in action and would only wish her wrath on his worst enemy. This was one woman who could take care of herself - with or without her tigers. "You're the best, you know that, don't you?"

Chynna waved the compliment away.

"Thank you in advance for helping me keep an eye on him."

"You're welcome. And I don't think there will be many humans around, if that's what you're worried about."

"It's just that, you know, he never really-"

"I do know." Chynna touched his hand again. "You're over-thinking. It will be fine."

Winter smiled. "You're right."

"Papa Winter?" asked Arnie.

"Hmm?" Winter glanced at him in the rearview.

"What's oral sex?"

Chynna snorted a laugh.

Winter's gaze shot to the twins, who had the good grace to look ashamed of themselves. He turned the music down. "It's, uh, it's when people get together and talk about sex, Arnie."

Arnie beamed. "We're having oral sex then!"

"It's not a nice term, buddy. Be polite, okay?"

Arnie frowned. "Okay."

Winter shot a warning glance at the twins, then turned the radio up and hoped Arnie would soon forget whatever it was the Darling girls had been teaching him. He looked at Chynna.

She sat, eyes forward, suppressing laughter. When she caught Winter's gaze, she fell apart.

Winter laughed too, but kept it quiet, not wanting to encourage the twins. "I need to stop for gas," he told Chynna. "You want to drive?"

"Sure."

"Shotgun!" Arnie cried from the back seat.

"You got it, buddy." It was exactly what Winter had intended - to get Arnie away from those wicked Darling girls.

21

ELVIS HASN'T LEFT THE BUILDING

Inside the True Grace All-Natural Market, Neil felt at home. Rows of vitamin supplements made him giddy, and of all-natural protein drinks, there were plenty. He took a deep breath, inhaling the scent of good health. A woman in a white tank and pink shorts passed him, a basket in her hand. She smiled.

"Hello there," he said in his deepest, sexiest voice.

Smiling coyly, she paused in front of the supplements and pulled out a bottle. "Do you know if this is a good brand?"

He took it and, stealing a glance at her jutting, obviously fake breasts, lost interest. As Sir-Mix-A-Lot had said a thousand years ago in that crappy rap song, silicone was for toys. He shrugged and handed it back. "I don't know."

Walking away, he looked for the fruits and vegetables. He needed snacks. As he passed a rack of organic nuts, he grabbed a small bag of them, then found the bananas and apples - all organic, of course. And gluten-free. He rolled his eyes. *All the posers think gluten is in everything. Little bitch morons, every last one.*

"May I help you?"

Neil looked up and almost staggered back as he stared into the face of the King himself, Elvis Presley. "Uh ..."

Elvis gave him that one-sided smile. "Alarming, ain't it?" He wore huge dark glasses, a white bodysuit complete with rhinestone adornments and, as an added bonus, blue suede shoes. His name tag identified him as "Elvis P."

Cute. "I'm looking for dinner," Neil said. "What do you have?"

"Our meat is all antibiotic and hormone-free." One side of his lip curled up and Neil expected him to break into a chorus of *Heartbreak Hotel.* "Our bodies are temples, but that doesn't mean we have to forgo animal protein all the time."

"Yes, it does."

Elvis pushed his glasses off his face and raised his brows. "All right, then. We have pre-made salads. How about quinoa and kale? Our customers rave about it. We bruise the kale and rub it with oil."

Neil smiled. "The kale gets a real nice tan, huh?"

Elvis just looked at him.

"From the oil," Neil said impatiently. It was a good thing this guy looked like Elvis because he was really stupid. "Got any tofurky sandwiches?"

Elvis gave a half-hearted chuckle. "Sure. Come on back to the deli and I'll make you one to order."

Despite Neil's aversion to Elvis Presley - the *real* one - he didn't mind this guy. Neil's body was a temple, too, and he respected anyone who recognized the importance of treating it as such. He followed Elvis, whose buttocks and thighs were sheathed so tightly in his Spandex pants it was surprising he didn't squeak.

At the deli, Elvis went behind the tall counter. The case beneath it displayed a plethora of meatless hamburgers, hot dogs, sausage, and bacon. Before Elvis could slice the tofurky, Neil said, "Stop."

Elvis looked up. "See something you like better?"

"I want a portobello burger."

"What do you want on it?"

"Everything. Tempeh bacon, all the veggies, on a multigrain roll. You have the kind with oats on top?"

"We do."

"Make that. With olive oil and balsamic vinegar for dressing. Tons of pepperoncinis and black pepper, no salt. And at *least* half a cup of dill pickle slices on the side."

"You want your roll regular or gluten-free?"

Neil blinked. "Are you serious?"

Elvis frowned.

"Gluten-free, of course."

"You got it."

"Thank you, Mr., uhhh ..."

"Presley."

He couldn't be sure but Neil thought he saw the guy wink. "Thank you, Mr. Presley." He felt like a tool calling him that.

"You might also like this." Elvis reached into the case, white tassels swaying, and pulled out the biggest dill pickle Neil had ever seen - it looked like a big warty green bratwurst. "They're made not too far from here."

"Sure." It was as if Elvis could read his mind. Neil took the pickle as well as a chocolate suicide brownie. *A guy has to have some fun.* "Hey, man, I was wondering - are there any good hotels around here? Got any recommendations?"

"Well, now, let's see." Elvis raised his hand to his chin, apparently in deep thought. "Plenty of places around, sure, but I'd recommend Dimples' Boarding House. Reasonable rates. Nice meals. Nice people."

Dimples' Boarding House? "It sounds more like a dog kennel."

Elvis laughed. "Well, I don't know that Priscilla would let me take her anywhere but The Dog's Age, but you may be onto something."

Neil squinted at him. "*Priscilla?*"

"My Yorkie." Elvis was dead serious now. "And you're likely to have better luck getting a room at Dimples' than anywhere else this time of year. It's busy right now and I imagine the regular hotels are booked up."

"Thanks, dude. I'll check it out."

Elvis gave him a crooked smile. "I could probably get Martha Ann and Elmer to cut you a deal if you're looking for a bargain. Going to stay a while?"

Neil considered. Given that his only cash was his mother's credit card, it might be best to get a personal rec from a local. People asked less questions that way. "I'd appreciate it, Mr. Presley."

"You got it." Elvis held out a hand. "And hey. Call me Elvis."

They shook. "Thanks ... Elvis."

"I'll go make that call and meet you at the register when you're ready. And thank you for shopping at True Grace. Thank you very much."

Neil watched him walk away, his hips swiveling in a perfect Elvis-affectation. There was no denying the guy was a spitting image of the King, if the King had been svelte enough to look good in Spandex, but Neil still couldn't help wondering what women saw in the guy. He nibbled the end of his giant pickle - it was as good as promised. *He got fat and died on the throne, for Christ's sake. The undertaker probably had to cut off his hemorrhoids to make him fit in the coffin.* Really, this impersonator was one crazy nutcase and had no business running a health food store at all, but if he was willing to get Neil a bargain on a room, he guessed he'd better be polite.

22

ON THE ROAD AGAIN

Plastic Taffy - Paul, Davy, Mick, and Ramon - pulled off Interstate 5 when they saw the sign for San Francisco because they needed to fill the tank. They found the gas all right, but then they took a wrong turn and somehow ended up tooling across the Bay Bridge. Then they hit Fisherman's Wharf, and ended up in traffic so thick and slow that they were starting to freak out.

"We gotta get up there before dawn," Mick said. "They'll find us and kill us if we don't."

"I know, I know," Davy called from the driver's seat.

Mick was right. They barely understood what was happening to them, but they knew that the dude at the Candle Bay Hotel wasn't kidding. They had to get up there. A moment later, they saw a sign pointing toward the most famous Frisco bridge of all time. "Google the Golden Gate to Eternity," Davy told Paul, who rode shotgun. "I don't want to go back through that traffic."

Right then, Ramon passed a half-empty bottle of blood to Paul. He took a swig, handed it back, then bent to stare at his cell phone. "Holy shit, Davy, just turn around. If we go that way, we'll be royally screwed for time."

"Motherfucker!" Davy made a U-Turn and headed back into the

crowds. "The sun's going to come up and kill us all!" But there was more than that. He felt - they all felt - a draw to the woman who had changed them. They would find her up ahead, and that was the most important thing of all.

~

"WE SHOULD HAVE SPOTTED the Plastic Taffy van by now," Natasha told Michael. She was in the driver's seat of her thunder-gray Murano and they'd been on the road for two hours.

"It's worrisome." Michael pocketed his cell. "Winter says they haven't seen them either."

"I wish Ivor had thought to put a tracking device in their van."

"Oh, well."

She glanced at Michael's silhouette. His glossy black hair was tied back in a ponytail just as it had been the first time they'd met, at the end of the Revolutionary War. He was younger than she - the Darlings went back to the late 1500s - but you'd never know it. These days, Michael seemed more mature than any vampire she'd ever known. And he wore it well. "Remember the night we first met?"

"Of course." Michael glanced at her and smiled. "We met in New York on November twenty-fifth, 1783. Near the witching hour." His eyes flashed a brighter shade of amber, betraying his desire.

"The day General Washington led the Continental Army into Manhattan," Natasha said. The last of the British troops had left New York City and the streets were filled with celebrating colonists that night, so drunk that she and her family were getting contact highs from the blood they drank. "It was a grand night."

"It was. I first saw you looking out at the harbor," Michael said. "You wore a green silk gown that picked up the moonlight and glimmered like the sea."

"I felt your eyes on me. I turned and there you were. You wore breeches and a brown waistcoat." She smiled to herself. "You had the look of a gentleman, but a rough one. A man of adventure. But of course, I knew you were no mere man."

He chuckled. "And I knew you were the most extraordinary woman

I'd ever laid eyes on. I wasn't very cautious back then. I wanted to drink you ... I was still so young that I didn't recognize you for a vampire until I came close enough to bite you."

Natasha laughed. "And I very nearly let you."

"Why?"

"I don't know. The merrymaking, the alcohol-laced blood ... that's why I bit you first."

"You did. But you were gentle."

She gave him a sidelong glance as she changed lanes. "I wasn't gentle, I was full and, after all, a little drunk. But it was hard not to overindulge. You tasted like nothing else." Normally, vampires didn't bite one another if they weren't already intimate – but there were always exceptions.

"You'd never drunk from a vampire before?"

"I had, in moments of passion, yes, but never a stranger. You were my first."

"Natasha."

"Yes?"

"These are wonderful memories, and I will always cherish them. But things are different now. As much as I wish otherwise, we cannot be what we once were."

"You mean lovers?"

Michael nodded.

"I shall honor that, but I would like to understand why." She turned to him. "It seems such a ... waste. The celibacy."

Michael looked away. "I have my reasons."

"I hope one day you will trust me enough to tell me."

"It is not a matter of trust."

Natasha sighed.

Michael looked out the window.

Natasha knew it would be a challenge to keep her hands, and fangs, to herself. She'd loved Michael Ward since that first night at the Battery. For her, the memories were as bitter as they were sweet. A change of subject was in order. "Washington was a great leader."

"What?"

"George Washington. I wish we could have turned him."

Michael chuckled. "That would be one frustrated vampire."

"Why's that?"

"Didn't he have wooden teeth?"

Natasha's boisterous laugh filled the car. "That's what they say. If it's true, I'm sure you could have whittled him some killer fangs."

"Your sense of humor has not changed."

"I'll take that as a compliment."

∼

THEY'D PULLED the van off at the Willows rest stop so Chynna could take the wheel, and Arnie, shotgun. Ivy got out, allowing Winter in - trapping him perfectly between the twins. Neither of them could take their eyes off the guy. *He's gorgeous!*

Then they were back on the road, *Indian Outlaw* blaring. Even Arnie, in the front seat, had gotten tired of singing and now peered out the window in silence.

The scenery was boring, but inside the van, the view was magnificent - Winter had one of the best bodies Lucy had ever seen; the guy was big enough to wrestle an angry bull to the ground. Pressing herself against him, she said, "I hear you have a great big sword."

Ivy giggled.

"What about it?" asked Winter.

Lucy touched his arm. It was as hard as she imagined other parts of him would be. "Natasha said it's very large and very dangerous."

"Snowfell," Winter said.

Lucy giggled. "Snowfell? That's the name of your sword?"

"You got it." He rested an arm across the back of the seat.

"Is it a *broad* sword?" Ivy tittered.

"Yes, it's a broadsword and I'm damn proud of it."

Lucy wiggled closer to Winter. "And did you bring your great big sword with you?"

He flashed a straight white grin. "I never go anywhere without it."

Ivy, seeing how close Lucy had gotten, nestled under Winter's other arm. "Have you ever *killed* anyone with it?"

"I have."

In the rearview, Chynna eyed them. Lucy wondered what – if anything – was going on between Winter and Chynna. She shrugged it off. There was enough of this guy to go around.

"And he has a Hummer named Frost," said Ivy.

"A hummer?" Lucy giggled. "I didn't know you liked hummers!"

Winter cleared his throat. "Yeah, I'd always wanted one, so–"

Ivy laughed. "Lucy will give you one!"

"Shut up!" Lucy giggled and reached across Winter to swat at her sister. "Hummers are *your* specialty!"

Both twins giggled.

Winter chuckled, too.

"So ..." Lucy ran a finger down his ribs. "Do you name *all* your toys after the cold season?"

He shrugged. "Just the ones I really dig."

Ivy nudged him. "What's your *real* name? I *know* it isn't Winter."

Winter, though generally ghost-white, pinked a little. "I'll never tell."

"But *why?*" the twins whined in unison.

"No way." Winter stretched his other arm out, resting it behind Ivy's head.

Lucy could tell he liked the attention. Men, whether living or undead, were always so easily maneuvered. She wondered what he tasted like. *If we're really, really nice to him, maybe he'll let us find out!*

"What's Winter's real name, Chynna?" called Ivy.

Chynna glanced at them in the mirror. "I can honestly say I don't know."

"Do *you* know, Arnie?" asked Ivy.

Arnie turned. "Papa Winter! His name is Papa Winter!"

Ivy sighed and looked to Lucy.

"All right, fine," Lucy said. "You don't have to tell us your *real* name, but I do hope you'll give us a ride in your Hummer one day."

"Next time you're in Crimson Cove, stop by." Winter stretched his muscular legs out, clearly enjoying the new seating arrangement.

The twins cuddled closer, snuggly, giggly, nearly naked bookends as they drove through the night.

"I'll be damned. That's Plastic Taffy's van." Eddie watched the eye-searing vehicle pass them just north of Shasta Lake.

"They look like they're in a hurry," Lois said.

Eddie glanced at the glowing clock. "Three hours until sunrise."

Lois stared at him. "You mean …?"

"I do. They're vampires and they're very new to it. I told the Darlings up at the hotel about them after one of them tried to snack on me, and it looks like they've sent them to Eternity." He shook his head. "There's no way they'd want them in Candle Bay. Those boys are lucky they're not dead." He grinned. "Not exactly dead, anyway."

"This is all just crazy," Lois said.

"You're telling me." Eddie decided keeping an eye on the boys would be a good idea, so he sped up and tailed them as he told Lois the story of the band and the first - and second - time he met Amanda Pearce, once a sweet young thing, now the bitchiest vampire of them all.

As he expected, the garish Plastic Taffy van soon exited the I-5 and headed northwest into the mountains. Eddie followed at a discreet distance and before long, both vans were on Eternity Highway, the last long leg of the journey.

23

BEFORE DAWN'S EARLY LIGHT

Neil had donned black sweats and crept out of his funky little room at Dimples' Boarding House at four a.m. to take his morning run. It was two hours earlier than his usual time, but he wanted to see what - and who - was up before dawn in Eternity.

It turned out to be a surprisingly lively place, considering the hour. He even saw a few other joggers in the park - most notably, a chick with gazongas that barely fit into her sports bra. Her eyes seemed to flicker amber and she smiled like she wanted to eat him up as she passed him. Neil turned to get a look at her ass, which wasn't bad at all - but it was vampires he needed to watch, not women.

It wasn't always easy to determine the difference but he'd know a vampire if he saw one. He watched a steady stream of tourists arriving in the predawn darkness, most of them in vehicles with dark-tinted glass. *Vampires, all of them. I knew it.*

The sprawling park, lit by old-fashioned street lamps, was paved with winding sidewalks that spread out around a small lake where people could go for rides in rowboats. No one was on the water now, but he imagined it would soon be filled with visiting idiots who thought sitting in a cramped boat in a park was pretty exciting shit.

Neil rolled his eyes, blew out air, and picked up his speed, hoping to counteract any bad fats and excess calories that would be impossible to avoid during his stay in Eternity. This was just one of the reasons he fucking hated vacations - they screwed up his diet and exercise program. *But this isn't a vacation,* he reminded himself as his legs pumped. *This is work. It's* more *than work! It's my duty. It's my calling!* And if it came at the cost of a few unhealthy meals, so be it. The mission was all-important.

Out of breath, he slowed, falling into a comfortable jog. While he was in damned good shape, a four-in-the-goddamn-morning run was no easy feat at this altitude. Reaching behind him, he squeezed his buttocks, enjoying the feel of the muscles flexing and imagining how great his ass would look when he was done. He did another full circle around the small lake but didn't see the girl with big tits again.

Bored with the scenery, he cut across the street, abandoning the park. He jogged along a main road - another one-way circular route just south of Main Street lined with various hotels and dotted with restaurants. The Bigfoot Inn looked like an old-time saloon that belonged in a fucking John Wayne movie. The St. Germain Bed and Breakfast was a miniature - and very creepy - German castle with its Tudor-style façade, and as he passed the Icehouse Inn, which stood tall and modern against the night sky, he had an eerie sensation of being watched.

By the time he realized his instincts were dead-on, the ominous feeling was replaced by excitement. He was staring at a vampire. And she was staring at him. As she got out of a gray Murano, she looked right at him, never blinking.

Neil slowed to a walk, his mouth suddenly dry. He hadn't thought to bring any of his vampire-slayer equipment, not even the vial of holy water he usually kept in his jock.

The vampire woman had long, glossy black hair, and was beautiful in the way Vivien Leigh was in *Gone With the Wind* - if Scarlett O'Hara had worn a form-fitting red sweater and leg-hugging black pants instead of a hoop skirt. There was a predatory smile on her crimson lips as she bent to one side, then the other, stretching after what he figured had been a long drive. Her eyes never left his face. She seemed to see through him.

A tall man got out of the passenger side, his hair just as black, his face just as pale.

Neil was sure they were both undead. *Dirty, filthy, fucking vampires!*

The man's eyes lit on him and Neil found himself unable to look away. His stomach filled with knots. *Don't be a little bitch!* Screwing up his courage, he glared right back at them. "I know what you are," he called as he pointed at them. "And I'm watching you both!"

They looked amused. Then the woman laughed. "I do hope you like what you see." She flashed some serious fang and, startled, Neil took off at a run, feeling like the little bitch he'd told himself not to be. *Next time,* he vowed as he sprinted away, *I'll be prepared!*

∽

"I never liked fang-boys," Natasha said. "They give me the creeps."

"I agree, they're a noxious bunch, the fang-girls, too. But this guy was more than that." Michael's eyes narrowed. "He knew what we were."

"And he threatened us. That kind of stupidity is disturbing."

They stood a moment, watching the young man jog away. "I made reservations at the St. Germain." Natasha led Michael to the charming peak-roofed and turreted building. "I had to pull some strings to get a room so near Biting Man, but it was worth it."

"*A* room?" Michael asked as he held the door for her.

"It's a small suite. Don't worry, we have separate bedrooms."

He nodded. "This place looks charming."

Wall sconces shaped like torches lit the rich but cozy lobby. The floors, furniture, and desk were all darkly stained and the chairs were upholstered in velvety red. Hunt tapestries lined the walls. It was very different from her own hotel, but every bit as lovely, even if the quarters were far more cramped.

Natasha signed them in, then Michael gave the Murano's key to a valet before they headed into the old-fashioned elevator. "We have a turret room," she said, handing Michael a key card.

"Is that good?" He smiled.

She almost said it sounded romantic, but caught herself; she didn't want Michael to think she was trying to seduce him. "It's a turret - it must be good, right?"

He chuckled as they stepped out onto the fourth floor. "I think it's this way." He pointed left and they found the room at the end of the hall.

Natasha stared at his hands as he slid the keycard into the lock. Large, graceful and long-fingered, they had explored every inch of her body, playing her like a harp, bringing her to ecstasy over and over. They had drunk from each other and made love and their times together had been the best of her life.

"Natasha?"

"Hmm?"

"Is something wrong?"

"No." She realized he was waiting for her to enter their suite. "Being here makes me nostalgic." She led them inside.

"Delightful," he said. They stood in a small living room. From within, the turret was simply an oversized oriole lined with an upholstered bench. A small oak table and two chairs furnished it. An overstuffed couch and easy chair faced a huge television that hung above a cabinet that held an aluminum bar sink and a microwave. A mini-fridge was built in below. Michael walked around the room, inspecting the art - pastoral scenes and thatched-roof cottages. "Quite romantic."

Natasha went to the turret and looked down. More cars had pulled into the hotels lining the street - the last of the vampire folk to arrive before dawn. "I wonder who that fang-boy was."

"Try not to worry about it." But Michael seemed uneasy as he brandished a bottle of A-Positive from Valentyn Vineyards. "Care for a nightcap?"

"Yes. I'd love one."

Someone rapped on the door.

It was a bellman with their luggage. After giving him a handsome tip, Natasha bade him good morning and closed the door.

Michael had found two glasses in the cabinet and poured an inch of ruby fluid into each. He handed her one. "To other times."

"And other places."

They clinked glasses and drank, then indulged a second time.

Someone knocked on the door. "I have a message for you, Ms. Darling. It came before your arrival."

She opened the door and read the folded paper. "Stephen says Julian called him. Amanda is at his place."

"That should be interesting. How is Julian responding?"

"Stephen says he didn't sound too happy about it. I hope he doesn't try to send her back to Candle Bay. She will not be welcomed." She looked at Michael. "I wonder why Stevie didn't text me."

"He probably tried. I doubt cell receptivity is very good up here."

Nodding, Natasha approached one of the bedroom doors and opened it. Small and cozy, like everything else at the Saint Germain.

Behind her, Michael said, "Nice."

"Very."

"Is this where you stay when you attend a Biting Man?" he asked.

"Yes. Well, about twenty years ago, I came up for a small festival and stayed here. It hasn't changed except for the flat-screen television and keycards. I find it peaceful. They welcome vampires. That helps."

"From the looks of things, most of the hotels are vampire-friendly."

"They'd be fools not to be," Natasha told him. But she knew there were a few that kept a strict no-vampire policy. They'd both rolled their eyes when they'd passed Perdet Towers - a squat round hotel with peeling gold paint and an arrogantly blazing sign that looked like it belonged in Vegas. The owner, Harry Donaldson, was one of the richest men in the state of California. And he was notorious for discriminating against the undead - and any other minority. It angered her.

"Don't let it eat at you."

Natasha turned to Michael, always awed by the way he seemed able to read her thoughts.

"The Perdet stinks. The Saint Germain is much nicer."

∽

NORMAN KEELER, satisfyingly full thanks to an errant park ranger who'd stumbled upon him while he was trying to catch a squirrel - that's how hungry he'd been - pushed the ranger's body over a cliff then continued walking along Pacific Coast Highway. He'd been too paranoid to risk hitching a ride so far, but a gas station was coming up and he'd try there, where he could pick and choose among potential rides. He smiled to himself as he trudged along, thinking he could probably pick up a trick easily for some extra cash - and maybe a ride, too - but wondered if he could control himself and not bite. *Time will tell!*

He was closer to the Woman - his Maker - now. He sensed that she was stationary. If she hurried, he would be with her soon.

And then what?

He had no idea. He just knew he had to go to her. She would have all the answers. He walked on and soon saw the lights of a gas station looming ahead.

～

"Plastic Taffy?" Neil Trinsky stopped jogging and watched the ridiculous yellow van cruise by. "What the fuck are they doing here?" He was trotting along a street beyond the downtown area. It was lined with huge rental cabins and many of them had vans and SUVs parked outside. The Day-Glo yellow Plastic Taffy van slowed down, its occupants obviously looking for something. Suddenly, it pulled off in front of a huge three-story cabin and edged in between two other vans. The doors opened.

Neil ducked behind a white Ford Explorer and watched as the band members, all dressed in black, piled out, jabbering.

They tried the cabin door, but it was locked and they began knocking and ringing the doorbell like a pack of rabid weasels. *What the hell is going on?*

Finally, the door opened and he heard a man's gruff voice. "Who are you?"

"Stephen Darling sent us," one of the moptops said.

"You're the band?"

"Yes," they chorused.

The man grunted and stood back, Plastic Taffy disappeared inside, and the heavy door slammed back in place. Neil even heard a lock click. *You can fucking hear everything in the mountains.*

24

FANGING OUT IN ETERNITY

The town had filled up overnight. Sheriff Zach Tully finished his cruise around Eternity, surprised at all the NO VACANCY signs glowing on Hotel Circle. Now, he parked in front of the King's Tart and strolled in, feeling like a cartoon character gliding on the aroma of coffee and donuts.

"You're late." Harlan filled a coffee mug. "Trouble in town?"

"No, no trouble." Tully took the mug and blew on it. "Thanks."

"I just made a batch of jelly donuts."

"You trying to fatten me up?"

"Never works. You have the metabolism of a sixteen-year-old. I envy you that." He patted his own belly.

Tully grinned. "I'll take two. Lemon."

The bakery was empty despite it being after seven, so Harlan came around the counter with his own coffee and a plate of pastries, and sat down. He snagged a donut. "So, what's up?"

"The town is packed. Is this all about that vampire convention?"

Harlan nodded. "I'd say so. It always fills up, even for the small ones, but the last big one, that was really something. You should have seen the carriages and coffins!"

"Coffins? Are you serious? Vampires really use coffins?" Tully couldn't believe his ears. As usual.

"It's a long journey to get here even now, but back then, it took a lot longer. Weeks, even months for some of them, but by God, they wanted to be here, and back then, vampires really did travel in coffins to avoid the sun. They had to. It was quite a sight." Harlan laughed. "It looked like Eternity was the epicenter of an outbreak of plague. I tell you, we lost most of the non-Lifers who lived up here back then - they hightailed it down the mountain, headed for Shasta, French Gulch, and Whiskeytown." His blue eyes twinkled.

"So, they were afraid of the vampires?"

Harlan shook his head. "No sir, they were afraid of the plague." He bit into a jelly donut and delicately licked cherry filling out of it. "We didn't think they'd take too well to the idea of vampires - we Lifers were afraid they might try to burn down the town - so *we* spread the plague rumors. Worked like a charm."

Tully remembered his donut and took a bite. "So ... Lifers aren't afraid of vampires?"

Harlan shrugged. "They're just people - as immortal as Lifers - but they happen to drink blood. They're as well or better-behaved as regular folk, as long as they don't get too hungry. Most will fill up on the occasional rodent, if necessary." He laughed. "Of course there are always bad apples - folks who were undoubtedly reprobates when they were human." His expression turned serious. "You don't need to worry, Zach. The vamps in charge of Biting Man keep a tight rein on those who come here."

"Why here?" Tully sipped coffee.

"As you know, Eternity is home to some pretty weird folklore."

"Sure, but-"

"Well, part of that folklore is vampiric."

"I've never heard that one before."

"We like to keep it under our hats. Vampires worry people."

"That's an understatement."

Harlan stood and refilled their coffees. "It's said a vampiric prince united his people here after his father - the king - slaughtered most of the half-breeds."

"Half-breeds?"

"Hybrid is the politically correct term now. They are the vampires of human folklore - vampires who are half human. The original vampires called themselves Trueborns and considered humans slaves and livestock, at least prior to the fall of Lemuria, and then Atlantis."

"Oh come on. Atlantis? Vampires are from Atlantis? Did they ride unicorns, too?" Tully guffawed. "You, Harlan King, are pulling my leg."

"I'm not. I swear to you, I'm not. After Lemuria sank into the Pacific not so far away, many Trueborns arrived here and founded a city inside Icehouse Mountain, in the huge fabled caverns none of us humans have ever actually seen. It's said they stayed there many centuries. It was a sort of base of operations as they traveled on to the Atlantic coast and beyond and they began colonizing the island they named Atlantis."

Tully finished his first lemon-filled donut. "Sure, whatever you say."

Harlan grinned. "A few stayed behind in the mountain. Eons passed and things didn't go so well on Atlantis under the rule of the particularly despicable Trueborn king. His son rebelled when the king began slaughtering the half-breed human vampires that were inevitably created - Trueborns were as frisky as we are, it seems."

"Uh huh."

"Don't believe me, Zach?"

"I'm listening. I've learned never to say never around here."

"Trueborns who supported human vampires began killing Trueborns who did not - it was all quite political, you see." Harlan picked up another donut. "Politics never change. Eventually, due to political infighting, Atlantis' population of Trueborns began to dwindle and truly suffered when the island was devastated by an earthquake."

"If you say so."

With a flourish, Harlan finished his donut. "The vampires who survived - Trueborn and human hybrid both - fled into the world. The unpleasant king did as well, but left a trail of bodies behind him. He headed for the west coast of what's now the United States, and when he arrived here, he first settled on the coast of central California, living among the indigenous humans who built him a fine castle. Eventually, he slaughtered most of them, but his son, Keliu, who had supported the hybrid vampires, arrived soon after and helped the remaining humans - and whatever hybrids he could find - rebuild their societies."

"Whatever you say." Tully sipped coffee.

"Meanwhile, the king traveled north, returning to Icehouse Mountain. There, he found a number of Trueborns still living in the Eternal City within the mountain, and he took the throne, killing those who opposed him. That lasted a while - quite a while in human terms - but he wasn't pleasant to the indigenous people and there weren't that many of them to begin with, so he turned many into half-breeds and put them to work as his slaves, sending them out to procure humans for consumption." Harlan shook his head. "He was not a kind monarch."

"Sounds that way." Tully started his second donut.

"Finally, Prince Keliu arrived and did what many thought impossible - he imprisoned his father. Immediately they tried to crown him king, but he refused." Harlan chuckled. "I guess his daddy left a bad taste in his mouth."

"And is he still here, living in the mountain?" Tully didn't bother to hide his sarcasm, but Harlan didn't rise to it. He rarely did.

"Oh, no, I doubt it. It's been a few thousand years, give or take. Now, the vampires make occasional pilgrimages here. It's kind of like the Christmas story where the three wise men go to Bethlehem. It's a celebration of the vampiric prince who is credited with saving the vampires."

"So ... You're telling me it's Christmastime for vampires?"

Harlan belly-laughed. "I have never heard it put so well."

"You're serious."

"As a pregnant nun."

Tully smiled. "That's pretty serious."

"Indeed."

"So as mayor and leader of the town council, how do you wish the Sheriff's Department to, uh, deal with our fanged visitors?"

Harlan laughed. "You really don't believe in vampires, do you?"

"No."

"You will." The baker finished his coffee. "Treat them like anyone else, keeping in mind that they are very, very good for our economy.

Except for the restaurants, but even those do good business thanks to the fang-boys and fang-girls who show up hoping to ..." Harlan stroked his chin. "You know, I don't know what they're hoping for, other than getting to rub elbows with the undead."

Tully chuckled. "I can't help you with that, but judging by the guy we ran into last night, you're right - these vampire fans are likely to be more trouble than the vampires."

Harlan nodded. "I'd say so. It's been a couple of decades since there's been a gathering here big enough to really draw much in the way of fans, but they're problematic. We don't want them hassling the vampires. You'll want your department to keep them under control."

"Am I going to be dealing with any, uh, vampire police or anything?"

"That would be V-Sec. I'll introduce you to those in charge and you can plan things out with them. More coffee?"

"Thanks, no." Tully stood up. "I've had about all I can take."

Harlan twinkled. "One of the vamps is quite a celebrity."

Curtis Penrose walked in. "Sheriff-"

"Just a minute, Curtis." He turned to Harlan. "Who?"

"Meet me here tonight at eight. I'll have some answers for you."

"Sheriff-"

"Thanks, Harlan. What's wrong now, Curtis?"

"My vending machine has been robbed again!"

Tully tried not to let his eyes roll as the litany began anew. "Call it into the station, Curtis."

"You're here."

"I'm not on duty," Tully lied. "And, as I've told you before, you need to put that machine indoors at night. Or put up a surveillance camera if you want to catch your vandal."

"I want to file a report-"

The bells jangled as the fang-boy from the night before walked in and approached the counter, giving Tully a bare nod. He realized the boy was really a man - pushing thirty, if he hadn't passed it already - but he had the kind of face that looked untouched by age, as if he spent all his time in a cave, careful not to make any expressions that might cause wrinkles. But there was age in his eyes - *the eyes never lie*. And these were cold, dark, questing. *He's trouble.* Tully had thought the same thing last night, and now, he was certain.

"Here for one of my famous jelly donuts? Or perhaps a cinnamon roll directly from heaven?" Harlan bellied up to the counter.

"My body is a temple," the guy said. "I would never eat such poison."

Harlan twinkled his baby blues. "Inhaling is free. Or may I interest you in some fine coffee?"

"Coffee is deadly," the guy said. "I'd like a glass of almond milk. A tall, cold one."

Tully managed not to react, but both Harlan and the annoying little Penrose burst into laughter. The fang-boy's face remained smooth as ice, but Tully noted the color creeping into his cheeks as his dark eyes turned to flint. He pivoted and left without a word.

"Touchy." Harlan laughed.

~

"Eddie," Lois said. "Are you awake?"

He grunted from the other bed. "Sort of."

"May I have the keys to your van? I want to get my suitcase. I need my toothbrush. And I need to take Renny down to do his business." At the sound of his name the little dog poked his head up. He'd been sleeping with Eddie.

Eddie grunted again and sat up, stretching. "I need mine, too. And some clean skivvies wouldn't hurt either."

Lois laughed. "No kidding. After sleeping in these beds, I feel like I need another shower."

They'd been so tired when they finally pulled into the Perdet Towers and wrangled a room that they hadn't even bothered going back down for their luggage. They'd turned on the TV - there was a *Twilight Zone* marathon playing - and conked out on the stained and ratty double beds, intending to rest a few minutes then retrieve the luggage. That never happened.

Lois waited while Eddie used the facilities. The Perdet Towers was five ugly stories of peeling yellow paint trimmed in gold. It looked kind of like a stack of pancakes, a small version of the other hotels in the tacky overpriced chain. The lobby contained a towering statue of Harry Donaldson, the notorious CEO. He stood staring above the guests' heads, his finger pointing in a way Lois assumed was significant. The faux man was dirty white from his shoes to the top of his forehead. His poofy hair was painted gold. The statue showed fingerprints as far up as people could reach. Lois smiled; there were dirty marks clustered in one area - guests had been grabbing his groin. *For good luck?* In any case, the hotel was a mangy mess but it was the only one with a vacant room, and she knew she should be grateful they didn't have to sleep in the van.

The room they were in carried on the unclean theme with a smirking portrait of Donaldson overlooking their beds. Despite the Snidely Whiplash mustache some guest had added to increase their viewing pleasure, Eddie had thrown a frayed bath towel over the portrait the moment they entered the room while mumbling something about corporate fraud and deception. *If he hadn't, I would have.* Overall, the room was pretty unpleasant with cockroach bodies behind the mostly-clean toilet, stinking mildew by the sliding glass window, and a gold carpet that was a constellation of stains. But it was still a heck of a lot better than sleeping in the van.

Eddie came out of the bathroom and they went downstairs.

Though it was high summer, the air at this hour and elevation was thin and chilly and Lois couldn't wait to get her hands on her jacket.

Eddie unlocked the back door of the van and pulled it open.

Lois saw her bag on the floor next to a pile of radio equipment that reminded her of something from a science fiction movie. As she reached for her bag, a blanket groaned and moved.

Lois yelped and wrapped her arms around Eddie.

A young woman with messy red hair and sleep-fogged, bewildered eyes stared at them.

"What the hell?" Eddie said.

"Oh!" The girl looked stricken. "I'm so sorry, I-"

"What are you doing in my van?"

Lois recognized the pretty waitress from the restaurant in Candle Bay. *What on earth is going on?*

"Bobby's Coffee," Eddie said, staring.

The young woman threw the blanket aside and tried to make a run for it, but Eddie snagged her by the shirt collar.

"Let me go!" shouted the girl.

"Mellow out. I'm not going to hurt you."

The girl's eyes landed on him. "I'm sorry. I needed a ride to Biting Man. I slipped into your van last night. I really, really have to pee, so if you don't mind-"

"Biting Man?" Eddie asked. "How do you know about Biting Man?"

The girl shrugged. "I'm a vampire expert. I know these things."

Eddie let go of her. "You can't just walk into Biting Man, young lady."

"I'm doing research for my thesis. I *know* people can't just walk in. That's why I hitched a ride with you! I was hoping you'd go straight there."

"We're not here to go to Biting Man. That would be a death sentence. We're here to track down my friend's son."

Lois nodded and put a hand on the girl's shoulder. "What's your name?"

"My name is Erin. Erin Woodhouse. And I *really* need to pee. I haven't gone since you guys stopped at Denny's last night. And I need to find some place to crash. A room or something."

"Good luck with that," said Eddie. "We got the last one."

"I have an idea," said Lois. "Why don't you come up to our room and use the bathroom? You're probably hungry, too." She ignored Eddie's look of disapproval. "It's been a very long ride. You must be starving."

"I *am* pretty hungry," Erin admitted.

"I don't think this is a good-" Eddie began.

"Well, we can't just set her loose!" said Lois. "She needs to use the restroom, Eddie. And I brought a lot of granola bars. We can feed the poor girl." Lois grabbed her bag and led Erin back to the hotel, Eddie staring after them.

25

FROM DUSK TILL DARK

Neil Trinsky had spent part of the day exploring Eternity, and part of it catching up on sleep in his room at Dimples' Boarding House. Hungry, he came downstairs and Mrs. Dimples bustled up, getting in his face, her granny-smile widening as she took his arm. "My, that cologne you're wearing is quite ... potent! And what nice muscles you have hidden under your sweat suit, young man."

"Yeah, thanks."

But she wouldn't let go, instead, tugging him along, talking incessantly. "We have our evening meal on the early side, Mr. Trinsky, and you're just in time. Tonight, I've made cornbread because Elmer has cooked up a big pot of his famous chili. Doesn't it smell divine?"

It wasn't bad, he had to admit. "Is it vegetarian?"

Martha Ann laughed. "Silly boy. You need protein to keep those nice muscles of yours big and strong!"

"There are plenty of *meatless* ways to get protein," he informed her. "Vegetarian beans are a perfect source. No one needs to eat meat. That's a myth."

"Yes, of course, dear. Whatever you say." She pulled him along. "You *must* meet your fellow boarders and have something to eat."

"I'm not interested in eating-"

"Of course you are, dear."

He tried to halt, but she just dragged him on, and he didn't want to alienate her since the other hotels in town were so booked up.

She drew him into a dining room with a long table filled with people. "Friends," Martha Ann said, "meet our newest guest, Neil Trinsky."

"Lifer?" asked a balding man with hawkish eyes.

Lifer? Does the old fart really think I'd live in this god-forsaken town?

"No, no, no. Neil is only staying with us for a little while."

"Fang-boy, is he?" the man asked.

Martha Ann ignored the question, and began introducing him to the motley crew of diners. The majority appeared to be over forty, but all ages were represented. And they all looked like assholes. He nodded greetings as Martha Ann rattled off instantly forgotten names.

"Now, sit down, won't you, Neil, and have a bite to eat." She paused and looked over the table. "Neil doesn't eat meat, you know. He's one of those vegetarians."

"No meat?" asked Baldy, sounding disgusted. "You don't eat meat, boy?"

Another man, dumpy and slumpy with watery green eyes and a pale blond comb-over that went on and on, smiled at Neil with rat-yellow teeth. He wore a short-sleeved plaid shirt and ear muffs. "I don't eat liver anymore. Not since …" He looked down at his plate, his words trailing off.

"Poor Jeremiah was involved in an unfortunate incident in the mountains quite some time ago," Martha Ann explained. "Come, have a seat."

"I'm sorry, Mrs. Dimples. I'm meeting someone for dinner. I need to get going."

"Oh, I understand." She twinkled. "A young lady. You must have to beat them off with sticks."

"I use stakes."

Martha Ann's mouth formed a surprised O.

"Fang-boy," said Baldy.

Ignoring him, Neil straightened his sweatshirt.

"Can I hitch a ride?" This came from Jeremiah Combover.

"Sorry, man. I gotta run." Neil left the house, stomach growling. Before he got down to vampire hunting, he decided to visit Crazy Elvis and buy a healthy sandwich. *Can't hunt on an empty stomach!*

In the parking area behind the boarding house, he got in Mom's stuck-up Altima and revved the engine, wondering if he ought to keep the car out of sight, just in case his stupid mother had reported it stolen. Then he grinned and pulled onto the road. *No way she's going to do that. I'm the only thing she has in her shitty little life, and she knows it.*

Lois watched as Erin Woodhouse ended the call and frowned. "There aren't any rooms."

Erin was a pretty girl, smart too, and Lois had taken a liking to her, despite the fact that she was a stowaway. During the day she'd explained it all, but Eddie still seemed put off by her, though Lois thought he was warming up. A little. It was a good thing because Eternity was apparently booked to the hilt.

"I don't know what to do," said Erin.

Eddie cleared his throat. "You seemed to know what to do when you hid in my van."

"I said I was sorry," said Erin. "If I do this thesis right, it will open doors for me. I wasn't thinking beyond that."

Eddie grumbled.

Erin sighed. "Look, I know you recognize me from the other night, not just from the cafe." She turned to Lois. "I asked Eddie to autograph my butt at the amusement park. There was this creepy guy following me around, and I thought that would turn him off." She beamed at Eddie. "But, I really am a big fan of yours, Mr. Fortune."

Lois laughed. "You autographed her ass?"

He nodded. "It's part of the job. You wouldn't believe some of the things I've autographed."

Lois turned to Eddie, who sat at the small desk, looking grim. "What are we going to do?"

He looked resigned. "I guess she'll have to stay with us."

Lois was relieved. She'd hate to toss the girl out - or make her sleep in the van again.

"I'm so sorry," said Erin. "I have money - I can pay you if you want."

"No need." Eddie gave Erin a weak smile. "Are you guys hungry? I was thinking we could go into town and get something to eat."

"I'll buy!" said Erin. "That way I won't feel like a *total* freeloader."

"Deal."

∽

"LET ME THE HELL OUT OF HERE!"

Julian Valentyn's eyes found the high ceiling of his bedchamber as Felix handed him a clean silk shirt. "She doesn't care for being locked up."

"No, Master Julian," said Felix. "She does not."

Julian smiled and brushed his long pale hair as he stared into the tall cheval glass. He looked no different than he had thousands of years ago, with milky skin, high cheekbones, and piercing onyx eyes that all spoke of Trueborn royalty. "It's a pity that Talai is, in her incarnation as Amanda, such a colossal twat."

Felix grinned. "She's certainly noisy. She kept up that racket all day long."

"She's an addict, you know. Too fond of Lixir. She abuses it."

"I thought it wasn't addictive."

"Not normally, but it happens on occasion if it's abused. Just like alcohol."

Felix nodded. "Perhaps when it's out of her system?"

"Let us hope, Felix. Let us hope."

Something crashed. "LET ME OUT OF HERE YOU BASTARDS!"

"My, my." Julian tied his hair into a low ponytail and took one final look in the mirror. "Patience is not her virtue."

"An understatement." His manservant followed him out of the bedchamber and into the great room.

"Felix," Julian said as Amanda loosed a new round of vulgarities, "do not allow yourself to be alone with her. She is dangerous."

"Yes, Master."

"Good man. Now go enjoy your breakfast and see to the servants. Make sure they know to stay out of her reach."

Felix nodded and left the room as Amanda demanded her freedom in the traditional language of sailors.

Smiling to himself, Julian sat down at the white baby grand and lifted the key cover. He ran one long finger down the keyboard as he wondered what to do with Amanda. She screamed a set of obscenities that hurt his ears. "Vile creature," he murmured, his fingers finding the keys.

He began to play *The Moonlight Sonata*, but the woman yelled louder, destroying the mellow mood he desired, so he switched up to one of Liszt's *Mephisto Waltzes*. While he didn't love the discordant sounds, they did cover up Amanda's obscenities and, in a strange way, both soothed and fed his irritation.

He didn't know his own heart, that much was clear.

When she'd arrived, it had been all he could do not to take her in his arms, but he was nothing if not a gentleman and he did not wish to touch a woman already taken, even if she was *the Woman*.

His fingers flew up and down the keyboard, hard and pulsing. She was different now; it wasn't just the way she'd acted, he'd smelled the difference, tasted it in the air around her. He was, as always, powerfully attracted to her, but there was something underneath her beauty, something that made him think of rotting fruit.

Incendarius. It was beyond doubt.

Julian picked up his phone.

∽

STEPHEN DARLING HAD JUST STEPPED out of the shower when his cell began ringing. "Damn it." Wrapping a towel around his waist, he snagged the phone from the counter, hoping to hell it wasn't Amanda.

He peered at the number: it was Julian Valentyn again, and that made his stomach twist almost as hard. Sighing, he answered. "Julian, how are you?" *Please don't let this be about Amanda!*

"I am well." The Trueborn's elegant, studied voice betrayed no hint of anxiety. "And you?"

"Fine, though I must admit that the very fact that you're calling me has me on edge. Is this about ... her?"

"Yes, Stephen, but don't fear - she is not making plans to return to Candle Bay."

"Good."

"Indeed." The Trueborn paused. "Stephen, have you considered what I said?"

"I have. Do you still think Amanda is Incendarius?"

"I do. Strongly. May I ask you a question?"

"Go ahead."

"Have you ever noticed that Amanda's blood has an unusual flavor?"

"Yes, I have. It's rather ... heady. Like overripe fruit. I have to admit it's been a long time since I tasted it, but I remember the flavor as if it were yesterday." He hesitated. "Julian, have you tasted her?"

"Not in this incarnation, and I don't intend to, but now I am certain she is Incendarius."

"Because of my answer?"

"There are many reasons, including the way you've described the taste of her blood. Most obvious to me is her strength; she is too newly created to have such power. And she tasks me, Stephen. She tasks me. It's more than her personality. Hybrid vampires have no such effect on me, yet here is an enormously rude and self-centered young vampire who ... What is the expression? Gets under my skin. Troubles me. Tasks me."

"Perhaps because she is an incarnation of your first love?" Stephen sat down on the bed.

"Yes, but there is much more to it than that. I never, not once, thought Talai's essence might be Incendarius. Not until now."

"But she was human."

"Yes. Stephen, Incendarius is not a trait in Trueborns. It is something born of the human essence. It is in the genes of the psyche, but incredibly rare. It is only revealed when the human is turned."

"You're serious?"

"Utterly. And Stephen, you are lucky to be among us. Incendarius is a soulless creature."

"Soulless. What do you mean?"

"I mentioned it before. As you know, hybrid vampires retain their human soul - their very essence - for better or worse. Like humans and hybrids, we Trueborns are also ensouled. But Incendarius is different. The trait lies dormant from lifetime to lifetime within any human essence that carries it. And it affects the body the soul dwells within."

"Affects it how?" Stephen's mind reeled.

"For one, it makes the taste of that human's blood cloyingly sweet. For another, they can turn anyone with one bite without being envenomated like our friends in Crimson Cove. Also, if a human - or a hybrid - is bitten by Incendarius and lives, they are often tied to it in atypical ways. This is related to the reason you've had a difficult time letting go of Amanda even though I sense you've wanted to for a very long time."

"That's true." Stephen felt a little better.

"Indeed." Julian cleared his throat. "If Incendarius turns a human into a vampire - and mind you, if they desire, it takes only *one* bite, not three - that newly born vampire will be tied to it with astonishing bonds; the new vampire will sense his Maker even if Incendarius is hundreds of miles away. Perhaps thousands."

"Julian, I have a question. A personal one."

"Go ahead, Stephen."

"The soul of Talai is the same soul that is now Amanda, correct?"

"Correct."

"So, does that mean Incendarius affects Trueborns as strongly as it affects human vampires?"

Valentyn chuckled. "No. It is far worse for Trueborns. Incendarius is a plague upon us. It is truly fortunate that the creature is so rare."

"How did you not realize that she, in all her incarnations, was Incendarius?"

"Simple. Between the rarity and my being smitten, I could not see it."

"Julian, you said Talai killed herself rather than become a vampire. Do you know why?"

"The soul that was Talai and is Amanda committed suicide in a number of incarnations to avoid becoming a vampire. I believe that the reason is that on some level, she knew - and when her soul was younger and more innocent, she feared losing herself to Incendarius."

"That makes sense," Stephen said. "But as Amanda, the soul is older and ..."

"Jaded might be the correct term."

"Jaded. Julian, is Amanda even in there anymore?"

"Once turned vampiric, the Incendarius aspect takes over. It becomes its own entity and will eventually destroy what is left of the original soul if it does not flee. I believe that has happened in Amanda's case."

"So, you're saying that Amanda isn't there anymore?"

"It would seem so. Though she still looks to be Amanda - or Talai - I don't see any other qualities that normal humans, hybrids, or Trueborns possess. You are a better judge than I, but I would say that, in my own brief experience with her, I see no sign of a conscience. No moral compass. She is like a shark; cold, deadly and very, very hungry."

Stephen felt horror and relief in equal measure. There would be no more guilt. And no more Amanda.

26

OF CABBAGES AND THINGS

"Ah, newborns." Karl Kohlkopf, big hands clasped behind his back, studied the four very poor excuses for vampires that Stephen Darling had stuck him with. Stephen had said they would be excellent entertainers. Karl wasn't so sure.

"What are your names?"

One of the leather-clad men cleared his throat. "I'm Davy, they're Ramon, Mick, and Paul."

Karl grunted and turned to his wife. "What do you think, Kora?"

"I don't think we have much choice but to make do since we owe the Darlings a favor or two." Kora, as tall, sturdy, and handsome as the day she'd turned him over two centuries ago, shook her round head. Tonight, she wore forest green. It suited her red hair. "If they can sing, and can follow rules, they'll do. And the youngsters might like something modern."

Karl nodded his leonine head. "Indeed." He turned to the aging boy band. "I want you all to stay in my sight at all times, is that understood?"

The band members looked at each other, then back at him, mouths slack.

"The reason for this," said Karl, pushing his own ginger hair out of his freckled face, "is that Biting Man is a very large draw, and as new vampires, your impulse control is weak. Should you do anything to compromise our position, make no mistake, you *will* be executed." He looked at Kora, who nodded agreement.

"You can't be serious!" said one of the men - Karl had already forgotten which name belonged to whom.

"Oh, I am very serious. We gather at Biting Man festivals all over the states to experience the *reality* of being Vampire. The festival here is the most important of all. Only vampires are allowed within Icehouse Mountain, within the Eternal City. However, Eternity draws plenty of tourists and it won't do for any of us to leave a trail of bodies. Touching humans is strictly forbidden and bears the ultimate penalty. The citizens and tourists of Eternity are gracious hosts and we must be gracious guests."

Kora stood next to her husband. "We'll make sure you have everything you need. Blood, shelter, and the like. You have no reason to leave this cabin."

Karl nodded. "But you'll get *only* what you need, no more and no less. Also, you'll be providing entertainment at the event. That is how you will earn your keep."

One of the mop-haired men stepped forward, a hard glint in his eye. "We're not puppets, man! We didn't come here to be-"

Karl raised a meaty hand, flicked his chest, and the man flew back several feet. He landed flat on his ass with a painful *Oof!* His bandmates stared in astonished disbelief.

"But you *are* puppets, all of you, until I say otherwise. You have much to prove. Frankly, you're lucky you're not dead already." Karl turned to his wife. "Kora, get them nourishment, then we'll drive them up to rehearsals." He smiled, deliberately showing plenty of fang. "We must make sure we give the audience the best show possible, wouldn't you agree?"

All four heads nodded.

As he walked away, Karl winked at Kora, who suppressed laughter. Karl and Kora Kohlkopf loved nothing more than acting like stereotypically wicked vampires. It was what was expected.

~

AT SIX STORIES, the Icehouse Inn towered above Eternity, looking so modern that it seemed out of place. It was nice, and even if it hadn't been, it was the only place with a suite available when Winter had called six months earlier. The penthouse had three bedrooms - one for himself and Arnie, the master bedroom for Chynna, and one for the twins. Winter set his bags on the bed and looked around. The room was done in pale corals and sea blues, more appropriate for an ocean room than one in the mountains. There was a mini-fridge in the corner and two queen beds faced an enormous flat screen TV. "I'll be right back. Arnie. Then we'll have some sustenance."

Arnie nodded absently, staring at the paintings on the walls.

Entering the living room, Winter realized this puffy-pastel penthouse probably served as a bridal suite as often as not. The lampshades featured big satin bows in various shades of lavender and blue, and the paintings consisted of romantic couples walking beaches and forest paths.

"Look!" Ivy, clad in a black bra and panties, came out of her room and crossed to the lavender-draped windows. "Come over here and look, Winter!"

Winter nearly walked into the built-in Jacuzzi near the slider because his eyes were on Ivy.

She flipped the hot tub bubbles on, and slipped her bra strap off one shoulder.

Winter grinned. Now, this was the kind of vacation he needed. When Lucy appeared in a red bra and panties, he sat at the edge of the tiled hot tub and crossed his arms, enjoying the view as the twins slowly helped each other out of their underwear, all the while casting him wanton glances and batting their lashes. They looked just as good out of their clothes as in them.

Winter was back on his feet, preparing to peel his shirt off when Chynna came out of the master bedroom. "Winter?" She was just in time to see the naked twins disappear into the hot tub.

"I, uh. It's hot in here." He tugged his t-shirt back down.

She eyed him, then glanced at the twins who giggled and splashed.

"Maybe I should trade rooms with the twins. The master suite has a jet tub nearly as big as this one. We - and more importantly, Arnie - wouldn't have to watch them ... *cavort*."

Winter laughed. "It's not so bad, is it, Chynna?"

She gave him an eye roll.

"Papa Winter! Papa Winter!" Arnie loped out of their bedroom, a big grin on his face. "Can we watch TV and-" His words dried up and his jaw fell open as his eyes landed on the nude twins.

Chynna took Arnie's arm. "I think Arnie and I ought to go unpack."

"But I want to stay here!" Arnie ogled the girls.

"Let's watch a movie, okay Arnie?"

"Can we watch *Tombstone*?" At last, his gaze left Ivy and Lucy.

"Arnie, if they don't have it, I'll buy you a copy." Chynna gave Winter an exasperated look that bordered on dirty.

He shrugged. "The guy's over two-hundred years old, Chynna. He's seen naked women before." He didn't tell her that he'd hired prostitutes for Arnie in the past. Despite his sweet childlike nature, Arnie was a grown man with a grown man's urges, but Winter didn't expect everyone to understand that, especially Chynna, who saw Arnie through maternal eyes.

"I know," said Chynna, "but ... it just seems ... I don't know ... *inappropriate*."

Winter grinned. "That's part of the fun."

He was glad to see a little smile on her lips. She led Arnie back to his bedroom.

Winter had no intentions of following.

Ivy pushed herself to the edge of the Jacuzzi. "Are you coming in?" She rose enough to show a pair of mammaries of a magnificence he hadn't seen since the swimming mermaids at The Crimson Corset.

"The water's great!" added Lucy, bobbing to reveal her equally fantastic flotation devices.

Without hesitation, he peeled off his t-shirt and flung it, rubber-band-style, across the room.

Lucy and Ivy laughed, whistled, and began crooning stripper music.

Winter obliged them with a slow, teasy, unbuttoning of his jeans.

He gave them his backside as he pulled his pants off, then, inspired by the girls' dreadful singing, twirled them on his finger and sent them flying.

"Ooh! Commando!" squealed Lucy.

"Always," said Winter, grinning. He stepped into the Jacuzzi.

"Wow," said Ivy. "You *do* have a great big sword!"

Lucy licked her lips.

Winter laughed as the giggling twins moved in for the kill.

27
IN A PICKLE

Neil Trinsky found a parking space in front of Kissel's Pickle Shoppe, a small Bavarian-looking business with big wooden barrels for decoration. It was tucked between a shoe store and a souvenir shop. Both of those were closed for the night, but Kissel's was brightly lit with the front door wide open. The scents of dill and vinegar wafted out, making Neil's stomach growl. Wondering if they made sandwiches, too, he followed his nose.

Within the shop, rows and rows of glass jars stood on wooden shelves and more huge pickle barrels served as end caps. The one nearest the entrance had a plate with a sliced pickle and toothpicks set in front of a toy tiger that wore a green apron that read, "I'm Sour Puss! Welcome to Kissel's Pickles!" Neil speared a couple slices and began nibbling as he wandered the shop, wondering where the owner was.

There were jars of huge foot-long pickles, tiny pickles, kosher, dill, and sweet. There were jalapeno-laced pickles and icebox pickles of every sort. Below his belt, Neil Jr. twitched to life. Another row was reserved for pickled carrots, onions, and oddities like pickled cauliflower and broccoli. Neil recoiled at that. Another row was entirely devoted to sauerkraut. Refrigerated cases lined the back and side walls of the shop, all full of pickled things. Neil smiled to himself, imagining a special section where the proprietor kept pickled babies and other delights.

"May I help you?"

Neil turned to see a small colorless man goggling at him through wire-rimmed glasses that magnified his pallid blue eyes in a most unfortunate manner. One eye was fixed on Neil. The other, a different shade of light blue, stared straight ahead. He wore a green apron that said "Kissel's Pickles are the Best!" and a name tag that read, *"Hello, I'm Flournoy. May I help you?"*

"Just looking. Do you do all the pickling here, on site?"

"Oh, yes, every bit of it." Flournoy rubbed his hands together in a washing motion. "Pickle Master Bill makes everything we sell himself."

"Pickle Master?"

"Yes, it was a title bestowed upon him in his home country when he was just a lad-"

"Flournoy, back to work with you!" A big man with a round face and a grin as wide as his long mustache clapped a hand on Flournoy's shoulder and set him on his way.

Seeing the pain on the clerk's face as he retreated, Neil smiled.

The man extended his big, square hand. "Bill Kissel. Proprietor."

Neil shook, squeezing hard. "Neil Trinsky. Pickle fancier."

Kissel's laugh filled the shop. "What's your pleasure?"

Neil grinned. "I was wondering if you have any pickled babies for sale?"

Kissel's face went blank, then the twinkle ran out of his eyes, and the smile slipped from his lips. "What?"

Guess I found a sore spot. "I'm sorry, I'm a little dyslexic sometimes. I meant baby pickles!"

Kissel regrouped, bellowing laughter that sounded too hearty. "Dill, kosher, sweet? What's your pleasure?"

Neil couldn't identify the man's faint accent. Something European. And he looked familiar, though he couldn't place him. Not at all. "Kosher dill." Neil watched the man.

"Very good." Kissel led him to a shelf and handed him a jar of pickles swimming in a salty green sea. "These have a lovely bite." He smiled. "They snap between your teeth."

They ought to give blow jobs for ten bucks a bottle. "I'll take them," Neil said. "Do you have sandwiches for sale?"

"Not tonight, my friend. I've a party to attend."

Maybe he's going to Biting Man!

Kissel led him to the counter and rang him up, looked at the Discover card dubiously, then put it through. "May I see some ID?"

"Sure." Neil pulled out his license. "My mom lent me her card. She's at the hotel, if you want to call and check."

Kissel considered. "Ah, what's to check? You're both Trinskys. A fine name. Yugoslavian?"

Neil had no idea. "I think so."

"Then you have good roots, young man." He bagged the pickles and handed them to Neil then took off his apron. "You're my last customer tonight, Mr. Trinsky. Thank you for your business. Come back again, won't you?"

He came around the counter and saw Neil out, then locked the doors behind him.

Neil opened the overpriced pickles and withdrew one. Kissel hadn't lied; it snapped perfectly. *Not as good as a bj, but close.*

Nibbling his pickle, seeing the sights, Neil headed down Main Street.

∽

STRIDER'S Steakhouse had sawdust on the floors, tables made of thick, heavily lacquered wood, and matching wooden chairs and benches. The lighting was low and atmospheric, a combination of amber lantern light on the walls and stained glass fixtures over each table.

Eddie took a handful of peanuts from the basket on their table and began shelling. Erin Woodhouse did the same and had eaten half a dozen before Eddie got his first one open. She was one hungry vampire fan.

"This is nice." Lois spoke between sips of ice water as she gazed out the window.

"It is," Eddie agreed. The park was lit by old-fashioned street lamps lining the sidewalk and illuminating the curving pathways within the park. Couples strolled, joggers jogged, and children ran and played around a huge pond - or a very small lake. A few paddle boats dotted the dark waters.

"Have you ever been here in winter?" Erin asked between peanuts.

"This place is almost impossible to get to in winter, but I've been here for ski season - it usually starts before October. It's beautiful."

"Eternity must look like a Christmas card by Halloween." Lois chuckled. "It must be gorgeous."

Eddie nodded just as the waiter arrived. He was about to order a burger since Erin was paying, but she ordered a steak as big as her head, so he did, too. Lois ordered scallops.

"So you aren't going to crash Biting Man?" Erin asked.

Eddie laughed. "No, no, no. We won't be attempting that. We value our lives." He paused. "And you need to get that idea out of your head, young lady. Don't even think about crashing the festival. Even if you could, it would be very foolish."

They paused when the waiter brought their salads. Once he was gone, Erin asked, "You guys both believe vampires are real?"

Eddie nodded and saw Lois hesitate then do the same.

"But you aren't here for Biting Man? You're only here to get your car back?"

"Exactly," Lois said.

"I'd like to help you," said Erin.

Lois reached into her purse and pulled out a photograph. "This is Neil, my son. If you see him, my car will probably be close by."

When Erin looked at the photo, Eddie saw recognition in her eyes. Recognition and distaste.

"I know him," said Erin.

"You do?"

"Well, not *know* him, know him, but I met him just the other night at the amusement park." She paused. "I shared a Ferris wheel ride with him. Um, he thought I was a vampire because I have a bat tattoo on my shoulder. He kind of scared me. It's why I ended up getting Eddie's autograph – he's the one I was getting away from." She paused. "I'm sorry. I don't mean to say anything bad about him."

"It's okay," Lois told her. "You're right to be nervous around him. He makes me nervous."

"He's been a fan for some time," said Eddie. "And he makes *all* of us nervous."

"He has problems," Lois explained. "He always has. I'm sorry he frightened you."

Erin shrugged. "So, did *he* come up here for Biting Man?"

Eddie nodded. "Absolutely."

"He fancies himself a vampire slayer," Lois explained. "He has pictures of Buffy all over his room. I'm not sure, but I suspect he thinks she's real."

"*That's* scary," Erin said.

"Hey, it's Zach Tully!" Eddie stood, knocked on the window, and waved at the uniformed man walking by. The cop looked surprised.

"Is he a vampire?" Erin asked.

"No. He's the sheriff." Eddie beckoned him inside.

A moment later, Zach Tully, his star gleaming, came in. "Sit down, Sheriff!" Eddie said. "You remember me, right?"

"Eddie Fortune. How can I forget you? What are you doing up here?"

Tully looked uncomfortable and Eddie didn't blame him. "I'm not here on business, don't worry. And I'm not going to bring up Jack the Ripper. I promise."

Tully nodded, still looking uneasy. "Vacation?"

"I'm on the trail of a vampire hunter," Eddie said with a grin.

Tully just looked at him.

"These are my friends, Lois and Erin."

"I'm doing my thesis on vampires," Erin explained.

"And I'm the vampire hunter's mother," Lois said. "He stole my car."

Tully brightened. "Have you reported it?"

"No."

Eddie spoke up. "We thought it would be better to get here first. We were afraid he might ditch it if he thought we were following."

Lois nodded.

"Do you want to report it?"

"Not officially," Lois said. "I just want to find it and take it home. My son can stay for the vampire convention or whatever it is. I'll be changing the locks when I get back, but I don't want to press charges." She hesitated. "Is that okay?"

"It's fine," Tully smiled. "Less work for me. Can you give me a description? I'll keep an eye out. Unofficially."

"I can do better than that." Lois handed him the photo.

∼

"Holy cluster fuck!" Neil Trinsky had been strolling along the street, sucking on a second pickle, and pulled up short when he spotted his mother, that cunt with the bat tattoo, and Coastal Eddie all sitting at a table with none other than Eternity's little bitch of a sheriff. "Holy fuck. I gotta hide the car!"

Dropping his pickle, he forced himself to walk, not run, in the other direction.

28

I NEVER DRINK ...WINE

"You're five minutes late, Zach," Harlan King said when Tully entered the bakery. "You're never late." He hung up his apron and began shutting off lights.

"Yeah, right. You remember Coastal Eddie, that conspiracy nut on the radio who comes around to annoy us with Jack the Ripper questions every so often?"

"Certainly. He's also very interested in Bigfoot and UFOs and our faux Jim Morrison who escapes from Shady Pines every so often." Harlan tapped his chin. "Of course old Jim isn't a Lifer, so he looks like a pot-bellied, balding Jim Morrison now. Even the tourists want him to put his shirt back on these days." He shrugged into a barnstormer jacket. "What does Eddie want?"

"He's here with a friend whose son drove up in her car."

"Stole it, you mean?"

"Yes, but she's not looking to press charges. She just wants her car back." Tully hesitated. "Her son came up here because of the vampire convention."

"Biting Man." Harlan raised an eyebrow. "What aren't you telling me?"

"We met him already - he's the one we sent to the True Grace

Market."

"Fang-boy. Fang-man, from the looks of him," Harlan said.

"Yep. I didn't like his looks and I don't think his mother is too crazy about him either. I caught a vibe from her - I think she's frightened of him."

"Too bad." Harlan shook his head.

"Keep an eye out for a late model white Altima. If you see it, let me know."

"We may see it again tonight." Harlan gestured Tully out the door, then followed, locking it behind him. "V-Sec - the vampire security people - are waiting for us by the bandshell in the park."

Tully felt a burst of anxiety as they began walking. "So what do vampires look like? Will I be able to tell one from a regular person?"

"Oh," Harlan began, "they have white skin, fangs, and you can't see them in mirrors. You're wearing a crucifix?"

"No."

"Have any garlic with you?"

"Only on my breath. Are you pulling my leg?"

"Only a little. They look like you and me; you won't be able to see any difference unless they want you to, not even with a mirror. They do tend to be on the pale side, as often as not."

"They won't bite, right?"

Harlan chuckled. "No, not even if you ask." They crossed the street and headed toward the bandshell. "I think those are our vampires." He nodded at three figures loitering in the shadows.

Tully wanted to laugh. *This is insane. A meeting with 'vampire security?' I need to have my head examined.* He hadn't even told his wife or son about tonight's meeting; they would have laughed.

"Gentlemen?" Harlan King called as they neared the bandshell.

Three heads turned, two male, one female.

Tully didn't see any fangs.

"Harlan King, Mayor of Eternity," the baker said with a smile. "And this is Zach Tully, our sheriff. You're V-Sec?"

The woman, a tall no-nonsense redhead, nodded. "I'm Marilyn Baker, security chief."

She shook both their hands and while her touch was cool, Tully thought it certainly didn't feel dead. *Or undead.*

"This is Cecil Trevor." She nodded at a stocky middle-aged blond fellow to her right then looked at the tall slender man with a black brush cut on her left. "This is Matthew Moon. Cecil and Matthew are my assistant chiefs. There are many more of us on the force. You can spot us by our badges." She touched a small gold pin on her lapel.

Tully nodded, noting the same pin on her officers. It was a simple gold disk with a black enamel "S" set into it. "Good to meet you."

"And you, Sheriff," said Marilyn. "Why don't we talk in the car?"

"The car?" Tully shot Harlan a look. "Where are we going?"

"Just up the mountain to the Ski Bowl turnout. Are you familiar with it?"

"Sure, but..."

"We want to be transparent with you, Sheriff." She led the group to a white SUV and unlocked the doors. "Sheriff, join me in the front, won't you?"

He obliged, while Harlan and her two assistants pressed into the back seat. "Seatbelts," she called out as the engine turned over. Tully was amused at the idea of vampires buckling up.

"We keep a very close eye on our kind," Marilyn said as they left downtown and took the winding roads toward Icehouse Mountain. "The last thing we want is for one of us to harm one of you."

"And vice versa," Harlan called.

"Yes. Most of our kind wouldn't dream of touching a human."

"How many of you are here?"

"There are thousands of us staying in the mountain, but you'll never see them."

"*In* the mountain?" Tully asked. Harlan had told him there was an ancient city inside Icehouse, but he'd assumed he was making up stories. Harlan did that a lot.

"Yes. The mountain figures large in our history and it's very dear to us. There are only a few places on earth that are considered as sacred to our kind. But that is unimportant. What is important is that several hundred *more* vampires are staying in your town and commuting to our celebration."

"Your hotels are full of vampires," said one of the guards.

"I see." Tully's head was spinning. He didn't really see. It all sounded ridiculous.

"If anyone staying in town creates a problem, we want to hear about it. We will find out if they are vampire, and if they are, we will remove them from Eternity. If they are not, we'll tell you and you can deal with them."

"Sounds fair," Tully said. "How can you tell the difference?"

Marilyn smiled. "Aroma."

Tully forced a chuckle. "I appreciate your honesty. Harlan here tells me we may have trouble with human fans trying to infiltrate your, uh, event."

"Your mayor is correct. The fang-boys can be very motivated and quite destructive. They will try to infiltrate the Eternal City but they cannot. So, they may attempt to break into hotels and cabins that our people have rented. During the day, most of our kind are rather helpless, as you might expect."

"Most?"

"Some use Lixir - something that helps them stay awake in daylight hours, or at least not sleep so heavily."

"The best of both worlds?" Tully asked softly.

Marilyn glanced at him then turned onto Icehouse Road and began the steep climb up the mountain. "Not necessarily. You might say that it's still controversial among us."

"Does that mean I'll have vampires walking around town by day?"

"Highly unlikely because direct daylight is not good for us. But at dusk, plenty will be out. You have nothing to fear," she added quickly. "It's the vampires who do. Some of these fang-boys attempt to meet vampires, or worse. Some try to kill us."

"Okay." Tully thought of Neil Trinsky. "What do you want me to do about that?"

"Cecil, do you have the list?"

"I do." The vampire passed a small notebook to Tully. It contained a list of hotels and room numbers as well as addresses of cabins.

"Most hotels are aware of their vampiric guests and have extra security - both their own and ours, but those of us staying in cabins are more exposed. We were hoping you might have your deputies cruise by the cabins once or twice a day? A police presence always helps."

"We can do that." Tully watched as a garish yellow van with fluorescent guitars and drums painted on its sides passed them on a curve. "Plastic Taffy?" he read. The lettering made him think of The Monkees with its Pepto pinks, baby blues, and lemon yellows. The name sounded familiar. "You need to tell your people to observe traffic laws."

"Yes. I suspect one of the Kolkopfs is driving. They're in charge of entertainment."

"Just because they're dead doesn't mean they can't set a good example," Harlan said with a laugh. "Right, Zach?"

Tully shot him a dirty look. "I remember them now. Many years ago I saw one of their shows while I was on vacation. Sort of a sunshine-and-rainbows group. A boy band. You mean to tell me they're vampires?"

"Newly turned," Marilyn said. "Baby vamps, we call them. They were sent up here to learn the ropes. You could say they're on probation."

"How so?"

"Babies don't have the self-control of older vampires. If they willfully misbehave, we turn to the Five Ss: Starving, sunlight, silver, staking, or severing."

"Of the head?" Harlan asked in surprise.

"Well, it wouldn't do much good to sever their hands," Marilyn said.

Tully nodded. "And how do you define 'willful?'"

"It varies. Young vampires slip accidentally and we certainly don't destroy them the first time, you know, unless they do something outrageous, something like you'd see in the movies. Blood everywhere, bodies ripped apart. If a baby vamp does that, it will always be a problem, so we don't allow them to continue their existence."

"Is Plastic Taffy staying in town?"

She nodded. "The talent always stays with the Kolkopfs and they run their place with an iron fist. You've nothing to fear. They won't be wandering and they won't have access to Lixir."

Tully wasn't too sure about safety, but since Harlan seemed happy, he tried to be agreeable. "If I catch one of these ... fang-boys trying to harm your people, what do you expect me to do?"

"Treat them as you'd treat any other criminal, but bear in mind that we won't be able to testify against them."

Matthew cleared his throat. "If you can keep them behind bars until Biting Man is over, that would be helpful."

Tully nodded, glad that the vampires didn't expect him to turn humans over to them. "I'll do whatever I need to do to keep the peace."

"Thank you, Sheriff." Marilyn pulled off the road into the huge parking area that led to the old Ski Bowl, the lifts, and the trailhead to the top of the mountain. It was packed with vehicles, including the Plastic Taffy van.

Beyond the cars, Tully could see Japanese lanterns and brighter lights, streamers, and balloons. People - *vampires!* - milled. The ski lifts were running. "What am I looking at?"

Marilyn turned off the SUV and jumped down. "The mixer. Few humans ever see it."

"Are we going inside the mountain?" Harlan asked as he and the security men joined them.

Marilyn smiled. "No, the Eternal City within is sacred to our kind. Only vampires may enter. You understand."

Tully nodded. "Why are the ski lifts running?"

"They take us to the city."

"Seems rather high in elevation for caverns."

"That's what the elevators are for. We've been working on them for years. Entering from above draws less attention."

"You have?" Harlan raised his blond eyebrows.

"Oh, yes. A small community lives in the mountain," Marilyn explained.

"I've heard that," Harlan said. "I've been here a long time but have never seen anything to confirm it."

"I'm glad to hear it. That means our people are behaving properly."

"How do you survive - I mean what do they eat?" Tully asked.

"Not people, Sheriff, don't worry." Marilyn smiled at him. "We're quite civilized. Our blood is bottled."

"Good to know." He decided against asking where they got the bottled blood. "Lead on."

Marilyn led them to the entrance and spoke to a couple of burly guards, then led them into the mixer. There was a string quartet playing classical music near the refreshments table. Tully eyed the thick-looking red punch. "Sangria?"

Marilyn chuckled. "Very good, Sheriff."

He decided not to ask any more questions. "Come along," Marilyn said when he dawdled to look at a group of vampires costumed in Renaissance Faire finery. "I want you to meet someone. I think you'll recognize him."

Tully sped up, seeing a man in a black cape standing with a few other people. He looked vaguely familiar, and Tully squinted in the poor light as they approached. *No, it can't be.*

But it was. Marilyn gave her hand to the man with the graying widow's peak, the deep-set eyes, the white vest and matching bowtie. Black satiny lapels showed beneath the black cape. "Sheriff Tully, Mayor King, I'd like to introduce you to our honored guest, Bela Lugosi."

"Good evening." The Lugosi ringer extended his hand.

Harlan shook it without blinking. "An honor, sir."

Tully waited his turn. "Are you really a vampire?"

Bela smiled. "I have been for some time. Ed Wood took pity on me during the filming of *Plan 9 from Outer Space*. I was having heart trouble that was nearly as bad as the movie itself, and he knew a vampire. He asked, I said yes, and the rest is history."

Tully nodded. "So ... I guess you never drink ... wine."

Bela had the good grace to laugh even though he'd probably heard that line a thousand times or more.

29
POUTY FACE

"I prefer fresh." Amanda sniffed.

Felix had done as Julian asked, seating Amanda at the far end of the long table, keeping her at half a dozen arms' length. It was as ridiculous as a bad English drawing room comedy, but he didn't want her any nearer. Despite her juvenile behavior - not to mention his suspicions that she was Incendarius - Julian could not stop thinking about her and this irritated him to such a degree that he'd even considered staking her.

Amanda stuck her lower lip out. "I want fresh."

He wanted to taste that lip, to bite it. He quelled the urge and kept his voice cool. "Unless one has willing human donors on hand, fresh blood is rarely available."

Amanda drained her glass. "Then how do you manufacture so much of this stuff?" She picked up the bottle Felix had left at her side and examined it, running her finger over the stylized bat flowers behind the lettering.

Julian smiled; he'd designed the label and it was stellar, if he did say so himself. "You know full well how we veintners obtain our supplies. Blood banks are a godsend and I own banks all over the world so that I may maintain strict control over the quality of blood we harvest. We use only the best."

"Do you have a blood bank nearby?"

"Not too far away." He knew better than to reveal the location.

"I'd like to go there and tap some from the source, if you know what I mean."

"Impossible."

"Then how about we drive down to the local skid row and do in a few homeless? Alcohol-laced blood is heady. I love it." She leaned forward, exposing her cleavage as she licked those red, red lips. "Don't you love it, Julie?"

"No, I do not care for the blood of alcoholics. It has a sour taste that I find repugnant."

"Picky, picky." Amanda poured herself another glass of French A neg and gave him a pouty-face worthy of a fourteen-year-old girl. "You're no fun, Julie! No fun at all. We could run down to San Francisco and pick off some hookers."

"We will not be dining on prostitutes and my name is Julian. I'll thank you to use it." He sipped from his own goblet of blood, a rather sweet little domestic A Positive with a delightful coppery nose. "The key to a long and peaceful life, Amanda, is abiding by the rules and not being greedy. Your gluttony will be the end of you."

She had the audacity - or the naiveté - to giggle . "Don't be so serious all the time."

"I'll also thank you to show some respect to your elder."

She puckered her lips and threw him a kiss. "Want to fuck me, Daddy?"

"I am not your father and I do not wish to have sexual relations with you." He wasn't sure if he meant the latter or not. He wanted to mean it, but seeing her and smelling her drove him wild, despite her repugnant Incendarius personality. He suspected that only his own self-respect prevented him from ravishing her.

Her face softened, her eyes glazing with crocodile tears. "Please forgive me for choosing Stephen. I was so young and rebellious that I didn't realize what I was doing. I wish I'd chosen you." She batted her lashes. "I'd love it if you'd taste me." She tilted her head to show off her long, white neck.

He felt temptation but knew better than to succumb. *False tears. It's all an act.* Julian rose. "I have business to attend to." He nodded to Felix, who sat reading in a far corner of the room.

"Yes, Master?" His man was by his side in seconds.

"Felix, would you call Bruno and ask him to keep our houseguest company for a few hours?"

"Certainly." Felix left the room.

Amanda stared at Julian, squinting her eyes in an unattractive manner. "A babysitter, Julian? You're having me babysat? What's the matter, don't you trust me?"

"Not in the least."

"You bastard-" she began, but stopped short when Felix returned with Bruno.

Julian rose. "Bruno," he said to the mocha-skinned vampire. "I have a job for you." At six feet, Julian was tall, but Bruno towered over him. "I need you to watch over my guest for a few hours. Make sure she doesn't wander where she shouldn't. And I'd advise you to keep her at arm's length. Are you up for it?"

"Certainly, Mr. Julian," he rumbled. "You can count on me."

∾

AT THE GAS STATION, Norman Keeler picked up a fat john with a skinny dick that needed attention. He'd done a good job and the guy handed him five twenties and his phone number and gave him a ride that took him to the northern end of Big Sur. Norman was proud of himself - he had wanted to attack the guy before, during, and after - but he'd refrained. The man had paid him well after all, and Norman was nothing if not professional.

Now he blew a fallen lock of blond hair away from his eyes, took his skateboard from his pack, hopped on, and cruised up the highway, figuring he'd be out of the park by dawn and hoping there were plenty of places to hide out during the day.

30

STRANGE ENCOUNTERS

It was after ten and raining steadily as Neil Trinsky strolled Main Street. Nearly every shop was dark, even the restaurants. Downtown was deserted. Most people hated rain, hated getting wet, but Neil loved it. He pulled his dark hair out of its rubber band and let it soak up the rain. So far, Neil had only killed two humans in his life, both homeless bums hanging out in the cemeteries in the hills above Candle Bay. Both times, he'd felt a minor rush but neither killing had been challenging. After that, he'd considered killing a jogger who ran past the house every evening - he thought perhaps a healthy young man might have more fight in him, but decided against it when a cop cruised by just as he was getting ready to attack. His heart hadn't been in it, anyway.

But the prospect of killing a vampire brought him fully to life, made his brain sharp and excited, and his body tingle from his toes to his cock to his head.

Tonight, Neil decided, before tackling any vampires, he ought to practice on a human. He'd been hunting for one and now, standing in the long shadows between street lamps, he spotted his prey. He watched as the unsuspecting man locked the door to his shop for the night and double-checked, making sure it was secure. He had an old-fashioned candy machine chained up under the awning of his shop and as the man turned, Neil fed quarters into it and pulled out an Almond Joy. He slipped it in his pocket.

The proprietor saw him now, and eyed him suspiciously.

"Sir," said Neil, putting on a perfect ass-sucking smile, "the machine took my money but didn't give me my Almond Joy." He suppressed a shudder at the thought of even putting such an abomination in his mouth.

The little man, still wearing his nametag - Curtis Penrose, Manager - swore under his breath. "Move over." He withdrew a little round key and stuck it in the lock. It popped and the guy turned it a few times, unscrewing. The door yawned open. "Almond Joy, you said?"

"Yes, sir." Neil glanced around, and seeing no one, watched as Penrose bent and stuck his head in the machine, peered around then reached past the thick steel edges, and withdrew a candy bar. "Damned machine, nothing but trouble," the man muttered. "I should–"

Neil slammed the heavy door shut on the man's neck, throwing all of his weight against it. Penrose's cries were muted by metal and rain; his arms flailed and his feet kicked as he tried to get away.

But Neil held firm, pushing harder and harder, until Penrose's movements faltered and weakened. Finally, he went limp. Neil let go and the man dropped to the ground, tongue lolling, his head flopping at an unnatural angle.

Penrose's neck, red and bleeding, was dented to half its normal width where the steel lips had kissed it. Pulling out a pocket knife, Neil bent and created two puncture wounds on the dead skin. That would create a nice diversion.

He smiled. "Don't you know candy's bad for your body?" Dropping the Almond Joy on Penrose's ass, he pulled his wet hair back into its ponytail and strolled away, glad he had worn gloves. You never knew when you might need them.

31

DAISY'S DIXIE CUP OF BLOOD

The party on the mountain was in full swing. In the half hour they'd been there, Natasha and Michael had recognized no one, and Natasha was about to suggest indulging in a second cup of sangria when she heard giggling behind her. Then someone tickled her ribs. She turned to see Lucy and Ivy. Lucy wore a long black 1920s-era sheath that dripped lace and pearls and left little to the imagination while Ivy wore a similar vintage gown in red. Both carried nearly empty foam cups of blood.

"Are Winter and Chynna here, too?" asked Michael.

"Chynna's here somewhere visiting some old friends. Winter and Arnie stayed at the hotel. They're watching movies, I guess," Ivy said.

"When did you get here?" Natasha reached out and pushed a stray curl off Ivy's cheek.

"Just after sunset. We've just been hanging out."

"And guess what!" Ivy chirped.

"What?"

"Daisy's here!" She glanced around. "Well, she was here a second ago."

Lucy pulled a face. "She just picked up on some baby vamp. He's like, only a year old, but he's hot as hell."

Natasha counted to ten while the twins waxed on about their cousin, Daisy Darling, one of the North Carolina Darlings who'd never moved west. Ori, ever the overachiever, had turned the cousins, too. While the twins had stopped aging at sixteen, Daisy'd been barely a teenager, but despite her age, she made the twins seem almost - *almost* - demure. Even before Ori had turned her, she'd probably made love to half of the Spanish Armada. Afterward, she single-handedly killed the other half. Natasha was not happy to know Daisy - *Crazy Daisy* - was at the festival, influencing the twins, who didn't need any encouragement to misbehave.

"Are you guys going into the Eternal City tonight?" Ivy asked.

"I don't know." Natasha glanced at Michael, who shrugged. "I doubt it. It will be more fun to go in once the festival really begins."

"I agree," Michael said. "I prefer the outdoors, even to the Eternal City. We'll be spending a lot of time in there within a couple days."

"Look, there's Bela!" Lucy said. "See you guys later!"

IN THE PERDET TOWERS, Eddie Fortune and Lois Trinsky sat on a ratty tarnished-gold couch and watched *High Noon*. It was one of Eddie's favorite movies, and Lois found herself enjoying the morality tale right along with him. Erin Woodhouse had gone out for a late-night jog around the park, assuring them she'd be careful, but that she just had to burn the excess calories she'd indulged in at Strider's Steakhouse. Lois hoped she meant it. It frightened her to think of a young girl out there alone, and now she moved a little closer to Eddie, putting herself in the path of his arm, should he decide to move it off the top of the couch.

A moment later, he did. She tried to relax and enjoy the closeness and the movie, but she still worried about Erin, especially when she realized Neil might be prowling the same streets as the pretty college student. After all, he'd already trailed her once.

MORNING WOULD COME EARLY in Eternity, and Zach Tully climbed into bed, spooning his wife, enjoying her warmth.

"Your feet are cold," Kate mumbled.

"Want to warm me up?"

She chuckled, low and throaty. "I thought you'd never ask." She rolled over and they kissed.

He put his hand on the swell of her hip, but before he could do more, she spoke again.

"What's on your mind? You've been off somewhere on your own for a while now."

"Eternity stuff," he murmured into her ear. "There's a convention in town."

"Biting Man," she said, soft as could be.

"You know about it?"

"Of course I do. I run Bigfoot Tours."

That brought him up short. "You tell the tourists about it?"

She laughed and kissed his nose. "Of course not. It's a load of nonsense, even for Eternity."

He didn't say a word.

"It *is* nonsense, isn't it, Zach?"

"Well ..." He kissed her and let his hand wander over her thigh.

"Well, what?" She ignored what he was trying to do.

"Well, if you'll kiss me, I'll tell you about it in the morning."

"It's real?"

"My lips are sealed unless you kiss them."

"In the morning, you promise to tell me?"

"I do, ma'am, and a sheriff always keeps his promises." His hand roamed and her thighs relaxed.

"Then kiss me, lawman. Kiss me good."

∽

"OH, MY GOD," said Ivy. "He is *so* big!"

"Everywhere," agreed Lucy. "Not just, you know, down there."

All three Darling girls giggled and from an outsider's point of view, Daisy may well have been Lucy and Ivy's missing triplet sister. They stood, huddled together under one of the colorful umbrellas that had bloomed after the rain began. They were well away from the crowd, catching up on old, wild, times.

"His muscles are amazing," said Ivy.

"Arms as big as my waist!" added Lucy.

"*Our* waist," said Ivy.

"What's this guy's name again?" asked Daisy.

"Winter." Lucy and Ivy spoke in unison.

"You have to meet him," said Lucy.

"We'll introduce you," added Ivy. "There's enough of him to go around - and I'm sure he wouldn't mind."

Lucy nodded and reached into her purse, pulling out a small vial. "Another thing you *totally* have to try is this!"

"What is it?" Daisy reached for it, but Lucy pulled it back.

"Lixir," said Ivy.

"Shh." Lucy put a finger to her lips. "It's a secret. It's too expensive to share."

"Does it really do what they say?"

Ivy smiled. "It lets you go out in the daytime."

"No way!"

"Way!"

"Here." Lucy reached over and tapped a couple of drops into Daisy's Dixie cup of blood.

~

AT THE ICEHOUSE INN, Winter and Arnie sat on the bed, watching *Tombstone* for the third time since they'd arrived.

"Did you *hear* that, Papa Winter?" Arnie asked when Wyatt Earp told Ike Clanton that hell was coming with him.

"I heard it, buddy." *Three times now.*

"He said a bad word."

"He did." Winter wished he'd gone to the mixer up at the Ski Bowl, but Arnie had wanted to watch movies. It was no real loss. Winter's reasons for going had only to do with the Darling twins. It wasn't as if he'd be able to run off with them somewhere anyway - Arnie needed constant supervision. And to be honest, he wasn't looking forward to exposing Arnie to the other vamps - or rather, exposing them to him. There might be repercussions when they realized he was mentally disabled. *There's nothing worse than a self-righteous vampire.* They had had centuries to hone their prejudices.

"Is it real?" Arnie's voice disrupted Winter's train of thought.

"Is what real?"

"Hell?" Arnie faced him, his soft brown eyes pools of worry.

Winter wasn't sure how to answer. Even if there were such places as heaven and hell, vampires would never see them. "No," he said with finality. "It's just a story."

Arnie watched him a moment, looking for signs of deceit. Though slow, he was sharp enough to usually know when he was being lied to. At last, he turned back to the television and within moments, he was in Tombstone, Arizona with Wyatt Earp, Doc Holliday, and the Clanton boys.

As he lay there, propped on pillows, arms behind his head, Winter wondered about heaven and hell. It had been a long life and would be even longer and there were times he wondered what living out his life as a human would have been like. He looked at Arnie. *We'd both be long dead now.* The thought was unpleasant - he enjoyed being undead - but every now and then, he couldn't help wondering how he might feel about his continued existence after another four or five hundred years. *And how will Arnie feel about his?* Winter didn't like this thought, didn't like the guilt that came with it, so he turned to pleasanter things. Sexier things.

The Darling Twins ... *My God, they're limber!*

32
STIR CRAZY

Amanda had spent the last two hours reclining on Julian's ridiculous yellow récamier thumbing through the copies of *Vogue* and *Elle* that Felix had picked up for her. Bruno sat in the corner of the vast drawing room, earbuds in his ears, his half-closed eyes avoiding her. He was gorgeous, but no matter how seductively she positioned herself, he wouldn't respond, wouldn't even look at her - which was irritatingly wise of him.

She caught his eye again, smiled at him.

He ignored her.

Finally, she opened her knees, showing him that she wore nothing beneath her tight red mini-skirt.

Again, he ignored her.

"So do you like guys?" she asked, leaving her legs wide open. "Or what?"

Bruno removed an earbud. "What?"

She ran her fingers along her inner thigh. "What are you into? Guys?"

He considered a long moment. "What makes you say that?"

"Well, for starters, I'm showing you my goddamned pussy."

"I see that." His eyes dipped, then flitted back up, stopping short of meeting hers.

"You don't seem particularly impressed."

He shrugged. "Seen one, you've seen 'em all."

Anger flared. "Well, fuck you too."

He shrugged, put his ear buds back in, and increased the volume loud enough she could hear Jay-Z blaring.

Amanda dropped the magazines on the floor and stood up. She had Bruno's attention now, but before she made it to the door, he was blocking her way.

"Sorry, ma'am. My orders are to see that Master Julian is undisturbed."

"I thought your orders were to watch me."

"That, too."

She stepped so close that she was speaking into his massively muscled chest. "Well, I need to talk to him." She ran a finger over his pale green t-shirt, feeling his pecs and six-pack. "Why don't you just come with me?"

"I'm sorry. He's not to be disturbed."

"Then I want to go for a walk and enjoy the night air."

"He asked that I see to it you remain inside the house. You may stay here or in your room."

Her hand dipped and rubbed his dick. She felt a twitch and smiled. "We could have some fun."

"That's not an option. Your options are this room or your bedroom."

Fury hissed in her ears. "How dare *you* - a lowly servant - try to tell *me* my place?"

"Calm down, ma'am." His dark skin stretched tight across his iron jaw. His face was placid but in his eyes - eyes that would not meet hers - fire burned.

"Calm down? Calm *down?*" Amanda swung, smacking him across that smug face.

Quicker than she'd thought possible, Bruno grabbed her wrist in a vise-tight fist. He jerked her forward till their faces were inches apart. He met her eyes now - and within them, Amanda saw no weakness.

"You get one of those, ma'am, and you just used it." His gaze was fixed and emotionless, his eyes dark pools of steely intent.

"You're hurting me," she whined, trying to bewitch him.

"Do I look like I give a damn?"

She gasped. He definitely didn't look like he gave a damn.

He turned her around and shoved her, hurling her face-down onto the chaise longue. "And keep your pussy out of my face."

Amanda turned on the tears. "I'll tell Julian how you treated me!"

"I'll happily tell him myself." Bruno replaced his earbuds and sat back down, legs stretched, eyes closed as his music thumped.

The tears weren't working, so Amanda turned over and hid her face in the magazine. Julian couldn't avoid her forever. Bruno or no Bruno, Julian was going to be in her thrall very soon. When she wanted something, she got it - and what she wanted was Julian Valentyn.

∽

MICHAEL GRINNED. "Want to blow this popsicle stand?"

Natasha laughed. "Slang, Michael? When did that happen?"

"I enjoy etymology and am partial to certain slang terms. Like blowing the popsicle stand. And groovy. And most recently, amazeballs." He chuckled. "I'd say it more frequently if I didn't fear it would damage my reputation as a serious student of the English language."

Natasha was happy to see the playful side of Michael. It was, she knew, a side few ever saw. It seemed like an honor of some sort. And in turn, he brought out the lighter side of her nature - a thing that was not easy to do. She looked at him. "Well, then, let's blow this popsicle stand and get something groovy to drink. I hear the blood bar at the St. Germain is amazeballs."

He laughed, genuine and full. "Let's go find out."

As they walked toward the car he put an arm around her waist.

She leaned her head against his shoulder, wishing ... wishing ... If only it could be as it once had been.

33

THE ALTIMA SACRIFICE

She thought she saw Neil Trinsky on Main Street. Erin Woodhouse wasn't sure - she'd only met the creep that one time at the amusement park - but she didn't want to take any chances, so she changed her jogging route, returning to Hotel Circle to take five shorter laps instead of two long ones around the park.

She couldn't wrap her head around the things Eddie Fortune had told her. *Vampires. Real vampires.* But she believed him - she had no doubt it was true. The knowledge created a blend of excitement and fear. On the one hand, she loved the discovery of unknown things and felt somehow vindicated, as if she'd secretly known - or hoped, anyway - that they'd existed all along.

On the other hand, it was terrifying. She felt vulnerable. It seemed like eyes - vampire eyes - were all over her, all the time now, and even if she hadn't thought she'd seen that creep Neil, she was uneasy.

Vampires. I'll never be the same after this, she thought. Once the mind was opened in new ways, it could never retain its prior shape. This knowledge would change her - it had changed her already. Not that it was a bad thing. She was more aware, more in tune to the things around her, and more conscious of the world and how little the general population really knew about the planet they inhabited. It was fascinating.

And it opened up all kinds of other possibilities. Werewolves. UFOs. Wendigos, soul-eaters, and ghosts! These myths must have come from somewhere, right? And she believed that virtually all legends and folklore were based in fact to some degree. It was dazzling - mind boggling - and Erin loved it.

As she jogged through the night, she wondered what it felt like to be undead. Did it make life easier or more difficult? Were vampire senses stronger than those of humans as it was so often portrayed in movies and books? She wished she'd bump into a friendly vampire so she could ask. She had so many questions, but knew if she dared claim vampires were real in her thesis, she'd be laughed out of the master's program.

She watched as a black Audi pulled up and a man in a suit got out and headed inside a hotel. *Maybe he's one of them.* How could she tell? She had no idea, but she couldn't wait to find out. *Stowing away in Eddie's van was the best thing I've ever done.*

∽

NEIL HAD HIDDEN his mother's car in the garage of a vacant cabin, but that wasn't good enough. It was obvious the lock had been broken and now that he'd killed that vending machine guy on Main Street, he'd have to be more cautious. Not long after he'd done the deed, before he'd left downtown, he'd spotted that little bitch, Erin, jogging in the dark - and was afraid she'd seen him as well. *What the fuck is she doing here? She must be stalking me!* Most women he met stalked him; it was a natural fact.

In any case, it was time to get rid of Mom's Altima. Keeping it wasn't worth the risk.

Now he drove the highway outside of Eternity, cruising the cliffs. He didn't want to go too far since he had to walk back, but after a mile, he'd still found no suitable place.

And then he saw it - a sharp curve with a nice turnout with orange cones blocking a break in the safety railing. He pulled over and walked to the edge. *It'll do.* The cliff was steep and rocky with a mass of trees at least a hundred feet down. The car, if it went over just right, might not be found for days. Or ever, if he was really lucky.

He moved the cones then returned to the idling car and inched it right up to the broken guardrail. Hopping out, he put the car in drive. It rolled up against the mangled railing but that was it. "Fuck."

Using his phone as a flashlight - that was all it was good for up here - he scoured the wide turnout and finally found a slab of rock that weighed at least forty pounds. He hefted it and returned to the car.

"Bon voyage, motherfucker!" He put the rock on the gas pedal and watched as the car revved high then pushed the railing out of the way. It sailed like a white bird down the cliff. He watched the taillights as it plunged.

When he heard the crunch of metal as it crashed, his cock stiffened in his jeans. Looking down, he realized the car had only traveled about fifty feet. It would be easily found. He was surprised to find himself even more turned on by that prospect. It was erotic, like having sex with the possibility of being caught.

Looking around, he unbuttoned and unzipped, dropped his jeans, and masturbated, hard, fast, and furious.

∼

"I've never rehearsed so hard in my life!" Davy complained. "It's like being in the goddamned army!"

Mick nodded, massaging his arms. He didn't care if he ever beat a drum again.

"Here." Paul handed him a bottle of blood. Mick took it with tired heavy muscles that didn't want to cooperate. He'd thought that being undead would have meant fewer aches and pains.

When the Kohlkopfs had taken them inside the mountain, their first glimpses had been unremarkable, probably because they'd been so forcefully ushered toward the amphitheater in the caverns where they'd be performing. While the acoustics were amazing, they hadn't been able to see a damned thing, including each other.

After working them like dogs without so much as a piss break, those bobbly-headed orange-haired motherfuckers had piled them back into the van and returned them to the big cabin, ordering them to get plenty of rest for tomorrow's even more vigorous rehearsal sets. But tired as they were, none of them wanted to rest. They wanted blood, lots of it, and they weren't going to rest till they got it.

"This sucks." Ramon sat on a ratty chair, legs spread wide, eyes hooded with fatigue.

"You know what we need?" asked Davy opening a fresh bottle of BO Negative. "Some good pussy." He grinned. "From Amanda."

"Yeah." Paul and Ramon spoke in unison.

"Where is that chick?" asked Ramon. "I'm really missing her."

"Me too," said Paul. "I can't quit thinking about those perky little tits of hers."

"And those lips," added Davy.

"And hips," said Ramon.

"Heh," said Davy "Tits, lips, and hips. I think I feel some new lyrics coming on."

Mick had also been consumed by thoughts of Amanda, but he was a little disappointed by the whole thing. Becoming a vampire was supposed to be cool as fuck. You were supposed to be glamorous, seductive, and powerful. So far, he'd been forced to rehearse for hours on end, denied the one serious blood craving he'd gotten, and now they sat, drinking and talking about pussy. It was the same as any other night in their lives except instead of a hotel room they were being held captive in a cabin in a tiny room with bunk beds and no TV, and instead of liquor, they were drinking blood.

"You know," he said. "It's not really all that great, is it? Being undead, you know?"

Three pairs of eyes blinked stupidly at him.

Ramon scratched his balls.

No one said anything. They just kept drinking and dreaming of Amanda.

34

DAYLIGHT

"Is it true, Zach?" Harlan King asked. "Curtis Penrose's head was severed by a candy machine?" He handed Tully a tall coffee.

"Thanks. Not severed. Severely dented." Tully sat down and sipped. "Let me tell you, Harlan, death by vending machine isn't pretty."

Harlan brought a plate of donuts over and slid into a seat, nursing his own coffee. "You told Curtis to lock up that candy machine. Too bad he didn't listen."

"Yeah." Tully took a glazed donut and savored it. There was a time when he couldn't have eaten after looking at such a mangled corpse, but that was long ago. Curtis Penrose's broken neck had been ugly, but his face, the color of a plum, had been frozen in a terrified scream. At least, that's how it looked. The candy in the machine had been splattered with blood and that, somehow, had been more sickening than anything else.

"Any suspects?" Harlan daintily bit into a chocolate confection and wiped a sprinkle from his lip.

"Well, there were puncture marks on his neck."

The baker looked up, surprised. "Really?"

"Yeah, but the doc said they were made with a pocket knife, post mortem. He said it was amateurish. So, I'm ruling out vampires."

"You've got somebody trying to blame the vampires, then."

"Yep."

"Damned fang-boy, most likely. Fang-boys are trouble. Can't trust them." Harlan raised his brows in a question. "I keep thinking about that car-stealing, health food fanatic fang-boy. There was something off about him ..."

Tully finished his first donut and reached for another. "He came to my mind, too. But there's no evidence. We can't accuse him just because he's a thief - and a weirdo."

Harlan nodded. "Fang-boy vegan - that's just wrong." He reached for another pastry. "You might let V-Sec know."

"Why?"

"Penrose may have been killed solely to incriminate the vamps."

Tully nodded. "Or maybe it's because Curtis was kind of an asshole."

"True that." King glanced outside at the bench where a couple of old geezers were already planted. "I wonder what the Death Pool odds on Curtis were."

∼

As the morning sun rose over Valentyn Vineyards, Julian was relieved to find out from Bruno that Amanda had already gone to bed, and except for one escape attempt, she had been sullen but compliant. Hopefully, she would remain asleep until evening - during the night, he had left the hydroponics lab and used a secret passage to enter the guest room and remove the bottle of Lixir from her bag. Despite the drug's lingering effects, even Incendarius would be hard-pressed to remain alert without a fresh dose. Lixir didn't linger in the hybrid body like his original bloodberry elixir did. Lixir was to elixir as aspirin was to cocaine. At least, as a Trueborn, he had the advantage of not needing chemical assistance to remain awake during the day.

The only wild card was Amanda's status as Incendarius. They were so rare that their powers were poorly recorded; little was known about them.

"Master?" Felix entered Julian's bedroom suite. "Did you have a productive night?"

"Indeed I did. The new crop of bloodberries is nearly ready to harvest, and both the veinery and the winery are doing well." He sat down and smiled at his manservant. "And did you have a good rest?"

Felix nodded as he removed Julian's boots. "I did. I'm glad Bruno is here - if I'd had to watch your guest last night, I would be exhausted."

"I wouldn't ask you to do that alone. She's far too dangerous to be guarded by a human."

"It was good of Bruno to return from his vacation early."

"Indeed." Bruno was the only vampiric servant that Julian trusted completely. Years ago, he had rescued him from near execution by a tawdry little cult who'd captured him while he slept and Bruno's loyalty to the Trueborn was impeccable.

"You checked the windows in our guest's room, Felix?"

"Yes, Master. Alarms will sound if she so much as touches a window. Bruno is resting in the alcove outside her door. He's using Lixir so if there's a sound, he'll hear it."

"Excellent." He watched Felix carry his boots to the door and set them outside - they would be freshly polished before dusk. "Felix?"

"Yes, Master?" He took Julian's blue pajamas from a drawer, and the matching dressing gown from the closet, and brought them over.

"There are things you do not know, and have had no reason to know until now." He handed his shirt to Felix who traded it for the silk pajama top.

"Yes, Master?"

Julian sheathed his torso in silk. He loved the feel of it against his pale skin. It touched him like a lover. "In case of emergency - if something should happen to me - I've left an envelope of instructions for you in the bedroom safe. You know the combination?"

"Of course. But-"

"Good man." Julian smiled at Felix's concerned face. "I've been meaning to do this for years, and I think this is the appropriate time."

Felix inclined his head in the direction of the guestroom, a question on his face.

"Yes. She's inspired me to action." Julian traded his pants for the pajama bottoms.

"Master, do I need to be concerned?"

"No. With Bruno here to help watch her until I can figure out just what to do about her, I believe we're safe."

"Dressing gown?"

"Leave it on the bed, Felix. I'm tired and going to rest immediately."

"Very good, Master."

Felix crossed to the windows and closed the drapes over the wooden blinds. "Have a good rest, Master Julian."

"I shall. And you, Felix, stay alert and do check the door to Amanda's room occasionally. And it would be best to keep all but the core human staff working in the winery or otherwise outside the house today. Just to be safe."

"Very well." Felix headed for the double doors. "Will that be all?"

"Yes. Wake me early, will you? An hour before sunset."

"Of course. Rest well, Master."

After the doors closed, Julian locked them then lay down on his bed.

35

THE GREAT ESCAPE

"Shit! Shit! Shit!" Amanda thundered. "Who the fuck took my Lixir?" She crossed to the locked guest room door, pounded it, shook the handle. "You bastards! How dare you steal from me!"

No one replied, so she screamed again. "Felix! You fucking little worm! Bring my Lixir back!"

But Felix wasn't listening. She crossed to a window and peeped out - the sun was up. Though it was full daylight, Julian wasn't necessarily asleep.

Unsure of where his bedroom was - he hadn't even given her a tour of his big yellow house - she didn't know if he could hear her, but she tried again. "Julian! Help! The blind won't close, I'm burning! Help! Help! Someone, help!"

She waited, but no one answered.

"Fuck. Fuck you, Bruno, fuck you Felix, and fuck you too, Julian. You'll pay for this! All of you!"

She opened her toiletries bag and dug out a travel-sized bottle of Listerine, uncapped it, and sipped from her hidden stash of Lixir. "That's better." Immediately, she felt more alert. And hungry.

Next, she opened one of the bottles of blood Julian had left in her room and gulped a quarter bottle of the O Negative down, licked her lips then stashed it in the mini-fridge. "You cheap fuck," she muttered. O Neg had been the house blood at the hotel - not bad but nothing special. Julian could have stocked her room with something more piquant. *But no... Julian, you're going to get on your hands and knees and apologize for this. You're going to beg me to forgive you for being a cheap fuck!*

Moments later, she was in the shower, scrubbing herself down with soap that smelled like jasmine, washing her hair with shampoo so expensive that Stephen, an even cheaper fuck, would disapprove. "Fuck you, Stephen! Fuck you all!"

As she stood beneath the hot steamy jets, she knew what she had to do. Biting Man would be in full swing soon and she - and Julian - would be there. "Here comes the bride," she sang and wondered if vampires used that song at their weddings, too.

~

It came as no surprise that Curtis Penrose had been one of the most disliked people in Eternity. Not only had no witnesses turned up, no one cared. Tully had talked to several of Penrose's neighbors on Main Street and had received everything from shrugs to "Good riddance," in response to the news. On top of that, the forensics department - his detective and one deputy - said the perp had left no evidence behind; not a fingerprint, not a fiber. The only surveillance camera in the area hadn't been working, but even if it had, it was unlikely it would have picked up anything useful in the rain.

It had been a long morning and the call about the car came as a welcome distraction. Tully had hurried to the turnout a mile outside of town to see who'd driven off the cliff. Search and Rescue had rappelled down the mountain before he arrived and the guys returned just as he got out to peer over the cliff at the white car.

"Well?"

"No one's in the car and there's no sign that anyone was thrown from it," Gordon Renquist told Tully as he climbed over the broken railing. He had an odd look on his face.

Relief and annoyance vied for Tully's emotions. "And?"

"And there was a slab of stone on the driver's side floor," Renquist said. "Tommy took some photos; he'll be up in a minute."

"Are you suggesting someone–"

"Placed it on the accelerator and sent the car flying. Looks like it to me. Here's Tommy."

The other S&R guy swung himself over the railing, dropped his backpack and pulled out a license plate then handed it to Tully. "It's a late model Altima," he said.

Lois Trinsky's car. Tully's stomach did a little flip. He recognized the plate and wondered why her son would ditch the car instead of drive out of town. *Maybe he had something to do with the Penrose homicide.* He shook his head. *Jesus, am I so hard up for a suspect that I buy into Harlan's musings? Yes.* But he bought it because he had the same feeling.

∼

Felix checked the guest room door every hour and not only was it locked, but Bruno lay slumbering only a few feet away, a small bottle of Lixir beside him. With alarm, he realized it was still sealed and quickly touched Bruno's shoulder. "Bruno? Bruno? Can you hear me?"

The big vampire didn't respond and his stillness made Felix realize he'd fallen asleep before dosing himself. If Bruno had taken it, his sleep would have looked more human and his breathing would be obvious; a hybrid vampire slept the sleep of the dead, going almost as deep as depicted in movies and books. With a sinking feeling in the pit of his stomach, Felix wondered if dribbling a little Lixir between Bruno's lips would work. *Unlikely since he's already asleep.*

The other vampires working at Valentyn Vineyards – those in the veinery and lab – slept in the guesthouse and it was unlikely any had been using Lixir. Felix wondered if he should alert Julian, but hated to disrupt his rest since he'd had so little of it in the last few days. *Amanda has no Lixir.* Since her bottle had been removed, and nothing had gone wrong yet, he decided it would be alarmist to disturb Julian. Instead, Felix pocketed Bruno's Lixir for safekeeping and would check the room every quarter hour until his master arose.

∼

AMANDA LICKED the opening of the Listerine bottle, then probed it with her tongue, tasting the essence of the Lixir. She didn't dare drink all of it, not until she had another bottle, but the mere taste and fragrance excited her. Besides, she'd had more than enough already. Her appetites were aroused; she was starving for blood. And sex.

She glanced at the door, smelling a human; a warm tasty human, just outside. *Felix.* She recognized his scent. She'd heard him trying to rouse Bruno. Amanda smiled, waited for Felix to leave then took a credit card from her bag, and crossed to the door.

It only took a moment to jimmy the lock - a trick she'd perfected at the hotel when sticking to bottled blood got old.

Closing the door softly behind her, she tiptoed, barefoot, to the cot where Bruno lay. He was out like the proverbial light bulb. *This is going to be easy.*

Quickly, she checked the hall - saw no one - and began walking, trying closed doors. It was a big house, but no castle, and when she came upon the set of locked double doors a corridor away, she laid her ear and a hand against the wood. *He's in here.* She sensed him as easily as if she'd seen him with her eyes.

The credit card gained her entrance. *Julian, you ought to have better locks on your doors.*

He lay there on the center of his bed, wearing silk pajamas, eyes closed. Trueborns slept lightly, so she would have to be cautious until he was hers.

Silently she moved to the bedside and stripped, leaving her short red skirt and black tank top on the floor before crawling onto the bed, slowly, so slowly, and inching her way toward her prize.

A hair's-breadth from his body, Amanda inhaled his scent: sex and old books. Odd, but that's what he'd always smelled like to her. She gazed at his face. He was handsome - painfully handsome, with sharp patrician features that would have been at home on a Greek statue.

With no warning, Julian's eyes shot open.

Amanda lunged, pinning him beneath her.

"Talai? What-"

She grinned and flashed her fangs. "Talai isn't here, my love."

～

JULIAN HAD BEEN DREAMING of Talai, of the first time he saw her working in his father's palace when he was still an innocent young prince of Euloa.

Talai had been a beautiful creature and he'd fallen madly in love and wanted to take her to wife, to give her eternal life, so that they might always be together. *Talai* ... And now that he knew her essence was Incendarius, he understood why he had always been captivated by her. His mind turned to Stephen Darling. Gone was the jealousy and hatred he'd felt, replaced by sympathy.

Then, suddenly, he'd sensed a presence beside him. A real presence, not a dream. He opened his eyes, saw her. "Talai. What-"

"Talai isn't here, my love."

Incendarius! The Trueborn's ultimate weakness. His downfall. Do not let her be yours!

And then she was on him, her fangs hot daggers in his throat.

It was heavenly.

She moaned as she drank and he wanted to push her off, to throw her across the room, to put a stake through her heart, to sever her head with the sword he kept beneath the bed.

"Julian, my love." He heard her voice in his head even as his own swam from blood loss. *"You are mine and I am yours. It has always been so."*

"You ... lie. Incendarius!" Even as he spoke, his arms, of their own volition, drew her naked body closer. His own fangs emerged. He put a hand on the back of her head and forced her neck down to his lips. His fangs sank into her flesh, and he drank, tasting her exquisite blood. "Talai."

Amanda's fangs retracted as she laughed softly in his ear.

36

FIRST BLOOD

The murder of Curtis Penrose stoked the fire that burned within Neil Trinsky. It had been an appetizer, a tease, and being here in Eternity, walking among the dirty undead, he could no longer suppress his nature. He needed to kill. Not another human - they were weak and ineffectual little things whose lives could be extinguished as easily as a snap of the neck. They died of flu, slips on the ice, and of heart disease - though not if they followed proper diets, but they were too fucking stupid to even do that. They choked to death on chicken bones, for fuck's sake. There was no dignity in killing a human. Neil needed to kill something that would put up a fight, something he could really put his balls into.

It's time to kill a vampire!

He'd stocked up on holy items and spent many hours forming a suitable plan of attack. It had to be subtle enough that he wouldn't get caught but bloody enough to satisfy. It'd be foolish to hunt the filthy bloodsuckers after nightfall when they had the advantage until he got a feel for it. While he liked a challenge, Neil was no fool, so he'd stalk them during the day, when they were vulnerable. He'd get them alone and then, when no one was around, he'd do what he'd dreamed of doing since he was a young teenager: slay vampires.

Now he crept through the trees, looking for suspicious cabins. The black backpack he wore over his shoulders brimmed with everything from wooden stakes and a mallet, to a couple of jars of holy water, cloves of raw garlic, and a Bible. He had no idea which - if any - of the items would work on real-life vampires, but no matter how you looked at it, a stake in the heart was bound to kill anything - except maybe zombies, of course. *But what kind of inbred Midwestern retard believed in fucking zombies, anyway?*

He trod slowly and deliberately, perfecting a silent walk and looking, he thought, like the perfect vacationer in a pair of loose-fitting jeans and a black t-shirt. In truth, he'd chosen the clothing because it allowed for plenty of movement should he have to attack, run, or both.

He passed many cabins, all of which raised no red flags and were obviously occupied by living tenants. They were spaced far enough apart that if he found what he was looking for - no, *when* he found what he was looking for - he'd have the privacy to do his job.

He'd begun to feel like he was in Bedrock, as if the scenery were repeating itself on a loop, and then, just ahead, he saw it. Windows shuttered up to keep the light out. A parked car in the drive, its tinted windows surely meant to serve the same purpose. Utter silence. No sign of life within or around the place, yet obviously, it wasn't empty. Neil's heart skipped beats and he began whistling a nonchalant tune - *The Flintstones* theme - and made his way casually toward the darkened cabin.

He hesitated just for a moment before he rapped on the door. It was perfectly possible the tenant was simply napping - but in that case, he'd just say he'd lost his key and gotten confused. Confidence soaring, he knocked again.

Several moments passed and there was no answer - another good sign.

He rapped harder.

Only silence.

Glancing around, he reached into his backpack and found a screwdriver. He rammed it into the lock, twisted it around, and within moments, heard it give.

The door creaked open and when Neil slipped inside, he froze.

The man on the bed was definitely undead. His face was as pale as a white onion, his arms were limp at his sides, and his chest was utterly still. Too still. Perfectly, wonderfully, deathly, still.

Neil grinned. Fascinated, he stepped closer, feeling the first stirrings of uneasiness. His heart hammered and blood throbbed in his ears, though that was more from excitement than fear. He'd never been this close to a vampire - a *real* vampire! - in his life. In his mind, his inner voice chanted to the beat of his thrumming heart: *I knew it. I knew it all along. I was right! I was RIGHT!*

The bloodsucker didn't look like anything he'd seen in the movies. Even the vamps in the parking lot the other night were different somehow - more *alive*. But they probably all looked like this when they slept.

On tiptoes, Neil stepped closer to the vampire, feeling its absence of life so palpably that it was like standing next to a corpse in a coffin. It was sickening, unnatural. Rage began nibbling at the edges of his excitement. *Dirty bloodsucker ... filthy piece of shit motherfucking dirty parasite ...*

Another step closer and now he was a foot away from the abomination on the bed. *And that's what it is,* he thought, *a fucking abomination!* Gently, he lowered his backpack to the ground and squatted to unzip it. His knee popped and he froze, holding his breath. It was silly, he knew. If the vampire had slept through the door-pounding, it was pretty unlikely a popping joint would rouse him.

But still, Neil moved with caution. As he pulled a stake and mallet from his bag, he wished someone was there to see him - preferably one of his online haters who'd made fun of him for buying into such "nonsense" as vampirism. *But here I am, fuckheads, Neil Fucking Trinsky, Vampire Hunter, preparing for my first kill.*

He grinned and rose to his full height, feeling taller than he was, with the mallet in one hand and the stake in the other. He knew he should just do it - drive the stake right into the fucker's heart, no muss, no fuss, but he wouldn't, not yet. He wanted to touch the filthy thing, even though - or perhaps *because* - it was an unclean freak of nature. *And how often will I be so close to a sleeping bloodsucker?*

Setting the stake on the bed, he reached out, willing his hand not to tremble.

As he crept closer, Neil inspected the vampire. He appeared to be in his early to mid-thirties, but Neil knew he could have been hundreds, even thousands of years old. He was dark-haired and well-dressed - *probably a rich fucker to boot!* - and if not for the unnatural stillness and unusually pale skin, he might have been any normal dude taking a midday nap.

So close ... Neil's breath was locked in his throat and his heart throbbed hard enough that he was sure it could be heard. He was just a hair's breadth away from the corpse's high white cheekbone. *So close ... so fucking close.* He just had to make sure it was real, had to see what its skin felt like, had to-

The vampire's eyes popped open and rolled toward Neil, fastening themselves like leeches onto his face. Its lips peeled back in a reptilian hiss and it shot up, flying into the air in a shrieking feral rage.

Terror shot into Neil's blood. He grabbed the mallet and swung it as the screaming vampire swooped down and clutched his shoulders with bony claw-like hands and pulled Neil into a fatal embrace, threw its head back and opened its mouth, preparing to strike.

Neil swung the mallet, slamming it into the bloodsucker's head again and again, a primal battle cry ripping from his throat, from his soul, as he pounded the fucker's skull. The bloodsucker shrieked, its razor-like nails tearing into Neil's shoulders.

With a wet crunch, the skull finally gave and the vampire fell onto the bed, the back of its head a ruined cave.

For a few seconds, Neil was paralyzed, staring down at the slack mouth, the sharp teeth, the lolling tongue ... and those pale, sightless eyes ... like burnt-out headlights.

But he had to act fast. The skull would repair itself and when that happened, the dirty fucker would be out for blood - *my blood.*

With trembling hands, he found the stake and centered it over the heart. Screaming, he brought the mallet down, again and again, relishing the crack and splinter of bone and the thick wet resistance under it.

The vampire screamed, its hands curling into claws, thin blue veins standing out against the papery skin, its mouth weeping blood, its eyes bulging until they looked like they'd pop right out.

Neil pounded and pounded as visions of *Buffy the Vampire Slayer* played in his mind like a slideshow. The wild dog was off its chain and, even as the vampire expired, Neil continued. "Die! DIE, you dirty fucker!" He thrust the stake in, deeper, deeper, until the rib cage caved entirely and Neil found himself wrist-deep in slick wet gore.

Losing the mallet, he pried broken ribs out of the way, snapping bone and tossing it aside until he found the heart, a torn unbeating lump of muscle. With a keening war cry, Neil stabbed it, over and over, destroying it, pulverizing it. "DIE!" He stabbed so deep and hard the stake met with spine. "DIE!" Flecks of blood and bone struck his cheek, his neck, got caught in his hair.

Stabbing, stabbing, stabbing, he plowed deeper still, so hard, so fast that his arm ached, sweat dripped off his brow, and his erection strained painfully against his jeans, so ripe with burgeoning lust that he knew he was going to nut himself like a teenaged boy in the throes of an erotic dream. "DIE!" Strings of drool slipped, dripped, and swayed from his mouth like the slobber of a snapping Great Dane. "DIE!" He was going to come ... he was going to ...

And then, at last, his pleasure mounted and exploded, his voice rising in erotic agony as his climax reached its highest peak. "DIE! DIE! DIE!" He'd never felt so alive, and as his throbbing cock shot hot jets of semen into his boxers and his body shook with exquisite spasms, he knew with perfect clarity that killing the undead was what he'd been born to do. *"DIEEEEEE!"*

His pleasure began its slow delicious descent - and then it was over. "Die ..." His voice was a trembling breathless whisper now. "Die ..." His knees felt like they might buckle and he trembled all over.

He'd come so violently that his balls ached and his cock was painfully, wonderfully sore. Every muscle in his body hummed with raw ecstasy and unharnessed power. Even his asshole tingled and buzzed, and he was sure he felt his prostate throbbing deep inside of him, empty and spent, like a deflated balloon.

This was the closest he'd ever come to a spiritual experience.

He wanted to collapse onto the bed, right into the bloody center of the job well done. He wanted to strip down and rub the slick blood all over himself, paint his body with it like a victorious warrior, masturbate with it. He wanted to climb into the gaping, torn, massacred body, find and fuck every cold, dead orifice that remained - perhaps even tear open some new ones - and spend himself again and again and again.

But he didn't. He was exhausted, and reality was settling on him like a bacteria-ridden housefly on a fresh-baked piece of apple pie.

I fucked up.

Somewhere along the way, he'd lost his head, gone overboard. He'd screamed and he might have been heard. Overkill, that's what the forensics experts would call it, and Neil knew what that meant. It meant outrage. Pure, black, unadulterated *hate,* and Neil could make no argument about that. What the experts would never know, however, was how fucking sexy it had been. Neil would keep that unexpected little detail all to himself.

But I fucked up. Bad. I shouldn't have ... no. Stop. He'd learned from his many therapists that there was no place for negative self-talk. He had to go easy on himself. It was his first vampire kill after all and he was allowed to make mistakes. It was only logical that his maiden slaughter would be a little untidy. *Yes, perfectly logical.*

But as he tucked the bloodied stake and mallet back into his bag, he realized there was one thing that wasn't logical at all - something he hadn't anticipated: He was not satisfied. Not even a little. The kill had brought him physical release but no freedom from the obsession, no peace. It had only given him an overwhelming urge to do it again - and again after that.

37
NIGHT HUNGER

"I'm hungry, Papa Winter." Having finally grown tired of *Tombstone*, the television was blessedly silent as Arnie slouched on the bed and sighed.

Winter sat at the small desk, staring at his checkbook, trying to figure out why the balance was off. He'd never been good at keeping books. "Isn't there any more in the fridge?"

"It's all gone."

Winter looked up over the top of reading glasses that no one but Arnie would ever see him wearing. He hadn't had great eyesight when he'd died a couple hundred years ago and, unfortunately, immortality had failed to improve the problem. "You drank all of it again, didn't you?"

"No, I promise I didn't."

"Well, then we'll go down in a minute and get some more, okay? Just hang in there, buddy." They'd stashed enough in the back of the van to last them a month. *Assuming I keep my eye on Arnie, that is.*

"Can I go down and get it now?"

"No." Winter didn't want Arnie wandering around alone. "I'm almost done."

"Fine." Arnie sounded like a petulant child. He flipped the TV on and now Winter had to try and concentrate around *Steel Magnolias*.

How the hell did I misplace - he checked the numbers - *one hundred and fifty-six dollars and seventy-six cents? Damn.* He started adding again, certain it was a mistake. Maybe he'd forgotten to add something in.

"Shelby won't drink her juice, Papa Winter."

"Huh?" Winter looked up, brow furrowed.

"If she doesn't drink her juice, will she die?"

On the television screen, Sally Field forced a glass of orange juice upon a quivering Julia Roberts while Dolly Parton, Daryl Hannah, and Olympia Dukakis buzzed about like worried bees.

"I don't know, buddy." He went back to the numbers.

"I think she should drink her juice." He paused. "I wish I had some juice. Well, not juice, but blood. I'm hungry, Papa Wi-"

"Damn it, Arnie." Winter slapped his hand down on the desk. "I can't concentrate with all this racket." He rarely lost patience with Arnie but when he did, the guilt was immediate. A new idea struck and he put on a gentler tone. "Why don't you go into Chynna's room and watch TV there? See if she has anything to drink."

But it was too late. Winter could see the hurt on Arnie's face. "But she's not there." He stared at his hands, speaking in a tiptoe voice.

Winter smiled, trying to inject it into his tone. "I know. She's out with some friends and said you're more than welcome to use her room and help yourself. Like I said, I'll be just a minute then we can get something to drink and hang out, okay?"

Not looking at him, Arnie slipped off the bed and disappeared into the adjoining room, shutting the door gently behind him, making as little sound as possible.

∼

TEARS WELLING IN HIS EYES, Arnie searched Chynna's room for something to drink. There wasn't anything in this room either. Not wanting to irritate Papa Winter more than he already had, he climbed quietly onto the bed, turned the TV on really low, and found *Steel Magnolias* where finally, Shelby had drunk her juice.

That made Arnie feel a lot better. He liked Shelby and had been very worried for her.

∽

Erin Woodhouse buzzed with pent-up energy. She couldn't concentrate on anything except vampires. *They're real. They're really real!* Belief came in waves and bursts. One moment she accepted their existence without question, the next she found herself thinking it was all some sort of joke. Right now, she was in another acceptance phase, and her mind was flooded with questions about life and death. Was it some sort of cosmic accident? Or were vampires, like everything else, part of the natural order? Assuming they *were* natural, anyway ...

I need to get out of the hotel. After throwing on a pair of sweats and pulling her hair into a ponytail, she told Eddie and Lois she was going for another jog. They sat on the couch watching *Steel Magnolias*, neither of them looking up. Erin let herself out and power-walked down the smelly, threadbare hall carpet, eager to hit the pavement outside and begin a long hard run that would hopefully burn off some of her nervous energy.

∽

Three knocks sounded on Winter's hotel room door. When he answered, it took him a moment to realize what he was looking at - and it wasn't because he'd ditched his glasses. The Darling twins stood there, smiling ... but now there were three of them. "Uh, hi ..."

"Winter!" chirped Lucy. "This is Daisy, our cousin."

"Doesn't she look just like us?" asked Ivy.

Daisy held her hand out and snapped her gum. "I've heard so much about you." Her tone suggested wanton things and Winter's mind shifted into a lower gear.

"I've heard so much about you - and it's all sexy!" She giggled. If she'd been human, she would have been jailbait - they all would have.

"It's a pleasure to meet you." Winter grinned. "So ... Poison Ivy, Juicy Lucy, and Daisy ... to what do I owe the pleasure of your comp-"

Lucy gripped Winter's crotch, giving it a firm squeeze.

Winter nearly let out a yip.

"We were just telling Daisy about your great big sword." She stroked her thumb over his already-stiffening manhood.

"It's true." Daisy giggled and looked coy. "I'd love to see it."

Winter cleared his throat. "Come in." He stepped aside to allow them entrance, watching their asses as they wiggled their way into the room. He couldn't believe his luck. *This is unreal ... I should come to Biting Man every year!*

"Make yourselves comfortable and-"

But they already had. He watched, transfixed, as they slipped out of their clothes and into the hot tub, their wet slick bodies glistening as they splashed and giggled.

He'd never seen so many perfectly-shaped breasts and round smooth asses at one time - not even in five-star strip clubs did the ladies look as good as these three. *Jesus Christ Almighty ...*

"Your turn, handsome." Ivy giggled.

Winter was just about to peel his shirt off when Arnie crashed into his thoughts. *Shit.* He held up a finger. "One moment."

They giggled and slapped at each other, lost in their kinky little world.

Winter cracked the door to Chynna's room and saw Arnie sitting crossed-legged on the bed, staring straight ahead. "Are you okay for a while, buddy?"

Arnie nodded, not looking away from the television. "I'm fine, Papa Winter." He sounded a little sulky, but he might have just been entranced by the movie.

Winter assumed he'd found sustenance in Chynna's room - he was glad about that; he didn't want to be interrupted.

In the Jacuzzi, one of the girls squealed and Winter tried to cover it with a deep cough.

Arnie took no notice. There were definite advantages to his one-track mind. He'd probably be engrossed in *Steel Magnolias* until it ended, and if he liked it, he'd even start it over.

"All right," said Winter. "Enjoy the movie. I hear it's really good."

"I will."

Winter withdrew and with just the slightest twinge of guilt, quietly locked the door between the rooms.

∽

AFTER DRINKING HER JUICE, Shelby wasn't nearly as interesting.

Arnie considered playing with his Matchbox cars, but then he remembered: They were in in the other room. And those ladies were in there with Papa Winter now, too - Arnie had heard them and he knew what they were doing. Papa Winter would definitely not like to be bothered right now.

He wished he hadn't upset Papa Winter. If he hadn't been such a menace, he could be watching Shelby with him right now. He didn't know if Papa Winter would like Shelby, probably not, but at least they would be together.

Tears stung his eyes. He didn't mean to be so bothersome but sometimes, like now, he felt so restless, like there was something he wanted to do but he wasn't sure what it was. It was like when you had to go to the bathroom really bad but there was nowhere to go and you just had to hold it and pretend you didn't have to go. But what was it he wanted? He thought about this, frowning with the effort.

His stomach rumbled at him and even though he knew the fridge was empty, he checked it again, just in case. Sometimes he was wrong about things - but there was still nothing in it. *Hurry, Papa Winter, so we can go to the van!* He sighed and watched Shelby, wondering if something better was on.

Then an idea hit him. If Papa Winter was with those ladies in the other room, how would he know if Arnie went to the van by himself and got something to drink? The idea grew more appealing, and soon, Arnie found himself on his feet, sneaking out of the room into the hall.

∽

ERIN ONLY HAD two more laps to go before she achieved her goal: five times around Hotel Circle. Her feet pounded the pavement and she wasn't surprised the jog had cleared her mind. Exercise, especially hard exercise, seemed to break up the cement in the brain and get things moving again.

As she ran, she kept an eye out for dangerous-looking people - especially Neil Trinsky. It struck her as funny that she'd rather run into a vampire than *that* guy. But she needn't have worried. She was alone. Utterly alone, and she loved it.

Vampires.

Her mind traveled back to the subject without her consent, and she found herself wondering as she ran. *What happens when vampires die? Are they really damned and soulless like in the books and movies? Do they have sex? Can they procreate? How have they been kept a secret for so many centuries? How many centuries? How far back do they go? What does it feel like to be undead?*

∽

"Stupid, stupid, stupid!" Arnie's reflex was to hit himself in the head, but then he heard Papa Winter's voice in his mind: *'Don't hit yourself, buddy. Never do that. You aren't stupid. Everybody makes mistakes.'*

But it had been such a stupid mistake. He couldn't open the door. Of *course* the van was locked. Papa Winter *always* locked the van - always - and it hadn't even occurred to Arnie. And now he was very, very hungry and there wasn't anything he could do about it but wait.

"I shouldn't have finished all of it so fast," he told himself. But it was too late for that. Earlier, while Papa Winter was showering, Arnie had guzzled all the blood in the fridge, then lied about it. Now, he was paying for it - his hunger was overwhelming.

With a heavy heart, he sat down on the cool grass and stared up at the night sky. He was hungry, so hungry, that he couldn't think of anything else anymore. "Stupid, stupid, stupid!" This time he did hit himself in the head. It hurt and that was good because he deserved it. "Stupid!" He did it again.

A scent floated toward him. It was warm, delicious. He stood, head raised, trying to detect where it came from.

And then someone rounded the hotel - a lady running on the sidewalk.

Without knowing why, Arnie darted to the van and hid behind it, watching.

She was slender and she smelled better than anything in the whole world. As she drew nearer, he saw that she was pretty too, with a red ponytail that swung back and forth as she ran. She was close enough he could smell her sweat - it was sweet. And beneath that, her blood. The scent of it made his mouth water, set his fingers trembling. She came closer, closer, and Arnie realized that if he stayed right where he was, he could catch her and ... and what? He wasn't sure. But whatever it was, it was right. It was what he was *supposed* to do.

∼

ERIN RELISHED the hum of blood in her veins, her muscles. Her heart pounded hard as she picked up the pace, preparing for her final lap. She sucked air in, let it out slowly, steadying her breath, imagining the crisp clean oxygen revitalizing her cells. She passed parked cars, feeling a kind of self-righteous pity for people who never got out of their vehicles and never walked anywhere. They'd never know the bliss of a good hard run. And it *was* blissful. She only wished she'd thought to bring her iPod. Exercise was better with some good hard rock and roll.

Just one more lap, she told herself. *Just one more.*

And then, several yards ahead, a figure stepped out from between the vehicles. A man. He stood on the sidewalk, breathing hard and fast.

Normally, Erin would have simply jogged around the guy, but something about him set off alarm bells. She slowed to a trot, then to a fast-paced walk, prepared to dart away if he made any sudden moves.

But as she drew closer, it became apparent that something was wrong with him. "Hello?" she called. "Are you okay?"

The man just stood there, breathing hard.

"Do you need help?" She was close enough now that she could clearly see him.

He was young, perhaps her own age, possibly even younger. His longish brown hair was mussed and his skin was covered in sweat. He might have been handsome, no, he *was* handsome, but his eyes ... there was something not right about his eyes. As she approached, she realized what it was - they were wild, feral. Then they flashed red, like a hunted animal's.

"Hungry." He whispered so low she wasn't sure she heard him. "Hungry." He was louder, more insistent, this time. "So ... hungry." He took a staggering step closer. Drool dangled from his bottom lip and his breath increased until he seemed to be panting. This wasn't a hunted animal - it was a *starving* animal.

Uneasy, Erin looked into his eyes. "You're hungry?" It was hard maintaining eye contact. He seemed to be staring through her. She was certain he could see her, but he wasn't seeing *her*. He was seeing something else, something beyond her.

She made to run and that's when he snapped.

With a roar, he hurled her into the parking lot, out of sight.

She hit the pavement between a white van and a black truck, smacking her head. Stars floated before her eyes and before she could make any sense out of what was happening, the man was on top of her, teeth and nails tearing her clothing, digging into her skin. She struggled, tried to scream and couldn't find her voice.

He pinned her by the shoulders and bit down on her throat. The pain was sharp and hot, like fiery pins burrowing deep into her. She rasped, coughed, pushed at the man on top of her, but it was useless. Her body was already going weak, the pain fading into bliss, and just as the last of her life drained out of her, Erin Woodhouse realized she'd just met her first vampire.

38

APPETITES FOR DESTRUCTION

The drinks at the St. Germain's blood bar were, indeed, *amazeballs*, and while Michael never imbibed alcohol, he made an exception this night. He was on vacation. He was with Natasha Darling, the woman he'd once loved - *still loved* - more than any other in his very long lifetime, and he simply could not justify foregoing the festivities. Festivities that, he knew, weakened his resolve and went against so many of his hard-won policies. He hadn't attended a Biting Man in many decades for this very reason, but it felt good to let go, to just *be*. Getting out of his own head on occasion, he told himself, was as imperative to his emotional and mental wellbeing as the meditations, all-natural lifestyle, and even his celibacy.

The St. Germain's drinks were blends of various blood types and alcohols. His favorite, the one he'd had far too much of, was called a *Scarlet Kiss*. One of the most expensive on the menu, this drink consisted of coconut rum, French AB Negative, and a dash of Grand Marnier.

Natasha's tastes were simpler. She enjoyed the *Tequila Sundown,* a blend of tequila, blood oranges, cherry grenadine, and O Positive. She was also a fan of the *Red Lady,* a simple vodka, lime, and B Negative concoction.

As he opened the hotel room door, Natasha staggered a bit, leaned into him and giggled. He realized that he was not the only one who'd had too much to drink.

Michael smiled. "I've never seen you like this before."

She laughed. "I'm sure if you think back far enough, you'll realize that's not entirely true."

Michael remembered those days so long ago. He and Natasha had particularly enjoyed bloodgrog back in Revolutionary times. In fact, that was the very drink that had begun his spiral into darker things. Not for the first time, he wondered if he'd made a mistake by hitting the blood bar tonight.

Natasha tossed her purse over the back of a chair, went into the living room, and slumped onto the couch. "I haven't drunk this much in ages."

She wore a sleek silky black dress that accentuated her curves. Her hair and makeup were slightly mussed and, because she always looked so pristine, so flawless, seeing her this way was charming.

And exciting.

Michael sat down next to her - but not too close - on the sofa.

"I had a wonderful time tonight, Michael. It was just like the old days."

"Indeed." He sat rigidly forward, hands clasped between his knees. "I suppose I ought to go to my room. It's going to be-"

"Wait." Natasha's hand touched his knee, sending an erotic trill through him. "Not yet. Stay with me a while longer." Her hand remained in place.

He cleared his throat, trying to ignore her touch - but he couldn't. It had been so long since a woman's hands had been on him that it was almost as exciting as the first time. And with Natasha Darling, it was always like the first time. He both relished and resented it. On one hand, their chemistry was like a drug, sending blissful, feel-good endorphins racing through his brain. On the other hand, he hated feeling so vulnerable and weak. So out of control. He was over 250 years old but when it came to Natasha Darling, he may as well have been seventeen.

"We should do this more often, Michael." Natasha's hand moved higher, resting on his thigh.

Michael's body began to respond with embarrassing enthusiasm. "I really need to get to bed, Natasha." The words croaked out, dry and thick.

"Not yet," she whispered.

"We've both had a lot to drink and I think we'd better call it a night." Michael felt shuddery and weak. A voice in the back of his mind told him to leave. But his body - which was now in the lead - wouldn't let him.

"You're right." She sat up, straightening her dress. "I'm sorry. I don't mean to make you uncomfortable."

"I'm not uncomfortable." He swallowed. "But I know from hard experience where this leads."

"And where does it lead?"

"To places I do not want to go."

"Is that why you meditate? To refuse those urges?"

He nodded.

"And the celibacy? That is part of it?"

"Yes." He looked at her, and the hunger in her eyes forced his hand. He touched her arm, running a finger up to her shoulder. Then he dropped it, making himself turn away. "I don't trust myself with you."

She put her hand over his. "But why? Please, help me understand."

He thought for a moment, considering how to put it, and when he opened his mouth, he found that the booze and blood had loosened him up more than he thought. "I am an addict in all things. Alcohol, sex, and free-feeding ... things like these have led to other things, to worse things. Things I do not ever wish to do again. It is a little like the domino effect. It has been this way all my life, and I simply cannot return to those places. I won't."

Natasha remained silent a moment. "But you drank tonight. With me. That says something, doesn't it?"

He shook his head. "I shouldn't have. I told myself I could handle it. I was wrong."

She touched his arm. "But I'm not afraid, Michael. I don't believe you'd hurt me." She smiled. "Even if you could."

"You don't understand. I am not afraid of hurting *you*. It's ... other things."

"What other things?"

But Michael had said too much already.

"Tell me the real reason for your celibacy." Her arm snaked through his and the warmth of her breath against his neck was more than he could take.

Willing his body to respect his wishes, he closed his eyes.

"No." Natasha touched his jaw. "Don't go into one of your meditative states. Stay with me. Here. Now. Talk to me. What happened to you?"

He opened his eyes, saw her face just inches from his own, and without any more thought, he kissed her.

~

Norman Keeler had feasted on a homeless guy just after leaving Big Sur and then had the good fortune to hitch a ride all the way to Muir Beach in Marin County. His Maker hadn't moved, and now she was less than an hour away. Tomorrow night, they would be together at last.

In town, he bought fresh clothes and toiletries, then cleaned up in a public restroom near the beach. It felt good to be clean again, to shave and brush his teeth. He spent a long time staring at himself in the mirror, only mildly surprised to find he had a reflection. He seemed a little paler than he had been before, but the jaundiced color was gone - his complexion looked healthy again. His wave of blond hair was shiny, his green eyes sparkled, and he no longer had the drawn malnourished look of an addict. He suddenly realized he hadn't had a craving for heroin since the Woman had turned him into a vampire.

Vampire. He'd more than come to terms with the notion - he was pleased with it now as, skateboard under his arm, he walked along a street in the shopping district, enjoying the sights, sounds, and scents. He still liked the aroma of food - even when he passed an Italian restaurant that exhaled garlic onto the sidewalk. But he didn't want to eat; food seemed like a perfume now, or a fragrant vase of flowers. It was something to enjoy with his nose, not his mouth.

The humans made him hungry. Their meaty scents, beneath their colognes and perfumes, their deodorants, soaps, and hair products, made his stomach growl with pleasure and he realized his sense of smell had sharpened.

It was getting late and he knew he wouldn't have time to find the Woman before dawn, so he decided to turn a few tricks and fill his wallet. It wouldn't be difficult in this rich beachside district and it would make traveling easier. He would find a place to weather the day and then work this last evening before meeting his Maker and finding his destiny.

~

"TALAI. I MEAN, AMANDA, MY LOVE." Julian Valentyn, drunk on Incendarius blood, lost in a haze of pleasure, could not recall ever feeling such happiness. He lay on his side gently stroking Amanda's face with the backs of two fingers, content simply to gaze upon her.

He couldn't believe how horrified he'd been when she first accosted him. She'd been so fast and strong that her teeth were in his throat before he could throw her off - and in that instant, everything changed.

Well, almost everything. After centuries of untold agonies and heartbreak, Talai - *Amanda, I must call her Amanda* - was in his arms. Not only that, but she had come to him, had fed upon him with a ravenous hunger that he'd rarely seen, a hunger that frightened him - and after all the millennia he'd existed, he had thought he was beyond fear.

So exquisite was her bite that he had only bitten her when he sensed his life force weakening, and then he had drunk deep of her sweet, exotic blood, taking all he needed, but no more, for fear of killing her.

Yet he still felt the fear. Despite the joy that filled his soul, a small aspect of him sat in the back of his mind calling out warnings. *Incendarius has enslaved you! This cannot be! You must fight!*

But then he looked upon her, at her blond hair fanning over his arm, her face half hidden against his breast, and wondered how anyone could fear such perfection, such beauty. He pushed a stray lock from her cheek and she sighed.

"Talai," he whispered. Then, "Amanda."

"Julian." She murmured his name and never had he loved hearing it as he did now.

He made no reply, only basked in love.

Then her lids opened, revealing light blue eyes surrounded by thick black lashes. "Julie?"

"Yes, my love?" He thought of correcting her, but on her lips, 'Julie' was charming.

She pushed up on her elbows and held him in her gaze. "Julie, will you marry me?"

That cautionary voice spoke loudly, but, again, he paid it no mind. "I'll do anything you desire, my love."

She sat up, golden embers sparking in her eyes. "We need to pack."

"Pack?"

"If we're getting married, we have to do it at Biting Man. It will be the biggest wedding ever!" She licked his neck. "This will be the best night of our lives!"

The cautionary voice screamed at him, but staring into those eyes, listening to that voice, made him unwilling to give it credence. "Anything you wish, my love. Anything."

39

CRUEL INTERRUPTIONS

They'd moved to the bed and there were so many arms and legs everywhere that if any Hindu gods were watching, they would have begun praying to them. The sheets were slick with sex and sweat and no inch of Winter's body had gone untouched by the hungry hands and mouths of the nearly identical Darling girls. He lay on his back now, arms behind his head, relaxing and letting the black-haired beauties do as they pleased.

Closing his eyes, he relished the feel of three velvety wet tongues that tickled, darted, and dipped, laving every last inch of him, giving him a tongue-bath of unprecedented proportions. In his ecstasy, it became impossible to tell the women apart - except for the gum-snapper: that was Daisy. He'd taken all three of them just the same - hard, fast, and savage - and this was a perfect end to a perfect performance.

"Don't get too relaxed just yet." One of the Darling twins - Ivy, he guessed - spoke from her position between his legs, then took him deep into her mouth, inciting a gasp and a low groan. Despite having spent himself several times over already, Winter found himself growing eager to go again.

He looked down, watching her bob, gobble, and stroke as the other two continued bathing him like cats, their breath cooling the sheen of sweat that had collected on his chest and stomach.

Then, as one, the giggling girls rolled him over onto his stomach and gave his backside the same attention. He shivered and fought off laughter as tongues tickled their way down his spine and across his buttocks. He felt a hungry growl building in his throat, and was just about to roll back over and ravage the first Darling girl available when gum-snapping Daisy dropped her wad into his ass crack and tried to fish it out.

Winter looked back. "What the hell?"

"Sorry about that!" Daisy popped the gum back into her mouth and grinned. "Kinky, huh?"

A hard pounding on the hotel room door saved him.

"Papa Winter!" Arnie's terrified voice brought him up from the tangle of arms and legs.

The giggling girls went silent.

"Papa Winter! Something bad happened!"

Winter shot to his feet, wrapping a sheet around him as he hurried to the door.

Arnie stood on the other side, hair mussed, eyes wide, his mouth stained with blood.

∽

NEIL PROWLED THE TOWN SQUARE, watching for vampires, but seeing few people at all, let alone the dirty fangers. It was nearing eleven and chilly - even the occasional joggers wore sweats tonight. He tugged his leather jacket closed as he crossed the park, heading for the businesses, all of them dark, on Main Street. He needed to kill something, anything - he burned with the need.

Last night, he'd found his victim, Curtis Penrose, among the buildings - maybe he'd find another there. Nobody'd expect a killer to return to the same area so soon. *They're so stupid.* Tonight at Dimples' Boarding House, the murder was all the boarders could talk about, and Neil had sat for a few minutes, drinking organic carrot juice, and nodding with feigned interest as Baldy held forth on the dangers of hosting vampires. He'd called them 'evil bloodsuckers' and that almost made Neil like him. Almost. Martha Ann Dimples declared her liking for vampires, and that made Neil want to stake her right through her frilly pink apron. *Stupid little bitch!*

Now, Neil jogged around the square without seeing a soul. He slowed at the bakery, wondering if Poppin Fresh was working late, but the place was dark and locked up tight. None of the old farts that sat on the bench out front by day were there. *Pity*. Killing one of them would've been easy ... and it would've at least taken the edge off.

He trotted to Kissel's Pickle Shoppe, hoping for a thick, wet kosher dill - *that* would take the edge off, too. There was a light on in back, but the doors were locked and if anyone was in there, they didn't respond to his knocks. "Fuck those little bitches," he muttered and began jogging again, blending into the shadows, when he spotted a patrol car. He watched the guy cruise by - it was a deputy, not the Rick Grimes-looking sheriff.

And then Neil realized he was on the wrong street - Hotel Circle was the place to be. The vampires would be awake and watching, but there were plenty of humans staying on the Circle too. If Eternity had a homeless population, this was likely the place to find it. And if there was anything Neil hated half as much as vampires, it was fucking homeless people. *Losers!*

He pulled a tube of strawberry Pucker-Buttons from his pocket and pushed a couple into his mouth, then headed for Hotel Circle.

∽

DESPITE HIS BEST EFFORTS, Michael's body was entwined with Natasha's, his mouth over hers, his hands hungrily roaming the exquisite contours and curves of her body when his cell phone jangled out Winter's ringtone. The sound shattered the spell and, equally relieved and infuriated by the intrusion, Michael pushed himself off Natasha. *Figures the cell would decide to work right now.*

"Don't stop, Michael. Please." Her eyes were hooded, her lips red from the crush of his kiss - but her clothing was intact. It wasn't too late to stop.

"I'm sorry."

The phone continued to ring.

Michael cleared his throat and answered.

"We've got a problem, Boss. A big one." Winter wasted no time with formalities and as he explained the situation, Michael's stomach turned to liquid lead.

"I'm trying to get him calmed down right now," Winter was saying. "He's really upset."

That was an understatement; Michael could hear Arnie's hysterical cries in the background. He glanced at Natasha, who now sat up, concerned. "You stay with Arnie, Winter," Michael said. "I will go check and uh, take care of the other matter." He hung up and looked at Natasha.

"What is it, Michael? What's happened?"

"Arnie," Michael said, still processing it. "He's killed someone. A young woman. I need to-"

Natasha was on her feet in an instant. "I'll go with you."

"I'M SORRY, PAPA WINTER!" Tears streamed down Arnie's face and Winter brushed them aside with the wet wash cloth, then dipped it into the water and continued scrubbing the blood off his young, simple friend.

After sending the girls away, Winter called Michael, then ran a warm bath for Arnie - with lots of bubbles, just how he liked it - but it was doing nothing to calm him down.

"I didn't mean to, Papa Winter! I don't want to be in trouble!" His racking sobs punched holes in Winter's heart.

"It's okay, big guy. You're not in trouble." Winter squeezed shampoo into Arnie's hair, trying to keep his voice calm. "It'll be all right. Michael's going to go-"

"I was just *so* hungry!"

It felt like someone had kicked Winter right in the gut. *This is my fault. If I'd listened to him, if I hadn't been so wrapped up in those girls, this never would have happened.* "It's all right, buddy. Just take slow breaths, okay?"

"I *can't!*"

Tears pricked Winter's eyes. "And after we get you cleaned up, maybe we can watch *Tombstone* again." His voice cracked and he cleared his throat. "Would you like that?"

But Arnie didn't even seem to hear him. He continued sobbing and shaking, his face buried in his hands as Winter slowly, calmly, shampooed his head, willing away the tremble in his own fingers.

This is bad. This is really bad. And again, Winter's self-loathing spread through him with deadly, razor-sharp focus, straight to the gut. *What was I thinking? I wasn't thinking - not with my head anyway. I threw Arnie under the bus for a romp with the Darlings ... and a young woman's life is the price.* Not to mention the guilt that would follow Arnie for the rest of his nights. *What the hell is wrong with me?*

"I'm sorry, Papa Winter!"

"It's all right. Now lie back so we can rinse out your hair."

Arnie did as he was told, and as Winter rinsed, he wondered what kind of mess Michael was looking at right now.

∼

THE GIRL WAS DEAD. Very dead.

She lay on the pavement between a white van and a black truck, arms splayed, her head gently tipped to one side, a look of horror frozen on her face. She was pretty - or had been, anyway - with delicate features and high cheekbones that would have been at home on the face of a fashion model. Michael's first guess as to the cause of death was blood loss - the young woman was pale, even for a dead girl - but looking closer, he was sure her neck had been snapped.

"She's so young," Natasha said. She stood next to Michael, both of them hanging back a few feet, staring down at the fresh corpse.

Michael scanned the area. It was dark, and there were no signs that anyone had seen or heard anything. He bent, checking for a pulse. It was futile - he knew a dead body when he saw one - but he wanted to be absolutely certain. After finding no signs of life, he looked up at Natasha and shook his head.

"What are we going to do with her?" she asked. "Your race can turn with one bite, as I recall."

"Yes, but only if we release a lethal amount of venom. Hopefully, that hasn't happened." Michael watched the corpse a moment, certain he was correct. *Arnie wouldn't even know how to release venom.* "We'll take her to the woods." It wouldn't be a *proper* burial exactly, but it was the only option that would keep Arnie safe.

"I think that's the best thing," Natasha agreed.

"I'll go get the van." Michael dug in his pocket for the key, and made his way toward the vehicle, a few yards away. He got in, and keeping the headlights dark, brought it back to where Natasha waited. She now had the woman's limp body propped against her own shoulder.

Michael hopped out and opened the back and helped Natasha load the body. After covering it with a blanket, they headed toward a thick stretch of trees he'd seen just outside of town.

As they drove, Natasha shook her head. "This is going to be very hard on Arnie, isn't it?"

Michael nodded. "And Winter as well." During the very short call, Michael had heard the self-blame in Winter's voice - and given that the man still carried the guilt of turning Arnie over two hundred years ago, Michael knew he would suffer from this just as much.

∼

NEIL TRINSKY BUSTED his nut on the gas cap of the silver Highlander he hid behind, then wiped his hands on his sweats. He'd lucked out, arriving on Hotel Circle just in time to see a pair of dirty undead in the midst of a crime. He'd masturbated as he watched the two vampires load a body into a van and take off. He was pretty sure it was the same couple who'd taunted him the other night.

Glancing around, seeing no one, he trotted across the street and bent to examine the area where the van had been. And saw spots of blood on the ground. "You dirty, filthy, bloodsucking freaks," he muttered, a smile on his lips and in his pants. Surely, they'd be back to clean up.

Neil moved across the lot and hunkered down between two black SUVs to wait.

∼

Eddie clicked off the television and looked at Lois. "I wonder where Erin is."

Lois glanced at her watch. "It's getting late." She picked up her cell and tried to phone Erin, then rolled her eyes and hung up. "Eternity has the worst reception."

"Yes, it does. Maybe we should take a walk. See if we can run into her."

"Good idea." Lois stood up and stretched.

Eddie scritched Renny under the chin. "You want to go for a walk, boy?"

The chubby dog turned a couple of excited circles. Eddie glanced at Lois. "That means yes, right?"

She smiled, bringing over a leash. "Yeah. Poor guy, he needs a good walk."

Eddie rose and shrugged into his jacket, telling himself that walking Hotel Circle or even the town square in the middle of the night was utterly safe. He was pretty sure it was, anyway.

40

THE DEAD AND THE RESTLESS

Michael brought the van as far into the stand of trees as possible and killed the headlights. They'd have to carry the body a few yards toward a clearing, but he was certain that this would be a perfectly acceptable resting place for ... *Well, for whoever she was.* He sighed.

"Michael?" Natasha faced him. "Are you all right?"

He nodded. "I don't enjoy this. I don't enjoy it at all." He wondered who the dead woman was - and who would be missing her.

Natasha touched his hand. "Me neither. But what choice do we have?"

"I know. It's just that-"

A rustling from the back of the van cut him off. Michael's stomach went cold.

"What was that?" asked Natasha.

Slowly, they both turned, facing the blanket-covered heap in the back, barely visible in the shadows. Nothing moved.

Michael relaxed. It was just the corpse's nerves. Newly-dead bodies often did all kinds of unpredictable things: moaning, twitching, vomiting, and the like, were perfectly normal.

"Well," said Natasha. "I suppose we ought to-"

The dead woman in back of the van shot up screaming, apparently not very dead at all. This was a new development – one for which Michael was not at all prepared.

"Oh my God," said Natasha.

Oh my God, indeed. Michael clambered into the back of the van to calm the screaming, newly-born vampire.

∽

NEIL REMAINED between the two black SUVs, hunkered low and cleaving to the shadows. "You filthy slut," he whispered under his breath when he spotted his mother and that queer Coastal Eddie strolling toward him along the sidewalk. And they had his fucking dog, too! As horny as he'd been since all the vampire-stalking – *and killing!* – his half-hard dick now went as limp as a wet noodle, his balls shriveling like deflated balloons.

How dare you? You dirty little slut! His eyes flashed to Eddie. *And how dare YOU?* He felt sick imagining it – the deejay taking his mother from behind so he could pretend she was a dude. *It's not as if he could just go straight all of a sudden.* He was no doubt doing it every chance he got. *And she's letting him! She's LETTING him!* An image of Mom sucking the greasy, hippie-loving fucker off set fire to his blood.

Neil Junior twitched.

But Neil himself remained silent and still, almost hoping Eddie would put his hands on Mom and give him an excuse to kill them both. Well, he probably wouldn't kill Mom – that would be too good for the little slut. But he *would* spend the rest of his life making her pay for her immoral, whoring ways.

As they passed him by, Neil cringed, hoping his Axe Body Spray wouldn't betray him. He crouched lower, glad the wind was in his favor, as he strained to hear. He caught a snippet of conversation, just enough to tell him they were looking for someone.

"Where could she be?" Mom asked quietly. Not *he* as in Neil ... but *she* ... as in ... *who?*

Neil watched them disappear around the bend and into the darkness and vividly imagined Eddie planting a hand on his mother's ass. *I'll fucking kill him! I'd kill him TWICE if I could! THREE times! SLOWLY! I'll cut his cock off and feed it to him raw!* Neil Jr. twitched again as Neil stepped out of the shadows and onto the sidewalk, hands fisted, chest puffed, cock hardening.

∾

"Did you hear something?" Lois turned her head to gaze back at the Icehouse Inn's parking lot just in time to see a figure emerge from the shadows. She'd recognize the stiff, hard-fisted stance anywhere. "Don't look, keep walking," she said.

"What? Why?"

"It's Neil. He's watching us."

"Then let's go have a chat with him." Eddie slowed. Renny whined and pulled on his leash, eager to visit a nearby fire hydrant.

"Not now."

"Why not?"

Lois hesitated. She always avoided Neil when his hands were fisted - she didn't trust him. He'd broken windows and wallboard before and she'd intuited that he might turn his anger on her. He nearly had on several occasions. But she was with Eddie and they were out in public. What could go wrong?

"You're right," she told Eddie. "Let's confront him. He stole my car then destroyed it. He's not my son anymore. I've had enough. I'm going to have the sheriff arrest him."

Eddie studied her. "Then maybe we'd better not confront him. He might disappear."

Renny whined.

Lois stopped moving and turned back, staring. Eddie did the same, speaking soft calming words to Renny as he did.

Neil's stiff silhouette still stood in front of the hotel parking lot.

"So, do you want to risk it?" Eddie spoke softly.

"I want to have a few words with my son."

"Okay. If you're sure."

They began walking back toward the Icehouse Inn. Neil remained under the streetlamp. Lois swallowed, screwing up her courage as her son began backing into the shadowed lot. Lois walked faster, Eddie and Renny beside her. She'd had enough - she wasn't going to let Neil intimidate her any more.

Just then, a white van turned onto the Circle and pulled into the lot, blocking her view. It parked in a slot next to the street. Eddie tugged Lois into the shadows of a potted fir tree. "Let's let whoever that is go into the hotel first."

"Why?"

"Caution is our best friend."

"Okay."

They waited.

Finally the van doors opened. A dark-haired woman got out of the driver's side and walked to the passenger door. Someone else - a man - got out, and then the side door slid open and a moment later, the two of them reappeared, a figure between them. Lois watched carefully, squinting to see details; it was nearly impossible until they approached the lobby doors. The man and woman both had their arms lightly around the middle figure. It was a woman with red hair.

"Eddie, do you think that's Erin?"

Eddie shook his head. "I have no idea, but the other woman is Natasha Darling."

"Who?"

"One of the owners of the Candle Bay Hotel."

"What's she doing here?"

"The Darlings are vampires."

"What?"

"Shhh. They're all right. If that's Erin, they won't hurt her."

"How do you know?"

"Tell you later."

Lois nodded and watched the trio disappear into the depths of the lobby, catching another glimpse of the red ponytail, and wishing she could recall what Erin had been wearing when she'd left tonight. "I hope you're right, because I'm sure that's Erin with them, but why?"

"I don't know. I wish I did. Lois, we can't be sure of anything. Let's go back to the hotel and see if Erin's back yet. She could be - we can't assume that's her." But his tone told Lois he wasn't convinced. He nodded toward the area where they'd last seen Neil. "And *he's* not going anywhere. We don't need to draw attention to ourselves tonight. In the morning, we'll go see Sheriff Tully."

41
VENOMOUS LIAISONS

Stephen Darling had spent hours researching Incendarius. In all his centuries as a vampire, he had never - not until tonight - considered this monster to be real. Vampiric lore was as rich and full of strange creatures as human lore, and Incendarius was one of the taller tales. Or so he'd thought - as did the authors of the books on his desk.

Incendarius was so rare that it was considered a myth. The tale went back to the era of the rule of the Trueborn and Euloa. Incendarians were human vampires - and Stephen suspected they were one of the reasons Trueborns had exterminated most hybrids on Euloa. Incendarius was like heroin to Trueborns. It enslaved them. The tale of Incendarius was similar to cautionary tales that human parents told their children to keep them out of trouble. Incendarius was the Trueborn equivalent of the bogeyman, banshees, and La Llorona all rolled into one - and was far more dangerous to Trueborns than to normal hybrids. Nothing else existed that could mesmerize and bend a Trueborn to its will.

Stephen picked up the phone and called Julian.

It rang five times before a deep voice rumbled, "Valentyn residence. This is Bruno. How may I help you?"

"This is Stephen Darling. I need to talk to Julian. It's urgent."

Bruno hesitated. "Please hold."

Stephen was about to hang up and try Julian's cell when another male voice said, "Mr. Darling? This is Felix Farquhar, Master Julian's personal assistant."

"I really need to speak with Julian."

"I'm sorry, he's not here." Felix's voice betrayed worry.

"When will he return?"

"I - I don't know, but Master Julian has spoken of you. You were engaged to Amanda, correct?"

"Yes, why?" Stephen's chest tightened.

"Well, I may be speaking out of turn, but Mr. Darling, I'm very concerned. My master is not himself."

"Please explain."

"Well, earlier tonight, he told me they are to be wed."

"What?"

"They will be married at Biting Man. They're on their way up there now."

"Amanda must have bitten him." Stephen said the words, knowing they were true.

"I- I think so, Mr. Darling. There was blood on his sheets. He never - he doesn't-"

"Julian is in her thrall. Did he tell you about Incendarius, Felix?"

"A little, yesterday. He said it's very dangerous. He also instructed me to open a letter he left in his safe if anything happens to him."

"Then I'd advise you to open it, Felix."

"I shall."

"Felix? Do you know where they're staying in Eternity?"

"No, sir, but Julian owns a cabin on the outskirts of town. He told me it's so well hidden that there's no address."

"I see. Do you know if he has his cell phone with him?"

"I believe he does, but service is spotty up there, assuming he will even answer." Felix hesitated. "Mr. Darling, all he was doing when they left was staring at the woman like a puppy dog. He was not the man I know and love." Felix cleared his throat. "She is Incendarius?"

"Yes."

"This is worrisome," Felix said. "What should we do?"

"We must rescue him. My sister, Natasha, is in Eternity now. I will contact her with this information. Hopefully she and her friends can stop this before it goes any further."

"Thank you, Mr. Darling. Let me know if there's anything I can do to help."

∽

"Do you mean to tell me I'm ... *dead?*" Erin sat in a chair by an oriel window, eyes wide, mind reeling, teeth chattering. The woman named Natasha had draped her own jacket around Erin's shoulders but it did nothing to combat the cold that pervaded her body – it seemed to come from *within* her, from the marrow of her bones, spreading outward to her extremities.

Memories of the past hour were clear – uncomfortably clear – and though she tried to will them away, they were like tiny slivers in her brain that she couldn't extract, no matter how she tried. First, the couple had taken her upstairs at the Icehouse Inn and spoken with a big white-haired vampire, then had taken her back down and over to their room at the St. Germain.

"You're not exactly dead, Erin." The man named Michael sat across from her, watching her with sadness in his eyes. "But rather ... you're undead."

Natasha stood beside him a hand resting on his shoulder, and stared at Erin with deep concern.

"But this can't be," Erin said. "It's not possible! It can't be *real!*" Thickness filled her throat, and tears – oddly cool ones – streamed down her cheeks. "Please, please tell me this isn't real!" But she knew the truth, she *felt* it. Something had changed in her since the attack, something she had no words for, something she might *never* be able to explain. Vampires were real, she'd just come to terms with that. *And now I'm one of them?* "Please, tell me it's a mistake – that I just got knocked out, and–"

"I am afraid I cannot tell you that, Erin." Michael shifted.

"It's not so bad, really." Natasha offered a wan smile. "It takes some getting used to, but–"

"But nothing! This can't happen to me!" Erin broke down and for several long moments, Michael and Natasha let her weep in peace. She wasn't sure how she was supposed to accept this. What did it mean for her future? How could she spend the rest of her life in darkness, feeding off the blood of innocent people?

Blood! Strangely, the thought wasn't as repulsive as she'd expected, and she felt a pang of panic when she realized that it not only didn't repulse her, but rather, comforted her. *Oh God! It's already starting!* A strange new instinct was blossoming inside her, making her feel pulled in two directions at once: drawn and repelled. She wept, burying her face in her hands, terrified.

"There, there." Natasha's touch comforted her. "You must pull yourself together, Erin. There are far worse things."

Erin wasn't sure she agreed - at least until she realized the alternative. *If I wasn't a vampire, I'd be dead. Really dead. Dead for real!* Despite her spinning mind and trembling body, Erin cleared her throat, wiped her eyes, and faced the two strangers - *the vampires!* - who'd rescued her. "What if I can't accept this?"

"You must and you will." Michael's eyes were grave. "Denial will only make it harder. I am sorry this happened."

"Sorry?" asked Erin. "Sorry for what? It wasn't your fault."

"No, but ...the man who turned you ... he was one of my own."

Erin blinked. "Your own? You mean ... you know him?"

Michael nodded.

For an instant, Erin felt a rage so deep, so razor-sharp, that she envisioned reaching out and cutting Michael's throat with the nearest-

"That would be a very big mistake."

Can he read my mind?

Michael's smile wasn't threatening, not exactly, but it told her that he knew how to handle attempts on his life.

She watched him, searching for signs he was reading her thoughts. If he was, he betrayed nothing.

After a few seconds, his body relaxed. "Arnie, the man who turned you, is of a simple mind. Unfortunately, he was left hungry and unattended, which is a matter I will deal with shortly."

"But why didn't he just kill me? Why did he *turn* me?"

"I am sure it was an accident. As I said, Arnie is simple-minded and was surely unaware that he'd injected you with venom. He is like a baby snake who hasn't yet learned to control venom expression." He paused. "In fact, I didn't think he even knew how to express venom."

"Venom? That's how it happens?"

"In some cases," said Michael. "There are several types of vampires. And my kind - Arnie's kind - has venom. A little will create a sense of euphoria, much like a drug. Too much, and the mortal body dies and the victim becomes undead. But as I said, there are different kinds of vampires, which contribute to the varying vampire characteristics in legend and lore."

Natasha spoke up. "I am of a different nature, one that doesn't secrete venom at all, only a chemical that numbs the site of our bite. We do things a little differently than Michael's group. For instance, it takes the traditional three bites for us to turn someone." She smiled. "Just like in so many movies."

Michael nodded. "Yet both of us are vampires. Different *races*, if you will, of the same species."

Erin grappled to understand. "So now I'm ...?"

"One of *my* kind." Michael's voice was like suede, comforting and narcotic, and the lived-in features of his face were soft, handsome, non-threatening. This was not a monster. Erin glanced at the beautiful black-haired woman beside him. *No, they aren't monsters, neither of them. But ... am I a monster?*

Michael's lips curved into a soft smile. "We are as good - or as wicked - as we choose to be. Just like humans."

Is he reading my mind again! Erin wondered if she had the same ability. *How would I even find out?* There were so many questions.

"We will answer your questions, all of them, but first, you need to feed." Michael nodded at Natasha and she headed from the room.

Erin felt a surge of anxiety - *I can't bite someone! I can't!* - and felt both relieved and suddenly very hungry when Natasha returned with a bottle of what could only be blood.

∽

"Why an Acura?" Amanda drove the SUV through the dark hills. "You could afford something a little more upscale. And white? That's so boring." She cackled. "I'm surprised it's not yellow!"

Julian looked away from the forested foothills - his Trueborn eyes picked up color and detail even in the dead of night and he loved watching the night creatures prowl the emerald depths of the woods. He turned his eyes on Amanda and at once felt a resurgence of something like pure love. "It's a very nice vehicle and doesn't draw attention to itself, my love. It is luxurious but safe, and holds plenty of cargo. It isn't wise to flaunt one's wealth."

"Oh, Jesus, Julie, you need to live a little." She took a curve at breakneck speed and the road steepened. "You'd look great in a Porsche or a Ferrari."

"I'm afraid that wouldn't be a good vehicle for me. For my business."

"Is that all you think about, Julie? Business?" She batted her eyelashes.

"Not anymore." He gazed at her, so in love it pained him. "I will buy you a Porsche, in any color you desire."

"That would make an okay wedding present." Amanda gifted him with a smile. "But, Julie, I'd rather have a Bugatti."

The request startled Julian, who had learned to value subtlety and privacy above all else. "My love, that's well over a million dollars."

"Closer to two mil." Amanda's perfect pink tongue poked out and wet her lips as she held him in a sidelong gaze. "You can afford it, can't you?"

"I-"

"For *me*?" She blew him a kiss.

He couldn't fight the wave of adoration he felt as she spoke. "Anything for you, my love."

He returned his gaze to the forest and as soon as he did, his blind devotion eased slightly. It wouldn't be long before they climbed into the mountains and began their approach to Eternity and Icehouse Mountain. He had secretly revisited the Eternal City within the mountain at least two dozen times in the last century; the place filled his spirit like nothing else. The hybrids who lived permanently within the

City had no idea he'd visited, such was the power of the Trueborn to remain invisible.

When his father, the king of Trueborns - the self-proclaimed Treasure - had traveled to the mountain after Euloa sank into the ocean, he'd left a path of death and destruction behind him. Julian - then known as Prince Keliu - had followed and tried to undo some of the damage, but his father was unstoppable. By the time Julian arrived in the Eternal City, the self-proclaimed Treasure had slaughtered thousands. Julian took it upon himself to stop his father and in so doing became the new leader. To his embarrassment, he found himself being worshipped as the Prince of Blood. He refused to let the hybrids or humans call him King - the word was anathema to him - but they did call him Prince; he allowed it because they had to call him something. In the following centuries, he remained in the Eternal City and tried to unite the remaining Trueborns and the hybrids and teach them to treat their humans well, as had been the practice on Euloa. It was the only way to survive and lessons were learned, though often hard-won.

But the Dead Agains had come together and continued to worship him, eventually establishing what was now called Biting Man as a festival in his honor. There were still statues and friezes depicting him within the temple. Except for legend, the Trueborn race was now all but forgotten. Some hybrid vampires still believed Trueborns had existed as a race, rather than as gods, but how much longer that would be true was anyone's guess.

He'd fled the Eternal City centuries ago and even now - especially now - he did not wish to be recognized.

His cell phone vibrated; he'd turned off the ringer to stop Amanda from ordering him not to answer his own phone. Surreptitiously, he pulled it from his pocket. It was Stephen Darling. Both he and Felix had phoned repeatedly in the last hour. He glanced at Amanda and realized her eyes were hard on him, even as she drove.

"Who is it?" Her words were as hard as cut glass.

"A business associate."

"Who?" Her blue eyes turned the color of night.

The haze insinuated itself into his mind again. *She's hypnotizing me.* He knew, but it didn't matter. He heard himself say Stephen's name.

She cursed under her breath. "You will not take his calls. Do you understand, my love?"

"I will not take his calls." *This is wrong. It's wrong. I need to talk to him. She's stopping me.* Never had anyone held such sway over him. He felt a wave of adoration as he looked at her and meekly returned his cell to his pocket, but he also felt something else, something foreign: Fear. *This is not possible.* But with Incendarius, anything was possible.

"Good boy, Julie." She blew him another kiss and spoke in sugared tones. "I think I'd like a red Bugatti. Will you get me one, my sweet, darling, Julie?"

42
TRANSITIONS

"Erin's not here," Lois said. They stood in their shabby gold room at Perdet Towers, not knowing what to do.

"Give her a while," Eddie said. "The police won't start hunting for a missing person for twenty-four hours anyway."

"But anything could happen to her. It probably already has. Eddie, we have to do something."

At a loss, Eddie undid Renny's leash then turned to Lois. "What do you think we should do?"

"I- I don't know." A single tear ran down her cheek. "I don't know."

Eddie put his arms around her and held her close, wishing he had an answer.

∾

"Excuse me, I have to take this." Natasha put the room phone on hold and moved to the bedroom to take her brother's call, leaving Michael and Erin to talk. The girl was in shock, but surprisingly knowledgeable about vampirism, though much of her information was incorrect.

Closing the door, Natasha picked up the phone. "Stevie? Is anything wrong?"

"Yes, I believe there is. You remember the stories about Incendarius?"

"Sure, but-"

"They're real."

"What? What are you talking about?"

"Julian told me that Amanda is Incendarius."

Natasha listened closely as he explained. "Well, that does make some sense. Is that why you couldn't bring yourself to get rid of her for so long?"

"I suppose that it played into it, but Incendarius has far more power over Trueborns than over human vampires. Amanda and Julian are on their way up to be married."

"Oh, bullshit. No one can make Julian do anything he doesn't want to-"

"*She* can, Tasha." Stevie's voice was so solemn that Natasha went silent as her brother explained in detail.

"That bitch," she spat when he finished. "I'll stake her myself!"

"It may come to that, but it won't be so easy," Stevie told her. "She has drunk Julian's blood, and now she's probably as strong as he is."

"But she's also ignorant, and ruled by her emotions, not her head." Natasha's rage was so great that her face felt hot. Her entire body did, and a fierce hunger kicked in as her fangs extended. "I'll drink her dry."

"I hope you do, but remember, Julian is in her thrall and he will defend her. You need a plan - and you need help from our sisters and Michael and his clan. Do not try to deal with her on your own, Tasha. Promise me."

She counted to ten. Her fangs receded. "I promise, Stevie. Now, tell me where to find them."

"Julian has a cabin, but it won't be easy to locate; you may have to wait for them to enter the Eternal City." His chuckle was dry as dust. "You may have to object to the marriage."

"Oh, I'll object, all right."

"Good. Just make sure you have lots of backup, no matter where you find them."

"Goin' to the mountain and we're gonna get marr-r-ied," Amanda sang for what seemed like the thousandth time.

Julian, torn between love and irritation, sat quietly in his seat.

"We're getting married," Amanda told him.

"Indeed." They were nearing Eternity now. Signs advertising restaurants, hotels, and even Little Stonehenge - *I wonder what they'd think if they knew Trueborns built it and what it's really for* - had begun dotting the roadside. Now, he watched for the dirt road that would eventually lead to his stone cabin. He hadn't told her about it yet, and wasn't sure he wanted to; she assumed they would be going to the fanciest hotel in Eternity, taking the honeymoon suite - by force if necessary - then march into the Eternal City tomorrow night when Biting Man officially kicked off and get married before beginning their rule as the new king and queen of the vampires.

Julian sighed. He knew this was wrong, all of it, from marrying Amanda to ruling the vampiric world as his father had. He had never wanted to rule anything but his own life, and now he was about to give them a queen as terrible as the Treasure himself. *I cannot do this to my people. But how can I refrain?* He glanced at Amanda. *My will is not my own.*

"Maybe I'd like silver better."

"Silver?"

"The Bugatti. Silver or red. What should we get me?"

Julian didn't reply.

Amanda pulled a frown. "Julie? Red or silver?"

"I don't know," he murmured, lost in dark thoughts.

"Maybe one of each, then." She glanced at him. "Julie?"

"Yes, my love?"

"You're the best."

"The best what?"

"Silly man. The best bridegroom ever." She cleared her throat. "We're going to the mountain and we're gonna get marr-r-ied."

As they passed a sign that informed them they were only ten miles from Eternity, Julian, basking in a haze of desire, wading in rebellion and terror, had never felt so impotent.

"I want to go with you," said Erin. "To Biting Man."

Michael and Natasha looked at each other – and Erin could see something pass between them. A flicker of doubt. Incredulity, even.

"I'm serious," she continued. "I was planning on getting in anyway. Somehow."

"Erin," Michael began, but she cut him off.

"It'll be the best thing for me. A quick way to learn who I am and to be around my ... my own kind." She sipped the blood Natasha had brought her, still surprised it not only didn't disgust her, but that she liked it. Loved it, actually. It was as if each sip she took tasted a little better than the last. She was no longer upset. She knew she should have been – and under normal circumstances, she *would* have been – but these were not normal circumstances and Erin Woodhouse was a different woman now. Her energy level was high, she felt strong and healthy, and even her appearance seemed to have improved; she couldn't help stealing glances at herself in a mirror that hung above the desk. Her hair was brighter, shinier, and more lustrous than it had ever been in her life, and her skin, which had always been a little too pale for her liking, now had a porcelain cast to it – an almost silvery glow that was very appealing.

As the evening wore on, she'd marveled at how quickly she'd come to accept her new state of existence. The shock – and then the terror – had dissolved and become something better than acceptance. It had become something not unlike delight. *I've been preparing for this my entire life,* she thought – and that's exactly how it seemed. *I was meant to become this.* She thought of the man who'd turned her. *What was his name? Arnie?* It seemed imperative that she meet him. No, not meet him – she'd already done *that,* hadn't she? She wanted to know him. She *had* to know him. She looked back at Michael, piercing his amber eyes with her blue ones, trying to convey her seriousness to him. "I want to meet my Maker."

"Erin, that might not be such a good idea right now."

"Michael." Natasha placed a fine, pale hand on his shoulder. "Perhaps we shouldn't dismiss the idea so quickly. It might be good for Arnie to see that Erin is all right."

All right? thought Erin. *All right? I'm more than all right, I'm fantastic!* She finished her glass of blood and Natasha immediately refilled it.

Michael remained reluctant.

"Please let me meet him."

Michael sighed. "I will call Winter and see if he agrees to this - but I am not making you any promises."

Erin grinned then downed her glass, knowing that this man, Arnie, would love her as much as she loved him. She could feel it. She could feel all kinds of strange, new things. Wonderful things. It was as if, despite being dead, she'd never been so alive.

~

WINTER ENDED the call with Michael and walked over to Arnie, who sat on the edge of the bed, hands folded in his lap, eyes downcast. "Are you sure you want to meet her?"

Arnie nodded. He currently wore his favorite pair of silky green pajamas - or as he called them, his *shinies* - and his face was puffy from crying. The Darling girls, having long since been sent to their room, had tried to cheer him up with a tickle fight, but the poor guy was completely despondent. However, when Michael had called Winter just now, saying the new vampire, Erin, had wanted to meet the man who'd turned her, Winter had finally seen something hopeful in Arnie's eyes. According to Michael, the girl had accepted the Transition wonderfully - she was one of the lucky ones - and was already eager to meet Arnie.

Winter, for one, thought it was a great idea. *Something* had to pull Arnie out of his slump. He sat down next to him on the bed. "They'll be here soon, buddy. Why don't we get you changed into something nicer?"

Arnie nodded. He liked being in his *shinies* and fought Winter nearly every dusk when it came time to get dressed, but now, he gave no resistance. And that told Winter he was looking forward to meeting the girl.

It will ease his mind. And with it, Winter's mind could rest as well.

~

ERIN'S HEART beat a little harder as they approached her Maker's hotel room. She had vague memories of being afraid - *no, terrified* - of the guy as he'd stepped out of the shadows and attacked her ... but it was a dull, distant fear now, as if the whole thing had happened decades rather than just hours ago.

Michael knocked softly on the door. Natasha placed a hand on Erin's shoulder and the weight of her touch was a comfort.

But the man who answered was not her Maker. It was the man with the mountainous muscles and white crew cut. And she could *feel* that he wasn't her Maker. She wasn't sure how to explain it, not even to herself, but even if she'd never seen the guy's face, she'd know the man who'd made her. She'd know him from across any crowded room in any city in the world. And what was more, she realized that she could sense his very nearness even now. It was as if her body temperature had cooled yet heated at the same time, just a little, and there was a pleasant hum under her skin that was ... delectable. Almost sexual ... but no, it wasn't sexual, not exactly. It was *far* more than mere sex that compelled her now. It was like being in the same room as a buffet table after being starved for a week. Her Maker was in the room, she knew it, and it took great willpower not to simply push past the muscular man who filled the doorway.

"Winter," Michael said. "This is Erin. Erin, meet Winter."

Winter's hand engulfed Erin's and he gave her a friendly nod, but his clear blue eyes betrayed apprehension. Erin became aware of a low humming electrical current that hung in the air and she realized what it was: It was the emotions of the other vampires - she was sensing them at a much deeper level than she ever could have as a human. She couldn't read their thoughts, not exactly, but she somehow knew the source of their trepidation: They were worried she might become angry and hurt her Maker. *Hurt his feelings.*

But Erin knew this was not going to happen. "Please," she said. "Let me see him. He's in no danger from me."

Winter stepped out of the way, and there, standing in the center of the room, was her Maker.

In a charcoal suit, cobalt tie, and polished shoes, he looked like an overgrown child dressed up for church. His hair was freshly-washed and slicked back and even from here, Erin could smell him: clean, somehow sweet ... it was a wonderful smell. A *perfect* smell. His eyes were downcast as if he dared not look at her. She willed him to meet her eyes, *needed* him to see her, but he was too ashamed, too frightened. She could feel that about him the same way she'd felt the others' emotions.

"Arnie?" As she took slow careful steps toward him, she knew one thing and one thing only: She loved this man. Not romantically, not exactly, but a little like the way a daughter loves her father, or a soldier loves the sergeant who saved his life.

A tear slipped from between his long dark lashes and fell to the floor, and Erin realized how beautiful his face was - how *perfect* - just like the smell of him.

"Arnie?" She stood just two feet before him now. The room hummed with silent expectation, and at last, the man's eyes captured hers.

"I'm sorry." His face crumpled and new tears spilled down his cheeks. "I didn't mean to-"

Erin surprised him - surprised herself - by walking straight to him and wrapping her arms around his waist, pressing herself close against him, feeling as if she never wanted to be away from him again.

43

MEET THE STALKERS

Neil Trinsky wiped his hands on his sweats. He was in the parking lot of the Icehouse Inn again, waiting. It was an exciting night. First, the dark-haired vampire couple had taken the Bat-Tat girl into the St. Germain; he'd trailed them. They were inside for at least an hour, and in that time, Neil's excitement grew so great that he'd fertilized a potted holly bush not once, but twice, while he waited.

Just as he was beginning to wonder if the vampires were in for the night, they reappeared, the couple still flanking Bat-Tat, but this time the little bitch of a redhead was walking freely between them, smiling and talking. There was something slightly different about her - she seemed paler, prettier - and Neil was sure he knew what it meant.

She's one of them, now. He thought about how Bat-Tat had behaved on the Ferris wheel, refusing him, laughing at him. *No wonder I thought she was a vampire - she wanted to be turned! Now she probably wants to turn me! She's stalking me!*

He'd waited until the trio was way ahead of him then followed them back to the Icehouse Inn. Now, hands smelling pleasantly of his own spunk, he saw the couple come out: Bat-Tat wasn't with them. They'd exited from the side door into the parking lot and were no more than ten feet away.

It's meant to be.

Screwing up his courage, patting his pockets to make sure the garlic cloves were still there, then pulling the crucifix out from under his sweatshirt, he stepped out from between the cars. "Stop right there, you dirty bloodsuckers!"

The man and woman paused, staring.

Neil held out the garlic, waving it their direction.

A smile crept onto the woman's lips. The man simply stared, impatience in his eyes.

Apparently, the garlic thing was a myth; Neil began feeling self-conscious. Stuffing the cloves back into his pocket, he advanced on them, the crucifix held out in front of him. The man-vamp seemed unnerved by this, but instead of cringing away, he grabbed Neil by the collar, lifted him off the ground, and brought him so close their noses almost touched.

Neil panicked. The crucifix clattered to the ground and the vampire kicked it away.

"Listen to me and listen well, young man," said the man-vamp. "You do not know who you're dealing with and if this harassment continues, you are going to make me very angry." His eyes, dead as a pair of burned-out headlamps, fixed on Neil's, piercing deep things inside him. Then those dead eyes flashed red.

Hot urine bloomed over the crotch of Neil's sweats and ran down both of his legs.

"Now stay away from us." The man spoke through gritted teeth, then hurled Neil into the air as easily and casually as if he were tossing an empty candy bar wrapper into the trash.

As Neil crashed into the nearby bushes, he thought he heard them laughing. And nothing made him angrier than being laughed at. *I'll kill you! All of you! TWICE!*

∽

"That idiot who tried to threaten us - he had an erection." Natasha grinned as she poured dollops of a nice domestic AB Neg into two brandy snifters. She handed one to Michael, who swirled the glass under his nose and smiled. "Indeed he did. And he worries me a bit."

"Why is that?" Natasha sat on the couch.

Michael joined her. "He's far more aggressive than the typical fangboy. When we first arrived, the boldness in his eyes concerned me somewhat. The way he watched us was atypical - but after this evening, I feel he is dangerous. Unhinged." He cleared his throat. "To old times." They toasted and sipped.

"True, but he's not *that* dangerous." Natasha chuckled. "You made him wet his pants."

"Indeed." Michael smiled. "Let's forget about him for now." His gaze flicked from her face to her body and back again.

His look sent a delicious shiver over Natasha. When Winter had phoned earlier, they were on the verge of reconsummating their relationship and as much as it frustrated her, she knew the interruption had been a good thing. *It wasn't the right time. Has that changed?* She was uncertain, but other things were on her mind now. "Michael, we need to talk about what happened tonight."

"You have no idea how badly I've wanted you, Natasha, but-"

"I meant what happened *after* that. We need to talk about Erin. And about my brother's phone call."

His relief was palpable. "Tell me about Stephen's call."

She'd already told him that Julian believed Amanda to be Incendarius; at least that was out of the way. "Julian and Amanda are arriving here tonight."

"What?"

"Stevie got a call from Julian's assistant. Amanda has bitten Julian; he's in her thrall. They're planning to be married during Biting Man."

"We can't let that happen. She'll destroy him."

"Exactly. Stevie wants us to stop her any way we can."

"And we shall. Where are they staying?"

"That's the problem." She explained about the hidden cabin. "Stevie says we may not be able to find them until they enter the Eternal City."

"That's certainly an option."

"Except that it would out Julian. He'd be mobbed."

"A second coming of the Prince of Blood. You're correct, Natasha. I'm given to understand that Julian has never wished to be a ruler."

Natasha refilled both their glasses. "That's correct." She sipped. "Right now, his will is imprisoned by Incendarius and he may not even know what he wants. Stevie says he will defend Amanda, even if he doesn't truly want to. He is not himself."

"It sounds like there's nothing we can do tonight, unless you want to alert V-Sec."

"No, not at this point. Julian and Amanda may not have even arrived yet. We need time to think about all this."

"Indeed, we do." Michael set his glass down and studied Natasha. "Now, what about Erin?"

"She mentioned that the people she's staying with will be looking for her. Fortunately, one of them is Coastal Eddie. We need to let them talk to her and see her, or they're likely to go to the sheriff." She paused. "My brother says Eddie is trustworthy–"

"Eddie Fortune, trustworthy? His intentions may be good, I'll grant you that, but the man spends his life on the radio talking about ghosts, UFOs, and vampires."

"I know. With the exception of one incident many years ago, he's never said a word about our family openly, and he's known all along. Has he ever spoken of the Crimson Cove vampires on the air?"

"No, he hasn't, and we do monitor the show. What are you proposing, Natasha?"

"Eddie knows vampires exist and, in his own way, he protects our clans by talking about Rogues and other undesirables, not about our legitimate communities."

Michael nodded. "Indeed, he's put us onto a Rogue or two before we knew about them ourselves. And I recall him making some very nasty innuendos about the Dantes before your family got rid of them."

Natasha smiled. "Those bastards had it coming." Just recalling their blatant attack on the Darling family and the hotel made her fangs twitch.

"Indeed." Michael raised his brows.

"Maybe we should double check with Stevie first, but I think we need to talk with Eddie before morning. Before they go to the sheriff."

Michael picked up the phone. "I'll let Winter know we're picking up Erin."

~

NORMAN KEELER, full of blood from a half-dead alky he'd encountered under a deserted pier was not only aware of the irony, he relished it. It was almost like some sort of karma. Now, logy with alcohol-laced blood, he looked around the deserted rental cabin where he'd spent the day. He was dismayed and annoyed that he had a headache - he thought being a vampire meant no more physical ills. But no, he was a little drunk and a little hungover. It was time to call it a night despite the fact that dawn was still a couple of hours away.

Doors secure, he slid under the bed. The windows were shuttered but he didn't want to take a chance on being hit by a stray sunbeam. He had turned four tricks and had plenty of cash for a hotel room, but hadn't wanted to risk being disturbed. Tomorrow night, he would be with the Woman. The one who had made him. He couldn't wait.

~

NEIL, EXHAUSTED, RETURNED TO DIMPLES' Boarding House. Happily, no one was awake, and he stalked upstairs, passing the other boarders' rooms. He heard Baldy snoring like a chainsaw and thought about stopping in to strangle him, but he knew better than to shit where you live.

After a shower, he stood in front of the bathroom mirror and admired his body. He had lost a couple of pounds since his arrival due to all the extra jogging he was doing, and it looked good on him. His pecs were more defined, and his high-cheekboned face had a sharp vulpine look that told people they'd better not mess with him.

Naked, he slipped between cool sheets that were only offensive if you looked at them - the Dimples' taste ran to apple pie and geese wearing bonnets - total stupid Americana - his sheets were printed with small, smiling cows. The Dimples deserved death for their bad taste, but then, most people did.

He lay in the darkness, faintly hearing Baldy's log-sawing, and fantasized about all the vampires - and maybe a few humans - he might kill tomorrow. After a time, he grew sleepy, and soon he was dreaming of pickles. Fat kosher dills so big his fists barely contained them. There were at least a dozen of them coming at him from all sides, and he took one after the other, bringing the thick wet pickles into his mouth, tickling their warty textures with his tongue and relishing the salty juices dripping down his chin.

He woke, soggy with sweat, and - he realized - other fluids. Raising the covers, he unstuck Neil Jr. from the smiling cows, wondering what had set the little guy off. He smiled at the Buffy tattoo rising from his sticky pubic forest. She seemed to smile back.

44

STRANGE RELATIONS

"My God, this hotel is a disaster." Natasha stared at the statue of Perdet Towers' founder, Harry Donaldson. First, she noticed all the fingerprints on the statue's groin - tourists had evidently been grabbing the Donaldson by the crotch for some time. She smiled, thinking about karma.

Michael grinned. "Do you suppose his hands are really that small?"

"You know what they say." Erin stared at the statue. "Small hands, small manhood."

"Small mind." Natasha chuckled. "Why did you choose this fleabag hotel, Erin?"

"It's all there was. Come on, Eddie and Lois are waiting for us upstairs."

Natasha's nose wrinkled as they entered the elevator; it smelled of ancient cigarettes, cheap vodka, spray-on tanning lotion, and urine. Michael looked pained, but it was nothing compared to Erin's expression.

"Oh my God, this place smells worse than I thought," she said. "I mean, it was funky before, but holy cow, with my new Spidey senses, it's beyond rank. No wonder it only has one star on Yelp."

"The good news is, you'll enjoy the fragrance of flowers and trees more now," Michael told her. "You'll be able to sense the smell of air in a cavern and differentiate it from other airs."

"And you'll either love the scent of the ocean more, or hate it." Natasha smiled as they left the elevator.

"I'll probably love it. I love the sea. This way."

Erin led them down a hall covered in - what else? - stained and threadbare gold carpeting. Toward the end of the hall, she knocked on a door and called, "We're here."

∽

"Erin, it's so good to see you! Eddie and I were worried sick!" Lois drew the girl to her and held her close, so happy that Erin hugged her back that she didn't pay any attention to the man and woman in the doorway.

Eddie ushered them into the room. "Ms. Darling," he said, shaking her hand. "It's a pleasure."

"Natasha. My brother tells me you've been quite helpful."

"I tried," he said as Lois and Erin joined them. Renny burst into the room and ran up to Erin, jumping, happy to see her safe and sound. She petted him, then the terrier greeted the other two visitors almost as enthusiastically.

"Michael Ward." Michael extended his hand and shook with Eddie, then Lois. "A pleasure."

"Won't you sit down?" Lois asked. "Would you like something to drink? Coffee?"

"No, thank you." Natasha smiled. "I never drink ... coffee."

Lois felt herself blushing. "I'm sorry, you seem so ... normal, that I forgot ... Anyway, your hotel in Candle Bay is so beautiful-"

"We all need to talk, Lois." Erin took her hand and led her to the ratty, stained sofa.

Worried, Lois sat down beside her. Erin looked a little different, somehow, but not in a bad way. She couldn't put her finger on it.

"I have news," Erin began.

"News?" Lois urged. "You didn't see Neil, did you?"

"No, it's not about Neil, but something happened to me tonight when I went jogging and Michael and Natasha saved me."

Lois felt a sudden chill. "Tell me."

Erin was silent a moment. "I was attacked. By a vampire. And I was … *bitten*."

Realization dawned slowly. Lois felt the blood drain from her face. She looked at Erin, taking in the subtle changes in the young woman's appearance. "You mean you're …"

"One of them now." Erin didn't seem upset. In fact, she seemed fine with it. So fine that Lois couldn't help wondering if the whole thing was a joke. She looked from Erin to Natasha, to Michael, and then to Eddie. No one smiled.

This was no joke. She watched Renny hop into Erin's lap and try to lick her face. "You couldn't be a vampire, Erin. It's a mistake. Renny wouldn't be on you-"

"There are many misconceptions about vampires, Lois." Michael's smile was gentle. "That animals dislike us is one of them."

"Really?"

"Well, it depends on the nature of the particular vampire. If a man was cruel to animals as a human, chances are animals will avoid him after Transition."

Natasha nodded. "Michael generally has a raven perched on his shoulder. I've never seen a bird and a man so in love."

Lois considered. "You know, that makes sense. Renny has never been affectionate with Neil. That's my son. He's not very nice and Renny knows it."

Eddie cleared his throat. "Her son is why we're here. I wonder if you might have seen him. He intends to crash Biting Man."

Natasha laughed. "If you came here to stop him, you needn't have. Security is tight - he can't get in."

"We came because he stole my car," Lois explained.

"I'm sorry," Natasha said. "What does your son look like?"

Lois glanced at Eddie, who took her cue. "Nice looking, thirty-two years old, but appears younger, dark shoulder-length hair, maybe five foot eight, in good shape. Very intense."

Natasha and Michael exchanged glances. "We may have seen him. A very bold individual?"

"Yes." Lois sat forward. "When?"

"Twice," Michael said. "Once when we arrived, and again earlier this evening. He approached us and was quite rude."

"Michael had words with him," Natasha added.

"Just words?" Lois asked.

"I didn't bite him if that's what you mean."

"I - I'm sorry. I guess that's what I meant. I don't mean to insult you, it's just-"

"I'm not insulted; I understand your concern. We do not bite people. Our sustenance is bottled."

"Michael *did* cause him to wet himself." Natasha smiled.

Lois looked from Michael to Natasha. "Well, he probably had that coming."

"Almost certainly," Eddie agreed. "Where did you see him?"

"He was lurking in the parking lot of the Icehouse Inn."

Lois glanced at Eddie. "That's where we spotted him, too."

He nodded.

"I've decided to press charges, even though he's my son," Lois explained. "After stealing my car, he ran it over a cliff. We'll tell the sheriff you saw him, too."

"Don't mention us, please," Natasha said. "We prefer not to have anything to do with human law enforcement."

"At any rate, I doubt he's staying at the Icehouse Inn." Michael scratched his jaw. "What's his name?"

"Neil. Neil Trinsky." Worry consumed Lois.

Eddie looked at the vampires. "I promise we won't mention you."

"Thank you."

"I do think you're right to have him arrested," Michael added. "I'm sorry to say this, but if it was your son we encountered earlier, he's unstable and probably violent."

Lois nearly cried. Erin took her hand and squeezed it. A mix of emotions filled her - sorrow as well as relief that Neil was no longer her secret to keep.

Michael and Natasha stood up. "It's getting very late. We need to get back to our hotel."

Erin rose.

"You're leaving, too?" Lois asked.

"I have to."

"You can stay here if you want, sweetheart."

"I would, Lois, but you don't really want me to sleep in that disgusting closet all day, do you?"

"What?"

"What Erin is trying to say is that some things you've heard about vampires are true," Natasha explained. "We do avoid sunlight and rest during the day. It wouldn't be safe for Erin to stay here."

"So this is it?" Lois asked.

Michael pulled out a St. Germain Hotel business card and wrote on it. "No, of course not. You can reach us here. That's our room number. After dusk, please."

"Thank you." Lois took the card then turned to Erin and hugged her. "I feel like I'm losing a daughter."

Erin hugged back. "You're not losing a daughter. You're gaining a vampire. A friendly one. I'll probably see you tomorrow night." She paused, staring at the beds. "If I were you, I wouldn't touch those bedspreads. They're disgusting."

"What?" Lois didn't understand.

"She's right," said Natasha. "Vampire vision encompasses the infrared range. Those bedspreads have more bodily fluids on them then you can imagine."

After the trio left, Eddie shut the door and turned to Lois. "How're you doing?"

"Frankly, I feel like I'm going crazy."

"I don't blame you a bit." Eddie smiled. "I could use a hug."

Lois held her arms out. "Me, too."

45

NO SHOES, NO SERVICE

"Jesus, Julie, why don't we just go stay in a hotel?"

"There will be nothing available."

"Oh, that's ridiculous. You're their king, you can get us a room, easy as pie."

Amanda batted her lashes, but it had little effect on him. "I am no one's king, my dear. I was once a prince, but I abdicated and no one will know of me," he lied. "My cabin is very comfortable."

"Nonsense. Everyone will know you and you're going to be a king, not a prince. And I will be queen!"

Julian cringed, unable to bring himself to argue. "Please, drive slower! The paint is getting scratched."

In the dark, he saw her roll her eyes as she slowed the slightest bit. He'd directed Amanda onto a hidden dirt road so narrow that tree limbs constantly scratched the Acura. This was only the first leg of several twisting tracks that would lead to the virtually invisible footpath to his stone cabin. The only signs of the path were cryptic marks on stones and trees that his trusted workers used when they visited twice a year to perform maintenance.

A branch pushed the passenger side mirror out of position. "Please, my love, slow down. It's fortunate we didn't lose that mirror."

"Oh, Julie, you worry too much!" Amanda punched on the CD player, bringing the sweet strains of Mozart's *Jupiter Symphony* to his ears. "God, why don't you have any CDs of *real* music in here? Some Britney or Christina? Or some Beyoncé, for Christ's sake. We've got to get you into some *modern* music." She shut the music off.

"To me, my dear, Mozart is modern. I do enjoy the Beatles as well. When you've lived as long as I have-"

"Fuck the Beatles, Julie. YAWN! They're so overrated! And aren't they dead yet?"

"There are some remaining members, but-"

"Jesus Christ, isn't there *anyone* in this godforsaken world who *doesn't* worship the fucking Beatles?"

"I suppose you would have us all bow to the feet of pop princesses such as Britney Spears - who, by the way is not as current an artist as she was when you were turned. We all tend to-"

"I know, I know, you told me already. We all tend to stick to the eras we liked as humans, but at least Britney, Christina, and Beyoncé are interesting to *look* at. Aside from those ridiculous hairdos, the Beatles were as boring then as they are now, a hundred and fifty fucking years later."

"I have seen the Beatles perform. And Mozart conduct. I assure you their talents exceed those of Ms. Spears."

"Oh, shut up, Julie! You wouldn't know good music if it sat on your face and wiggled."

"Slow down. There's a trail coming up on the left. You need to turn there." He could find nothing else to say - and it infuriated him. *How can she hold such sway over me? How can I feel anything but contempt for her?*

But he could not deny the attraction. He would do anything for her. *Even though I don't want to.* "There's the turn."

She shot right past it, and giggled. "Oops." Slamming on the brakes, she threw the Acura into reverse, then made the turn, quickly speeding up again even though this pine-needle covered path was even narrower than the first one.

She has bewitched me. Incendarius has glamoured me. I must resist. I must not allow her manipulations. "Slow down, my love, turn right just past that big boulder. It's a *very* tight turn."

"No shit, Sherlock! Why didn't you warn me sooner?" She careened onto the final track.

The door raked against the rock; metal screamed. Julian cringed.

Amanda laughed, then sped up again. "How many points for a coyote?"

He saw the animal just before she tried to smash it. "Why did you do that, Amanda? Have you no respect for life?"

She snorted. "You're a fucking Trueborn, Julie, and you ask *me* that?"

I need to distance myself from her, from her influence. I need help. He thought of Natasha Darling, who would be at a hotel in town. He cleared his throat. "We're going to come to a copse of six fir trees in a moment. Park among them. We will proceed on foot from there."

"On foot? Why?"

"The cabin is hidden. No road can take us there. It's not a long walk." The walk was three miles, but he kept that to himself.

A moment later, they parked. She started to take the keys from the ignition. "Leave them. No one will disturb the vehicle. I would rather the keys remain with it than risk losing them. It's many miles to walk to Eternity." He decided exaggeration was in order. "Likely a full night."

She eyed him dubiously.

"If we lose the keys, it would delay our marriage, my love."

She leaned over and pecked his cheek. "You're so romantic, Julie. Okay, let's go." She opened her door and Julian opened his.

For an instant, he heard crickets; they silenced as they passed, then began again. He saw the trees in detail with his Trueborn eyes. There were animals all around - a doe and a fawn watched them from behind a clutch of bushes. He glanced at Amanda; she seemed unaware, and he wondered how her night vision and hearing compared to his.

They walked on. At first, she put her arm through his, but after the trail got rougher, she withdrew it to climb over rocks and push branches out of the way. After about a mile, she stopped walking and sat on a boulder. Removing a stiletto, she rubbed her foot. "I wish I'd worn my sneakers. Julie, why didn't you tell me we had to hike?"

"I'm sorry, Amanda. I should have."

"Well, you could have said something. I left my walking shoes in the car."

Julian smiled, trying to look sympathetic. "Why don't you rest here, my love? I will go back and fetch them for you."

She looked at him. "Really? But it'll take forever."

"Not at all. I am Trueborn. I can move so quickly that you'll barely know I'm gone."

"Okay. There are three pairs of sneakers in there. I want the black ones, the Nikes with the purple shoelaces."

"I shall fetch them." He turned.

"Wait a minute, Julie." She removed her other stiletto then waved both shoes at him. "Here, take these back with you. I can't take another step in them."

"Yes, of course." Julian's smile was quite real.

"Don't be long, okay, Julie?"

"I promise I will be very quick. You're sure you'll be all right by yourself, my love?"

"What could happen to me?"

"Nothing. I dare say that even a mountain lion would stay out of your way."

"I'd kill it and drain it before it could touch me. Now go, Julie. Just hurry."

"Your wish is my command."

He ran.

~

AMANDA SAT RUBBING her feet as she waited for Julie. She was bored, and she hated this business of having to spend the night in his cabin, but dawn was nearing. Julian was a bore; too proper, too old-fashioned, but he had what she wanted - he would be king.

She pulled her travel-sized mouthwash bottle from her pocket and had a small sip of Lixir. Instantly, she felt better. "Hurry up, Julie," she whispered. "Your queen is waiting."

And then, in the distance, she heard an engine roar to life and a vehicle began moving, the sounds quickly receding.

She stood up, her bare feet tender against pine needles and pebbles, and screamed, "JULIAN, YOU SON OF A BITCH! GET YOUR ASS BACK HERE!"

But Julian did not return.

~

JUST BEFORE DAWN, someone pounded on the door of Natasha and Michael's suite. As she came out of her bedroom, Michael came from his. "Who could that be?"

"I have no idea, but we'd best answer it." Natasha unlocked the door and peered out. Julian Valentyn, looking surprisingly unkempt, peered at her. "Excuse me for intruding, Natasha, but I am on the lam, as it were. May I spend the day here?"

46

BANANAS FROM PACOIMA

It took Neil fifteen minutes to escape Martha Ann Dimples, who insisted he join the rest of the boarders at the long dining table for breakfast. They were all there, like a Norman Rockwell painting, except instead of a turkey, old Martha Ann was holding a platter of bacon and sausage. The aroma made Neil's traitorous stomach growl, but he held steady, sitting down between Baldy and a spotty woman in a big gray wig and a floral pastel dress who smelled of elderberry wine and cigars. Her name was Miss Finch and she told him she was a schoolteacher. Neil feigned politeness the best he could while he ate a few slices of melon and two big blue grapes that looked like squirrel testicles. He thought Baldy was staring at him, but when Neil rose, it turned out the old fart was staring at the spotty woman. *Old, smelly lust. Keep it in your pants, you shriveled up gasbag.* He'd hidden his thoughts behind a smile and got the holy fuck out of there, Martha Ann behind him, trying to force him to take along a cinnamon roll as big as his head. *What are you trying to do, poison me?* It was all he could do to keep from punching her in her stupid face.

After leaving Dimples' Boarding House, he jogged to Main Street. He had a big yen for a dill pickle and he went straight to Kissel's Pickles, but the store wouldn't open for another hour. He trotted down the street to the True Grace All-Natural Market and waited around, tapping his foot, until Elvis showed up, ten minutes past the posted opening time. The weirdo, dressed in cowboy-esque 50s Elvis togs, grinned. "You're my first customer of the day." He unlocked the door and stood back, allowing Neil to enter first.

"What can I get you, son? Organic bananas from the wilds of South America? Fresh blueberries straight from Snapdragon, California? Perhaps some tofu-"

"From Pacoima, I know, I know."

Elvis laughed. "Not from Pacoima. From-"

"I want a pickle. A big kosher dill. Straight from your pickle barrel."

Elvis went behind the deli counter. "Let's see what I have." He opened the cold case behind him and peered inside. "I'm sorry, friend. My cupboard is bare - but I'm expecting a shipment before noon."

"A shipment? Why don't you just get them from Kissel's Pickles? I thought you got them locally."

"Not quite that local. I believe in giving my customers what they want at a decent price. If I bought them from Bill Kissel, I'd have to charge twice as much just to cover my cost." Elvis' lip twitched. "And I do believe in buying local. My pickles are crafted in Crimson Cove, a little town in the Santa Cruz Mountains-"

"Yeah, yeah, yeah. Crimson Cove is a vampire breeding ground - I wouldn't want pickles that come from there. Or from Candle Bay, for that matter." Neil watched Elvis' twitchy lip, knowing the guy was getting pissed off, and enjoying it to no end. *He might be fun to kill. I could shove one of his fucking blue suede shoes down his throat. And a pickle up his ass.*

"Mr., uh-"

"Call me Neil. Like in Neil Diamond, the best singer ever born."

Elvis didn't take the bait. "Neil, I don't know much about vampires, but aren't you here because ... for the, uh-"

"Biting Man?"

"Yeah."

"I just want to get a look at the filthy bloodsuckers. Size up the enemy, know what I mean?" Neil Jr. woke up and he adjusted himself.

"Most people who get wind of Biting Man are fans of vampires. We rarely have any, uh-"

"Vampire hunters?"

"Yeah, those are rare."

"Vampires cower when I'm around." Neil slid a snakey smile onto his lips and artfully cocked one eyebrow. He watched Elvis, noting the look of concern flitting over his face before the man hid it with a lazy grin.

"Different strokes, I guess. So, Neil, can I get you anything else? I can whip you up an egg white and tofu burrito real quick."

Neil shook his head then glanced at his watch. Kissel's would be opening soon. "Gotta go," he told the idiot behind the counter. "Catch you later."

As he pushed the door open, he heard Elvis say, all snarky-like, "And Neil has left the building."

He let the door slam behind him. *Stupid fucking douchebag can't even keep his store stocked. Vampire pickles. Stupid little bitch.*

He took off at a jog, going the long way around Main Street to kill time before arriving at Kissel's. The circular street was already busy with tourists, some wearing ridiculous Dracula capes, some still window shopping for their costumes, others jogging like himself. He wanted to stake them all.

Most shops were open by the time he rounded the far end of the oblong street on the last leg to the pickle store. When he got to the corner where Kissel's was located, he followed a whim and turned off, heading into the rear parking lot.

Bingo. Flournoy Grebble of the jolting Adam's apple was unlocking the backdoor. An old teal Honda Civic was the only car in the lot. It was warm, the engine still ticking.

"Mr. Grebble?" Neil called, his voice as warm and welcoming as milk and cookies.

Flournoy turned, his thyroid eyes bulging at Neil, making him look more like a guppy than a man. "Uh, can I help you?"

"I'm Neil, remember?"

Flournoy looked him up and down. "Not sure - there are a lot of tourists in town right now and-"

"Not to worry, I understand." Behind his smile, Neil saw red. *How could this sorry little bitch forget* me? *Fucking jerkwad.* "You helped me choose some pickles the other day."

"I did? I hope you're pleased with your purchase."

"I'm so pleased that I already ate them all and need more. You could say I have a craving for them."

Flournoy's wide, thin smile and long, scrawny neck made him look like a ventriloquist's dummy. "Just so long as you aren't craving ice cream, too." His Adam's apple bobbed as he yucked it up.

Neil, proud of his ability to keep his temper, managed to crack a smile. "I know it's early, but do you think you could let me come in? I just need a big kosher dill from your barrel."

Flournoy looked him up and down. "I guess it'd be okay this once. My boss wouldn't approve, but he won't be here for an hour." He stepped inside and waited for Neil to follow him into the fragrant building. "Turn the deadbolt, would you?"

"With pleasure." Neil looked around the workroom. It smelled delightfully of vinegar, dill, and exotic spices. Ropes of garlic hung near a massive commercial stove and a glass jar full of dried red peppers sat on the counter. Boxes of pickling cucumbers - from midget to humongous - filled one wall. A huge pickle barrel, enamel-lined, stood empty by the worktable. "Are you going to fill that with pickles?"

"We are. You can't beat pickles made the old-fashioned way."

"How do you do it?"

"Well, you have to pour in the brining solution and add the spices and herbs and seal it all up for a month or two. Check this out." Flournoy opened a massive refrigerator. "Ever see so much dill in your life?"

Masses of ferny dill filled an entire shelf, awaiting its fate. The smell woke Neil Jr. right up again. Neil adjusted himself and beneath the vinegary perfume, caught a whiff of his own briny sauce. He'd jerked off earlier today and wondered if Flournoy detected the scent of his musty dried man-seed. This thought only aroused him further and this time, when his cock began to stretch and stiffen, he did nothing to hide it. "What's in all those tall pots?" Most of the other refrigerator shelves were lined with them.

"Brine, all ready to go." Flournoy grinned.

"So you just pour the brine in with the cucumbers, right?" Neil backed against the barrel, jutting his hips out, proudly displaying his raging hard-on.

"That's it. We also add garlic and-" Flournoy's already bugging eyes strained as if trying to escape their sockets when his gaze landed on the front of Neil's tented sweatpants.

"Pretty impressive, isn't it?" Neil cocked a crooked smile.

Flournoy's Adam's apple jitterbugged.

"There's just something about pickles that really tickles *my* pickle, you know what I mean?" Neil gave himself a squeeze.

"I - um ... I'm not gay, young man."

Neil's jaw tightened. "You think I'm a queer? I'm not a fucking queer! *You're* a queer, you queer!" Enraged, he pushed himself off the barrel and went at the guy, wrapping his hands around Grebble's scrawny neck.

Flournoy gasped for breath, his eyeballs all but popping from his head.

"Queer!" Neil squeezed and shook Flournoy's bobble-head back and forth. "Queer, queer, *QUEER!*"

Flournoy grasped at Neil's hands but his own thin fingers and limp wrists were no match for Neil's hard-earned strength. If the guy had had a purse, Neil was sure he'd be trying to beat him with it. "QUEER!"

Flournoy sputtered.

Neil let off the pressure. "You want to say something, queer?"

"Please! Stop!" Grebble's voice was a raspy gasp, his larynx half-broken already.

But Neil didn't stop. And he'd heard enough from this cock-gobbler to last a lifetime. He found the man's Adam's apple and pressed inward with his thumb, using all the considerable strength in his hands.

Flournoy's eyes bulged with panic and his arms flailed.

Neil pushed and pushed until, finally, something popped and Flournoy's insect-looking face turned blue before his arms fell uselessly to his sides. Neil let go and Flournoy crumpled to the ground like a woman with the vapors. *A dead woman with the vapors.*

"Call *me* a queer." Neil spoke between heavy breaths. He spat on the corpse, then rolled it over onto its stomach. Looking around, he retrieved a huge cucumber from a nearby box, jerked the dead man's pants down, and shoved it deep into Flournoy's ass crack, pushing hard until he felt the sphincter give. Neil did the same to the man's mouth and when Flournoy had a great big warty cucumber jutting from each end, Neil hefted him into the empty barrel.

Flournoy's bulging eyeballs stared in dead disbelief as Neil poured pot after pot of brine into the barrel, then added a bouquet of garlic and topped it all with a bouquet of dill. As Flournoy Grebble sat pickling, Neil reached into his sweatpants and gave Neil Jr. what he wanted. His man-sauce floated lazily just above Flournoy's submerged head.

After just a few strokes, Neil washed his hands then found the barrel lid and pounded it on, before using a dolly to take the keg into the store and hide it among the others. Smiling, he helped himself to a pickle - a big fat one - and let himself out back, careful to wipe his prints away.

Outside, Main Street was still fairly quiet, so he strolled, his appetite for killing even stronger than his appetite for pickles. And that was saying something. But when he smelled Poppin Fresh's bakery and saw the sheriff's SUV out front, he left the main drag, taking the backstreets toward Dimples' Boarding House. In his haste to leave, he hadn't brought his backpack and if he was going to take down a few more sleeping vampires, he needed his stakes and mallet, his silver crucifix and other implements of destruction.

47

INSOMNIA

Julian, tired but unable to fall asleep despite the daylight, cracked the door to his bedroom - Michael had insisted he take his room - and peered into the suite's living area. After closing the room-darkening drapes, Michael and Natasha had fallen heavily asleep on the couch, resting against one another in a familiar, comfortable way that stirred odd feelings in the Trueborn. They looked right together; it was subtly - but significantly - different from his intimacy with Amanda. He envied them that, even as he felt a longing for Incendarius. And a loathing.

He realized his inability to sleep had to do with worry. He had deserted Amanda, shoeless and miles from the road, and he knew she would not forgive him. He closed his door and locked it, knowing it wouldn't be long before Incendarius found a way to town. To him. *Rest while you can,* he told himself. *You will have to deal with her soon.*

He knew she wouldn't try to kill him for his transgression, at least not until after they were wed, but he also understood he was in danger until he could destroy her. *Will I even be able to destroy her?*

He truly did not know, but as he sat down in a chair across from the sleeping couple, a line from a Beatles song gave him hope. *I get by with a little help from my friends.*

❦

THE SIMPLE CABIN was nothing that a king or queen ought to be caught dead in. Amanda licked Lixir from her lips, glad that she'd finally found the building. She would see that Julian paid for his tricks. *How dare he leave me alone in the woods!* She shook her mouthwash bottle: the Lixir was more than half gone, and she'd have to be careful and wait for evening before heading for town.

There was nothing whatsoever interesting about the stone-sided cabin. Wood floors, plastered walls, beamed ceilings and a stone hearth, cold and black like Julie's heart. The living room had sheeted furniture and she ripped one cloth back to reveal an overstuffed easy chair. *Plaid! What is the matter with him?* She spat on the offensive seat and figured that Julie was probably trying to fit in with the plebes. *He couldn't like this mess, could he?*

She walked into a small sparse kitchen and rifled around in the cabinets, looking for something to drink. Finally, she found a dusty bottle of AB Neg at the rear of a bottom shelf. Smiling, she withdrew it, searched the drawers for a bottle opener, and at last, pulled a butcher knife from a drawer and sliced off the top of the bottle. Blood spattered the walls and hit her face like tasty little raindrops. She lifted the bottle and gulped down half before continuing her explorations.

The bedroom wasn't bad, at least if you were only looking to spend the day there en route to a luxury hotel. Flopping across the white down bedcover, she finished the bottle then let the dregs stain the quilt. "Serves you right, Julie, you fucker."

Checking out the closet and drawers, she found one of Julie's satin robes. "This'll do." She stripped and took the robe into the bathroom, pausing to admire the room. "Now, this is more like it." The bath was luxurious with a huge waterfall shower and an oversized whirlpool tub. She turned on the faucets and filled the tub, flipped on the jets and sank into the warm bubbling water. *This is more like it.*

❦

"I WANT TO PRESS CHARGES," Lois told Zach Tully.

That was the last thing Tully had expected to hear when she and Coastal Eddie entered the King's Tart. He'd nodded an innocent hello, and they'd taken that as an invitation to join him. Tully looked at his cream-filled donut and sighed. It was going to be a long day. "Charges against your son?"

Lois nodded.

Eddie cleared his throat. "Maybe we should talk with the sheriff after he's had breakfast."

"Oh, yes, of course. I'm sorry, Sheriff."

Her expression was so sincere that Tully relented. "Why don't you try one of Harlan's pastries and have some coffee? Then we'll talk."

Harlan came out from behind swinging doors, a platter of donuts and a pot of coffee in hand. As always, he'd been listening.

"On the house," the baker announced, a smile decorating his rosy-cheeked face.

Tully watched Lois and Eddie choose donuts - chocolate glazed for her, an orange-frosted cake donut with colorful sprinkles for him. Lois took her coffee black, while Eddie liked it white and sweet. Very sweet. Tully nearly gagged as he watched the deejay dump enough sugar in his coffee to put an elephant into a diabetic coma.

Harlan nodded at Tully then disappeared into the kitchen, giving the civilians a false sense of privacy. It was best that way.

Tully finished his donut and folded his hands. "So you've changed your mind about pressing charges against your son, Ms. Trinsky?"

"Lois. Yes, I have. I realize I can't let him get away with what he's done. Stealing my car, destroying it ..."

"I think it's a good idea, Lois. Do you have any idea where he's staying?"

She shook her head. Eddie cleared his throat. "Last night, we were out for a walk and thought we saw him outside the Icehouse Inn."

"We aren't positive, though," Lois added.

"We'll find him," Tully assured them. "We'll be arresting him for theft and destruction of stolen property. He'll go to jail."

Lois nodded. "That's where he needs to be."

Tully, relieved, knew Lois wasn't going to back down. He pulled the photo of Neil she'd given him from his breast pocket. "How old is this photo?"

"About five years. His hair is long now, but he usually keeps it in a ponytail, so he pretty much looks the same as he did back then." She paused. "Sheriff?"

"Yes?"

"Neil can be ... violent. I mean, I don't know if he's actually violent, but he makes a lot of threats and he's very jealous. He frightens me."

"I understand," Tully told her. "If it helps, you're doing the right thing."

"I know. It's hard, though."

Across the table, Eddie patted Lois' hand.

"Where are you staying?"

"The Perdet Towers."

Tully hid a cringe. "I'll be in touch."

He watched them leave. They looked like an ordinary couple as they walked out onto Main Street. Tully wished Lois Trinsky didn't have such a weight on her shoulders on this beautiful, clear and breezy day.

Harlan returned with fresh coffee and more donuts and sat down across from Tully. "Poor woman."

Tully looked at the photo. "I've gotta say, I'm going to enjoy arresting him."

The entry bells jangled and Elvis walked in. "You two look as thick as thieves. Harlan, I ran out of bran muffins. Any chance you'd sell me some?"

"Carrot-raisin okay?" Harlan rose.

"Perfect. Thanks." He gave Tully one of his sleepy grins. "Ever try Harlan's muffins?"

"Not the healthy kind," Tully admitted as he finished another donut.

"They're delicious. So, who's that?" He nodded at the photo.

Tully handed it to him. "Neil Trinsky. I believe you've met?"

Elvis whistled, low. "Sure have. He was in this morning again. That's one weird guy, if you ask me."

"Tell me."

"Chip on his shoulder as big as Kentucky. I don't like him. First thing this morning he came in wanting a dill pickle. He was waiting for me."

"A pickle for breakfast?"

Elvis shook his head. "Takes all kinds. He bothers me, though. Got righteously pissed when I said I was out of them. Wanted to be sure I bought local, so I told him my pickles come from Crimson Cove. You know what he said?"

"Not a clue."

"That he wouldn't buy pickles from a place like that because it's a hotbed of vampires."

Tully nodded. "So what did he do?"

Harlan came back and handed Elvis a big pink box of muffins. "Thirty-six hold you?"

"You bet, thanks." Elvis nodded at the photo. "Neil was headed for Kissel's last I saw him. You know, he told me he's a vampire hunter. Takes himself seriously, too. I'll be glad to see that boy leave town. You keeping an eye on him? Has he been threatening our visitors?"

"I'm looking to arrest him."

"Did he harm uh...?"

"Not that I know of. He stole his mother's car."

"A real charmer, that one," Harlan said.

"Sure is."

"Elvis, do you have any idea where he's staying?"

"Dimples' Boarding House. I sent him there myself."

༄

"You're all going to die." Neil stood in the park behind a big holly plant and watched Poppin Fresh's bakery through a cheap pair of binoculars he'd bought at a tourist shop near Kissel's. First, the donut-loving sheriff went in and a few minutes later, that fucking queer Coastal Eddie and Mom walked in and sat down with the sheriff, and had some kind of deep conversation. And when they left, in came Crazy Elvis. They were all looking at a photo or something.

He knew they were talking about him. *Knew* it. *Mom must be worrying herself sick by now, the little bitch. She's looking for me. Well, she's not going to find me! Let her worry! She deserves to worry.* This made him smile. It was about time his dear mother found out what it was like to be ignored - *the way* she's *ignored* me *my whole life!*

Against his own will images of his mother, on her knees, sucking Coastal Eddie's queer cock, invaded him, filling his brain and invading every cell in his body. Neil Jr. twitched as he envisioned her licking a pearl of man-dew off the tip of Eddie's tool. But this image quickly brought a new, stronger emotion: pure, black, unadulterated rage.

That fucking whore! How long has she been fucking him anyway? That dirty whoring little bitch! Neil envisioned that, and after another twitch beneath the belt, he decided it was time to do something about this nonsense once and for all.

But first, he needed to clear out of the boarding house.

48

ROUND ABOUT TOWN

At midday in Eternity, Hotel Circle was quiet. A few tourists strolled the sidewalk, searching for lunch, costumes, or souvenirs, but most of the hotels' clientele remained in their rooms, awaiting sunset. At the Icehouse Inn, Winter and Arnie slept soundly in their room; Erin shared Chynna's room, and the Darling twins, Lucy and Ivy, were blessedly gone, having opted to spend the day with their cousin Daisy in a cabin hidden from the view of all but the most knowledgeable denizens of Eternity. Michael and Natasha continued their peaceful sleep on the couch in their suite at the St. Germain, unaware that Julian, too caught up in worry over Amanda's Incendarius capabilities to sleep, watched over them.

∽

AFTER MEETING WITH SHERIFF TULLY, Lois and Eddie took a tour of Icehouse Circle, then had come back to eat lunch at a dog-friendly outdoor cafe on Main Street, happy to be away from the peeling Perdet Towers. Now they were in the park where they played fetch with Renny and tried to forget the troubles that loomed ahead. It didn't work. Lois could think of nothing except her son and what would become of him. She smiled at Eddie as he tossed a frisbee for Renny. She liked the deejay, and though she knew it was her relationship with him - however innocent - that had caused Neil to go over the top, she had no regrets. It was nice to have a friend. It had been years since she'd been able to have any kind of relationship with anyone. *Except Neil.* She wondered where her son was now, and what he was up to.

∼

NEIL'S only regret in leaving Dimples' Boarding House, was that he hadn't had time to murder any of the boarders before departing. He had carried his few possessions in his pack as he hiked a series of back trails. Finally, he found an empty cabin to make his new base of operations.

He came upon it after only an hour and broke in easily, half-disappointed that there were no vampires to slay. The cabin was small but nicer than the boarding house, and the power was on. Now, he hid his possessions and made ready to go out on another daytime hunt.

∼

IN THEIR HUGE cabin a few streets away from the town square, the Kohlkophs slept soundly, their bulbous heads resting heavily on their massive pillows. And not one of them didn't snore. This struck Davy and his Plastic Taffy bandmates as a very peculiar vampire fact - he'd always assumed that vampires slept like the dead - but the Kohlkophs sawed wood like lumberjacks.

After taking a small sip, Mick passed the half-full sixteen-ounce bottle of Lixir to Davy, who did the same. The stuff was oily and thick, but not at all unpleasant. Someone had left it behind in the auditorium inside the mountain. Davy suspected it belonged to the Kohlkophs but wasn't sure. All he knew was that they had to keep it hidden - and they had to make it last. They all had to try hard to keep their minds off of Amanda. The blood helped.

"Hey man, don't Bogart that shit." Paul scowled and Davy passed it over.

They'd been careful with it, sipping just enough to keep them awake during daylight hours, and it occurred to Davy that they really ought to be doing something fun if they were going to be up all day. He looked over at Mick, who scratched his balls and yawned, and wondered when they'd become so old and boring. Even undead, they were like a group of old ladies sitting around sipping sherry and playing bridge.

"This sucks," Davy said.

Three heads swiveled to face him.

"What sucks?" asked Paul.

"This." Davy made an expansive gesture with his hands. "All of this. We're acting like a bunch of old women. We're rock stars for Christ's sake! And vampires, to boot!"

Heads nodded agreement and they murmured among themselves.

"We should be out there, stirring shit up and having fun!"

"But what about the bobble-heads?" asked Paul. "They said to stay put."

Davy shrugged. "Since when do we care about following the rules? Plastic Taffy is all about breaking rules, man! Remember when the record label told us we had to be the boys next door and we wore eyeliner and faux-hawks on stage just to spite them? That's the Plastic Taffy *I* remember!"

Heads nodded.

"That was like, last week, man." Mick scratched again. "We could go streaking."

Davy sighed. Mick always wanted to go streaking.

"No. Something better than that, something ... *dangerous*."

"Like the time we threw our poop from a hotel room window at the police?" asked Mick.

Davy rolled his eyes. "No, something *way* more dangerous than that."

"Then what did you have in mind?" That was Ramon.

Davy considered, then an idea began to form, weak and anemic at first, then bright and hard. Brilliant as a diamond. "I've got it." A sly grin slid onto his lips. "Let's take the Lixir and go party with some vampire chicks!"

"Far out!" Ramon grinned.

"Guys?" Paul said, rubbing his chin. "Do you think we cum blood now?"

"Definitely not." Mick patted his package. "Definitely not. I checked."

∼

AMANDA, pruny from her long bath, drummed her fingers. There was nothing to do in the cabin - Julie had no television or magazines, just a few shelves of boring old books. Classics. *Reading is such a waste of time!*

She looked into the wooded shade beyond the window. It was still too early to head for town - she wasn't even sure she had enough Lixir left to see her through until dusk. "But I'm going to lose my mind in this boring fucking cabin!"

She paced, considered napping, paced some more. *Damn you, Julie!* "Damn you! You'll pay for this!"

∼

"FLOURNOY? FLOURNOY? WHERE ARE YOU?" Bill Kissel shut the back door of his pickle shop and strode out onto the sales floor. His assistant hadn't opened this morning, and that wasn't like him. "Flournoy Grebble? Where are you? Answer me!"

He nearly opened for business then decided it would be better to find his employee first. "Flournoy?" He reentered the workroom and that's when he noticed the pickle barrel was missing. *What's this!*

He opened the refrigerator and found it full of brine pots - but when he touched them, he realized they were empty. Had Flournoy done the keg of pickles himself? Anything was possible, he supposed, but it would be a first. Flournoy was good at following directions, but not at taking the initiative. He glanced at the crates of pickling cucumbers, but none seemed to be missing.

In his long, long lifetime, Bill Kissel had seen and done it all, and now he turned and reentered the shop itself, his eyes scanning for an extra barrel. He spotted it within moments, nearly hidden by two others.

With a grunt, the big man wrestled the heavy barrel out. A moment later, he had the lid off and was staring down at the scalp of his assistant, whose thin hair waved like scant seaweed in the brine. A bouquet of dill tickled the man's cheek.

"Oh, my."

49

SEX AND VIOLENCE

Inside a cabin on a back road just outside of town, Neil pulled his dagger from the dirty vampire's chest. The blade scraped bone as it slid free - a sound that made him hungry for more. Neil held the knife up, watching as a drop of ruby blood dripped from the wet glistening tip of the blade onto the hardwood floor. This was his second slaying. Neil Jr. twitched. If there was any such thing as God, He would be pleased.

But Neil wasn't satisfied. It might have been because the sleeping vamp hadn't given him any challenge at all, but more likely, it was that his inner nature, so long repressed, had finally awakened and was rampaging like a wild beast. He wished he knew how to satisfy it - to scratch that ever-elusive itch that compelled him on. And on.

As he rinsed the blade in the bathroom sink, he caught a glimpse of himself in the mirror. His hair looked amazing - but he'd changed. His eyes were wilder now, his features harder than they'd been just days before. It was only his nose that threw off his face. It was delicate and ... *cute*. Even if a lot of chicks had complimented him on it, he fucking hated it. It was his mother's nose.

He thought of her again, on her knees, choking on Coastal Eddie's great big queer tool. He didn't know why he thought Eddie was packing some serious pipe – the deejay just had that look about him, Neil supposed. *And she likes it. My mom likes his great big dick!* Thick, black rage bubbled under his skin. *Fucking whore.* But as he vigorously rinsed the knife, Neil Jr. stiffened. *I'll bet he pulls her hair while she sucks it. Maybe even calls her his dirty little girl. And after that, he probably bends her over and slams it into her till she screams.* Neil hoped it hurt like hell. He smiled. *He probably smacks her ass while he rams her, too.* Neil Jr. was raging now. He looked down and frowned, torn between fury and ecstasy. His balls had grown heavy and full and the need was upon him.

As he unzipped, it briefly occurred to him what he was about to do: Masturbate to thoughts of his mother – and a queer! *Well, what other fucking choice do I have?* There was no other choice. His cock was raging, demanding satisfaction, and though he knew he'd feel dirty and ashamed later, he began stroking. *This is* YOUR *fault, Mom! Look at what* you're *making me do!*

Even as his pleasure mounted, his anger rose, reaching a boil as he drew closer and closer to bliss. Though Neil was usually a speeding bullet, it took a little longer this time – probably because he was distracted by the hate growing within him as he stroked – but he didn't mind. That blend of hate and desire was pitch perfect for a mind-blowing orgasm, and when it finally came, it was enough to take him out at the knees.

They buckled as he shot his seed, and Neil smacked his head on the edge of the sink – adding pain to the delicious mix – and though it hurt like hell, he continued pumping, shooting hot jets of semen, and groaning out his orgasm as he writhed on the floor. He quaked, jerked, and twitched, and when the last tiny spurt of seed spat out of him, he lay there long moments, catching his breath and enjoying the cooling sweat on his skin.

But the rage remained. In fact, it worsened.

I just beat off to my mom. It was far from the first time she'd forced herself into his fantasies, but the thought that followed nearly made him vomit. *And Coastal Eddie, too.*

Now there was shame as well – and it was his mother's fault.

You fucking whore. Look what you made me do!

He got to his feet on wobbly legs to check the gash where he'd hit his head. It was bleeding. "You fucking whore. You ruined my face!" This, too, was his mother's fault. When he tried to meet his own eyes, he couldn't, and that's when the hate turned sour and black - that's when he remembered what he had to do. He had to kill the whore. Kill her - right when she's fucking queer old Coastal Eddie. And he wanted her to see him coming, too. It was time to teach her the ultimate lesson.

Neil smiled, realizing that *this* was what he'd been craving all along.

∽

"DID YOU HEAR SOMETHING?" Lucy, full of Lixir and dirty thoughts, swung her bare legs off the arm of the easy chair and stood.

"Hear what?" Ivy didn't bother to look up. She was painting Daisy's toenails gold in preparation for the first night of Biting Man.

"I think somebody's walking around outside." Lucy peeked out a window of Daisy's cushy two-story cabin but saw nothing below.

Ivy giggled as she finished Daisy's pinky toe. "Maybe we've got a peeper."

"Maybe." Daisy wiggled her gold toes and smiled. "Wanna strip and give him a thrill?"

"Daisy, what if it's a bear or something?" Lucy shook her head. Daisy was so crazy that she felt like an old lady in comparison - *like Natasha!*

"I'll give the bear a thrill." Daisy giggled and pulled off her tank top.

Ivy's head swiveled as a branch snapped outside. "I heard that!"

"Me, too." Snapping her gum, Daisy stood up, Ivy on her heels.

Lucy pointed. "Ivy, check the front windows. Daisy, go look out the back. But put your top on first." *I can't believe I said that. I really am turning into Natasha.* Not waiting to see if she obeyed, Lucy crossed the hall and entered a small bedroom to look below. Nothing.

Ivy tiptoed up behind Lucy. "There're some guys down at the front door. I think they're trying to break in."

Lucy grinned. "Boy, are they in for a surprise." She adjusted her red crop top. "Let's go see who they are. Quietly."

Ivy grinned then followed her sister down to the first floor. The front door knob was wiggling. "Not very good burglars."

Lucy, feeling alive for the first time today, smiled. "Let's find out if they're good for anything else."

She crept to the door, Ivy behind her. After putting her finger to her lips, she waited an instant before grabbing the knob with one hand and flipping the deadbolt with the other. She pulled the door open and four middle-aged guys dressed in ridiculous fringed black leather tumbled across the threshold.

"Who the fuck are you?" demanded Ivy.

The guys just lay there goggling up at them.

"I know who you are," Lucy said after a long moment. "You're that boy band from Candle Bay. "Old fart band is more like it."

One of them reached out and touched her ankle, a worshipful look on his face. She kicked him away. "Plastic Taffy. What the hell are you doing here?"

"Maybe they're fang-boys," Ivy said.

"We won't hurt you," one of them promised.

Lucy broke out in laughter. "*You* won't hurt *us*?"

"We won't," stammered another one. "You're so beautiful. We promise not to bite."

Roaring with laughter, Lucy and Ivy looked at each other. Ivy wiped away a tear. "They promise not to bite!"

"What's going on?" Daisy was coming down the stairs. Her tank top was on but pulled so low that one nipple peeked out.

"Company. They've promised not to bite us." Ivy started giggling again. "Isn't that nice?"

"Maybe we should bite them!" Daisy walked forward and poked one guy with a golden toe. "What's your name?"

"Mick-"

"Knock it off, Daisy." Lucy looked down at them, murder in her eye. "Did you follow us from Candle Bay?"

"No!" said one with foot-long fringe on his vest and gray hairs on his chest. "My name's Davy and we were just out walking and-"

"And, my ass." Lucy glared. "How did you find us?"

"We were just taking a walk," said another.

"We were hoping to find some girls to party with," piped up the third.

Daisy grinned at the twins. "They're kinda cute."

"No way, Daisy. We can't mess with humans."

"We aren't humans!" the fourth one cried.

"You're claiming to be vampire?" Lucy asked.

"We're new, but yeah-"

"Bullshit. You wouldn't be out here in the daylight if you were-"

One of the old boys waved a big bottle of Lixir at them.

"Why didn't you say so?" Lucy purred.

"Come on in, boys." Ivy stepped back.

Blowing a bubble, Daisy took her top off. The girl possessed no subtlety.

∼

TULLY EXAMINED Flournoy Grebble's briny body and found no sign of bite marks on his neck or anywhere else. "Thanks, Doc."

"Like I said," John Henry drawled. "He's been strangled. Nothing more, nothing less." A small smile tickled the edges of his mouth. "Once I delve into his interior mysteries, I may find poison." An eyebrow cocked. "Though, sir, I expect we'll only find pickle juice."

Tully nodded. "Anything new on Curtis Penrose?"

"He certainly wasn't killed by any vampire. No blood loss, no *real* bite marks. You saw that for yourself."

"Thanks. I've got to get going. Let me know about this one as soon as you can." Tully let himself out of the doctor's office. He liked John Henry just fine - he'd been with them since the last doctor, Phil Katz, had left a decade ago.

Climbing into his SUV, Tully felt disgust that murder had come to his town once more, but was pleased that no vampires were involved. "Leaving the Holliday Medical Clinic, heading in," he told the radio.

"Ten-four," came Connie's voice. "We've got an 11-44. Deputy Hapscomb requests you meet him at 84 Firty Road."

Crap. "On my way."

Connie came back on. "Sheriff, it's not a regular one."

"What?"

"It's - you know-"

He nearly said *A vampire?* but caught himself. "Got it."

He signed off then began driving, cursing so steadily that if his mother had been alive to hear him, she would have washed his mouth out with soap.

∽

AFTER WASHING his stake and showering in the dead bloodsucker's cabin, Neil added a fresh coat of Axe Body Spray then headed out in search of his whoring mother and her lover. "Whore." Just thinking of the look on her face when she saw him cutting Coastal Eddie's throat brought a smile to Neil's lips.

As he made his way through the forest, keeping near the dirt road, he plotted his next move. The first thing he needed to do was figure out which hotel his mom was staying at - there were only so many choices so she wouldn't be hard to find.

From within a nearby cabin, he heard giggling. He paused, staring at the tall log house, listening. More giggling. A soft moan. *The sounds of sex!* Glancing around to be sure he wouldn't be seen, he slipped closer to the cabin, to the window. The curtains were drawn, but not entirely, and through a small gap, he was able to make out what was happening inside.

It was definitely sex. Group sex, and from what he could tell, there were three curvy brunettes and several men. They were all sprawled on and around a fold-out couch, a tangle of arms and legs, and as he watched them, he suddenly realized who he was looking at: *Plastic Taffy! What the ...*

One of the women threw back her hair and bared her teeth - her very sharp teeth - before biting down on the lead guitarist's neck.

Vampires? In the daytime!

Neil's mind reeled. He brought his face closer to the glass, studying the pale skin, the dead eyes. *Vampires! All of them!* He was sure of it. But it made no sense.

One of the women disengaged herself from the locked bodies on the fold-out and sauntered toward a buffet in the corner. She was hot as hell - they all were - and without even realizing it, Neil began giving himself a rub-down below the belt.

The black-haired woman lifted something off the buffet top - a bottle - and sipped from it.

"Don't drink so much!" said another woman. "You want to be able to go outside tomorrow, too, don't you?"

Outside? Tomorrow? As in daytime?

The girl - who'd been bringing the bottle to her lips - paused, frowned, and set it back down. "I guess." With a pouty look, she made her way back to the orgy, her hooters swaying with each step.

Neil was intrigued. A liquid that allowed vampires to go out in daylight? This was a game changer. Until now, he'd only been looking for vampires at night ...

Now, I'll never be safe from them! They'll be everywhere, all the time, looking for me! Filthy fucking bloodsuckers!

A new thought struck him: *I have to get my hands on that bottle.* If he took it away from them now, it stood to reason that he could come back tomorrow and stake them while they slept - every last one of them.

They're not playing fair! And this outraged Neil Trinsky more than anything.

A plan began to form. He glanced from the hide-a-bed to the buffet, gauging the distance between them. It wasn't far, and the buffet stood near the front door. The bloodsuckers were fully absorbed in each other and if Neil could get inside, he could snag the bottle, unnoticed.

50

TWILIGHT IN THE TOWN OF GOOD AND EVIL

"I wonder if Erin's awake yet." Lois picked at her ravioli.

"Soon," Eddie said. "You really need to eat more, Lois. You look pale and I can see how tired you are. It's in your eyes."

She tried a smile. "Are you saying I should have worn makeup?"

Eddie laughed. "Nothing of the sort. I'm just concerned about you. Worried, in fact."

"Don't be. I'm fine." She forked up half a ricotta and spinach ravioli and chewed. "I love this little restaurant. I'm surprised it's so empty."

"That's because we're here during early bird hours." He glanced around. The other people there were almost uniformly of retirement age. He'd suggested an early dinner at Mario's to try to get Lois to stop worrying about Erin - and about what Neil was up to. They'd waited all day for a call from Sheriff Tully, hoping to hear her son had been picked up, but none had come. It was nerve-wracking, to say the least, but Eddie sublimated his own worries and concentrated on Lois. She was really hurting.

He saw a police cruiser pull up and park across the square. A moment later Tully walked into the King's Tart.

Eddie realized her eyes were on him and he quickly locked into her stare. Pretty eyes, deep and rich. It was a pity she had suffered so much at the hands of her psychopathic son. He smiled at her. "It's going to get better soon," he said. "I promise."

"I hope so. If you'd asked me a week ago what I'd be doing today, I would have said hopefully selling a beach house on the bluffs. Never in a million years would I have guessed I'd be here."

"With me?" Eddie smiled. "That's pretty weird."

"No, trying to have my own son arrested. Worrying about a vampire." She chuckled. "Believing that vampires are real." She touched his hand. "Being here with you is the only pleasant aspect of this whole thing. I feel like I've found a new friend."

He squeezed her hand. "Me too. I'm sorry we had to meet under such bizarre circumstances."

"You're Coastal Eddie, the crazy conspiracy talk show host. What other circumstances could we have met under?" She chuckled again, and this time it wasn't forced.

"Indeed. Strange has followed me my entire life. I saw my first UFO when I was five." He smiled. "I think it was something the military was testing. I saw quite a few more before I left Brimstone. There were plenty of bases out there."

"Brimstone?"

"A little town in Arizona. Strange place, full of legends and ghosts and ... other things."

"I've never even heard of it."

"Have you ever read Holly Tremayne's novels?"

"Sure. I love her books."

"She grew up there. Still lives there, I believe. I met her when she first came to town - cute little girl with blond curls. Her grandmother was Delilah Devine."

"The movie star?"

Eddie nodded, happy to see Lois thinking about something besides Neil and Erin. He wished he could do the same, but there was a block of ice in his solar plexus that wouldn't melt. *Something's coming down.* He could feel it. "Delilah owned the Brimstone Grand. She lived on the top floor and the rest of the building was a hotel. A grand one. It was a hospital in the old days and was supposed to be full of ghosts."

"Did you see any?"

Eddie grinned. "Maybe."

"When did you leave?"

"I got a college scholarship. I worked my ass off for that." He laughed.

Lois ate one more ravioli then pushed her plate away. "I'm stuffed."

"Let's take a walk."

"Sounds good."

Though it was still light, street lamps were beginning to come on. And Tully's SUV was still parked near the bakery. "Look." Eddie pointed at the cruiser. "Want to talk to the sheriff?"

"Yes!"

They cut across the square and were outside the King's Tart in record time. "May I buy you a pastry, Ms. Trinsky?" he asked.

"You may, sir." She smiled as he opened the door.

∽

"V-Sec will meet us here after dark. It won't be so bad."

Harlan pushed another donut at Tully, but he shook his head. "Kate says I'm about to start popping buttons."

Harlan looked at the glazed donut for a fraction of a second before biting into it. "I know you don't want to talk to them, but believe me, there's nothing to worry about. That vampire may have been another victim of the murderer who took out Curtis Penrose and Flournoy Grebble. It could be coincidence. The killer might not have known he was doing in a vampire."

"Maybe." Tully rubbed his chin. "Probably. He'd been dead at least a day before we found him - I wish it had been sooner." He paused. "And I'd sure like to question Neil Trinsky." He'd vacated the boarding house and left no forwarding address, which wasn't suspicious on its own, but Elvis had told him he'd gone to Kissel's after leaving the True Grace Market. That was plenty suspicious.

"Maybe he left town?"

Tully sipped coffee. "Maybe, but I don't think so. It feels like he's here somewhere. Probably holed up in an empty cabin. I've had deputies checking all day. Nothing yet."

"Zach, I think you're right to suspect Neil Trinsky." Harlan finished the donut with a flourish.

Bells jangled as the door opened. Eddie Fortune and Lois Trinsky entered. Lois looked exhausted and Eddie didn't look much better.

"Is there any news?" Lois asked while Eddie ordered donuts and tea.

"No, I'm sorry, Lois. We're searching for Neil, but so far haven't had any luck."

"You won't hurt him, will you?"

"Of course not." *Not unless he tries to hurt us first.* He was glad the pair hadn't overheard his conversation with Harlan.

"Thank you, Sheriff. I'm just a little nervous about all this."

"That's understandable. Don't worry. I'll let you know the minute we find him." Tully paused, glancing at Harlan, who raised his brows and gave a slight nod. "I want you both to be careful. If Neil shows up at your hotel room, don't let him in."

Eddie set the teas and pastry on the next table.

Lois' eyes filled but didn't overflow. "He's never gone this far before. I don't know what he's capable of."

Tully saw the pain in her eyes. "I'm sorry you have to go through this."

Eddie put his arm around her shoulders. "How about a donut?"

She smiled. "Yes."

Tully nodded at Harlan. "I'll see you later."

51

THE PURLOINED BOTTLE

The purloined bottle was heavy, square with a thick glass stopper, and looked a little like that expensive tequila. Neil sat at the little table in his secret cabin and eyed the bottle. It was a third full and the amber fluid within looked oily, clinging to the glass long after he'd swirled it. The label was old-fashioned and ornate, edged with weird-looking embossed gold flowers. There was no manufacturer listed: All it said was LIXIR.

"Something's fishy," Neil muttered. Without a manufacturer listed, it seemed like it might be illegally made and Neil wondered if it was against the law for vampires to possess the miraculous fluid. He doubted it; there was no way that bloodsuckers could be civilized enough to have laws, let alone follow them.

He twisted the glass stopper and, with agonizing slowness, it began to slide from the throat, revealing an old-fashioned cork. Suddenly, with a loud *plop,* it pulled out, leaving the bottle like Coastal Eddie's queer dick left his mom's ass.

The thought made Neil Jr. twitch, but he paid no attention. He was a professional vampire hunter and he had to find out what this Lixir was, for the greater good. It was his duty.

He brought his nose to the lip and immediately recoiled. It smelled like metal shavings – but underneath there was the scent of something sweeter. Berries, he realized, but berries unlike any he'd ever smelled before, weird and exotic. With great caution, he brought it closer to his face and poked his tongue out. When the tip made contact, several things happened at once: his eyes began to water, his mouth filled with an anticipatory flood of saliva, and the taste of the stuff – like fermented cough syrup with a dash of wet skunk – seemed to leap into his mouth, filling it with the nasty flavor. He couldn't taste the berry smell at all until he exhaled, then there it was.

"Jesus fuck!" Wincing, he held the bottle out, wondering how in the name of God he was supposed to go through with the experiment. *There's no way!* But as he spat on the floor and rolled his tongue in his mouth, trying to wash out the flavor, another thought occurred: *What Would Buffy Do?* It was the thought that had gotten him through so many tough times that he'd once considered having the initials of that question – *W.W.B.D.* – made into a ring or a pendant to wear around his neck. But that was pretty gay, he'd realized, and decided instead on the Buffy tattoo on his groin. He'd made the right choice.

He glanced back at the bottle. *And what she'd do is drink the stuff,* he decided. Never one to shy away from her duties, Buffy would have gulped it with abandon, he was sure.

And if I want to be a pro like Buffy, I've got to do shit I might not want to sometimes. Taking a deep breath, he brought the bottle to his lips and tipped it back, letting it slide down his throat quickly, swallowing one mouthful. It was like swallowing something thick and mucousy, and despite the speed with which he'd ingested it, the taste wouldn't be ignored. Neil felt as if he'd just bitten into something dead.

The moment it hit his stomach, his insides tightened around it, shocked. Neil brought the bottle down, sucking in deep breaths. As he wiped his hands across his mouth, a bubble of acid rose from his belly to the top of his throat, floating a moment like some toxic gas from the bottom of a poisonous pond, before popping and filling his mouth with a sour, rancid taste. There was a bubbling and rumbling deep in his belly, as if the contents of his stomach had been brought to the boiling point – and the pot was about to boil over.

Neil thrust a hand up to his mouth as he felt the liquid rise, rebelling against him and threatening escape. He swallowed convulsively, forcing it back down, and after a moment, the nausea passed.

"Wicked shit," he said, waiting to see what else was going to happen.

∽

MARILYN BAKER, head of V-Sec, sat in Harlan's twilit bakery, flanked by her officers, Matthew Moon and Cecil Trevor. Tully and Harlan, equipped with hot coffee, sat across from them. Tully had been dreading the meeting; dreading telling the vampires that one of their own had been murdered, but he was pleasantly surprised when the security team took it in stride, showing more understanding than most humans would have.

"We appreciate your candor, Sheriff." Marilyn folded her hands. "Do you have any leads on the perpetrator?"

"We are following up on a suspect - we have no evidence yet, but we're trying to find him and bring him in for questioning." He paused. "He may have left town already, but we suspect him in two, uh, human homicides as well. It's a hunch, though. The only thing he's actually wanted for is car theft."

"Is he a fang-boy?" Trevor asked.

"We believe so." Tully didn't want to give anything away. While he was impressed with the professionalism of V-Sec, he didn't know for certain that they wouldn't turn vigilante, despite their - and Harlan's - assurances. It was a risk he couldn't afford to take.

Marilyn Baker rose and her officers followed suit. "You have my number, Sheriff. Please let me know if you find out anything." She paused. "Now that Biting Man has officially begun, my officers and I will be using a medication that will allow us to function normally during daylight hours as well as nighttime, so contact me anytime."

Tully glanced at Harlan, whose face betrayed nothing, then shook Marilyn's hand. It was cool but not cold; he'd never take her for anything but human. "I'll do that."

"And don't worry," she added as if reading his mind, "I meant it when I told you that daytimers are your forte. We won't take human law into our hands and we appreciate you not arresting any nighttimers." She paused. "It's too dangerous, and we have our own laws, which are, without doubt, harsher than yours. They have to be. But they only apply to vampires. If we happen to catch your human perpetrator in the act, we will do nothing except deliver him to you."

Tully gave her a genuine smile. "Thank you, Ms. Baker. I couldn't ask for better."

After more hand-shaking, the vampires exited into the falling night. Tully and Harlan watched them cross to their SUV and drive off. "I like the vampires," Harlan mused. "They're so much more civilized than we are."

"They are civilized. I especially like that they call us 'daytimers,'" Tully said. "It's so much nicer than 'dinner.'"

～

"Where the hell is the Lixir?" Daisy bitched. "Did those idiots take it with them when they left?"

"I don't know," Lucy called from the bathroom, where she was finishing her makeup. "Unless one stuffed it down his pants, I don't think so."

"They were all wearing tight leather." Ivy smoothed seamed black hose up her legs and fastened them to her lacy black garter belt. "There's no way they could've carried it out."

"Well," snipped Daisy. "It's gone. It was on the buffet downstairs before." She came into the bedroom and pirouetted where both twins could see her. She wore a leopard-print mini-skirt so short her ass cheeks showed even when she stood still. When she moved, her lacy black thong would have showed if it hadn't been so snugly up her ass crack; her transparent black crop top prominently displayed her nipples.

Lucy strode out of the bathroom to eye her cousin. "You sure don't leave anything to the imagination, Daisy."

She'd told Ivy that the more she was around their forever fourteen-year-old relative, the more she understood their big sister, Natasha, and felt like an old fart. Daisy laughed and blew a big pink bubble. "You don't approve?"

"You can wear whatever you like." Lucy ran her hands through her mass of just-made curls. She wore red lace leggings under a red leather mini skirt and a matching scoop-neck top with lacy sleeves that matched her leggings. A red velvet choker with an onyx cameo drew attention to her graceful neck.

"But you think-" Daisy began again.

"Lucy just means that you're not making anybody work for it." Ivy wiggled into a form-fitting purple dress that emphasized her tits and ass.

"It's not like you two are hiding anything," Daisy sniffed. "When you move, I can see the tops of your nylons, Ivy. And your boobs are almost hanging out."

"No, you can only see a flash of my bare thigh if I want you too, Daisy, and my nipples aren't showing. Anyone I choose has to unwrap me before they can get a look at the goods." Ivy fastened a gold chain with a purple-black enamel bat flower pendant around her neck. Julian had given one to her and one to Lucy when he'd opened his business. She adored him; so did Lucy, but not like she did. She wished he were here and it almost felt like he was, but it was wishful thinking.

"I think Cousin Daisy dresses to get laid as quickly as possible," Lucy said. "Right?"

"Right!" Daisy finished applying glossy red lipstick, then worked her gum and grinned. "I really like to fuck, you know?"

"Then let's go," Lucy said. "There's a shuttle to the Ski Bowl every half hour. If we hurry, we can make the next one."

"What about the Lixir?" Daisy tried to pout.

Lucy patted her crimson handbag. "I have ours. There's enough left for morning. We'll find the one the boys left tomorrow - it's around here somewhere. We won't need it until then anyway."

"I bet we can buy a bottle in the Eternal City," Ivy said. "There are vendors. Davy told me it's like a big-ass fair in there."

"Cool." Daisy said. "Let's go."

∽

NEIL WAS DISAPPOINTED. Having taken two more sips from the allegedly "magic" liquid, nothing had happened. Aside from giving him a slightly upset stomach and practically killing his taste buds, it hadn't done a fucking thing. He supposed that if he were a vampire, it would have done something, but apparently it didn't do anything for humans, which was just one more way those dirty bloodsucking little bitches discriminated against the living.

Prejudiced is what they were - racist against humans, and if there was one thing Neil wouldn't stand for, it was bigotry. He hated them for it, all of them, with their secret clubs and their special magic liquids that allowed them to go out in daylight - and as soon as he took care of the little problem with his mom and Coastal Eddie, he intended to kill every last one of them, kill them slowly and painfully, like the dirty fucking hateful dogs they were. He didn't care if it took him the rest of his life.

"Fucking little bitches, all of them!" He stormed out of the cabin, slamming the door behind him, and made his way into the woods, his backpack slung over his shoulder. In a way, he figured it was a good thing the magic liquid hadn't done anything for him - that liquid was just one more dirty little secret those bloodsuckers were keeping from the human race and that added the extra fuel he'd need to put a hard painful end to his mother's wanton love affair with that queer Coastal Eddie. He thought of them fucking again and grimaced. "And you're little bitches, too," he muttered as he stalked through the forest. "*Dead* little bitches." This made him chuckle, a sound that was eerily resonant in the silence of the falling night.

Neil paused as his stomach suddenly rumbled, full of threat and discontent. There was a hot sloshing deep in his bowels that he didn't quite trust. *If that so-called magic liquid makes me sick, I'll kill those fucking bloodsuckers TWICE!*

And then the sickness passed and aside from a sudden film of cool sweat on his forehead, Neil felt fine. He even ate three pickles from the jar in his backpack to soothe his stomach. High on his fantasies of committing bloody murders, he stalked on, enjoying the fresh scents of the forest air and the sound of the earth beneath his powerful, determined feet. He likened that sound to the encroaching footsteps of a monster in a classic horror movie - probably one with that haggy old former scream queen Maisy Hart, whose movies had always been a little too dull - and her tits too saggy - for Neil's blood. It was fun to be the monster in the woods. It suited him somehow and Neil smiled.

That was when the cramps seized his belly.

Neil doubled over, his hands on his abdomen. It felt as if a hot slippery eel were snaking through his guts - and cutting him up as it did. An acrid taste filled his mouth and the nausea hit him like a wrecking ball.

Fighting the rising gorge, a vicious sweat broke out over his entire body and he was suddenly struck by an urge - a cruel, demanding *need* - to do more than toss his cookies. He needed to void his bowels. Except void wasn't the right word; purge was more accurate, or perhaps even eject, but *void* was far too gentle a term for his body's desperation to unload whatever evil currently sloshed hotly around within him.

"Fuck! Are you fucking kidding me?" Once the cramps subsided enough that he could walk again, he tight-cheeked it behind a tree, tossed his backpack down, and hurriedly unbuckled and unzipped, squatting just in time to release a torrential fury so violent and spiteful that it ached deep in his guts, as if his body were spewing streams of fire-hot barbed wire. Neil winced, breathless as he bore down on the agony, his fingers digging deeply and painfully into the bark of the tree.

52

AT VALENTYN VINEYARDS

As soon as dusk fell, Norman Keeler hitched a ride back across Highway 1 with a man who appreciated a good blow job. Less than half an hour later, he was at the gates of Valentyn Vineyards, skateboard under his arm. So hungry that he regretted not dining on his driver, he blew blond bangs from his eyes, and pressed the call button.

Beyond the gates, he sensed vampires. The only disturbing thing was that the Woman's presence was not as strong as he'd expected.

A camera by the gate moved, training on him.

"Valentyn Vineyards," came a voice over the call box. "We're currently closed. Our hours are-"

"I'm here for the Woman."

"The woman?"

"She's here. Or she was. Where is she?"

"To whom are you referring?" The man's voice was polite and measured.

"You know. The Woman. The only Woman."

"Can you describe her?"

"Blond, petite, beautiful."

"Did she bite you, sir?" The voice dripped with something that was neither sarcasm nor honey.

Taken aback, Norman fell silent as he realized he was probably talking to another vampire. *If he knows that, he has to be!* "I am hers," he replied simply.

"She isn't here at the moment, but may I ask, have you had sustenance this evening?"

Norman's stomach growled at the question. "Why?"

"One recognizes a certain timbre of the voice when someone such as yourself has a ... need."

"I need sustenance." Norman's hunger suddenly overwhelmed him. "But I need to know where the Woman is."

"Very well. Remain where you are. We will be down momentarily."

"Can't I come in?"

"I'm afraid that's impossible."

Norman wanted to yell, to break the camera and climb the fence, but instead, he counted to ten, refusing the hunger pangs that made him feel weak. He waited for ten minutes then saw a canopied golf cart coming down the road from the hills beyond the gate. It was driven by a slender man in a suit, his red tie nearly glowing in the falling darkness. Beside him sat a huge figure with dusky skin and an outdated Afro.

They pulled up about five feet from the gate. The cart was white with "Valentyn Vineyards" written on the sides. Exotic gold flowers encircled the words.

But as fancy as the cart was, the two men were fancier. The one in the black suit was perfectly coiffed, not a lock of hair daring to stray. His suit was immaculate, his posture as straight and stiff as an English butler's. His companion was right out of the movie, *Shaft*, and he towered over the butler-guy. He was at least six-foot-five, not counting the hair, and his chest was so muscled that it threatened to rip his red wife beater.

"I am Felix and my companion is Bruno. May I ask your name, sir?"

"Norman. Norman Keeler. I'm a friend of–"

"The woman's. I understand that." Felix turned to his giant friend. "Bruno?"

The big guy nodded, picked up two bottles and approached the wrought iron gate. "Here you go. Make it last." He thrust one bottle between the bars.

Norman made to reach for it but Bruno pulled back, a grin revealing sharp white fangs. "You're new, aren't you?"

"Yes."

"You drink this," he said. "You don't drink from humans, understand?"

"Yeah."

"If you kill anyone, I'll find you and stake you myself. Understand that, too?"

Norman nodded, swallowing. Bruno passed both bottles through the gate and returned to the cart.

"Mr. Keeler, the woman you are seeking–"

Norman cut in. "What is her name, sir?"

The man hesitated, then said, "Amanda."

"Amanda ..." It was like honey on his tongue. "Amanda ..."

"Mr. Keeler, she has gone to Eternity."

"*What*? She's dead?"

"No, the town of Eternity, about five hours north. She's attending the Biting Man Festival there."

"Biting Man Festival?"

"A vampiric gathering. I don't know where she's staying, but I suspect you will track her down easily since you belong to her."

"What do you mean?"

"Because she's your Maker, you are connected to her. Just use your senses, as you did to find this place, and I assure you, you *will* find her."

"I don't have a car."

Felix and Bruno conferred. "My friend will drive you into town. From there you are on your own. Do you have money to rent a car?"

"Yes." Norman patted his wallet. No way was he going to risk renting a car, but he wouldn't tell Felix that. He'd steal one.

53

FULL DISCLOSURE

"I thought you'd never wake up."

Natasha blinked and sat up on the sofa. She'd been leaning against Michael, who roused as she moved. "Julian, how long have you been sitting there?"

"For some hours now, watching over you."

Michael yawned. "Watching over us? Are we in danger?"

Julian folded his long fingers together in his lap. "I doubt it, but one never knows." He paused. "I, however, am in danger, and did not rest well."

"Amanda." Natasha tried not to spit the name. "I understand from Stephen that you drove up with her."

Julian studied his hands before pinning her and Michael with his dark eyes. "Indeed. My man did the right thing in contacting your brother. I was unable to speak with Felix directly."

"Because of Amanda?" Michael spoke softly.

Julian nodded. "She is Incendarius. Are you familiar with the term?"

"We are," Natasha told him. "Stephen explained."

Absently, Julian rubbed the large cabochon ruby in his gold ring. "Then you know that I am not the complete master of my fate at this moment. I feel great affection - or at least lust - as well as loathing toward Amanda. I did not comprehend why she attracted me through so many lifetimes until recently. While I understand now what is occurring, it is difficult for me to overcome when I am near her. You might even say I'm fighting an addiction of sorts."

Michael stood and retrieved a bottle of domestic AB Neg, then poured three glasses of the ruby fluid. He handed one to Julian. "We understand and we will help you. My clan and Natasha's."

Natasha nodded. "Of course."

Julian held the glass under his nose, inhaled, then sipped. "Understand that in Amanda's presence, I may become ... untrustworthy. I could hurt or even destroy you."

"We understand that." Natasha swirled her glass, inhaled, then took a delicate sip, savoring the deceptively simple flavor. "Where is she now?"

A closed-lip smile crept across Julian's mouth. "Most likely at my cabin, perhaps twelve miles distant. I deserted her in the woods near it. I can feel her anger in the back of my mind. I've felt it all day." He paused. "Amanda abuses Lixir and I don't think she's slept. Felix removed her bottle, but I'm certain she has some hidden."

"Is it possible she's in town now?"

Julian shook his head. "Unlikely. She felt distant and tired today. Only since twilight has she strengthened. She is probably on her way now." One side of his mouth quirked up in a half-smile. "I did take her shoes. That should slow her down."

Natasha grinned. "So she's barefoot."

"She is."

Michael cleared his throat. "I pity the driver who picks her up."

"Indeed. I'm relieved that it will take her hours to reach the highway."

~

EVEN THOUGH THE Darling twins had spent the day at their cousin's cabin and the third bedroom in Winter and Chynna's suite was empty, Erin, still rattled by her new state of existence, had eagerly accepted Chynna's invitation to stay with her. Erin and Arnie were slowly bonding, but the human part of Erin still wavered in and out of caution and there were moments when Chynna had seen apprehension and even distrust in the girl's eyes. *It will pass, and soon enough Erin will want to spend as much time with Arnie as she can.* Chynna knew this not only from personal experience, but from the experiences of the many others she'd met over her long lifetime.

As the sun set, Chynna sat up in bed, surprised to see that Erin was already sitting in a chair, staring out a window. When she heard Chynna moving, she looked over and smiled sadly.

"How did you sleep?"

Erin only nodded. There was still something haunted in the depths of her eyes but Chynna could see she was going to be okay.

"It won't be so frightening forever." Chynna slipped out of the sheets, walked to the girl and smoothed her auburn hair.

"I still just can't believe it, you know?" Erin held back tears.

"I know exactly where you're at, and believe me, it gets better." Chynna spoke in positive soothing tones, but in truth, she *was* concerned for the girl. It always bothered her when anyone was turned against their will. "I think you can be quite happy as one of us."

Erin wiped a rogue tear from her cheek. "I know. I believe that, too. I feel so stupid for sitting here crying, but it's just ..."

"Such a shock. I know. It takes some getting used to."

"How long did it take you to get used to being a vampire?"

She sat down beside Erin and gave her a thin smile. "My situation was a little different from yours."

"How so? What do you mean?"

Chynna considered. "I worked with big cats in a circus and I was terminally ill. I wasn't ready to die. I was terrified for my tigers. When I was offered immortality, I took it without hesitation. It's easy to be afraid of eternal life when nothing is wrong - but when your own mortality knocks at the door, well ... it wasn't a difficult choice for me."

Erin's eyes, which had been deep, sad pools, changed now as something new came into them - a firmness Chynna hadn't seen before. "You're right," she said. "There are far worse things than being a vampire." There was no humor in her chuckle. "The funny thing is, I always wondered if vampires were real - and what it was like to be one." She looked back out the window, her face taking on a contemplative expression. "I'm even starting to think that maybe this is my destiny, you know? Like, maybe some part of me always knew this was what I was supposed to be." Her eyes snapped back to Chynna. "Do you believe that?"

Chynna shrugged. "I believe anything is possible."

"Me too." She smiled, but it didn't last. "Arnie," she said. "I really like him, but ... well, I'm a little frightened of him. I know I shouldn't be, but I am."

"Of course you are. It's perfectly natural after what happened, and I promise you, you can come to terms with Arnie at your own pace."

"I feel so drawn to him - I *want* to be his friend ... but what if I never make peace with this?"

Chynna smiled. "You will. I promise."

"Because he's my ... Maker?"

"That's right. Know that he would never hurt you. The bond between a Maker and his creation is a lot like that between a parent and child. You're frightened right now, but time - and exposure - will erase that fear."

"Exposure?"

Chynna nodded.

Erin looked lost in thought. "You said earlier that you were terrified for your tigers. Do you still have them? I mean, can animals be what ... what we are?"

"I'm afraid not. Those tigers lived long happy lives, but they've been gone for many years now." She paused. "But as far as I'm concerned an existence without tigers is no existence at all, and that's why I always have at least two of them."

"You have some now?"

"I do. Back in Crimson Cove. We have a compound for them where they pretty much run free."

Erin beamed. "That's amazing. What are their names?"

"Absinthe and Hyacinthe." Pride bloomed within Chynna - it always did when she spoke of her babies. "Perhaps you'll meet them one day."

Erin's eyes went wide with excitement. "I'd love to!"

Chynna stood to answer a soft knock on the door.

"Are you two ever getting up?" Winter stood outside, grinning.

Chynna glanced over her shoulder. "I want to talk to you. Can we go to the living room?"

"Sure." Winter shrugged and followed Chynna into the painfully pastel living area, joining her on an ivory sofa that strained beneath his heft. "What's up?"

"I don't think we should go to Biting Man tonight."

The silky half-smile that rested on Winter's lips slipped out of place. "Why not?"

"A couple of reasons. First, I think we should check the place out before we take Arnie along. I think we need to get a feel for the ... *culture* of Biting Man before taking Arnie in. If there's still any prejudice against the mentally challenged-"

"Then I'll handle it." Winter's jaw was firmly set, his icy blue eyes fixed on Chynna's. She'd always considered him handsome in a generic way - it was his size and musculature, his height, his white buzz cut, and his beaming smile that caught the eye (and usually brought it back for a second glance) but now, with such determination on his features, she realized he was more than generically handsome. In fact, his face, all sharp angles and planes, missed that degree of downright gorgeous by only the slightest of margins. Though his attractiveness was at its height - perhaps because of his firm resolve - there was also something threatening about him now, something that told Chynna not to argue with him.

But she did anyway. "All I'm saying is that maybe we shouldn't *all* go tonight."

"I promised Arnie we'd go, and I'm going to keep that promise, Chynna. I can protect him if we come across any issues; I didn't drag him all this way to tell him he can't come."

"There's something else, too."

Winter's jaw flexed. "What's that?"

"Erin is so new that I'm a little worried about taking her as well. And obviously we can't leave her here alone. She and Arnie haven't quite bonded yet, so I was thinking maybe one of us could stay back with the two of them. The other could go get a feel for the festival and-"

Winter shook his head. "A promise is a promise, and I promised Arnie we'd go tonight."

And there was the stubbornness that always managed to wriggle under Chynna's skin. It seemed to her that every time she really started to like the guy, that pride of his reared its head, striking like a cobra, and turning off whatever he'd just turned on. She spoke in measured, mellow tones. "Couldn't you just ask him if he'd reconsider? He might be perfectly content to-"

"I don't really see how this is your business anyway, Chynna."

His words were like a slap across the face. She was angry now, and felt no need to disguise it. "It's my business because it could hurt Arnie. And Erin. You might think you're the only one who cares about Arnie but-"

"I never said that. Now you're just being belligerent."

"-but I care, too. And I care about that young girl in the other room."

"And you didn't say anything about this before because ...?"

"Because I'd hoped you would have considered it on your own. I didn't want to be the one to say it because I know how you are about matters that concern Arnie."

"How I am?" His brows rose. "And how am I, Chynna?"

She sighed, tamping down frustration. "You're overprotective. I don't think I need to tell you that."

"It seems to me you just did." His nostrils flared. He reminded her now of a threatened bull, preparing to charge and Chynna knew her next words needed to be carefully measured if she didn't want a fight on her hands.

But knowing that didn't help. *And maybe I* do *want a fight.* She wasn't sure what had brought the thought on and she had no time to analyze it now. "I really hate you when you're like this." *There I said it - and I'm not going to apologize for it.*

Winter seemed unfazed. He shrugged a massive shoulder and that slippery grin lifted the corner of his lips. "Then I guess it's a good thing

I'm not trying to win any popularity contests." The anger in his eyes went out like a smothered fire and Chynna despised his ability to completely unplug himself from situations he didn't like. It infuriated her.

"And now the conversation is over." Her voice was steely and barbed with sharp things. "Just like that." She snapped her fingers. "You've made up your mind and, as usual, there's nothing else to talk about." She felt her anger rising, gaining ground. "This is just like you, Winter. You always have to call all the shots, all the time. You make decisions without any thought about anyone else's feelings, and if anyone dares to defy you, you simply shrug it off and do what you were going to do anyway. You're selfish, and-"

"Oh, *I'm* selfish?" Winter was on his feet, towering over her. "You're the one who waited until the day of the festival to voice your concerns about this, and that's just like *you!* You sit back and say nothing, then, when it's too late, suddenly you've got a problem! You're passive-aggressive, Chynna."

She gained her feet and although Winter was nearly a head taller, she would not allow this barbarian to intimidate her with his size. Her hands were tight fists at her sides and she almost wished he'd give her a good reason to use them. Her own hostility surprised her, but she was in no position to analyze. "Listen to me, Winter, and listen good. I'm not going to be bullied by you. I-"

"Oh, now I'm a bully?" He laughed, deep and booming.

"That's exactly what I said, and if-"

"You guys?" Winter and Chynna both turned to face the new voice.

Erin stood in the doorway, looking uncertain. "I, uh ... I want to stay back tonight. With Arnie, if he wants to."

Chynna felt suddenly guilty, the way parents must feel when their children catch them fighting. She felt an urge to apologize and though she didn't look at him, she knew Winter wore the same look of contrition. Chynna could sense it in the shift of his posture.

"Really," said Erin. "I want to spend some time with him. Alone. And I think tonight would be a good opportunity for that. If he wants to, that is."

Chynna glanced at Winter. She no longer saw hostility in his eyes.

"I'll talk to him," Winter said.

"Let me do it." Erin's voice was firm. "I want to talk to him about it myself."

"Okay," Winter said.

"I think that's a good idea," Chynna added.

Erin gave them a thin smile and left the room.

The seconds stretched on in heavy silence, so long that Chynna began to feel self-conscious. Suddenly the entire argument seemed ridiculous - but she wasn't about to apologize for merely voicing her concerns.

Fortunately, she didn't have to.

"I'm, uh, sorry about that." Winter spoke low and she could hear the self-consciousness in his voice. It broke down what leftover barrier still stood between them.

"I'm okay with whatever Arnie decides to do, I guess. I'm just worried about him, that's all."

Winter grinned. "I know. And I love that about you."

Love? Something lurched behind Chynna's ribs and she realized - not with pleasure - what had been eating at her these past days, what had caused her irritation toward Winter. It was the twins - how easily he'd slipped into bed with them. *Am I being possessive?* Yes, she was, and this brought on a whole new set of uncomfortable questions she wasn't ready to answer. Pushing them aside, she said, "I'm sorry, too. Not for being worried, but for calling you names. I shouldn't have done that."

"I think I called you a few of my own." Winter's handsome smile lit up first his face, and then the room, warming Chynna. "Friends?"

She smiled. "Friends."

Winter pulled her into a hug and placed a kiss on the top of her head. He smelled like aftershave; Chynna luxuriated in his powerful embrace. It felt, oddly, like this was where she belonged.

"And speaking of names," Winter added in his typical smartass style. "What kind of name is *Chynna*, anyway?"

She laughed. "I don't know, *Winter*, why don't you tell me?"

He let go of her and she looked up at him. "I've always suspected it's not your real name. Am I right?"

Winter crossed his arms. "I'll tell you mine if you tell me yours?"

Chynna considered. "Promise?"

He nodded. "That way, if we ever have another fight, we'll know the best names to call each other." Another broad smile. "But there's one rule: You can never repeat it. To anyone. Ever."

"I only ask the same."

"Shake on it?" Winter held his hand out.

She took it. "It's a deal."

Then, at once, they both blurted out the names with which they'd been born.

"Charlotte Clutterbuck," said Chynna.

"Wilberforce Bishop," said Winter.

And then they fell apart with laughter.

∼

As soon as Bruno left to drive the interloper, Norman Keeler, to town, Felix let himself into Julian's bedroom suite and opened the safe. Within were dozens of vials of elixir- the highly addictive pure form of the bloodberry extract that Lixir was derived from. Julian would never leave the elixir where his vampiric workers might encounter it; it was far too dangerous. In addition, there were rare jewels, antique gold coins, other valuables, and finally, a neat stack of papers. Underneath those, Felix found a simple oak box with his name taped to its lid.

He took it to Julian's writing desk, and undid the seal - deep blue wax imprinted with Julian's signet ring. The first paper named Felix executor should anything happen to Julian and directed him to consult with the Darlings on all matters. Under that was a handwritten memoir bound in leather. Julian told Felix to read it and to allow Natasha and Stephen Darling to as well if he didn't return. There was a will that made the Darlings the trustees of Valentyn Vineyards, with the stipulation that Felix be kept on. If Felix so desired, he could be turned into a vampire himself and eventually inherit the vineyards and veinery as long as the Darlings felt him capable and remained on as advisors until they felt it was no longer necessary.

Felix's head spun with the revelations, but he forced himself to move on rather than read in detail. Next, he found directions to Julian's cabin in Eternity, along with a number of other properties, most located on the west coast, but others in New England, New York, Europe, and Asia. There was another sealed envelope under that. Within, he found pages and pages written in Julian's small, elegant handwriting. They began, "*There is another Trueborn in addition to the Treasure, and you, Felix, and Stephen and Natasha Darling, must be made aware of the presence on the chance this Trueborn shows up. You must know what to do to protect yourselves.*"

Though he wanted to linger, Felix moved on, knowing these were all things that could wait. His mind still reeled at the thought that Julian would allow him to become a vampire. It had been his dream - and his nightmare - for a decade.

Finally, he found a single sheet of folded parchment. He began reading. "*My dear Felix, If you are reading this, I am in peril or dead. All the other items within this box are important to you if something has happened to me. Guard them with your life and share them with no one except Stephen and Natasha Darling. They are trustworthy, but only those two.*

"*If I am merely missing, what, if anything, will help you find me, I do not know, but I sincerely hope there will be something of use here and that I shall see you again, my most faithful Friend. Share nothing of my will or other instructions - save for the property locations and the missive concerning the other Trueborn and other notes concerning certain vampires - with the Darlings unless you know with certainty that I am no longer in my body. I sincerely hope that you will not have to share.*"

By the time Bruno returned from town, Felix was on the computer researching Norman Keeler. He found him all too easily: he was a young male prostitute who had been murdered in Candle Bay mere days before - and his body had gone missing from the morgue.

When Bruno opened the door moments later, Felix was already in deep conversation with Stephen Darling in Candle Bay, telling him how to find Julian's cabin.

54
IN EXTREMIS

Every time Neil thought there was nothing more within him to be expelled, his abdomen cramped, the nausea overcame him, and he was forced to make another mad dash behind a tree to find some relief.

He hadn't always made it in time. The seat of his pants was ruined - as were his socks and shoes. And now, his body was no longer content to evacuate the poisonous contents from just one orifice - he'd begun vomiting as well. And it was just as vicious on one end as the other.

Ragged, his insides feeling like shredded ribbons, he gingerly made his way up the stairs - his asshole felt like a burning ring of fire - and his hand found the cabin doorknob just as he was seized by another bout of sickness. He lowered his head to spew a stream of acrid liquid between his feet. He was tired, too tired to fight against it, and to an onlooker, he may have appeared to be an English butler giving a courteous bow to an arriving houseguest. Except for the projectile vomit that shot from his mouth, anyway.

He let it out soundlessly - opening his throat and just letting it happen - and wishing very much that he were dead. It splashed noisily onto the wooden porch where it could sit and stink and dry out and feed the fucking forest rodents for a week for all he cared. He needed sleep, blessed, blessed, sleep.

After wiping his mouth with the back of his hand - which came away with a long string of green slime - he entered the cabin and felt for the lights. Illumination bloomed hard and bright and painfully, bringing on yet another round of gastrointestinal hell. Slamming the door, he hurried toward the bathroom, relieved that he finally had a place to sit and do his business properly.

He was just outside the bathroom door, however, when his body made the immediacy of its situation unbearably apparent. Even as he lowered his pants and positioned himself above the bowl, his insides betrayed him, spewing out unspeakable grotesqueries. He slid onto the now slippery seat and let nature takes its course, no longer concerned about the mess - that ship had sailed - and groaned. It was like passing rubbing alcohol or liquid fire - and he never would have believed his insides were capable of containing so much of ... well, anything. It was as if a pipe had burst within him - a pipe whose point of supply was the goddamned Atlantic Ocean.

As he sprayed down the toilet's porcelain walls, tears dripped from his eyes - he wasn't crying, but his body seemed desperate to cleanse itself by any means - and thick ropes of saliva continued forming and dangling and swaying and snapping from his lips. Even as he emptied out his bowels, the nausea came again, bringing another furious clammy sweat, and Neil parted his knees, lowered his head, and shot out a fresh round of hot vomit - most of which splashed off his thighs and ran down his trembling legs. Buffy, rising from his wet, matted pubic hair, seemed to frown at him from beneath the coat of sick that covered her. Neil frowned back.

That was when the fever began. He felt it like glowing coals burning hotter and hotter within him until he was certain they'd burn his brain to a cinder.

55

FANG-BOYS

Frustrated, Stephen Darling hung up the phone and walked out into the foggy hotel gardens. They smelled sweetly of night-blooming jasmine and evening primrose, but even those scents did not ease his worry.

The St. Germain had rung his sister's room for him despite the fact that she and two male companions had been seen leaving no more than half an hour before. He'd wanted to tell her about his conversation with Felix.

"What's wrong, Stephen?" His hulking brother, Ivor, silently emerged from the fog.

Briefly, Stephen explained about the call from Felix Farquhar, Julian's assistant. "Natasha's already left for Biting Man. Michael and Julian are with her."

"Julian's there?"

"The hotel clerk described him perfectly. That means Amanda is there, too. Somewhere." He searched his brother's face. "This isn't good, Ivor. This isn't good at all."

"Her cell isn't working?"

"Service up there is terrible - and she'll be in the Eternal City by now, where there's absolutely no chance of contacting her."

"What precisely is it that you need to tell Natasha?"

Stephen opened his mouth, then closed it. "You're always the voice of reason, Ivor. If Julian is with them, they already know Amanda is nearby. But he may be under her thrall. Incendarius can do terrible things to a Trueborn. We need to make sure Natasha and Michael are aware that they can't trust Julian right now."

"I believe they know this. You've already passed on the information about Incendarius, correct?"

"Yes."

"Then don't worry. They'll be on the alert." Ivor paused. "If I were guarding Julian, I wouldn't leave him by himself for fear of Amanda locating him. I would keep him with me at all times." He paused. "After all, we human vampires are not in such danger as a Trueborn and he needs their protection."

"They're guarding him," Stephen said softly, embarrassed he hadn't reasoned it out on his own.

"I would wager on it."

∼

"It's like Halloween," Eddie said. He and Lois sat on a park bench beneath the glow of an old-fashioned lamp. They waited for Renny to do his business, while watching the fang-boys and girls party. Most were dressed in fantasy garb, mainly vampiric, but there were plenty of werewolves, wizards, and Wonder Women in the mix. A band that looked straight out of Bobby Pickett's Monster Mash, performed in the band shell with more enthusiasm than talent. The atmosphere in the square was giddy; the fang-kids were there for a good time, nothing more, and that pleased Eddie. "It's nice to see them having fun," he told Lois.

She nodded, her eyes on Renny. "Yes. I wish I could enjoy it more."

"I know you do." Eddie gave her free hand a squeeze. "It'll be okay." He hoped he was right, but he could barely push away his own worry.

And, he wouldn't tell Lois, but he felt like they were being watched. He'd had plenty of stalkers in his years as a talk show jock - mostly female, jealous with imagined love - and he had quickly developed a sixth sense about the crazier ones. He would feel a certain twist in his solar plexus and if he looked out the radio station window, he'd see his stalker's car sitting on the street below. If the internal twist happened right before the phone rang, he'd know it was one of the women who thought he should belong to them. And he was always right.

He felt like that now, only it was different, oozing with a confusion of violence and lust. The feeling had come and gone since they'd arrived in Eternity, and had grown stronger earlier this afternoon. It was there now, but weak, as if Neil - *I know it's Neil* - wasn't concentrating on him or Lois at the moment. He wondered if Lois sensed it, too; he hoped not.

Happy shrieks and giggles punctuated the Monster Mash band. Frankenstein and his bride, in perfect costumes, strolled by, holding hands and smiling. A Lugosi-style vampire told them *Good Evening* as he passed. It was a cool, perfect night, full of happy partiers, yet Eddie had to force himself not to tremble.

～

THE EVENING WORE ON. On his post on the toilet, Neil briefly gained consciousness. After more violent expulsions, his body was worn out and his mind could take no more. Leaving the safety of the porcelain throne, however, was not an option - and Neil had begun to wonder if it would ever be again.

He raised his head, groaning deeply as his eyes - blurred and seeing double half the time - rolled around like bloodshot marbles in their sockets. His leg muscles ached, his lower back protested, and Neil didn't have the strength to move. The fever was high enough now that his vision blurred and every inch of his skin felt as though it were being pricked by invisible needles. His throat burned furiously with acidic bile and each time he succumbed to another round of the shits, his ass screamed out agony.

But Neil remained helpless against it. As unconsciousness threatened to overtake him once more, he tipped over and collapsed onto the floor, splatting into a puddle of something cool, wet, and malodorous. As he lay there shivering, his soiled pants around his ankles, his mind circled around the same subjects: Eddie, Mom, and the vampires. *This is their fault,* he thought. *And if I survive this, they're going to pay for it - every last one of them.* He opened his mouth to allow another stream of noxious vomit to escape.

When he finished, Neil felt an invisible hand on his shoulder. Then the voice: *"Neil, this is good work. I am pleased."*

Neil blinked, unable to move. "Who's there?" he croaked.

"I think you know," said the deep, beautiful, disembodied voice.

Neil squeezed his eyes shut. *No. I'm imagining things. That stuff I drank ... it's playing tricks on my mind. There's no such thing as-*

"That's right, Neil," the voice interrupted. *"It's Me. The Lord. I've come to guide you, My child."*

"No way. You're not really-"

"Real?" The Lord chuckled. *"Oh, I'm real, all right. And I'm here to help you complete your mission."*

Neil couldn't believe it. *I'm going crazy,* he thought. He opened his mouth, loosing another hot stream of unmentionable sludge before fully losing consciousness.

56

ENTERING THE ETERNAL CITY

Julian sat between Natasha and Michael as they rode the lift from the Ski Bowl down to the hidden elevators that would take them into the Eternal City. The elevators were modern - last time Natasha had been here, they'd traversed thousands of stone steps to enter the sacred mountain.

It had been Julian's idea to ensure his safety by accompanying them to Biting Man and it had been a good one. Not only that, but Natasha had to admit that his chosen disguise - a Bela Lugosi-style tux, complete with white vest, bow tie, and red-lined cape - was brilliant. The costume was available throughout the town and it seemed like nearly half the males - both vampiric and the fang-boys - had chosen to wear it, making the disguise even more innocuous. She wondered what the real Lugosi thought of such an honor.

When they'd arrived at the Ski Bowl, Natasha had been pleased to see that at least half the attendees were, like she and Michael, not in costume. Natasha wore a sleek little red dress that hugged her figure in the best way possible. Her accessories - shoes, bag, and jewelry - were black. Michael had chosen the same colors. He wore black trousers and a vest over a red long-sleeved shirt. His dark hair, as usual, was pulled back in a low ponytail that accentuated his square jaw and high cheekbones. His garments made Natasha think of Mick Fleetwood's clothing on the *Rumours* album cover - minus the ridiculous dangling wooden balls. She glanced at him now. Fleetwood could only dream of being as well-built and handsome as her companion. She smiled and Michael caught her eye, a subtle gleam in his.

"Are the two of you lovers?" Julian asked, dry as dust.

"We have known one another in the past," Michael said after Natasha gave a vague nod.

"Well, you look as if you are in need of more knowledge. I am sorry to intrude tonight."

"You're not intruding," Natasha told him. "We're glad you're with us."

"As am I."

They rode another hundred feet in silence then slipped off the lift bench at a deceptively normal-looking cafe at the bottom of the hill. Two vampires, a man and a woman dressed in rich Victorian costumery, nodded at them as they boarded the lift back up toward the Ski Bowl.

A sleek vampire in black guided them into the closed cafe, then down a set of hidden stairs and into a cavernous area below. He pressed a hidden button and a door - disguised as a granite wall - slid open to reveal two elevators. "Hotel or festival?" the vampire asked.

"Festival, please."

The vampiric guide motioned them into the correct elevator and a moment later, they were traveling down at a startling rate.

"Julian," said Michael. "Are you certain Amanda isn't here yet?"

"I sincerely doubt it. She's probably still in the woods - I doubt she's even made it to the highway as yet. I barely feel her."

"Good."

Natasha was relieved that Julian was so sure; she wanted to have a little time to relax and enjoy the festival without having to play bodyguard - they were planning to meet up with Michael's group, as well as her sisters and Cousin Daisy before long. That Julian would remain with all of them was not a concern. There was safety in numbers and while Natasha and Julian had once been at odds, that time was long over. She valued him now and wanted to ensure his safety.

The elevator slowed and as it came to a stop, they heard merriment and music beyond. When the doors slid open, they caught their first glimpse of Biting Man in all its glory. Natasha gasped, Michael's eyes narrowed, and Julian pulled his cape closer, disguising his face as best he could.

∼

"I CAN'T HELP FEELING a little sad for them." Chynna stood beside Winter in a cavernous ballroom and watched two child vampires moving with swan-like grace over the dancefloor. They wore Regency-era finery and despite their undeveloped bodies, they carried themselves with the dignified manner of a couple much older and much wiser than their appearance suggested.

"Nonsense," Winter said. "They look happy." He watched them smile at each other as they step-danced in a slow semicircle, their fingertips entwined. "And I can't help noticing no one's giving them the stink-eye, which bodes well for Arnie." If the vampire extremist groups disapproved of anything more than a mentally or physically challenged vampire, it was a child vampire.

"I noticed that, too. It's such a relief that things seem more liberal now." Chynna looked dazzling in her modern all-silver attire - faux-silver hoop earrings and half-moon pendant, and a silver tunic over silver pants. She wore the color often - as if in defiance of her inability to get close to the real thing - and this, more than the vampiric children on the dancefloor, drew shocked looks. *Screw them,* thought Winter. *Screw them all.* He thought Chynna looked fantastic - she smelled fantastic as well. Despite her vampirism, silver became her. Even her eyes seemed silvery, and her pale blond hair glinted the same shade.

He felt like a bit of a clod in his white wife beater, tight white jeans, and clunky black boots, but it wasn't all the elegantly dressed festival goers that brought the feeling, he realized - it was standing next to Chynna that had him self-conscious. She was attractive - he'd always been aware of that - but these past few hours, he couldn't seem to take his eyes, or his mind, off her. *It's the way she stood up to me when we were talking about Arnie,* he realized. Winter wasn't used to being defied and was surprised to find out he rather liked the challenge. *As long as she doesn't sic her tigers on me, that is.* He chuckled at the thought.

"What are you grinning about?" Chynna glanced up at him. She was tall, but next to Winter she seemed petite.

"Nothing," said Winter. "Do you want something to drink? I'm buying."

Chynna shrugged. "Let's see what they have."

They stepped out of the ballroom and into the midway. The options were endless; the place was brimming with stands and kiosks and bars all selling something you just couldn't live without. There was a Lixir vendor and several Slater Bros. stands, which only slightly outnumbered their competitors - Hemo Farms and Sanguine Spirits - where you could purchase bottled blood, alcoholic or otherwise, in plastic wine glasses. At the libation bars, there were claret cocktails and plasma shots. The lines were long and daunting and Winter was relieved when Chynna declined his offer.

Over the clamor of voices, Winter heard the unmistakable beat of hard rock coming from a nearby cavern. It was a sound that pumped a happy buzz into his blood and instinctively, he said, "Let's go see who's playing." He hadn't realized he'd put his hand on Chynna's lower back until he felt the silkiness of her tunic - and the firmness of her flesh beneath it. She made no objection and as Winter shouldered his way through the mass of loitering, half-drunken vampires, he found himself growing aroused.

He was almost disappointed when they arrived and he no longer had any excuse to touch her. The amphitheater was crowded - undoubtedly beyond the legal limit - and Winter scarcely recognized the eyeliner-wearing, leather-clad, head-banging band onstage.

Chynna pointed. "Is that ...?"

"Plastic Taffy. Yep."

"What on *earth* have they done to themselves?"

Winter shrugged. "Not a clue, but they've been turned or they wouldn't be here." These were not the same boys who'd stared out from the posters on Arnie's bedroom wall ten years ago when the band had briefly caught his attention, and were it not for the lead singer's shock of blue-black hair, which was now ratted into a semblance of something from the 1980s, Winter wasn't sure he would have recognized them.

They played one of their old songs - one he'd heard on the radio and from Arnie's bedroom a thousand times many years ago - but it was like a demonic clone of itself. Gone were the bubblegum sounds of synthesized instruments. Instead, guitars crunched, hair flew, drums pounded, and leather-cupped genitals bulged. At musical high points, the lead singer squeezed his crude package in a vulgar display of middle-aged teenage rebellion. But the Plastic Taffy band members were no longer teens and it was the most unseemly performance he'd seen since a fifty-something Madonna had strutted, shimmied, and strained in full cheerleader gear for the Super Bowl halftime show.

In the audience, a platinum blond in a red corset hopped onto someone's shoulders to throw devil horns. For an unsettling instant, Winter thought he was looking at Gretchen VanTreese who, as far as he knew, was still at the bottom of the lake in Crimson Cove, stake through her heart. He shuddered at the memories of the destruction that tiny woman had caused Michael's group and, not for the first time, wished that Michael had taken off her head and buried it somewhere deep, very far away.

∽

JULIAN HAD BEEN in the Eternal City many times, but this was his first visit during a modern Biting Man Festival. It was obscene. *But what were you expecting? Quiet reverence? Trueborn choirs singing beatific high hymns to the moon and stars, to nature and night creatures, music not unlike Gregorian chants but so much sweeter?*

For a moment, Julian was transported to his youth on the island of Euloa. The rolling hills, the alabaster buildings, the spires and columns and courtyards. His father's palace had atriums devoted to night-blooming flowers and the art in the palace rivaled that in the museums and public places of their land. And there was Talai, the human servant girl he'd fallen in love with. Talai, who had destroyed herself at sunrise rather than accept the bite that would give her immortality.

If Julian had been a hybrid vampire, he might have shed a tear, but his kind did not allow themselves to indulge in such emotions. But when Talai reincarnated as a woman, no matter where or when, Julian always found her and, usually, attempted to turn her - not in one traumatic bite, but with three gentle ones done with romance and understanding. Yet it had never worked.

Until she became Amanda. And even then, Stephen Darling, a mere hybrid, had turned her. And she had become a monster.

Incendarius.

His darling Talai must have possessed some inner knowledge of what she would become, for although she always expressed love for him, she inevitably took her own life rather than permit the change. She had known, on some level, that she would destroy him if she allowed the Transition.

He loved her for her sacrifice. *If only I'd realized.*

Walking with Natasha and Michael deeper into the caverns, he heard a cacophony of voices and music, smelled an array of bloods, most cheap and vulgar, some exquisite, and wondered what had happened to Talai when she reincarnated as Amanda. Amanda had been a lovely young human, sweet and sincere, and she had allowed Stephen to turn her. *Why? Did she not sense this time what she was? Did she not feel Incendarius lurking within her?*

She had not. Her human nature had been as lovely and kind in Amanda as it had been in her other incarnations. No, she hadn't known. Something was different within her, something that kept her from knowing.

And now she is Incendarius. And she had drunk of his own Trueborn blood, making her, quite possibly, his equal in strength of will and body. And she had bewitched him. He nearly smiled to himself, thinking of the humans' heroic invincible Superman, who only lost his strength to Kryptonite. Amanda was Julian's Kryptonite. The irony might have amused him if the danger hadn't been so real.

"Julian?" Michael touched his arm.

He shook off his reverie, became aware of the noises and odors of this crowded place once more. "Yes?"

"There's a Lixir vendor over there." He pointed at a small booth doing a landslide business. "Did you send him?"

"No. He is illicit." A rush of rage killed Julian's melancholy. He stalked quickly toward the vendor, vaguely aware of his companions on his heels. The booth was sandwiched between a t-shirt vendor (*I've Been to Biting Man!, Bloody Good Show, Crimson Tides are Best*), and a comic book merchant featuring Vampira, and an undead Archie Gang.

He approached the Lixir booth, and pushed to the front of the line. "Who are you to sell-" he demanded just as Michael's hand came down hard on his shoulder.

"Excuse our friend," Michael said to the vendor. "I'm afraid he's had too many plasma shots this evening."

Julian whirled, fire in his heart, forgetting to mask his face, but Michael caught his gaze. His supremely stern gaze. Beside him, Natasha's eyes pleaded.

All at once, he understood that if they had not intervened, the illegal vendor would be on the floor, his head torn from his body. Shocked at his own lack of control and hoping no one had recognized him, Julian quickly raised his cape to cover his lower face and let Michael and Natasha lead him to a deserted alcove.

"Are you all right?" Natasha asked.

"I am. But I am not myself and was about to act without thought."

"I'll tell the festival administration that the vendor isn't licensed to sell Lixir," Natasha said. "They'll handle the problem."

"I thank you. Both of you." Julian paused, looking around at the garish, costumed hybrids, at the fairground-style booths lining the walls, raking in money. *They are no different than ordinary humans, driven by greed and lust and little else.* "Michael, Natasha, I am in your debt. I am not myself. Incendarius has seen to that."

"Incendarius," Natasha repeated, her voice so soft that he only read her lips. "Do you sense her?"

Julian closed his eyes and scanned for Amanda, opening his mind to her wiles. Finally he looked at Michael and Natasha. "Though still far away, she is nearing. She is out there somewhere, but there is still time."

"Time?" Michael asked.

"Time for you to enjoy this festival without worry." He paused. "It would be wise to locate your clans and visit with them soon."

Michael pulled an antique pocket watch from his vest. "We are supposed to meet outside the temple in fifteen minutes." He raised his brows at Julian.

"That should work out well. I believe it will take nearly that long to walk there. I suggest we begin."

His companions nodded and, once again, they flanked him as they walked along halls full of hybrids wearing bat flower leis and selling souvenirs. Their protectiveness annoyed him, but he also appreciated it. However, his companions, strong as they were, could not protect him from Incendarius, not if he could not find the strength to fight her alongside them. Still, he appreciated the gesture.

57
SHAMELESS

The red Camaro drove as smoothly as a kitten's purr. Norman had found it in the parking lot behind a chichi bar and grill in Mill Valley that had paid more for its tall outdoor neon sign than its building, which was little more than an aluminum box on a patch of landscaped dirt. Under different circumstances, he might have taken some time to enjoy his find, perhaps driven the Camaro up some of the local canyons, but tonight he had only one thing on his mind - his Maker. And She was close. He could feel Her.

He sped north on Interstate 5 on his way to Eternity, knowing that with every passing mile, he was that much closer to his goal. It was all-consuming now. Thoughts of his Maker burned like brushfire in his head, leaving no room for anything else. His skin buzzed with Her very closeness, the tiny hairs on his body stood on end as if in response to an electrical storm, and though he wasn't sexually aroused, his penis was stiff in his jeans, resting against the flat of his belly like a sun-hot stone. His entire body was on alert; he thought he could even detect the ghost of Her scent in the air and taste the salt of Her skin on his tongue. Yes, he was getting close.

AMANDA'S bare feet hurt and she kept getting lost as she tried to find her way out of the forest and onto the main road. "Fuck you, Julie, fuck you!" was her mantra. She walked, stubbing her toes and ruining her pedicure as she tried to stick to the dirt track they had driven into the woods the night before. But it was nearly impossible since the path barely ever even looked like a path. It was all pine needles and sharp stones and ruts and rocks and sticks. "Fuck you, Julie, fuck you!"

After her bath, she'd had to dress in the same outfit she'd worn yesterday since the bastard had taken off with her clothes. She felt funky. "Fuck you, Julie, fuck you."

Now she walked on in darkness. The moon was hidden behind a covering of trees so thick that even her vampiric night vision was severely impaired, making her stumble into unexpected boulders and trip over windfall trunks. "Fuck you, Julie, fuck you."

But he wouldn't win. He wanted her to be stuck out here and she wondered if he'd even been sure she'd find his cabin. *Probably. He's addicted to me. He wouldn't let me die.* But he did dare to strand her.

She heard cars, like rushing water, in the far distance. When she made it to town, Julian Valentyn would be one sorry sonofabitch. "Fuck you, Julie, fuck you."

∼

"THERE'S NATASHA AND MICHAEL." Ivy pointed.

"Where?" Lucy asked.

"By the temple entrance. Remember? We said we'd meet them there, you silly twat."

"I remember, I remember. Jesus, there's so many people in here I can't see shit!" Lucy stood on tiptoes. "Oh, there they are. Is that Julian with them?"

"Who's Julian?" Daisy asked, adjusting her leopard-print skirt and snapping her chewing gum.

Ivy spotted a platinum blond man in a Dracula cape talking with her big sister and Michael. "I can't tell if it's Julian." She paused. "I thought he never came to Biting Man."

Lucy squinted. "It looks like him, but I'm not sure."

"Who the hell is Julian?" demanded Daisy. She was carrying a six pack of plasma shots in a little cardboard carrier and she lifted one before sticking her tongue out, coated with Double Bubble, and blowing. Once it popped, she poured the shot down her throat.

"You're going to OD on that shit," Lucy told her. "It doesn't even taste like human plasma. I think it's like cow or rat or something. And it's mixed with really crappy vodka."

"Mind your own beeswax, Luce." Daisy, so drunk she was half-staggering, defiantly downed yet another shot. "And who the hell is Julian?"

"A friend of ours." Ivy threw Lucy a concerned glance. If it really was Julian, he wouldn't want anyone outing him, that was for sure.

"Well, let's go check them out," Daisy said, her voice too loud. "And who the hell is that tall drink of water talking to your big sister?"

"That's her friend, Michael."

"Michael who? He sure is good looking." *Snap. Pop.*

"He's in charge of the clan in Crimson Cove," Ivy said. "And he and Natasha are real friendly."

"Are they fucking?"

"How should I know?" Ivy suddenly wished they could ditch Daisy, but didn't know how.

"Why don't you ask them if they're fucking, Daisy?" Lucy winked at Ivy.

"Good idea. I want me some of that. Who cares if they're fucking? I'll take that any way I can get it. Mm-mm, good!" Daisy snapped her gum. "Hey look! It's Winter and that bitch from yesterday. I could use some more of him, too. In the hot tub. Couldn't you?" *Snap, snap, snap* went the gum.

Winter and Chynna were heading right for them and as Ivy watched, he waved. Daisy waved back enthusiastically enough for all three of them.

The big man - he looked like a hotter version of Mr. Clean to Ivy, who'd always had a little thing for the well-muscled cleaning guy - came closer.

"I wish he'd left that silver whore at the hotel," Crazy Daisy muttered.

"Ladies," Winter boomed. "Are you having a good time?"

Daisy looked him up and down. "We are now."

He ignored her. "Have you seen Michael?" As he spoke, he drew Chynna's hand through his arm and patted it, confirming Ivy's suspicions that the two of them had a little thing going on. Daisy was scowling. That made Ivy smile.

"Yeah." Lucy pointed. "Come on. They're waiting by the temple doors."

Ivy and Lucy led the way and as they approached, Ivy saw that it really was Julian in the Dracula costume. When he'd told them the stories of his Trueborn roots, of when he had led a revolt against his father, he said he'd ruled here in the Eternal City and had been worshipped, but that he never wanted anything to do with all that. *So why is he here?* Ivy tapped her sister's shoulder. "We need to be cool around Julian."

"I know."

"What about Daisy?"

"Good thing we didn't tell her jack shit about him."

Ivy nodded, and an instant later, the families - hers and Michael's - were all together.

∾

THE WOMAN.

It was She.

Even when Norman could make out no more than a lithe black shape on the side of the winding two-lane highway, he knew this was his Maker. He pulled the Camaro over and She brought Her thumb down. As She headed for the car, his bones rang out with the electric buzz of Her very nearness. It was as if every cell in his body had been pulling him magnetically toward Her, and now that he had found Her, he crackled with new life. Even his teeth felt alive. He lowered the passenger side window and grinned.

She leaned in, showing what seemed like miles and miles of milky-white cleavage. "Where are you headed?" But there was no hint of recognition in Her luminous eyes, and Norman felt a stab of rejection.

"Eternity," he said. "The same as You."

She eyed him. "How do you know where I'm going?"

Seeing that She clearly didn't recognize him, Norman decided to give it to Her straight. His Maker seemed like the kind of woman who could take it straight - it was something he knew without knowing how. "You're the Woman who tore my throat out the other day under the pier in Candle Bay. I was hoping I might get to know You a little better."

She stared at him, long and hard.

"I'm not interested in revenge," Norman said.

A slow smile spread like a stain on Her red lips and Her eyes went as hard as Norman's manhood. "I fear no such thing, I assure you."

Norman caught the subtext: *Bitch, I could kill you a second time without even smearing my lipstick* - and he had no doubt it was the truth. "Don't you want a ride to Eternity?" There was a childlike desperation in his voice, a vulnerability he didn't much like - but it didn't matter. He *had* to be with the Woman, and his dignity was a small cost. "It's a long walk and You're barefoot. I don't think You'll have much luck hitching. The roads are dead tonight."

The Woman smiled, flashing straight white teeth that glistened like freshly-painted fence posts under the silvery moon.

Norman's mouth watered with a need to run his tongue across those teeth.

"I'll take the ride, sure - but I have just one question first."

"Anything. Ask me anything." *God, just get in! Please get in the car!* He needed Her closer, closer.

"What business do you have in Eternity?"

Norman spoke before he thought. "You. You're my only business. Eternity is where You're going so it's where I need to be."

"I remember you now." Her smile broadened. She slid into the passenger seat and for a moment, Norman just sat there, unable to peel his gaze away. She knew he was looking and seemed to enjoy it. Reaching up with a pale fine-boned hand, She removed her black leather jacket. The motion jutted Her breasts out and Norman could see the peachy-soft circles of her nipples beneath the fine fabric - and now he really was sexually aroused; it was as if his cock had simply been waiting for the rest of him to catch up. "Amanda?" he whispered.

"Yes, that's me," said the Woman, eyes narrowing. "But you can call me Mistress." Her gaze slid down to his lap and took in the straining spike that stood there. "And I'll call you Surfer Boy."

"You can call me anything You want. I don't mind."

"I don't care if you *do* mind. Quit staring at my tits and drive."

Norman slammed the car into gear and took off, raising dust and spewing gravel behind him. For the first time in his existence, all was right in the world - and if this Woman had wanted him to drive Her to the moon, he would have found a way to do it.

∞

"Natasha. Michael. May I speak with you alone for a moment?" Julian, seated between them in an exclusive blood bar that catered to a quieter clientele than the stands in the cavernous midway, was growing uncomfortable. They - Natasha and Michael, Chynna, Winter, the twins, and the odious, drunken Daisy - had whiled away nearly an hour catching up on old times, and if Daisy popped her gum once more, it was Julian who would snap.

"Of course. Excuse us for just a moment," Natasha told the table.

Michael Ward - a vampire Julian had respected ever since he and the Darlings had helped quell Gretchen VanTreese's uprising in Crimson Cove - raised his brows and accompanied them to a quiet corner.

"Is anything wrong?" Natasha asked. "Is Amanda-"

"She is somewhat closer, but fortunately, she is not here. Not yet. I suspect we might have an hour or more before she arrives." He paused. "I am certain, however, she is on her way and I would like to absent myself from this place before she appears."

"We will leave now, Julian." Michael and Natasha spoke simultaneously.

"No, it's not my intention to drag you away from the festivities."

"I've had all the excitement I need for one night." Natasha said.

Michael nodded agreement.

"No." Julian gave them a thin but sincere smile. "I believe you two have unfinished business. I do not want to intrude-"

"You're not intruding."

He raised a finger to his lips. "Listen to me, both of you. I understand that there is an unused bedroom in Winter and Chynna's suite and I believe I would be better off varying my location - that may keep Amanda from sensing my presence so easily. Would you check and see if they are amenable?"

"Of course," Michael said.

"Are you sure?"

"I am, Natasha." Julian reached out and brushed the back of his fingers against her perfect porcelain cheek. "You must take happiness where you can find it. And you, as well, Michael. See that you do."

"I-"

"You know of what I speak." He hooked his eyes into theirs. "I sense that the two of you have known one another a very long time."

Natasha blushed. "Yes, but-"

"There is longing in you both." He gently kissed Natasha's forehead then briefly took Michael's hand. "I have lived longer than even you can imagine, and I tell you this with the utmost sincerity. Find happiness. It is the one thing that matters most in this world."

They stared at him.

"And now I wish to spend a few moments alone in the temple. Perhaps half an hour." This smile was even thinner than the last. "I wish to indulge in a few memories."

"I'll ask Winter to meet you outside the temple in thirty minutes."

"That would be excellent. If he can simply give me directions and a key, he can rejoin the party. I shall find my own way to the hotel."

58

ARE YOU THERE GOD? IT'S ME, NEIL

Neil woke, finding himself feeling well enough to at last leave the bathroom. Getting to his feet, he wandered into the bedroom, half dragging his left leg, which had become numb, and flopped down onto the bed, not caring at all that his soiled body and clothes would render the bedsheets profane.

He had heard the voice of God - he was sure of it - but now, all was silent.

"Hello?" he mumbled. "Are you there, God? It's me, Neil!"

Only silence.

"Jesus Christ in a picnic basket, where *are* you?" *Some people are so fucking rude!*

Or maybe I was just hallucinating...

Either way, Neil couldn't lose sight of his mission. He wiped a glob of mysterious bodily fluid onto his pant leg, and stared up at the ceiling. He was certain he was feeling better - a little, anyway - but he wanted to hurry his recovery along. He had shit to do and was tired of being held up. *Those little bitches aren't going to kill themselves!*

He looked down at his lap, wondering if he had it in him to administer a little self-gratification. That *always* made him feel better. *But what if God's watching?* Neil shrugged. *Oh, well.*

There was not a day in Neil's memory that he hadn't choked the chicken at least half a dozen times. Sure, the number dropped slightly when he had the flu or a cold, but he still pumped the python at least two or three times daily, no matter how sick he felt. He could be dying and still crank his shank at least once or twice before he kicked off.

It's worth a shot. He freed Neil Jr., but try as he might, nothing made his man-pickle perk up. He thought of a girl with gigantic titties and pubic hair showing through her white bikini he'd seen on the beach when he was thirteen.

Nothing.

Of Buffy, naked and begging for it.

Still nothing.

Of the times he'd spied on his mother while she showered.

Not a twitch.

Of Coastal Eddie's faggy-sack hitting her filthy bitch snatch as he pounded her. He felt something then - anger - and Neil Jr. responded. He fed the fantasy, picturing the old hippie giving it to Mom in the ass before spewing on her tits. *Twitch, twitch, twitch.* "That's it ... Come on boy, sit up and beg."

He reached down and started to stroke the beast, pulling back momentarily when he felt air bubbles, like Rice Krispies, snapping, crackling, and popping under the skin. "What the fuck?"

It still felt good, though. But it made it hard to concentrate. His skin sounded like frying chicken. His stomach growled at the thought - then spun as if to rebel against such a heinous idea. For a moment, Neil thought he might shit the bed ... but the feeling passed. He sighed, relaxed his sphincter, and continued trying to buff the banana. But the banana wasn't having it. It was like playing with a blob of silly putty. Neil Jr. was *not* in the mood.

Maybe later.

Neil coughed - a deep, wet one that nearly brought up his insides. He rolled over, hacking and trying to get air - and that's when he noticed the blood. There were just a few specks of it dotting the pillow. A coppery taste filled his mouth. Whether it had come from his stomach, his gums, or his lungs, he didn't know, but regardless, he was suddenly terrified. Terrified, but more determined than ever to carry out the mission he'd been born to execute.

The fear was like an injection. It shot new life into him, and despite the still-lingering nausea, he gained his feet, grabbed his backpack, and headed out of the cabin, more resolved than ever before to kill whatever - and whoever - needed to be killed.

I'm coming, Mother.

He only hoped she and Eddie would be fucking when he arrived.

59

MY NEW HEROIN

"And then," Norman droned on, "when we get back to Candle Bay, we could get a place together - or at least, two places that are close to each other. And then, when You're ready to take the next step, we can-"

"I've told you, Surfer Boy," Amanda interrupted. "We are *not* getting married."

But he didn't hear anything except the sound of his own irritating, blathering, infuriating voice. "I'll give up turning tricks, of course. Now that I'm one of you, I haven't had a single craving for smack since!" He turned and grinned, and Amanda wished he'd shut the fuck up and keep his eyes on the road. "I always wanted to be an astrologer, and now, I finally can be. What's Your sign?" He didn't pause for an answer. "Of course, blood is kind of my new heroin, but I think You can teach me how to-"

"I'm not teaching you anything, Norman. I just needed a goddamned ride."

"-feed without making a mess so I can live a normal life with You. It's so exciting! To think, just twenty-four hours ago, I was ..."

Amanda tuned him out. She needed to get away from this guy, and bad. She looked at him, feeling nothing, and realized that if she weren't so tired, she'd kill him. Again. Right here and now. Then she'd take the car, and find her way to Biting Man by herself.

As Surfer Boy prattled on, Amanda fantasized about her upcoming wedding ceremony with Julian and smiled, thinking of what she'd wear.

60

IN THE TEMPLE

Julian stared at his own face on the wall. He had passed by numerous stone statues, most of the Treasure himself, but they were of no interest, even the one of Keliu in Euloan finery. But the mosaic was beautiful, the detailed art colorful and precise. He drew his Dracula cape closer to his face, hiding everything but his eyes, wishing for a hood or a wig to disguise his platinum hair. At least it was pulled back and hidden beneath his shirt collar.

A temple priest, garbed in a traditional emerald and white robe, had managed to approach without Julian's knowledge. He stood next to him now, his hands hidden beneath the long, belled sleeves. Julian looked at the gold embroidery that decorated the hem. The old runes were beautiful but Julian thought that the translation was probably long lost. He hoped so.

"My name is Diego and I am one of the priests here to help. Do you know the history of this place?"

"The history? Indeed, I have studied the history of the Eternal City at some length." While he dared not lock eyes with the priest, he stole furtive glances, thinking there was something familiar about him.

"If I may say so, sir, you have the look of a scholar." The priest spoke with a slight Spanish accent. His eyebrow shot up. "Despite your costume."

Julian nodded. The costume, while necessary, embarrassed him, but he could not be there without it. *I should not have entered the temple.*

Temple Vampirus was a place that few festival goers frequented. Silence and respect were expected and those were not things that were willingly given, except during tomorrow's Passion Play, which included the traditional reenactment of the Prince's overthrow of the Treasure. A century ago, Julian had slipped in, in a more appropriate disguise, to watch and had been relieved that so little of the original tale remained extant.

The cella was huge, the walls hewn from the natural limestone and granite of the cavern. Along them, were columns and pillars carved in what appeared to the modern eye as Doric columns, but they were Euloan, not Grecian, and far older. The differences were subtle but obvious to Julian's eyes. Most of the perceived columns were not carven at all, but were natural stalagmites and stalactites. Many of them were cavern pillars and served more beautifully than any carven ones. Julian himself had stopped the carving of pillars and decreed that the cavern had to be kept in its natural state. His father had already removed many small natural cave formations when Julian - then Keliu - had arrived, but he hadn't managed to destroy the natural beauty.

After Keliu deposed the King, he had declared the cavern sacred and ordered it protected. Before that, it had been his father's throne room. Much blood - human, hybrid, and Trueborn - had been spilled there by the Treasure. It had flowed into the stream that still bubbled across the room and into a great waterfall in the darkness beyond the Treasure's throne.

The throne remained and at the moment, another temple priest sat in it, enjoying a hookah full of bloodweed. Julian found it offensive. The throne was a natural formation that resembled a tall chair with carven stalagmites at all four corners. Only the marble steps to it had been created and set into place. He stared up at the ancient throne now, remembering what it had been like to sit there.

Glancing at the priest beside him, he caught him staring. "I did not know that it was permissible now for anyone, priest or otherwise, to occupy the throne."

The priest seemed to notice the smoker for the first time. He raised his voice. "Cornelius, it is not seemly to sit there."

The other priest looked up, his eyes red with the effects of bloodweed, saw Julian, and muttered something as he rose and carried his massive water pipe into the darkness. "I apologize for his behavior," the priest said. "He is not himself. He lost a very good friend. Security informed him earlier tonight. He was murdered as he slept in a cabin in town."

Julian nodded, barely hearing him. He stared at the throne, remembering. After he vanquished the Treasure and imprisoned him in a small cavern many miles distant, he had enjoyed the feeling of accomplishment, knowing that at last he had stopped his father's reign for all time. But sitting on a throne soon grew wearisome. He hated that many vampires insisted on worshipping him as a god-king - as they had his father. He disliked the politics, the constant talk of battles, and he'd yearned to wander the world again, as he had for eons.

He heard familiar voices drift into the temple. Winter and Chynna had arrived. With a last look at the mosaic depicting his reign, he took his leave and approached the waiting vampires, knowing that they would not allow him to leave alone and secretly glad of it. Amanda's presence was much stronger now.

61

THE MAD SHITTER

Zach Tully yawned. He'd always been a morning kind of guy but had decided that, for the Biting Man weekend, he'd have to work the nightshift.

It had been a weird couple of days. Most of his deputies had no idea the town was full of *real* vampires; they thought that the festival was simply a very serious convention - an academic one as far as the festivities on the mountain went - and that the fang-boys and girls in town were all they had to concern themselves with. Essentially, it was the truth, and Tully always preferred to stick as close as possible to the facts.

But Tim Hapscomb, his right-hand man, knew the truth. Tim had been with him since Tully's arrival and always knew - and accepted - everything and anything without comment. He was the only non-lifer besides Tully himself who believed - who *knew* - that Jack the Ripper had been the real thing. He knew that dearly departed Mayor Abbott had really been Ambrose Bierce. He was the one who asked postmistress Amelia Earhart questions about her air travels and who had Elvis autograph his collection of vintage LPs. In the first years, Tully had half-thought that Deputy Hapscomb was a little simple, but he'd been wrong. Tim Hapscomb, seemingly laconic, was one of the canniest cops he had ever met.

Tim had volunteered to man the radio in case anything happened that other dispatchers wouldn't understand. He was probably sleeping, but Tully took comfort in the knowledge that Tim was there.

Tully had cruised Main Street earlier, checking out the fang-kids in the park. He wasn't needed there - it was covered. After that, he cruised the back roads, paved and gravel both, keeping his eye out for strays - human or vampire. *Hopefully only human.* As he rounded a hairpin curve, his headlights flashed over a few cabins, all but one, dark and deserted. The exception glowed with lamplight but there was no car parked out front.

It was probably a rental waiting for the return of a pack of fang-boys. *Or maybe a vampire.* He pulled over and picked up the handset, dispensing with codes. "Tim? Come in."

After a beat, the deputy's voice crackled through. "I'm here."

"Can you check on an address for me? 884 Pine Tree Lane. See if it's currently occupied."

Tim would know he meant by a vampire.

"The cabin is empty right now. The Stratons own it; they come up most weekends from Shasta, so they don't rent it out."

"The lights are on."

"They keep the power on during the summer."

"I'd better check it out."

"10-4. Closest backup is Car 54."

"Got it. Out."

Tully turned off the engine, attached his personal transmitter to his jacket and exited the SUV. As always, a little thrill ran through him as he checked his Glock before approaching the cabin.

He knocked on the door, called out his identification then, receiving no response, he began a walk around the single-story cabin, looking for a view inside. Just as he wondered if he was on a fool's errand, he caught a whiff of something nasty.

As he approached a small window, the stink nearly took his head off.

At least it isn't a body he told himself as he peered inside. No, the cabin smelled of vomit and-

"Shit!" he muttered. He hadn't seen anything so disgusting since he was a young cop called to a college dorm where a dozen frat pledges had gotten shit-faced on Thunderbird laced with Ex-Lax. *This is worse.*

The walls were painted with vomit, most of it green fizzy stuff that smelled of yellow bile. And it only got worse. Sour, foul, diarrhea, coated the toilet and floor with brown ichor like wallpaper paste. The smell was beyond anything he'd ever imagined. *It's worse than a two-weeks-dead corpse in a trunk on a warm summer day.*

"Hello?" he called. "You okay in there?"

No reply. He tried several more times, then returned to the backdoor and jimmied it. As usual, it was way too easy to break in.

The kitchen was fairly clean. There was an open jar of pickles on the table, the vinegary scent mixing with the smell of sick coming from the next room. Two half-empty water bottles were on the counter as well as a half-eaten carton of tofu. *I'd get sick if I ate that shit, too.*

"Hello?" he called again as he stuck his head in the living room.

A mad shitter had obviously been squatting in the cabin. There was a pillow and a blanket tossed on the sofa and brown handprints and smears on the wall by the front door.

Tully called in to let Tim Hapscomb know that the Straton cabin had a squatter of the worst kind, but to wait until tomorrow to tell the owners. *Nothing they can do tonight.* He looked around and sighed. *Whoever the Mad Shitter is, he's doing the job up brown.*

Tully searched the living room, hoping to find something that would ID the perp, and hit pay dirt when he opened a magazine dedicated to 'vampire aficionados.' He strummed through the pages until a yellow sheet of paper fell out and drifted to the floor.

In crabbed handwriting, it said *Perdet Towers, Room 526.* It didn't mean much, but he supposed he ought to check it out since it might be connected to a fang-boy or even a vampire.

62

CONNECT FOUR

They sat at the table, facing each other, a game of Connect Four standing between them. Erin slid a black checker into the plastic slot, blocking Arnie from his goal. She fully intended to let him win, but she didn't want to be obvious about it.

Arnie's grin brightened. "You're almost as good as Papa Winter." He was clearly pleased that the game would be a challenging one. After discussing what to play - Arnie had everything from Operation to Dominoes to Hungry, Hungry Hippos in his suitcase - they'd decided on this one, which Erin hadn't played since childhood.

And she was having a good time. "I am the Connect Four master." She gave him a wry smile.

Arnie shook his head. "Nuh-uh. Papa Winter's the master." His face went serious.

Erin could see the love and admiration when Arnie spoke of his Maker and realized she already felt the beginnings of a similar affection toward Arnie. *My Maker,* she thought. She wondered if those feelings would continue to grow, turning into something comparable to the love she felt for her parents. She suspected so. *Vampirism is just like a family.* Which made Winter her ... what? A grandfather, of sorts? So what did she call him? *My grandmaker? Maybe I'm overthinking this.*

"Connect Four!" Arnie bounced in his seat and pointed excitedly at the four consecutive red discs lined up diagonally. "I win!"

Erin smiled. "Yes, you do." And she hadn't even let him. Looking at the grid now, she realized he'd created several contingency plans for himself - at this point, he would have won no matter where she'd put her token - and it occurred to her that the guy was sharper than she'd thought. While she'd been busy blocking him, he'd been strategizing. She felt a surge of pride for him - which was strange given that she barely knew him, and even stranger considering this was the same man who'd quite literally ended her life in the parking lot. *Ended my life, or given me new life?* It was both of those things, she realized.

"Let's go again!" Arnie emptied the grid. Red and black plastic tokens bounced and rattled on the table top. "I want to be red again. Can I be red again?"

"You sure can."

Someone knocked on the door, and Erin stood abruptly. She'd been on edge since she'd been turned - which was understandable - but only now did she recognize how relaxed she felt with Arnie. He seemed to be a kind of balm for her frayed, exposed nerves ... and now, someone was removing the Band-Aid. "I'll get it."

Arnie paid no attention as he separated the red discs from the black ones and prepared to start over. "I won so I get to go first."

Erin headed to the door and was relieved - and even excited - to see Eddie and Lois. Between them, Renny looked bored at the end of his leash.

Eddie was stiff, cautious. "We, uh, just wanted to make sure you were okay."

Lois, however, was already moving in for a hug. "How are you?"

"I'm fine, really." Erin hugged her back, enjoying it.

Lois broke the embrace, her hands on Erin's shoulders as she took her in. "You look fantastic, Erin."

"Thanks! I feel pretty great, too. Would you ..." Erin felt the brightness of her smile dim when she thought of inviting them in. *What if Arnie hurts them? He wouldn't, would he? Well, look what he did to me. Better safe than sorry.* She stepped into the hall, closing the door behind her. "I miss you guys." She bent to scratch Renny behind the ears. He responded by thumping his tail on the carpet. "I missed you, too, boy."

Eddie cleared his throat. "Is everything *really* okay?" His voice was low, serious, and conspiratorial. "They're not holding you against your will. Blink twice if—"

Erin laughed. "I'm fine. I promise. I'm just spending time with ... well, with my new friend."

Lois nodded.

Eddie still looked guarded but he nodded, too.

"Honest-to-God. I'm fine." Erin smiled. "Now, what are *you* two up to?"

Lois and Eddie exchanged glances.

"Well," said Lois, "we were thinking about going to the park and listening to the bands. We're not sure who's playing, probably some teeny-bopper nonsense we won't be interested in, but you're welcome to come with us if you'd like. You can bring your friend along, too."

This earned her a subtle but pointed look of disapproval from Eddie.

"No, thank you," said Erin. "I'd really like to spend the evening here." *With Arnie*. But she was flattered that the pair had been concerned enough to stop by. She'd come to think of them as friends and felt a great deal of affection for them both.

Lois nodded. "You'll call if you need anything?"

"I absolutely will." Erin bade them both goodbye and slipped back into the room, smiling. She was eager to get back to Arnie and had a feeling she was going to like her new life just fine.

63
ADDICTED TO LUST

After returning to their suite at the Saint Germain, Michael and Natasha sat together on the love seat, enjoying goblets of AB Negative. Michael, trying to keep a safe distance from Natasha, was keenly aware of the few inches of empty space between them - and he could feel the warmth of her skin, smell the soft scents of soap and lotion. He felt like a pubescent boy sitting next to his crush in the classroom.

"Julian is terribly perceptive, wouldn't you say?" Natasha's voice broke Michael's thoughts, which were headed down dangerous paths.

"What do you mean?"

She brought the rim of her glass to her ruby lips and sipped. "He sensed our history, our attraction to one another."

Michael cleared his throat. He'd gotten the same impression and it made him feel exposed, like he'd been walking around with his zipper down. It was unsettling. "Yes. I suppose he's had a lot of practice. He's very, very old."

Natasha laughed. "That he is. And he's Trueborn; that sharpens his senses further." She was silent a moment, then added, "Do you think our ... uh, history shows so clearly to others?"

Michael, growing increasingly uncomfortable with the topic, shifted. "I would not dare say."

Natasha inched closer to him. Despite his better judgment, he allowed it - and soon, her head rested gently against his shoulder. Michael's body began to respond and he silently cursed his anatomy for its betrayal. "I don't think-"

"Shh." Natasha's fingertips swept the back of his hand, feathered across his thigh.

Images - dark, terrible, unforgettable - flashed across Michael's mind with the intensity of strobe lights, and his hands knotted into granite-hard fists. "You are being foolish, Natasha." He spoke through gritted teeth. "This cannot happen."

Natasha brought her face in front of his. "But why?" Red fire flashed in her eyes. "You won't tell me why and until you do, I can't understand. And Michael, I deserve to understand."

His growing fury shrank when he saw genuine pain in her eyes - such pain and confusion. "Why do you force me to relive such terrible things, Natasha? Why is it not enough that I have made this decision, that I am celibate for reasons that are personal to me?"

"Because it isn't fair, Michael. I know you want me as much as I want you. It comes off your skin in waves."

"It isn't fair?" Michael gave a humorless laugh. "Perhaps you should take more into consideration than your own desires. Perhaps-"

"But I am, Michael. When I say it isn't fair, I mean that it isn't fair to *you*." She gave him a wry smile that softened the hard knot of rage that had built within him. "As much as I want you, I *can* survive without having you. It won't please me, but I can." Then the smile faded. "It's you I'm worried about. You have to come to terms with whatever's been holding you back all these years."

"That's why I have-"

"Meditation? It's not enough, Michael. You know it and I know it."

There was such violation in Natasha's insistence that if she'd been anyone else, he would have stormed out, perhaps after throwing his goblet against the wall. But this was Natasha Darling - Natasha who, he knew, genuinely wanted what was best for him. But was any of this for the best? He wasn't sure. He turned to face her, holding her gaze steadily, fiercely, in his own. "If we were to ... be together now, tonight, I couldn't be sure of the effect it would have on me. There are things you do not know; things you may not *want* to know-"

"I want to know, Michael. I want to know all of it."

He gave a clipped laugh. "Be careful what you ask for, Natasha Darling."

"I'm well aware of what I'm asking."

"And if you do not like the answer?"

She shrugged. "I don't believe there's anything you could tell me that would change my opinion of you - and if there is, then that's my business, isn't it? Since when were you so concerned with outside opinions, anyway?"

She was right, of course - Michael generally gave very little thought to the impressions he left on others, but what Natasha failed to understand was that she was the sole exception, that if she were to turn against him, it would destroy him as surely as a silver dagger to the heart.

But his resolve was weakening, perhaps because he'd carried the burden too long; perhaps because he believed he could trust Natasha. Perhaps both.

"Please, Michael. If not for yourself, then for me. Tell me what happened that made you this way. Tell me. You know I won't hate you for it, whatever it is. I can't hate you. Not ever. Look into my eyes and see the truth of what I say."

He did look into her eyes then, and when he opened his mouth to give more objection, he found his tongue speaking words his mind hadn't yet consented to. "I am an addict, as I have told you," he began. "And it runs deep, very deep. Dangerously deep."

Natasha gave a subtle nod of encouragement.

"Imagine a row of dominoes. You tip one, just one, and it tips the next and the next until the entire design is in a shambles." He paused, recalling something someone had said in an opium recovery meeting when he'd tried his hand at that, before discovering meditation. "A drink is a drug is a cookie is a woman," he said. "Do you understand that?"

She nodded, but a little uncertainly.

"If I were to ..." he cleared his throat, "be with you tonight, then what is next? Fresh blood, I suspect. Murder."

"But Michael, we all fight that! It's part of our nature."

"There is more."

She watched him. "Go on."

Michael sighed and ran his hand over his face, then leaned forward, hands clasped between his knees, hanging his head, concealing his face from her. "The last time I made love to a woman, I killed her." He waited for a response. When none came, he continued. "It was many years ago, but it may as well have happened the day before yesterday. My desire grew so strong that I couldn't control myself. And Natasha?" He looked at her now, wanting her to see the seriousness of what he was about to say.

She swallowed. "Yes, Michael?"

"It wasn't an accident."

A long stretch of silence. Heat burned through Michael's body. The room felt hot, the air thick.

Natasha didn't flinch - just watched him - but Michael saw the change in her eyes. Caution had replaced compassion. It was still there, her compassion, but it paled in the wake of her worry.

"I killed her. In cold blood. And I enjoyed it."

There was another stretch where neither spoke, then Natasha's voice cracked the silence. "But ... why?"

Michael shrugged. "Because I lost control. I lost control of my emotions because I let that first domino tip over. And it didn't end there, either. I killed again and again after that. Sex with that woman was like opening a vein and for months, the violence inside of me bled out in torrents. I rampaged each night, often looking for fights, an excuse to kill. And afterward, the guilt nearly destroyed me. I'd made up my mind to walk into the sun when Winter confronted me."

Natasha touched his hand.

"He told me he knew all about my behavior. He'd been following me. But he wasn't angry - he wanted to help. He began taking me to recovery groups where we posed as drug addicts, or whatever the theme happened to be - because the addiction is the same. Only its avenue of expression changes. And Natasha, addiction never dies. It's a shapeshifter that simply changes form. When I discovered meditation, I was able to turn that into my new addiction – but I am always aware of how easily it could reshape itself into something malicious, something deadly."

"I had no idea." Natasha seemed to be speaking to herself.

"No one does. Only Winter. And now you. And I am trusting you with it the same as I have trusted Winter."

She nodded. "Of course, I would never say anything."

"And now you can understand why we can never be physical again."

"But all those years ago ... when ... when we were together ... "

"All those years ago, the addiction hadn't developed into what it is now. Making love to you left me hungry, it made me wild – but nothing like what it became later. It grows. It grows and grows and the more you feed it, the more it consumes you. I was so young then. I hadn't yet acquired such dangerous tastes." He looked at her with meaning. "But I assure you, even then, I was working on it – or rather, it was working on me."

Something new came into Natasha's eyes – something hard, something daring. "It doesn't have to be this way."

"But it does."

"I don't believe that, and deep down, I don't think you do, either."

Michael got to his feet, throwing his hands in the air as he paced. "And still, you persist! Fool!"

"I'm not a fool, Michael. I'm ... I'm in love with you and I want to be with you. More than that, I want *you* to be with *me*."

Her words stopped him mid-step.

"You heard me. I'm in love with you."

"I ..."

"What if I promised you I would show you another way? What if I swore to you that I wouldn't let you go off the deep end?"

"You couldn't stop me."

Natasha raised a brow. A playful smile flickered on her lips. "I hope you aren't suggesting that I couldn't *handle* you."

Michael shook his head. "This is not a laughing matter."

"You're right. But Michael, I think you're going about this the wrong way."

"How so? When an alcoholic seeks treatment, he must abstain from liquor if he is to remain sober. It is the same here."

"No, it isn't, because *intimacy* is not a drug, and intimacy is not a drink. Intimacy is necessary. Think of a compulsive overeater. He can't *abstain* from food, Michael. A food addict must be helped to acquire a different attitude toward sustenance and learn healthier ways of handling food. Not eating is not an option any more than not breathing, not sleeping, and not loving. You can't abstain from some things, Michael. It will destroy you."

"Yes, but …" But there was nothing else to say.

"You know I'm right about this, Michael. I can see it in your eyes. You *know* I'm right."

"And what if …"

Natasha stood. "I told you. I won't let you. I'm older than you and, at the risk of offending your sense of masculinity, I'm stronger than you." She moved closer to him. "I can handle you, Michael. And I can stop you from spiraling out of control." Her face was close enough now he could feel the warmth of her breath feathering across his lips. "You'll do no damage under my watch, Michael, none at all. That's a promise." Her lips brushed his, barely, and Michael's hand shook with desire, with *need* as he ran a knuckle down the smoothness of her jaw.

"I love you, Michael."

"And I love you." Speaking the forbidden words made the moment real. Speaking the words dignified his desire, so long repressed. Speaking the words meant no turning back. And tonight, no matter the cost, Michael would not turn back.

64

SKIDMARKS

A plan formed.
 As Neil Trinsky bent to pluck a handful of sad yellow chrysanthemums from the hotel flowerbed, his back popped painfully - a series of ratcheting snaps that rode the length of his spine. "Ugh." For a moment, he was suspended there, half bent over, unable to move. Then, when the pain lessened enough, he pulled up the flowers and continued toward the hotel.

It was too late to make himself presentable exactly - his clothes were soiled by heinous things that stank to the heavens above and his once-smooth skin was cracking in places, oozing sluggish blood and thick yellow mucus. But he smoothed his hair anyway - and came away with a handful, leaving a bald patch. "Jesus, Mary, and motherfucking Jehoshaphat!"

Still, he had to try.

He straightened, rubbed his blurry eyes, cleared his throat, put on his most winning smile, and headed inside the Perdet Towers. The place smelled almost as bad as he did - with any luck, no one would even notice him.

Neil coughed into his hand, frowning at the tar-like goo that came up. He looked around, not sure what to do. Then he saw the life-size effigy of Harry Donaldson and continued toward the main desk, smearing the lung-goo across the ridiculous statue as he passed. He wasn't the only person who'd wiped something nasty on it. He could see the crusts of dried boogers all over the thing. A fresh clot of bright pink bubble gum adorned Donaldson's crotch.

Behind the desk sat a reed-thin balding man who faced a small television. He was unaware of Neil's presence. On the screen, a fat man in a bad toupee grabbed a half-naked woman between the legs and gave her a firm squeeze. She screamed, acting momentarily scandalized, but soon enough, the cheesy music began and the crotch-grabbed woman was writhing and moaning and begging - in a thick Russian accent - to be nailed. The fat man in the toupee complied all too happily.

Neil cleared his throat. "Excuse me, sir?"

Without even the decency to lower the volume of the porno, the scrawny desk clerk faced him, blinking stupidly. "Yeah?" He looked Neil up and down, his nose wrinkling.

"I, uh ..." Neil cleared his throat again. His voice was funny, as if he'd swallowed a bucket of rusty nails. "I have a delivery for room, uh, 528." He was pretty sure that was it. He held out the flowers and grinned.

Desk Guy blinked. "So, why are you telling me?"

Apparently Perdet Towers' security policies left a lot to be desired.

"Fifth floor. If you can count, you can find the room." Desk Guy returned his attention to the TV screen where the fat man in the bad toupee was taking a generous leak on the previously scandalized Russian woman. She seemed to be enjoying it.

Neil stumped his way toward the only working elevator, leaking something warm and wet. It dribbled down the back of his leg.

∼

"AND THEN," Norman the Drudge droned on, "after I get my astrology degree, I'll get a job that will support us both, and-"

"I already have all the money I need, Surfer Boy." But it was senseless trying to get a word in. Amanda rolled her eyes. She was sick of him and the endless curving highway. They had to be nearing Eternity, but she still hadn't even had a glimpse of the damned town.

"It will have to be a night job, of course." He laughed. "I learned the hard way that I can't go in the sun and-"

"I need to piss, Norman."

"Huh?" He looked over at her, his concern palpable.

"I need to piss. Bad. And now. We need to stop."

"Oh, of course. I don't know why I didn't think to stop at the last rest-"

"I'm not waiting until the next rest stop. Just pull over right here."

"But-"

"But nothing. Pull over."

At last, the idiot obeyed.

Amanda, a plan already forming, got out and crouched behind the car, relieved herself, then walked to the driver's side. "Get out. I'm driving."

Norman hesitated.

"I don't know if You want to do that. It's a really fast car and I don't want You to get hurt and-"

"I know how to fucking drive, Surfer Boy."

"Are You sure? I mean-"

"Move over and let me drive."

Reluctantly, he complied. She'd been hoping for a chance to punch the gas and leave him in the dust, but he was too quick. She rolled her eyes and began driving, not even bothering to make sympathetic noises as he blathered on about their future together. A future that would never exist beyond his trite imagination. *And this is why you don't turn just anyone,* she scolded herself. But it had been an accident. She looked over at the idiot beside her. It was a very unfortunate accident. Except for one thing - now she knew that she could do something the Darlings couldn't - she could turn someone with a single bite. *Fuck you, Stephen!*

A new idea arrived.

Amanda found the cruise control and, after raising her speed another fifteen miles an hour, set it. She leaned her seat back enough to allow more room to move, then lifted her right leg and laid it across Norman's lap. "Massage my foot, Surfer Boy."

He looked at her, baffled, his eyes resting on her crotch.

"If you make me ask twice, you're going to be wearing your balls for earrings."

"Yes, Mistress." Eagerly, he slipped her shoe off and began massaging. She hated having her feet touched, but it was a small price.

"Does that feel good?"

"It feels amazing." She felt the sudden rigidity of his cock straining at his jeans. "Go higher on my calf."

Norman's hand moved up her leg.

"Tell me again what we'll do when we get home from Biting Man, Surfer Boy."

Excitement sparked in his eyes. He looked like a child with a brand-new toy and as he evangelized the pleasures of their imaginary future together, Amanda stretched her toes out, reaching, reaching, until she got to the door handle. She wriggled a toe beneath it and pulled. The door flew open.

Norman didn't even have a chance to look alarmed - which was kind of a shame, really - before Amanda brought her leg back and kicked him in the ribs as hard as she could.

He hit the rushing pavement, screaming, skidding, rolling.

Amanda laughed until tears came.

∾

THE ROOM WAS a snap to break into - the lock was total shit.

A thousand things were going through Neil's mind as he entered the hotel room and looked around. In the distance, he saw the bed - and the shapes of Eddie and Mom beneath the sheets. He wanted to kill - he was ready for it - but he had to be stealthy ... and there were other things weighing him down, distracting him.

He was growing quite concerned about his health, which he'd always cherished above all else. He was exhausted, he still had no appetite and, when he caught his blurred reflection in the mirror above the hotel room sink, he stared at himself in disbelief. He couldn't be seeing this. He rubbed the blur from his eyes, squinting ... and what he saw staring back at him made him want to render himself blind with the stir-sticks beside the cheap coffee maker.

His hair - what hadn't fallen out, anyway - was stuck in dull-colored patches to his scabby, spotted scalp like chunks of a cheap wig haphazardly glued to the head of a scarecrow by a five-year-old. His eyes bulged out of the slack sockets giving him the stunned appearance of someone who'd just witnessed something unspeakable, and his face was covered in sores and seemed to be melting - he looked like a wax statue in a sauna. His body had grown thin and wispy which gave his head an oversized, bulbous, very *wrong* appearance.

He gasped; the inhalation loosened an incisor. It came unmoored, filling his mouth with blood, then fell and plopped onto the floor. Neil slowly backed away from his own image. *This can't be happening! It can't be!*

Even as he stepped away, he was aware that a continuous bubbling stream of his hot and rotten insides dribbled from his ass like the mouth of a rabid drooling weasel, or a faucet that couldn't be turned off.

He realized he was leaving his DNA all over the place - aside from the continuous diarrhea, more skin and hair had fallen - and this snapped him back into the moment. He wasn't here to bemoan the loss of his good looks - he was here to kill the traitors. The fornicators. The bloodsuckers. If anything, he should be flattered by the ruin and sickness that had befallen him. Neil Trinsky, like Job, was being tested - and this confirmed for him that God, though silent, was surely on his side. Neil had never given much thought to God until he'd heard His Holy Voice on the bathroom floor, but he was certain now that he hadn't been mistaken. *Yes. God is testing me.* And it was clear that the Almighty hated those bloodsucking sons-of-bitches (not to mention his lying, whoring, fornicating mother) as much as Neil did. *God's a pretty cool dude, after all.*

He sent up a quick prayer of apology for having doubted, then brought himself back to the now, back to the mission. He was aware that his thoughts had grown fuzzy lately; it was as if his brain were a piece of old fruit covered in furry mold - but he didn't waver. Quietly, he stepped into the bedroom and stared down at the two sleeping shapes beneath the sheets. *That bed's way too small for the size of nuts Coastal Eddie must have to think he can bang my mom in the ass and get away with it!*

The deejay snorted in his sleep. *He must be exhausted after all the hours of anal olympics!*

Rage overcame Neil. Neil Jr. tried to twitch.

Slowly, carefully, he brought the knife out of his backpack – and that was the last careful thing he did.

Neil lunged onto the bed, bringing the knife down like a sewing needle, jabbing, cutting, stabbing – stabbing before his victims could loose a scream, stabbing until there was nothing left but two blood-covered lumps beneath soiled blankets.

At last, Neil pulled the covers away, wanting to get a good look at their shocked, death-frozen faces.

But the couple in the bed were not Mom and Eddie.

This couple was young, probably in their early twenties. "Fuck! Fuck a fucking motherfucker in the motherfucking ass!" Neil was on his feet, stomping out his rage in deranged circles of fury. "Fuckety-fuck-fuck-FUCK!" He smashed a lamp, kicked over the desk, swiped the old tube television off the stand.

Then he saw the Gideon Bible next to the bed. It was a sign, he realized, a sign that he'd been making too much noise and needed to flee. It was also another sign that God was on his side.

God must have wanted me to kill this couple. They were fornicators and the Lord Almighty used me as a vessel to smite them! He was sure this was the truth, but his thoughts were growing more disjointed and he became aware he'd been standing in the center of the room, staring at the blank wall, thinking about an episode of *I Dream of Jeannie* he'd seen many years ago. Suddenly, his synapses fired up, and Neil was back on the move.

∼

TULLY WAS DRIVING TOO FAST, window down, enjoying the way the night air cleansed his nose of the stench of the Straton cabin. The easiest way to get back to town from that location was to catch the main highway and circle around from the south, then head into downtown. He was curious about the note – and the Mad Shitter – but couldn't see calling for backup. There was nothing really to go on. *The Mad Shitter's gone on everything already.* He chuckled, then pictured Kate making that, *What are you, ten?* face at him. And chuckled again. He'd be telling her the story just to get her to make that face. He liked it when she pretended she was more grown-up than he was when it came to bathroom humor. She wasn't. He grinned.

Light bar flashing, he was only a half-mile from the turn-off when he rounded a curve – and found a man standing in the middle of the road. "Jesus Christ!" He swerved to miss the guy, then screeched to a halt.

The young man staggered toward him. His clothes were torn and bloody. He looked like he'd already been hit. Tully backed up and got out.

"What happened? Are you injured?"

"I'm fine. I was massaging my fiancée's leg and the door opened. I fell out."

"You mean she kicked you out?"

The guy's jaw dropped. "Mistress wouldn't do that."

Mistress? S&M? "Well, it looks like she did. Can I see some ID?"

The young guy shook his blond head. "I don't have any. I lost it." He paused. "When I fell. I lost my backpack too, and my skateboard."

The youth looked like he could use a doctor. "Okay." Tully patted the guy down and opened a side door on the SUV. "Get in. I'll take you to Urgent Care."

"No. I don't need a doctor." The guy climbed in, smearing dirt and blood on Tully's upholstery. Tully shut the door and returned to the driver's seat. The door was locked and the rear caged, so if this guy was a killer or a vampire – *or both* – he was safe.

"Are you sure, son? You look a little–"

"I'm not going to the doctor."

"Okay." Tully took off, heading for Perdet Towers.

"Are you arresting me?"

"No. I'm just taking you to town. What's your name?" Tully called over his shoulder.

"Norman." The kid hesitated. "Norman … Jones."

"Well, Norman Jones, what's your business in Eternity?"

"My fiancée is here-"

"The one who kicked you out of the car?"

"Uh, yeah."

"Why is she here?"

"She's - we - are going to the festival." He paused. "Burning Man."

"Biting Man, you mean?"

"Yeah, sorry. We're going to Biting Man."

"Fang-boy, are you?"

"How could you tell? I've only been one a few days, but I already learned how to keep my fangs from-"

"Your fangs." Tully was extra glad of the bars now.

"Yeah. Amanda - my girlfriend - she turned me just a few days ago, but I already learned-"

"To keep your fangs in," Tully finished. He wanted to laugh - it sounded like nonsense, but he knew better. "Your girlfriend is a vampire, too?" As he glanced in the rearview, Tully saw that the scratches on the young man's face had all but healed already.

"Of course. She's my Maker and I love her. Sheriff?"

"Yeah?" Tully exited the highway and headed for Hotel Circle.

"Are you one?"

"A vampire?"

"Uh huh."

"No."

"You-you're not going to stake me or anything, are you?"

"No." Tully slowed, seeing the round gold shitstack that was the Perdet Towers. The place was filthy and dirty and had a horrible reputation, yet the Health Department never bothered it. No doubt Harry Donaldson's people paid out a lot of bribes. Tully only wished he could force them out of his town. The place was an embarrassment even to the hookers, drugs, and filth that resided there.

He parked in the loading zone in front of the Shitstack Towers and turned to face Norman. "Do you want to get out here, or wait for me? When I get back, I'll help you find someone who can help you."

"I'd like to wait, thanks."

"Okay. I'll be back in a few minutes. Sit tight." Tully picked up his radio set. "Come in, Tim."

Tim's sleepy voice came on. "This is base."

"Leaving the vehicle. Checking something out at Perdet Towers."

"10-4. If you need back-up, it'll take a while. There was a situation out at the old Snakes Alive! Building. Most everybody's out there - a break-in and vandalism. Fire, but it's already out. Some drunken fang-boys."

"I don't need back-up."

"10-4."

65
A CONSTELLATION OF STAINS

The last musicians, a Cars tribute band, petered out near the end of their fifth number. It was late, the crowds had thinned and the remaining fang-boys and girls were tired. Eddie looked at Lois beside him on the bench, thinking he was getting too old for this shit. Lois looked exhausted too; only Renny seemed happy and alert.

"I guess it's time to head back to the hotel," Eddie said.

Lois nodded. "I'd almost rather sleep on the bench then go back to that rat-trap."

"Can't say I blame you, but it gets cold here at night. Really cold."

"I know." She smiled at him. "I've enjoyed spending the evening out here, though, away from that horrible room. I guess I should be grateful to have it, though."

He smiled back. "We could sleep in the van."

"If it had a toilet and running water, I'd say we should." She smiled again. "Less chance of bedbugs."

They stood up, stretching. Eddie glanced around, but saw nothing and no one to worry about; just other tired people getting ready to go back to their rooms. He glanced toward Icehouse Mountain. Within, the vampiric partying must be in full swing.

Eddie scritched Renny behind the ears. "Ready to go, boy?"

Renny panted and licked his hand.

"I guess it's time," Lois said. "Eddie, I have to admit, I'm glad we didn't run into Neil. This was a nice night."

"I agree."

"Maybe he's left town."

"I hope so." Eddie meant what he said and hoped Lois was right, but still, there was an edginess in him. Neil was around. Like a stalker. He could feel him.

They began walking through the park, heading back to the sidewalk and then around to the cross street that would bring them back to Hotel Circle and the Perdet Towers.

∼

TULLY WANTED to cite the sleazeball desk clerk for playing porn where kids could see it, but he had more important things to do and knew he could probably catch the perv at it any night of the week. Besides, any kids out this time of night probably had fangs and were older than God.

The clerk was so involved in the bad porn that he didn't even realize that Tully was behind him. "Hey."

The clerk turned in his chair and the look of long-suffering boredom swept off his face at the sight of the sheriff. He fumbled for a remote, dropped it, then settled on slamming his palm against the old TV - it went black.

"Yes, sir. What can I do for you, sir?"

"You can start by washing your hands and doing your job."

"Ye-yes, sir."

"Who's staying in 526?"

The clerk jumped up and crossed to the desk, punched the computer keyboard. "It's registered to Edward Fortune."

Tully felt a wave of dizziness. He turned away and spoke into the receiver attached to his shirt. Quickly, he told Hapscomb to send backup. He turned to the clerk. "Do you know if Mr. Fortune is in his room now?"

The clerk shrugged. "How should I know?"

"Give me a key. I'm going up. Some deputies will arrive soon, but don't allow any guests to go upstairs until I say so."

"But-"

Tully glowered at the sleazeball. "I could arrest you right now. You know that, don't you?"

"No guests go upstairs, got it." He handed over a key.

Tully spent two more seconds glowering at the clerk, just to be sure the guy knew he meant business. "You leave that TV off. Pay attention."

The guy nodded.

Tully headed toward the elevators and punched the button for the only one without an out-of-order sign. It immediately opened, letting him in - and belching out cheap cologne and an underlying rancid smell. Tully groaned, entered, and punched number five on the panel of buttons. It dinged and did an awful lot of creaking and groaning as the car labored upward.

Staring down at the ugly gold carpet, Tully noticed a couple of small fresh brown splotches among the constellation of stains. Then two more. He bent cautiously and when the stink worsened, he realized what he was looking at. "Well, shit," he muttered.

When he arrived at room 526 and knocked, no one answered, so he unlocked the door. There was nothing wrong. The room looked untouched. Relieved, he left, pulling the door shut behind him.

And that's when he spotted more stains, dark red, mostly hidden by an ice machine. Alarmed, he approached the not-quite-latched door to 528.

He tapped on the door. "Hello?"

There was no answer.

All the hairs on the back of Tully's neck stood at attention as he pushed the door open.

The smell hit him like a wall of August heat, so thick he could taste it. The entire room was covered - no, spattered - with blood. Underneath it all were puddles of feces and vomit. *The Mad Shitter's been here.*

Then he saw the murdered, mangled couple on the bed.

There was so much blood.

More blood than he had ever seen in one place.

EDDIE STARED at the police vehicles sitting outside the Perdet Towers, their light bars flashing red and blue. There were two squad cars and two SUVs. One, Eddie knew, was Tully's and there was someone in the backseat. He turned his attention to the hotel.

"I wonder what's going on." Lois shortened Renny's leash and joined Eddie, peering into the hotel through smeared windows.

"Something's gone down. Let's go see what we can find out."

They entered the lobby. The snotty little desk clerk was looking edgy and a single deputy was on guard. Eddie took Lois' arm and approached the officer who looked too young to be in charge.

"Excuse me, Deputy..."

"Deputy Black, ma'am."

"Deputy Black, would it be possible to go to our room?"

"What floor?"

"Fifth."

The cop blanched. "What room?"

"We're in 526," said Eddie.

"Wait here." The deputy turned and spoke into his transmitter, got a staticky reply, then turned back to them. "Are you Mr. Fortune?"

"I am." Eddie fought down a curl of fear. "Why?"

"Sheriff wants to talk with you. Follow me. You too, ma'am."

Trading glances, Lois and Eddie trailed the deputy into the elevator. One side was cordoned off with yellow crime tape. The deputy pushed a button and the elevator lurched upward.

"I smell him," Lois said.

"Sorry, ma'am?" Deputy Black looked worried.

"Neil. I smell him. His body spray." She looked at the deputy. "I didn't mean you, officer. I meant my son."

"I can smell it, too." Eddie stared at the cordoned-off brown spots on the elevator's faded gold rug.

The car came to a stop. The door slid open and the deputy led them along the curving hall until they neared their room, then halted.

Eddie and Lois stared. The room just beyond theirs was lit up and wide open. There was more crime tape, and cops were everywhere, going in and out, plastic booties over their shoes. Eddie could see blood on the carpet. A lot of blood.

The deputy waved at his boss, who was just exiting the room. "Sheriff? They're here."

Zach Tully, looking grim, approached. "I'm happy to see you two."

"Sheriff?" said Black.

"Yes?"

"The lady, here, ID'd the cologne as possibly belonging to Neil Trinsky."

Tully nodded slightly and stared at her. "How-"

"He *always* leaves the bathroom smelling like that." Lois looked unwell.

"Okay." Tully appeared to be searching for words. "Good to know. And if you're correct, I have to tell you that you two are *very* lucky to be alive. The couple in 528 was murdered tonight. I believe you were the intended targets."

"Oh, my God." Lois turned white. "Neil killed them?"

"Looks that way."

Eddie put his arm around Lois. "Are you saying he got the room number wrong?"

"It's just a guess at this point." Tully glanced around. "Lois, would you like to sit down in your room for a few minutes?"

"Our room is okay?" she managed. "There's nothing *wrong* in there?"

"That's right."

"I don't want to stay here another night." She turned to Eddie. "We can camp in the van."

Eddie nodded. "Would it be possible for us to take our belongings, Sheriff?"

"Yes, but don't leave just yet. I have questions for you."

"Of course," said Lois.

"Just a minute, I have an idea." Tully went to Deputy Black and conversed quietly, then the deputy took the elevator downstairs.

"We're going to find you a room on a lower floor. That'll work, right?"

"I don't know," Lois shook her head.

"What if Neil comes back?" Eddie asked.

"We'll post a guard. You'll be much safer than you would be in your van."

"But there aren't any rooms," Lois fretted. "We got the last one."

"Never believe anything a hotel clerk tells you." Tully tried a smile, but it didn't work. "There's *always* a room. We'll make sure it's yours."

∽

HALF AN HOUR LATER, Tully left the Perdet Towers. The pervy clerk had given up a suite on the second floor as soon as Tom Black told him what happened in prison to guys who played porn in front of children. Once Lois and Eddie were safely inside their new quarters, Tom took the first two-hour shift outside their door. The pair would be safe, though how anyone as physically ill as Neil Trinsky could have the strength to kill, Tully didn't know. However, anything - obviously - was possible.

When Tully finally walked out into the fresh night air, once again grateful for the cool breeze that cleansed the stink of shit and death from his sinuses, he remembered his passenger. "Holy hell," he muttered. Trotting to the SUV, he got in and started the engine. "I'm sorry I left you so long. There was an emergency."

"Heck, it's okay," said Norman. "I'd only worry if sunrise was closer."

Tully didn't want to deal with the kid, but he couldn't desert him. He pulled out and drove to the other end of Hotel Circle, leaving the crime scene activity behind. "Let me get you to your people."

"My Mistress?"

"No, someone who won't leave you in the road." He searched for Marilyn Baker's business card - V-Sec could help the guy.

Tully looked up when someone tapped on the passenger window. A huge man with a white buzz cut and muscles bulging under his equally white wife-beater, was smiling at him. An attractive blond woman dressed in silver stood beside him. A third man, mostly hidden in a Dracula cape, was staring into the backseat. Norman stared back, as if hypnotized.

Vampires? They had to be – they were different somehow, larger than life – *especially the big guy* – but they looked friendly. Tully rolled down the window an inch. "Can I help you?"

The big guy studied his badge. "Sheriff Tully?" he asked.

"That's me."

"We were told that you are aware of our nature, that we could speak with you if necessary, and you'd understand."

Tully lowered the window another inch. "Yes, that's right."

"My name is Winter, this is Chynna, and our caped friend is Julian. We've just come back from Biting Man."

"I suspected that." Tully tried a smile. It didn't really work.

Winter grinned. "Thought you might. The fellow in your backseat, he's one of ours, isn't he?"

"I believe he is. A very new one of you."

"Do you know anything about him?"

"He says his fiancée dumped him."

"Now that we've been introduced," the caped man said in a deep, cultured tone, "might you open the backseat window so that I may converse with your prisoner?"

Tully complied. "He's not a prisoner. In fact, you could say I rescued him." He paused, considering his next words. "I found him on the road. Evidently, his fiancée dumped him out of a moving car." Tully hesitated. "She is one of … your kind … as well."

"Amanda," said the caped vampire.

"Amanda!" repeated Norman, suddenly eager. "Do you know Her? Can you take me to Her?"

"Indeed, I know her," Julian said softly.

"His … *fiancée*," said Winter, "is dangerous. She is here stalking Julian, and we are guarding him. We would be happy to guard this one as well." He nodded at Norman.

"Please," said Norman. "I'd like to go with them."

Tully, exhausted, and with a murderer on the loose, wasn't sure he should comply, but then vampire business was beyond his domain. "Maybe I should call your security team."

"We would prefer not to involve V-Sec." Chynna spoke in a soft, musical voice. "It's better if we handle things ourselves. Our friend,

Julian, is in immortal danger. We can keep him from harm only if the woman seeking him can't find him."

"And I can help this young man get past his obsession with this woman" Julian added.

Tully almost argued. Almost. Instead, he got out and came around the vehicle. At six-two, he wasn't small, but Winter towered over him - and Chynna wasn't much shorter. Julian was his height and their eyes met as Tully unlocked the door to let Norman out.

Julian's obsidian gaze left Tully dazed, mesmerized, as if the pale, handsome man knew everything about him. Tully looked away and opened the door, gesturing for Norman to get out.

"Sheriff, I wish to thank you for your understanding and goodwill," Julian said. "Come," he added, motioning to Norman. "We will speak. I will help you."

With that the vampires turned and walked into the lobby of the Icehouse Inn.

66
THREATS AND PROMISES

Amanda had driven the red Camaro into Eternity. On Main Street, lamps glowed but the park was deserted and the cutesy-ass tourist shops were closed. The entire time she drove, she tried to sense Julian, but beyond knowing he was in the general vicinity, she couldn't get a bead on him.

She'd taken the Icehouse cutoff at the far end of Main and headed up the mountain even though Julian wasn't likely to be at the festival. But she didn't really care; she was eager to see the city and tell the elders, or whoever the hell was in charge, that tomorrow night the Prince of Blood himself was returning to take the throne and a bride. She would make sure they prepared a wedding ceremony worthy of royalty.

When she arrived at the Ski Bowl entrance, no one questioned her - the lift keeper and the guard at the cafe that led her down to the elevators both knew she was one of their own and smiled approvingly, despite the fact that she was barefoot and still dressed in the same outfit she'd worn for days.

When the elevator doors opened on the Biting Man festivities, she smiled. *I'm home.* The partying, half-drunk vampires, the brilliant costumes and colors, the dozen strains of music assaulting her ears from all directions were welcome. The scent of alcohol-laced blood made her mouth water. She stepped out of the elevator.

This is how vampires are supposed to act!

As she strolled the main corridor brimming with wares, she only occasionally tried to sense Julian's presence - tonight, she was more interested in plasma shots, clothing, and jewelry. Pleased Stephen hadn't thought to cancel her charge card, she bought a new pair of red stilettos with blade-sharp heels made to look like gleaming silver knives, then moved on to the clothing booths, buying a gypsy-esque translucent black skirt and crop top with a profusion of colorful chiffon scarves worthy of Stevie Nicks in her glory days, a sleek Spandex mini-sheath dress in metallic gray that would hug every curve of her perfect body, and, for fun, a Dracula cape - maybe she'd wear that with nothing underneath. For now, she donned the metallic gray sheath and stilettos.

She searched fruitlessly for the perfect wedding gown, moving from shop to shop, growing angry and frustrated. Then she spotted the entrance to the temple. Approaching, she saw darkness first and then, beyond, the huge softly-lit interior, nearly empty. A few temple priests in their jewel-toned robes - emerald green and diamond-white - tended the vast room. The handful of visitors within were quiet, solemn. *A real drag.*

Hefting her shopping bags, she stepped inside and came face to face with a priest. "You may leave your things here." He gave her a mewling smile and gestured at a long stand of shelves snugged into the back wall. A few bags and boxes dotted the mostly-empty compartments.

"Thanks, I'd rather hang onto them. I don't want anyone walking off with my stuff."

"I'm sorry, but I must insist; the rustling packages disturb the peace of the temple. I assure you, no one will touch your property. I will keep it safe."

Amanda looked him up and down, then demanded, "What's your name?"

The little priest cringed and put his finger to his lips. "My name is Milo."

"Okay, Milo, I'll hold you to it."

After shoving her packages into his hands, Amanda turned and strutted into the temple proper, enjoying the tap of her silvery heels against the marble floor. The priests and visitors all turned to look at her. *Just as they will tomorrow night when I become their queen!* Old stone statues were carved into the walls in some places; other areas were natural, just cavern formations. She picked up a powerful scent - a heady aroma she'd smelled before but at first couldn't place. Then it came to her: bloodweed. The vampiric answer to cannabis, only far more potent. She'd only smelled it once or twice before - the Darlings didn't allow it in the hotel. *Fucking prudes.*

A tall priest with a dark complexion and peaked eyebrows that put Jack Nicholson's to shame glided up the main aisle, looking like he had a hair up his ass. She grinned at him, but his expression didn't change as he drew near.

"Hello, Father," Amanda said, trying to be nice.

"You *are* a young one," the man said. His accent made her think of Ricardo Montalbán on *Fantasy Island*. "My name is Diego."

"Nice name." She eyed him.

The priest allowed himself a slight smile. "Why do you visit us, young one? To learn?"

Amanda hid her irritation. "Sure, to learn, but also to bring you news."

"Come. Walk with me. I will show you the sacred murals. We can teach one another."

"Sounds good." Amanda walked a few feet down the aisle with the priest, then stopped, her eye on a huge mosaic set into a wall. She veered toward it, Diego following.

"It's Julie," she murmured, staring at the central image, a young man on a throne gesturing to servants. "He's barely aged."

"What did you say?" asked Diego.

"How long do Trueborns live?"

"If any were still among us, they would be considered immortal."

"How fast do they age?" She stared at the mosaic, thinking that Julie looked only a little younger than he did now - *but it's just a fucking mosaic, who the hell knows?* If she had to guess his age now, Amanda would think he was in his thirties, maybe even younger.

The priest hesitated. "It is said that a Trueborn grew to adulthood quickly - in a century or two - but once attaining a certain age, they virtually stopped aging." Diego paused. "Of course, we don't really know the facts anymore." He hesitated again. "There are rumors that a few Trueborns still walk among us, but they are only rumors." He looked at the mosaic. "For centuries, there have been rumors that *he* has been seen on the mountain at times. I'm afraid it's nonsense. I've been here centuries and have never witnessed such a thing."

"It's not nonsense. I know him." Amanda nodded at the mosaic. "The Prince of Blood is alive and well."

Diego shook his head. "If that is so, you know more than the rest of us. That is Prince Keliu. Thousands of years ago he freed us from his father, a tyrant called the Treasure. But Keliu only stayed among us a few centuries; he did not care to rule and hasn't been heard from since."

"The Prince of Blood is here," someone said.

Hearing a collective gasp, Amanda turned - a small group of vampires stood nearby, eavesdropping, along with another priest. She turned and smiled at them, showing fang. Another gasp. Diego gave them a paternal look of disapproval, then spoke to the other priest. "Cornelius, be about your duties and show your guests the rest of the cella."

Once they departed, he turned to Amanda. "You have been fooled, young one. If Prince Keliu is still among us, he is far away from here."

"Who the hell do you think makes Lixir? Ernest and Julio Gallo?"

Diego's eyebrows shot to his hairline. "Do not say such blasphemous things. Whoever this vampire is, he is toying with you."

Amanda looked down, then back up into the priest's eyes, letting her true nature come forth. "Do you know what I am?" she asked, even as she sensed the priest's recognition of her strength.

"You are a young vampire." His voice shook and while he was only a hybrid, she knew that she had a strong measure of control over him.

It's because I drank from Julian. She smiled. "I am stronger than ten of you. I have drunk Trueborn blood."

Diego said nothing.

"Do you believe me? I could show you if you don't." She looked toward Cornelius. "Would you like me to throw him across the room?"

"That is not necessary."

She sensed that Diego was transfixed, a mouse ready to do her bidding. "Then listen to me, priest. The Prince of Blood, Keliu, will be here tomorrow night to reclaim his rightful place." She nodded at the throne. "You shall be here to honor him. Do you have his crown?"

"Of course. It is a sacred relic, well-protected."

"Well, get it out and polish it up." She paused, eyeing the gold embroidery on his cassock. "You're the head honcho here, right?"

He nodded like a good little puppy.

"Once Keliu is crowned, you will immediately officiate at our wedding."

"What?"

"We're engaged. We will wed tomorrow night and I will be his queen." She smiled, her eyes locked on the mesmerized priest. "I will be *your* queen as well, so think twice before crossing me or ignoring my wishes. Or my orders."

"I understand."

"Find me an appropriate crown as well. And you will speak of this to no one."

Diego nodded slowly. "Yes."

"Yes, what?"

"Yes, my queen."

∼

"Juicy Lucy and Poison Ivy! You guys have the best nicknames!" Daisy, drunk off her ass, snapped her gum. "I need a nickname, too."

They were standing in an alcove not far from the temple, an area less crowded than most. Ivy and Lucy looked at each other and giggled. "You already have one." Lucy downed a plasma shot. She was pretty drunk herself, but at least she wasn't blowing big pink bubbles every few seconds. She was getting sick of her cousin and her cunting gum. Listening to it was worse than hearing a dog eat peanut butter.

"Then what is it?" asked Daisy. "What's my nickname?"

The sisters exchanged another glance.

"Crazy Daisy!" said Ivy.

Daisy laughed. "You bitches! What is it really?"

Lucy and Ivy bent over in laughter, but Daisy wasn't amused anymore.

"I'm serious," said Daisy. "What is it?"

"We're serious, too," said Ivy.

Daisy's eyes flashed red. "So you guys make fun of me behind my back?"

The twins giggled.

"And how come you guys get cool names and mine just ... sucks?"

"Oh, come on, Daisy," Ivy said. "It's perfect for you."

"Why? Because you think I'm crazy?"

Ivy looked at Lucy.

"Well, yeah." Lucy didn't think that was such a bad thing, but the look on Daisy's face made it clear their cousin disagreed.

Daisy took a step closer, gum snapping, her hands fists at her sides. "I'm *not* crazy."

Lucy giggled, high-pitched and merry with alcohol.

"Don't laugh at me!"

But Lucy couldn't help it. "We really struck a nerve, I guess," she said to Ivy, who giggled harder. "The truth hurts, huh, Crazy Daisy?"

That's when Daisy lunged. She was on top of Lucy before either of the twins could react, her face in Lucy's, screaming and spitting, fangs extended. Daisy's hands locked into Lucy's black curls as she banged her head on the floor.

"Ouch! Stop it!" But Lucy couldn't get the crazy drunken bitch off her. Her own fangs flashed.

Neither could Ivy, who was at Daisy's back, trying unsuccessfully to pry her off.

"Say you're sorry!" screamed Daisy. "Say it right now, you scuzzy cum-slut!" The wad of Hubba-Bubba fell from her mouth, disappearing into Lucy's mass of curls.

"Never!" cried Lucy. "Fuck you and your bubblegum, too!" She brought her knee up hard, felt it connect with Daisy's pelvis just as Ivy yanked her off by the hair.

Daisy crashed into the alcove wall, looking dazed. "Dazed Daisy," Lucy roared. "Is that a better nickname, you rancid twatsicle?" They broke into laughter all over again, until Ivy gasped, covered her mouth, and pointed at Lucy's hair. "The gum's in your hair. It's all over the place!"

Frantic, Lucy felt for the glob of bubblegum, which was now a soft mat, a snarl that was never going to come out. "I'm going to *kill* her!"

"Lucy, no!" cried Ivy, but it was too late.

Lucy charged at Daisy who was still slumped against the wall, looking lost and confused.

Lucy raised her stilettoed foot to drive into Crazy Daisy's face. But a voice rang out that stopped her.

"If it isn't the Darling twins, in trouble, as usual."

Lucy and Ivy whirled. Amanda - the biggest, most rancid, twatsicle of them all - stood before them, smiling like a shark with PMS.

"What the hell are you doing here, bitch?" demanded Ivy.

"Oh, wouldn't you like to know?" Her voice dripped with superiority.

"Yeah, we want to know. You aren't supposed to be here. Stephen kicked your ass out." Lucy stepped closer.

"Stephen can't do shit to me. He's as weak and stupid as you two." Then she and Lucy were only a foot apart. "Now, why don't you tell me where Julian is."

"Julian? How should I know? He left hours ago." Lucy forced herself not to take a step back, and to avert her gaze from Amanda's eyes; their pupils were too big and black. Red flashed in them like lightning.

Amanda reached out and grabbed Lucy's arm, dragged her closer. "Look at me. Where is he? Where's Julian?"

Ivy stepped forward. "We don't know where Julian is, you pinch-faced bitch! Now leave my sister alone!"

Instead, Amanda grabbed Ivy's arm too, yanked her around, then flung both twins across the corridor as if they weighed nothing.

Lucy and Ivy flew, hit the ground, and slid several feet, scraping painfully across the terrain.

"I SAID, WHERE IS HE?" Amanda's shriek ricocheted off the cavern walls.

Lucy and Ivy sat up and looked to one another, stunned.

In the alcove, Crazy Daisy laughed her crazy ass off.

∽

DAISY DARLING KEPT LAUGHING until the twins were out of sight. They'd disappeared in a hurry after Amanda had humiliated them - and they weren't just pissed off - they looked scared.

Daisy continued giggling as she stood, straightened her leopard mini-skirt, and smoothed her dark hair. Even as she began chewing a fresh piece of Hubba Bubba, she kept her eye on the little blonde. She'd thrown the twins at least ten feet through the air. *Holy shit, whatever she's on, I want some!* Daisy had never seen anything like it.

"You okay?" the blonde asked, approaching. She set a bunch of shopping bags on the floor.

"Sure." Nervously, Daisy brushed dust off her skirt. She didn't want to be thrown, too.

The blonde smiled, approaching and extending her hand. "Don't worry, I won't bite."

She smiled back and shook hands. "I'm Daisy."

"I'm Amanda."

"You know the twins?"

"I dated their big brother. He's an asshole. They are, too. No offense, but you're related, right? You look like them."

"They're my cousins. I'm from the Carolinas. We're not that close. They're so mean."

Amanda smiled. "You have a little dirt right there." She pointed at Daisy's transparent black crop top.

"I don't see it."

"May I?"

"Sure!"

Amanda reached out and touched her right on the nipple. She held onto it a beat, looking into her eyes the whole time. Daisy felt a strange thrill course through her. "Got it," the blonde said, tugging the nipple as she let go.

"Thanks." Daisy didn't normally go both ways, but she found herself wanting to do sexy things with Amanda.

"You know where a girl can buy Lixir around here?"

Daisy brightened. "I think we have to ask around. I haven't seen any stands. Lixir is so great! I had some but the stupid twins used it up." She frowned. "That's the last time I ever ask them to spend the day in my cabin with me. What a pair of cunts."

"They used up your Lixir? That's terrible. Let's get a drink - my treat - then scout out a new bottle. Come on." Amanda handed Daisy half her shopping bags and off they went.

67

PEANUT BUTTER AND HAIR

"Then Arnie and I joined up with Michael Ward in Sleepy Hollow, New York," Winter told the others.

"Papa Winter saved me."

Something flashed in Winter's eyes. "No, Michael saved *us*." He smiled at Arnie, who sat at a small table across from Erin. A deck of cards lay forgotten between them.

"A fascinating story." Julian, ensconced in a high-backed upholstered chair, had been listening to Winter and Chynna's stories - and a few from Arnie, Erin, and Norman Keeler - for several hours. He'd concentrated on their tales, trying to keep his mind clear and free of Amanda. *Of Incendarius.* He knew she was near and felt her searching for him every now and then; it had been intermittent for quite a while, but now her intent was growing stronger. Normally, it was simple for Julian, as a Trueborn, to hide himself, to remain invisible to those who sought him. But with Incendarius, it was another matter. Now, he glanced out the window - dawn would arrive before long, but that was no guarantee of safety if she had obtained more Lixir. He knew she would not hesitate to hunt him by day if she could. He looked at Norman. It had been relatively easy to remove most of Amanda's hold over the boy with a simple glamour; he only wished he could use it on himself.

Winter was watching him, a question on his face. Julian gestured - *everything is all right*. "Please, continue," he said. "Tell me about your compound in Crimson Cove, won't you? I've heard wonderful things and hope to visit soon."

"When you come to Eudemonia, you must meet my tigers and-" Chynna fell silent when someone pounded on the door. She and Winter stood, both looking to Julian.

"It is not she," he told them.

Ever cautious, Winter stood back, out of sight, ready to pounce, while Chynna opened the door.

The Darling twins tumbled in, looking out of breath and unkempt. Lucy's makeup was smeared. "Shut the door! Lock it!"

After peering into the hall, Chynna threw the deadbolt. Julian watched as Lucy and Ivy looked wildly about the room before they saw him and simultaneously cried out his name. They ran to him, falling all over themselves until he was smothered in twins.

"My dear girls." He kept his voice calm even as he smelled Incendarius upon them. "Speak to me."

"Amanda!" cried Ivy.

"She threw us across the hall!" Lucy's eyes went wide. "Like we didn't weigh anything."

"Amanda's in the Eternal City." Ivy spoke the obvious.

"Tell me." Julian slowed his breathing. Chynna and Winter stood close, but the others didn't dare approach. "Catch your breath, speak slowly. You're safe here."

"We got in this big-ass fight with Crazy Daisy," Ivy said. "I mean, she was so drunk and she wouldn't stop snapping her gum and being nasty and she got mad because she liked our nicknames but when we told her hers, she went ballistic."

"She's obviously insecure about being crazy." Lucy smirked.

"Ladies, I understand." Julian had no doubt the twins had fed the girl's anger in their own inimitable way, but that was not important. "Tell me what happened next."

"She put gum in my hair!" cried Lucy.

"Daisy and Lucy got in a fight, right there in front of the temple," Ivy explained. "It was all Daisy's fault! She's such a juvenile snatch-cracker! That's when she dropped her gum in Lucy's hair—"

"I got really mad and shoved her against the wall and was telling her off when that bitch Amanda showed up."

"Yeah!" Ivy reached across Julian to pat Lucy's hand, high on his thigh. "And you know what? Amanda grabbed us and started staring at us and her eyes were all black and flashy and creepy—"

"I think she was trying to hypnotize us!" Lucy interrupted.

Julian nodded. "I'm certain of it. I will explain after you complete your story."

Ivy sighed. "When we wouldn't tell her where you were, she just picked us up and threw us through the air!"

"I think she wants to kill you, Julian!" Lucy hugged him closer.

"That is not her intention, at least not at this point." Julian put an arm around each twin and eased them up onto the chair arms, off his lap, before the smell of Incendarius overwhelmed his senses. "What happened after that?"

"We ran like hell is what happened!" Ivy tried to wiggle closer.

"Straight to you, to warn you!" A tear rolled down Lucy's cheek. "She's not a regular vampire, Julian. She's really scary! I mean, she's been weird almost from the time she was turned. It's like she changed personalities. When she was human she was so nice that I wanted to slap her all the time. Once she changed, she got meaner and meaner. And strong, strong as us, maybe stronger, in just a couple years."

"Yeah." Ivy wiggled nearer. "She's a real twat."

"So you left the festival at that point and saw nothing more?"

"No, nothing."

"What of your cousin?"

"Fuck her!" Ivy said.

"And shit down her throat!" seconded Lucy. "We're not staying in her stupid cabin anymore!"

"We're disowning her!" Ivy said. "She's no Darling!"

"She's undead to us!" Lucy cried.

"Indeed." Julian gently pushed them away, lured and repelled by Amanda's scent on their clothing. "Lucy, Ivy, you're welcome to stay here." He glanced up, but Winter was across the room, on the phone, no doubt telling Natasha and Michael the news, so he looked to Chynna, who nodded agreement to his invitation. He turned back to the twins. "I think you two should bathe now, particularly if you would like to share my room."

"Really?" Ivy asked, her eyes lighting up.

"Only if you bathe."

"We'll scrub our skin off!" Lucy giggled, then paused. "But my hair–"

"Get started, you two," Chynna told them. "There are plenty of towels. I'll go downstairs to the mini-mart and buy some peanut butter. It'll fix your hair right up." She looked from one to the other. "Okay?"

"Okay!" they chorused. Giggling, they headed for the bathroom.

"Did you speak with Natasha?" Julian asked as Winter put the receiver down.

"No. It will have to wait until sunset. The desk said they'd asked not to be disturbed."

A small smile tickled Julian's lips. "Indeed."

68

SWALLOW THE LEADER

"Damn it." Amanda looked up and down the midway. It was less crowded now than it had been an hour ago; dawn wasn't far off. They'd just dropped their packages with a delivery service. "Why isn't anybody selling Lixir?"

"Got me." Daisy had stuck with Amanda since she'd tossed the twins, and had immediately invited her to spend the day in the cabin. When she accepted, Daisy had been thrilled; she was already half in love with the blonde, admiring her audacity and sense of style, among other things. Her admiration only grew as minutes passed. By now, she thought the two of them had hit just about every merchant in the Eternal City, and Amanda had bought shoes, clothes, and jewelry galore, for both of them, all the while asking where they might get some Lixir. No one knew.

Even when they licked their lips and made promises of three-ways, no one knew. "There's gotta be Lixir here somewhere." Daisy stifled a yawn. After all the drinking with the twins, she hadn't stopped, matching Amanda shot for shot. Now it was getting really late and she was ready to sleep, even if it was still full dark. But she wasn't about to admit that to Amanda. *Not now, not ever.* There was something about the woman that made Daisy want to impress her, to keep her respect. That, and she was just a little afraid of her.

"I know!" Amanda turned. "Come on. We're going to the amphitheater."

Daisy was in awe of the speed with which her new friend moved in those high stilettos. She could barely keep up as Amanda strutted down the midway. "Amanda!"

"What?"

"Why are we going to the amphitheater?"

Amanda didn't reply until they reached the turnoff, then she paused and gave Daisy one of those dark stares. "Musicians. They always have the best drugs. Let's go."

Daisy followed. "We did a band yesterday."

"What?" Amanda didn't stop walking. "Who's we?"

"The stupid twins and me. It was this band from Candle Bay called Plastic Taffy."

Amanda stopped walking. "Plastic Taffy is here?"

"Yeah. They're here. And they aren't much good in bed. Why?"

"Because they're mine, sweetcheeks. I *made* them." She eyed Daisy. "How'd they end up at your place?"

"It was daytime. They were ripped on Lixir and hanging around and we wanted some, so we let them come in." She paused. "I stole their bottle, but Lucy and Ivy drank it all, those stupid bitches. I told them-"

"Shut up, Daisy. They'll have more."

Daisy followed Amanda into a huge, empty cavern that served as the theater and thought that the blond vampire was fucking brilliant.

Amanda slowed, took her heels off and gestured to Daisy to do the same. Then they padded further in, silent as death. The crescent seating was empty, and high overhead, a circle of stars twinkled in the natural skylight, letting Daisy see that there was barely an hour left to get back to the cabin. *Unless we stay here.* Either way, she was unconcerned because she was with Amanda.

They crossed to the darkened, silent stage and went up the stone steps. Daisy paused to look out over the tiers of seats, imagining an audience there all for her. She took a step toward center stage before being yanked back.

Amanda glared at her, eyes gleaming onyx. "Follow me, you little twit."

Daisy obeyed.

A moment later they were backstage. Light shone under only one of the doors. Amanda led her to it, then slipped her shoes with the silver heels back on, reapplied lipstick and checked her hair and makeup. Daisy followed suit.

Finally, Amanda knocked on the door. "Hello?" she called in a voice that dripped sexual promise.

Daisy tingled with excitement at the sound of that voice. Unbidden, her mind filled with craven images of Amanda.

"Who's there?" The voice was male, drunken.

Amanda licked her lips. "You asked me and my friend to come backstage after the show, remember?"

The door opened and one of the guys Daisy had screwed - she didn't know which one - peered out, lust in his foggy, froggy eyes. "The show ended hours ago." He took in Amanda with something like awe, then peered at Daisy. "Come on in."

He doesn't recognize me! Daisy wasn't sure why, but she felt relief. She stepped over the threshold into a pall of bloodweed smoke. Under that pungent scent, she detected blood and alcohol. The other Taffy guys - she couldn't even recall their names - stared at them, just as high and bleary-eyed as the one who'd opened the door. They hadn't changed out of their black leather clothing, which looked like the same pants and vests they'd had on when they'd come to the cabin. *They're kind of gross.*

"You look familiar." The one with chest hair leered.

"I get that a lot." Amanda stepped closer and slapped his face. "I'm your Mistress, you little idiot."

"I have a mistress? Far out!"

"I'm Mistress to you all."

The guy was too drunk to do more than goggle at her, his awe apparent. "You want a drink? Some smoke?"

"We'd love a drink," Amanda said. The other three had gathered around her, sucking in their middle-aged paunches, drooling like rabid mutts, yet somehow respectful. It was clear that they worshipped her.

The balding one with the ponytail went to the fridge and got out a bottle of BO Neg then slopped it into a bunch of paper cups. With an undignified eagerness to please, he handed one to Amanda, then another to Daisy. The other guys grabbed theirs. "Cheers!" called out the cutest one. *Which isn't saying much.*

"Cheers," purred Amanda in a voice that made Daisy want her for her own.

The men responded the same way and Daisy saw bulges bloom inside their sweaty leather pants. *What is it about her? I'm straight and I want to fuck her!*

They drank. It was horrible and cheap tasting. It made Daisy's head spin, but not in a good way. She needed to go to bed.

"You know what?" Amanda said in that silky, sexy voice.

"What?" asked one.

"What?" chorused the other three, all leaning in close, hanging on every word.

"My friend, here, she likes four-on-ones."

"What?" Daisy yelped.

Amanda put an arm around her waist and used her other hand to turn her head, then kissed her on the lips, her tongue playing so the men could see. "Play along, Daisy. I made these assholes. They'll do anything I say."

Daisy couldn't refuse Amanda's soft whisper. No one could.

"What about you?" asked one of the men, leering at Amanda. He adjusted the long, stiff bulge in his leather pants.

"Call me Mistress, you little scumbucket. I don't fuck the vampires I create." She blew them a kiss. "But I like to watch my children play. So, why don't you boys get to it?" Amanda nudged Daisy toward them.

"Yes, Mistress!" The guy nodded enthusiastically.

"Let's get you out of those clothes," said another one, putting his hands on Daisy's hips.

"Hey," Amanda cooed. "I need to use the john. Where is it?"

The ponytailed guy pointed. "Back that way. Can I watch?"

All four heads nodded eagerly.

"Fuck that," said Amanda. "I'll be right back."

"But ... wait ..." said one of the band members. "I thought you wanted to watch us bang this one." He hooked a thumb at Daisy.

"Of course I do, so don't undress her until I get back, understand? That's my favorite part." She blew another kiss. "In fact, I'll undress her for you."

The thought of Amanda undressing her made Daisy so hot that she almost wanted group sex. Almost. *I really only want Amanda.* Then, *But I'm not into women!* She didn't understand. *I guess I'm just drunk.* She smiled at the guys surrounding her as Amanda disappeared.

A few seconds later one of the guys asked, "What's taking her so long in there?" He was staring at the shut bathroom door, rubbing his hand along the length of his leather-clad erection.

"She always takes a long time." Daisy tried to sound like Marilyn Monroe. She was beginning to feel a little self-conscious. It was obvious the guys had virtually no interest in her. They had eyes only for Amanda - not that Daisy blamed them. "She'll be back soon."

"She better be," said the bearded one, also rubbing his crotch. "I got a beast that needs taming." He looked at Daisy. "How about a little BJ while we wait? You could keep your clothes on."

The thought of putting her mouth on that damp, smegma-crusted thing turned her stomach. "Sorry, can't. Amanda wouldn't like it. She wants to watch, remember?"

And then Amanda reappeared, one hand behind her back, her eyes huge and black. She walked forward slowly, and the men were riveted. "Hello boys. Stay right where you are."

Half-drooling, they obeyed.

"My friend and I have to go now, but we'll be back tomorrow night to do this right. I want you all to stay right where you are while we leave. Understand?"

They murmured assent.

"We don't get to do your friend?" asked the ponytail guy.

"No. But I'll give you something else to do tomorrow night if you're good boys." Amanda did a far better Monroe voice than Daisy. "Will you be good boys?"

They murmured and drooled assent.

"That's not good enough. What do you call me?"

"Mistress. Yes, Mistress." They spoke in a chorus, their crotches bulging and straining.

"That's better. Now, come on, Daisy. It's late."

Joining Amanda, Daisy saw the Lixir bottle behind her back.

"Okay, boys." Amanda called as she opened the door. "I want you all to suck each other off as soon as we leave. Understand?"

They nodded.

"Oh, and boys?"

"Yes Mistress?" they chorused.

"Swallow."

69

THE SQUATTER IN THE WOODS

Neil had barely eluded the cops at the hotel, but once he did, he ran like the wind, making it to the woods in record time. But then he made a mistake while scouting for an empty cabin; it was occupied.

The fat little bitch had nearly gotten away. After finding her inside the cabin, Neil had no choice but to kill her. He needed a new place to stay and he'd assumed this cabin was vacant. It wasn't, but that was fine. He enjoyed a good fresh kill, even if it was only a human. The trouble was, the fatty hadn't gone down easily.

After he'd whacked her over the head with an ugly blue Tiffany lamp, she'd stunned him by not falling down, instead taking off at a run for the front door. She made it out of the cabin but Neil managed to bring her down on the porch with another whack to the head with the lamp.

The fat little bitch wailed as she toppled down the stairs and Neil wasted no time. Before she could get to her feet, he bashed her head in - over and over and over - until the lamp's crystal base shattered. Then he used one of the jagged shards to cut a wide bloody grin into her throat - and as her body went still and that mortal wound smiled up at him, Neil found himself smiling back – and thinking not only of the couple he'd sliced and diced at the Perdet Towers, but of his mother, who would soon be stew meat herself.

He looked around.

Surely, no one would come wandering out here at this hour; it was nearly dawn and all the good little vampires would already be tucked in for the coming day.

Certain that he wouldn't be disturbed, Neil unzipped and freed Neil Jr. who, by now, was a slick, dripping slab of crackling raw meat. Even his balls were covered in sores, but Neil didn't mind. As he stroked himself, he felt no pain, only pleasure.

"Oh, Mom," he moaned as he went to work on himself.

～

"I NEARLY GOT gang-banged for a couple of measly swallows of Lixir!" Daisy tramped through the woods with Amanda.

"Hey, it's better than nothing. The sun's about to come up." Amanda tipped the empty bottle to her lips and tongued the opening. "Without it, we couldn't have made it back to your cabin." She didn't mention how pissed off she was that there wasn't enough to allow her to search for Julian during the day. Not only wasn't it the little twit's business, Amanda didn't trust her half as far as she could throw her. No, it was best just to keep the girl's mind on sex and spend the damned day in her cabin.

Daisy was so busy watching Amanda's tongue that she nearly tripped on a pinecone. "Yeah, I guess. I just wish we could've parked closer."

"Eh, exercise is good for you." They'd picked up a V-Sec van when they left the highway so they'd parked the car among a bunch of others in a lot by a huge chalet and walked the rest of the way to Daisy's cabin.

Amanda stared Daisy in the eye and licked the bottle's opening again. "Are we close?" *The girl wants me sooo bad.*

"I think so. I never expected to have to walk to it, though."

Daisy had partied too hearty and was conking out fast, wobbling on her stilettos like a five-year-old in her mommy's heels. Amanda thought about leaving her out in the sun to fry. *She's a Darling, after all; they* all *deserve to die.* But all the packages were being delivered to the cabin tomorrow and Amanda didn't want to risk losing them because of a charred body out front. "Come on, Daisy, you can find it."

"There!" The girl pointed through the trees. "See the upstairs window with the red curtains half open?"

"Is that it?"

"Yeah. I left a light on upstairs so it'd look like I was home."

"Good girl. Shhh." Amanda put her hand out, stopping Daisy in her tracks.

"Wha-"

"Shh!"

Up ahead, she could hear breathing and something else. Something wet, a slapping sound.

What they saw when they moved closer brought a strange hybrid of revulsion and amusement to Amanda's heart. A man covered in filth - based on the smell it must have been blood, feces and infection, and something else she couldn't quite place - stood over a bloody corpse, its head bashed in. He was masturbating. Blood dripped from his fap-hand, and in fact, the man dripped blood - and yellow-black pus - from just about everywhere.

He tossed his head back and groaned. "Oh, Mom."

Amanda realized the sick fuck was younger than she'd first thought.

"What the-" Daisy couldn't finish.

"Mom, Mom, Mom!" With just a couple of short terse strokes, the man shot his seed - which looked more like something that should come out of a pimple than a penis - all over the broken-headed body at his feet.

Amanda's curiosity was beyond control. Before the guy had even tucked himself back into his pants, she stepped closer. "Are you seriously jerking off on your dead mother?"

She expected him to run, or at least be surprised, but instead he appeared annoyed. "Of course not!" He tucked himself in and Amanda caught sight of a large crusted Buffy tattoo rising from his bush. "I was just *pretending* she's my mom, you dumb fucking bitch." He rolled his eyes.

Amanda and Daisy exchanged glances. The guy was off-kilter, there was no doubt about that, but something about his casual attitude appealed to Amanda. She could use a servant as wicked and self-assured as this guy. Someone not at all like that stupid besotted Norman. As she stared at the guy, he seemed familiar. Then the wind brought his scent toward her and beneath the stink of rot and infection, she recognized the sweet powerful cologne. *It's Coastal Eddie's little stalker*. It was clear he didn't remember her. "Now if you little bitches will excuse me, I need to find a new cabin! This one," he jerked a thumb at the one behind him, "smells like fat chicks."

The swaggering pus-ball had the nerve to look them up and down, his eyes crawling over them both. "Hey, you guys aren't fat, though." He paused to run a hand through his hair, trying to slick it back, but a clump came away with his fingers. He threw it behind him and smiled, half-toothlessly. "So tell me, what are you lovely ladies doing out here? Don't you know there're dirty stinking vampires on the loose? It's not safe, but I'll protect you."

He didn't look like he could protect shit from a fly. Amanda laughed. "Well, we-"

"*SHHHH!*" The man suddenly hunkered, his eyes darting around nervously. "Do you hear Him?"

Amanda and Daisy exchanged another glance. There were no sounds but the distant chirps of crickets. A breeze brought his stink into her nose again and this time, Amanda smelled Lixir strongly. But he was no vampire and she'd heard that Lixir destroyed humans. That would explain a lot.

"Hear who?" asked Daisy.

"The Lord." The man slowly returned to normal; Amanda could practically see the sanity refill his eyes. "Never mind. Only certain people can hear Him - people on a *mission*. *I'm* on a *mission*. An important one."

"Are you?" Amanda suppressed a smirk.

He nodded. "So do you guys want to fuck or what?"

Amanda nearly threw up. "Um, no. But we'd love to hear about this mission you're on."

"Vampires," he said. "I'm going to kill them all. God has spoken and it's His will."

Amanda felt a smile sneak onto her lips. This was getting better by the moment.

"At the Biting Man Festival," he continued. "I'm gonna kill them all! I'll walk in there with fifty pounds of C-4 strapped to my chest. It'll blow the place sky high and send all the dirty vampires to Hell, where they belong." He suddenly threw his head back and laughed. When he finished he looked at them gravely, worried. "You won't tell anyone, will you?"

"Of course not." Amanda turned somber. "As a matter of fact, I think we may be able to help you."

Daisy started to object, but Amanda silenced her with an elbow to the ribs.

The loon stared at Amanda. "I don't *need* any help, baby."

"Are you sure about that?" Amanda asked. "Are you sure we haven't been sent by God to assist you on your mission?"

He considered this for much longer than it required, then nodded. "Okay."

"Okay?"

"Okay, I accept you as part of the mission." He lowered his voice to a conspiratorial tone. "*He* works in mysterious ways and even though *He's* a bit of an asshole sometimes, I think I better do what *He* wants."

"All right then, it's settled." The first thing Amanda was going to do after having him ditch the body was have Daisy give the guy a bath. The second thing was figure out how advanced his deterioration was and how much time she had to work with him - she was certain he'd been hitting Lixir and it was destroying his body and mind the same as it would any mere human who'd ingested it. Though why one would ingest it, she had no idea.

And finally, she needed to start planning. He was the perfect weapon against the Darlings, she just needed to figure out how to use him. "Pick up your backpack and come with us." She batted her eyelashes. "We'll take care of you ..."

"Neil."

"We'll take *good* care of you, Neil."

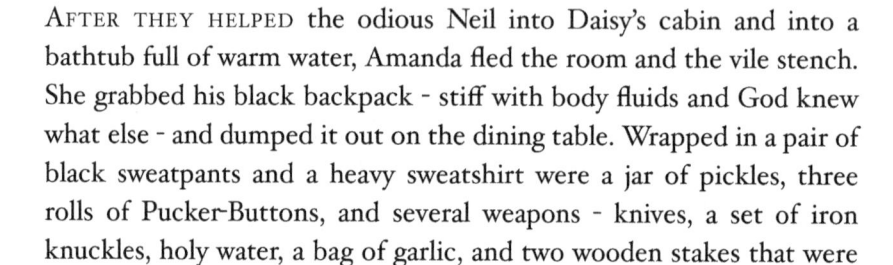

~

AFTER THEY HELPED the odious Neil into Daisy's cabin and into a bathtub full of warm water, Amanda fled the room and the vile stench. She grabbed his black backpack - stiff with body fluids and God knew what else - and dumped it out on the dining table. Wrapped in a pair of black sweatpants and a heavy sweatshirt were a jar of pickles, three rolls of Pucker-Buttons, and several weapons - knives, a set of iron knuckles, holy water, a bag of garlic, and two wooden stakes that were obviously - and badly - hand-carved. Wrapped in his underwear - bright clingy shorts and black T-shirts - was a Lixir bottle. And a silver crucifix on a chain.

"Oh, fuck you!" Amanda let the cross fall to the floor, kicked it across the room into the fireplace, then turned her attention to the Lixir.

"Damn it!" She turned the bottle upside down, but there was no more than a swallow left inside. *Not enough to let me go after Julian.* She took the bottle to the sink and rinsed Neil's slime away, then opened it and consumed the dregs before replacing it in the backpack and shutting it. Then she sat down to wait.

Dawn was near breaking when a bedraggled Daisy came out of the bathroom, Neil in tow. A white towel was wrapped around his waist and he looked dazed. "Here he is." Daisy pushed him forward. "I have to take a shower now."

"You go ahead, Daisy. Enjoy." Amanda stood up and smiled at Neil. He was still a horror show, covered in pustules and boils, his hair half gone, his body oozing brackish yellow and red disease. Where one nipple should have been, a huge carbuncle pulsed, ready to spew its particular form of lava. But he had good bones and probably there'd once been a nice face under the bubbling skin. *There could be again.* "You work out, Neil?"

"Of course. My body is my temple." He tried to wink but his eyelid didn't work right. "Are you a vegetarian, like me?"

The walking pustule is trying to pick me up! "Not exactly." Amanda smiled, all sympathy. "How are you feeling?"

"SHHHH!" His eyes weren't focusing. "He's back!"

She watched him as he hunkered down to listen to absolutely nothing, his eyes darting wildly. As she watched, the skin of his forehead split, opening a small channel of fresh blood. He wasn't going to last much longer – certainly not long enough to help keep the Darlings from interfering while she married Julian.

It was time she told him what he was up against. Suppressing a smile, she began talking.

When she finished, his swimming eyes found hers. "You shitting me?"

"You're very ill, Neil."

He looked at her a long moment, his bleeding scabby lips twitching. He scratched his nose, which was little more than a ledge of raw gristle, and frowned down at his blood-covered fingertips.

"It's going to get worse until ... well, until you die." She kept the sympathy coming.

He blinked at her.

"Do you understand me?"

"We're all going to die, you dumb ass."

"Yes, but you're going to die *very* soon. I've seen this before, Neil," she lied. "I know what I'm looking at."

He scoffed. "God won't let me die. He wants me to–"

"It's a matter of hours, Neil. Not weeks, not even days. Hours." She let that sink in while she gathered her thoughts. "First, your skin breaks down. It begins with little more than a rash. This is a sign that your immune system is failing. Then, your mind starts to go fuzzy. You've undoubtedly experienced some mental disturbances in the past hours." She saw the beginnings of anxiety in his eyes. "Then comes the infection. Since your body can't fight anything off, you become infected, and that's what ultimately does you in. It gets in your blood, goes to your heart. And your brain." She pointed at his arms. "Do you see all that pus? You're infected."

He looked down, touched the festering wound on his arm and looked at her, his eyes wide with worry. "But the Lord ... I'm ... I'm on a mission."

"That's all part of your delusion, Neil."

"But I am! It's important!"

"I don't doubt you're on a mission, Neil, and I want to help you. But God is not speaking to you."

"Yes, He is!"

Amanda shook her head. "Neil? Has He ever spoken to you before?"

"Well, no but I never had a mission before, so-"

"I want you to tell me what you think when someone tells you that God has spoken to them. What kind of person do you think they are?" She watched him. "Think about it really hard, Neil."

Clarity distilled in his eyes. "A ... a crazy person!"

Amanda nodded. "But you're not crazy, Neil. You just drank too much Lixir."

He nodded. "I'm going to die."

"Well ... there is one option, Neil."

He looked at her. "There is?"

She nodded. This was more fun than she'd anticipated, but she kept that to herself. She could have used hypnosis to get what she wanted out of him, but it seemed more fitting, ironic somehow, that he should make the decision of his own free will. If he refused, then she'd resort to using her powers, but she'd much rather he choose to become the thing he most hated, all on his own.

"What is it?"

"You can let me turn you." She nearly chuckled. She pictured him as one of those glittery angst-filled vampires that teenage girls swooned over.

"Turn me? Into a ..." His eyes darkened. "Wait, are you saying you're ... you're a vampire?"

Amanda smiled, showing fang. "What did you think I was, Neil? If you become one of us, you'll get to destroy my enemies. And *they* are vampires."

"Fuck that! I won't be a goddamn, dirty bloodsucker, no way!"

Amanda shrugged. "It's that or you die."

"But I can't! I won't be one of you!"

"That's fine. I just thought I'd make the offer." She sighed. "Well, it was nice knowing you, Neil. We won't be seeing each other again because, you know, you'll be dead and all that, but it really was a pleasure." She frowned. "Such a shame. We could have destroyed them. But as it is ... well, you'll be lucky if you make it until noon."

His lips moved but no words came.

"So long, Neil." She turned to leave.

"Wait."

Amanda faced him, smiling, eyes twinkling. "Yes?"

"Why do you want to destroy your own kind?"

Amanda laughed. "They are *not* my kind. They are lesser beings. *I* am royalty. You've made the basic human mistake of assuming all vampires love other vampires. Well, they don't, and there are vamps up at Biting Man who are the kinds of creatures I can't tolerate. With your help, I might have been able to take down my enemies, but alone ..." She shrugged. "Well, I guess the Darlings will just have to get away with being the filthy fucking things they are."

"The Darlings?" he gasped. "Those dirty bloodsuckers at the Candle Bay Hotel?"

"Those are the ones." She watched him a long moment, aware that the wheels were turning, aware that he was considering it. "We could kill the Darlings, our greatest threat, then rule the rest of them together. Turn them into our slaves. Or ..." Amanda sighed. "You can die and I can go on, never knowing what might have been. The choice is yours."

Neil fidgeted with his bleeding decaying fingers, pulling a nail out of its bed.

"And you know what else?"

"What?"

"If you were one of us, everything would go back to normal for you. Your face would be beautiful again. Your body would return to how it was before. Your hair would come back immediately. And your teeth. You'd be gorgeous again, Neil."

His gaze brightened, then he squinted as a ribbon of bloody pus dripped into one eye. Slowly, his lips peeled back into a terrible grimace, the skin splitting and bleeding all around his mouth. "Will it hurt?"

"I'll make sure you don't feel a thing." She stepped toward him.

70

SUNDAY MUSINGS

The town of Eternity looked as peaceful as a greeting card under the warm rays of the morning sun. Birdsong filled the pine-scented air, waking human inhabitants to a brand new day. On Main Street, bicyclists cruised, joggers trotted park paths, and old men sat on the bench in front of Harlan King's bakery, inhaling the heavenly scent of cinnamon rolls, and laying odds on who would be the next to die.

"I never expected Flournoy to kick the bucket," old Willy Wilkens complained.

"Kicked the pickle barrel is more like it." Arley Mordred cackled.

"Between Flournoy and Curtis, a whole lotta people made a whole lotta nothing on the Death Pool," Creighton Davies observed in his affected Maine accent. "Makes a body wonder."

Arley cackled again. "Leastwise, nobody misses that bastard, Curtis Penrose."

Creighton stood up, bones creaking. "Amen to that. Anybody for a cinnamon roll?"

"Zach?" Kate called from the kitchen. "You ready for coffee?"

Tully rolled over and put the pillow over his head. "Give me another hour. I was up all night."

"Okay, I'll leave it on warm. See you tonight?"

"Probably not. I'll be on duty. Want to meet at Strider's for a late lunch?"

"You bet your sweet ass I do, lawman. Two-thirty?"

"It's a date." Tully was asleep again in thirty seconds.

∼

Eddie Fortune and Lois Trinsky had breakfast delivered to their slightly odiferous suite at the Perdet Towers. The deputy on guard duty accompanied the hotel worker inside and Lois invited him to eat with them. The hotel was going overboard trying to keep them happy, trying to avoid the bad press they deserved, and had sent up a ridiculous amount of food. But the deputy declined all but slightly burnt toast and coffee.

Lois still felt shock when she thought about Neil going crazy and trying to kill her and Eddie. She thought of the slaughtered couple on the fifth floor and could barely eat. She wanted out of this seedy hotel, but didn't want to leave the room, so she remained inside, blindly staring at the babbling television while Eddie took Renny for a morning walk.

As for Eddie, despite all his bravado and reassurances to Lois that they were safe, he was just as worried, and during the walk never stopped watching for Neil. Crazy Neil, who wanted to kill vampires - and his own mother.

∼

At noon, Neil Trinsky slept handcuffed and locked in one of the bedrooms in Daisy Darling's cabin, though he wasn't actually sleeping. He was transforming. The bite Amanda had administered had slowed his body to a death trance, and now it was beginning to change, cell by cell. Already, the pustules were smaller and little black hairs were regrowing on his scalp. And Neil slept peacefully through it all.

∼

IN THE MASTER BEDROOM, Daisy and Amanda lay sprawled nude on silky lavender sheets, their bodies tangled together after an hour of lovemaking in which Daisy did everything that Amanda asked. Now, she was deeply asleep. Amanda, merely drowsy, absently stroked the fine expanse of Daisy's thigh and thought about the coronation.

∼

LEAVING the twins curled up like kittens on his bed, Julian Valentyn sat in the high-backed chair in the darkened living room, hands folded together, too lost in thought to take rest. Even if he could have, he would have shunned it, because he faintly felt Amanda's mind; she was awake though it was three in the afternoon. He couldn't risk her finding him, for his own safety as well as that of the other vampires sleeping in the suite.

He had a full bottle of Lixir hidden away in his room; one that he'd secreted in the mountain some years ago in case of emergency. He had extricated it last night and was glad of it; if indeed, Amanda somehow ferreted out his location, he would pour a few drops into the other vampires' mouths to wake them. Chynna and Winter, in particular, would give her a good battle - *at least as long as I don't fall under her spell.*

Amanda's presence became weaker as the sun rose higher. *Incendarius,* he reminded himself, *think of her only as Incendarius. Do not allow yourself to be drawn to her!* He closed his eyes, considering. She would have to be dealt with, and soon; otherwise she would plague him for eternity. *Or until she has killed me.*

∼

MICHAEL AND NATASHA, lovers entwined, slept peacefully, dreaming of nothing but each other.

71

I, VAMPIRE

Dusk settled over Eternity like a fleece quilt, with the promise of rest for the living - and unrest for the dead.

As consciousness slipped through the fine cracks of his slumber, slowly lifting the nets of fog from his mind, Neil Trinsky became aware of three very pressing matters. First was the pain that shot through his wrists and arms where he'd been tethered to the bed with pairs of Daisy Darling's steel handcuffs. Agony screamed down his sides, burning like hot oil under his skin as his muscles stretched to accommodate his position - which was reminiscent of Jesus on the cross. He tried moving his arms to get his circulation going, but it was impossible.

And this was when his second quandary made itself known. Neil's cock was literally throbbing. Hot and hard it strained with such fierceness that its head had worked past the elastic waist of his boxer shorts and found freedom. Neil looked down, reminded of the time Renny had gotten his head stuck in the doggy-door, and admired his cock's enthusiasm. While it wasn't unusual for him to wake with morning wood, this was more like morning cement. He was certain it was the stoniest, most adamant hard-on he'd experienced since he was thirteen and he'd glimpsed the shadowy outline of his mother's brown-pink areola through her white silk nightgown as she tucked him into bed. Despite his physical discomfort, a swell of pride blossomed in Neil's now barely-beating heart as he smiled down at Neil Jr.

The final - and most nagging - item that he became conscious of was an overwhelming hunger. A new hunger - one that was unlike any other he'd experienced - and it had nothing to do with food. Not the usual food, anyway. What he wanted was raw meat. No, not the meat - just the blood. He wanted blood. Lots and lots and lots of blood, and even though he'd never drunk blood before in his life, he knew this was what his body needed as surely as a pregnant woman's body knows what it needs to sustain the life within it.

Blood. That's what he needed - that's what would keep him alive, and though he was well aware of the fact that he was now one of the filthy bloodsuckers he'd so despised, Neil didn't mind admitting to himself that he wanted nothing more than to slice open the vein of some healthy and supple man, woman, or child and swallow down the very life that pumped through them.

I'm one of them. I'm a filthy bloodsucker. He waited to be disgusted and outraged ... but it didn't happen. All he could think about was blood - and the pain in his wrists, arms, and sides. He needed one of those silly little bitches from last night to come in and uncuff him before his arms straight-up died and fell off. He opened his mouth to scream for them when the bedroom door yawned open.

Amanda stood in the doorway, a distinctly female shape in a white silk robe reminiscent of his mother's own, all those years ago. And like his slutty mom, Amanda lacked the modesty to try to conceal her nipples. She displayed them proudly through the whisper-thin fabric, so pink and so ripe that they begged to be ogled.

And touched.

And bitten.

And suckled.

Neil thought of his mother as his eyes roamed down Amanda's body to the cozy little V of her groin where a shadowed thatch of hair was just visible. Neil realized that even from here he could smell her - her skin, her sex, all of her.

Neil Jr. thumped his abdomen enthusiastically.

Amanda's gaze settled on his pecker and she frowned.

Neil could hear her soft, slow breathing - he even thought he could hear the beat of her heart. It was as if his senses had been given a shot of steroids.

"I see you're up," she said, unamused.

Neil grinned. "More than I've ever been up in my life, baby." He winked, noting that the skin of his face no longer cracked, ripped, and bled with each new expression as it had done the night before. He ran his tongue over his teeth. *I'm healed.* And that alone made it worth becoming a filthy bloodsucker. With a nod, he gestured to Neil Jr. "Want to take a seat and go for a ride?"

"Oh, please," said Amanda. "Spare me your pathetic attempts at seduction. We have a busy night ahead of us and we need to get moving."

"Fine." Neil frowned. "Get me out of these fucking things, damn it." He wiggled his hands, rattling the chains.

"That's why I'm here." As Amanda bent over him to unlock the cuffs, Neil's eyes were glued to her perky little tits and his nose brought the scent of her - the very *essence* of her - into his lungs.

"Don't get any funny ideas, loser." She unlocked the final cuff. "You need to follow my instructions to the letter. Do you understand?"

Neil sat up, grateful to be free of the shackles. "Yeah, I guess."

Amanda's hand shot out and clutched his jaw, forcing his eyes on hers. "There is no, 'Yeah, I guess.' There is only 'Yes, Mistress,' or 'No, Mistress,' and if I hear a single 'No, Mistress' that I don't want to hear, I'll kill you, bring you back to life, and kill you again. Got it?"

Staring into those blazing black and beautiful eyes, something within Neil changed, and suddenly, he couldn't imagine wanting anything more than to please this woman, to make her happy, to do her bidding. "Y-yes, Mistress."

"That's better." Her vise-like grip loosened. "I'm sure you have a lot of questions and I'll try to answer them, so long as it doesn't distract me from my plans or inconvenience me in any way. The best thing I can tell you about being a vampire is that you'll learn as you go. I'm sure you're thirsty, so the first thing we're going to do is go into the other room where Daisy is getting some blood out for us. After we take sustenance, we're going to town. I need a wedding dress."

"A wedding dress?"

"I'm getting married tonight and I need your help."

"Married?" An odd and powerful wave of jealousy burned its way down his throat and into his heart.

"Yes. I'm royalty, you see, and those damned Darlings and their pals are trying to cheat me out of my proper place. You're going to help me claim my crown." She studied him. "Unless you're no longer interested in slaying vampires, that is. Do you still want to kill vampires, Neil?"

"I'll kill whoever you want me to, Mistress."

"That's a good boy."

Neil felt a twinge of arousal as she tousled his hair - hair, he realized, that had grown back just as thick, lustrous, and long as it had always been. No. More so. Everything was more so now. More colors, more sounds, more scents, more everything. But Neil wasn't interested in counting the ways he'd improved. Amanda had promised him blood, and that took full residence in his mind now.

72

THE PRIEST'S STORY

Diego Villanueva, high priest of Temple Vampirus in the Eternal City, was troubled and had been ever since the blond vampire had informed him that Keliu had returned and would be crowned king this night. He stood before the mosaic of the Prince of Blood, studying the image, recalling the old stories. While he did not believe what the blond vampire had said - if Keliu were extant and nearby he would never have truck with such a brash, arrogant woman. Yet, the woman had unusual powers, he had no doubt of that. Not only had she very nearly hypnotized him - he had sensed the intent as well as the violence within her and allowed her to think she had succeeded. Later, he observed her throw not one, but two females across the main hall outside the temple. Few males had such strength; for a female of her stature, it was unheard of.

He had briefly considered that she might be Trueborn herself, but his instincts, honed over centuries of study, told him she was not. She was unusual, certainly, but no Trueborn ... *Or is she?* He knew his view of Truborns was colored by Keliu's gallantry and wisdom, his refusal of power. But the prince's father, The Treasure, had been a terror. He reminded himself not to think of all Trueborns as cut from the same cloth as Keliu.

He first encountered the prince centuries ago at Machu Picchu. Back then, Diego's name was Tupa and he was a priest of Inti, the Sun God. One evening, Keliu simply appeared, having trekked the steep paths to the holy city. The inhabitants were intrigued by his pale skin, moonlight hair, and regal bearing, and it wasn't long before he was identified as Viracocha, the Great Creator, who had fathered Inti himself. Viracocha was said to travel the world doing great deeds and though Keliu did not use the god-name, the pale man matched the description in all the other ways. A great fuss was made over him and Keliu was quickly accepted among the people of the holy city.

The pale man seemed to enjoy his time in Machu Picchu, and spent much of it with the priests, especially Tupa, learning their ways and beliefs, and telling tales of his travels. Tupa had learned much, too. Privately, Keliu never quite denied to him that he was Viracocha, nor did he claim to be the god, either, whereas in public, he freely implied that he was.

When he first arrived, Keliu said that he would not linger long, but then he met and fell in love with a dark beauty named Paqari, a Virgin of the Sun. She was renowned as a weaver of ritual garments, and sometimes tended the sacred fire as well.

Keliu, in the guise of a god, was allowed to court her; indeed, he could have taken her as his bride if he'd chosen. But he did not. Instead, he spent the evenings in her company until, weeks later, Paqari vanished as if she'd never existed. It was thought she fell - or threw herself - from a steep cliff as others had before her.

Keliu was devastated, blaming himself, though Diego - Tupa - did not understand why until one night, shortly before Keliu left, he told him he wished he were immortal like Viracocha. "Do you?" Keliu asked. "It is a lonely life."

"I would spend my days in the company of wise scholars and books such as you carry; I would not be lonely. I would study the ways of nature. I would travel, as you do."

"You would have no days, only nights." Keliu stared at him with great someberness.

"It would not matter to me."

"You would not eat as others do." Keliu explained.

Diego listened with open ears and heart to all Keliu told him. "I would like this life very much. This eternal life."

"I will give it to you if you still wish it tomorrow night." Keliu added, "Most would not want it. Paqari did not."

"Did you kill her?"

He shook his head sadly. "I feel responsible." With those words, he rose and wandered into the night.

The following evening, they met again. Diego had not changed his mind. Keliu transformed him and then he left, never to be seen again.

～

JULIAN WATCHED from the high-backed chair as the rest of the vampires assembled in the living room of the suite at the Icehouse Inn. Ivy and Lucy were preening each other. They wore matching costumes; red lace-up bustiers trimmed with short, black netting meant to suggest skirts. Garter-belted black net hose sheathed their legs and black fingerless evening gloves covered their arms. On their heads they wore little jauntily-tilted top hats trimmed with feathers. Their considerable charms were displayed to perfection.

Chynna and Winter, chatting companionably near the window, were not the sort to wear costumes. Winter wore a simple white t-shirt with black jeans and his ever-present black boots, while Chynna wore her silver jacket again, this time over a black blouse and pants. Julian approved. *A charming woman, a strong woman.*

For better or worse, Arnie and the new vampires, Erin and Norman, would be accompanying them to Biting Man. Chynna had purchased Dracula capes for all three, her theory being that they would draw less attention that way. Julian, all in black beneath his own ridiculous cape, thought her decision a sound one.

A moment later, Natasha and Michael arrived. As Winter opened the door and bade them enter, Julian was pleased to see a tell-tale sparkle in both vampires' eyes. He stood up and crossed to greet them, taking Natasha's hand, then Michael's.

As soon as everyone was seated (except the twins who were still off in their own hair-and-makeup-centric world) Michael looked to Julian. "Are you sure you want to go tonight?"

"Michael and I," Natasha added, "would be glad to keep you company here or somewhere else of your choosing."

"I must go," Julian told them. "There is no choice."

"There is always a choice-" began Michael.

"Not in this case. It would only put off the inevitable." Julian looked around the room, his eyes stopping on the twins. "Young ladies, you must sit down and listen now. It's important."

Lucy and Ivy obeyed.

Julian folded his hands together. "Now, I have explained to you all what Incendarius is. It is incredibly powerful physically, and has as much ability to hypnotize as a Trueborn does, and is particularly poisonous to Trueborns. Amanda is Incendarius and while a hybrid vampire with self-control is capable of resisting her suggestions to a great extent, a Trueborn is not." He paused. "She does not know what she is, but she does know her own power. And she knows she can manipulate me as she pleases." He looked at the others. "However, I don't believe she realizes she has far *less* power over you. I would keep that in mind at all times.

"Tonight, after the Passion Play, she plans to have me crowned king. If she gets this far, do not interfere. There is no real harm and it may work in our favor. However, she then intends to make me her husband so that she can take that which is mine and become queen. You must *not* let this happen." Julian studied each of his companions in turn. All paid close attention.

"She is going to attempt to take control of me, and if she succeeds, it will not bode well for any of us. You must work to prevent this. If she succeeds, you may have to kill me. Do not hesitate."

Natasha blanched.

"If we capture her, what do you want us to do?" Chynna asked.

"Kill her. Show her no mercy - she will only use it against you."

Even though it was Saturday night, most of the shops in town were closed. Amanda, Daisy, and Neil stalked the lamp lit streets, finding only one open business that would serve their purposes - a shop called *Surprises and Disguises*. There, they'd found a simple black cape for Neil - which he'd refused to wear until his mistress commanded it - but Amanda had found nothing for herself. As for Daisy, she needed nothing - the Vampira costume she'd brought with her blended in perfectly.

"Where are we going *now*?" Daisy whined as they made their way past the line of darkened shops and boutiques. She blew a bubble and popped it.

"We're looking," said Amanda.

"For what?"

"Something to wear."

Daisy began to speak but Neil cut her off. "I'm hungry."

"You just took sustenance," Amanda told him. "You're going to have to get used to exercising moderation." She could tell that Neil hadn't been the kind of human who'd been on good terms with moderation, and this meant that as a vampire, he'd be hard to control - but Amanda was determined to train him properly from the get-go. She'd begun by throwing out his body spray and forbidding him to ever use it again.

Once Neil had served his purpose and she no longer needed him, if she decided not to kill him, that loser could do whatever the hell he wanted. But until then, Amanda wasn't about to spoil him by catering to his every whim. "Perhaps when we've achieved our goal, we can think about blood, but we have more pressing matters to contend with right now."

"Our goal?" asked Neil. "I don't even know what our goal is!"

"Yeah!" Daisy snapped her bubble gum.

Just then, a young human female with long, dark hair rounded the corner, heading their way. She wore a glittering tiara and carried a sequined handbag that matched her red shoes and filmy red flowing gown. It was this, the gown, that drew Amanda's attention. "Follow my lead," she told Daisy and Neil.

They continued toward the young woman and she toward them,

and when they were within speaking distance, Amanda paused, putting on a bright smile. "Well, look at you!"

The young woman paused uncertainly.

"And who are you supposed to be?" she asked the girl, whose eyes were appraising Neil.

"One of Dracula's Brides!" The girl displayed pathetically fake fangs.

"Isn't that precious," said Amanda. "What is your name, dear?"

"Carrie."

"Well, Carrie I like your dress. Where did you buy it?"

"I sewed it myself."

Amanda couldn't have cared less, but rapport was important. "Where are you headed, Carrie?"

"I'm on my way to a party at the Bigfoot Inn!" She twinkled at Neil. "You guys should come!"

"We'd love to, but unfortunately, we have other plans." Amanda grinned wide enough to flash fang. *Real* fang.

Carrie's eyes betrayed uneasiness. "Wow. Where did you get your fangs? They look so real!"

"I made them myself," said Amanda.

Carrie looked confused.

"They glow in the dark, too." Amanda bared her teeth.

Carrie squinted and frowned.

"It's not dark enough with these street lamps burning. Step into the alley with me and I'll show you. It's really cool!"

Carrie hesitated, but Amanda took her hand and led her into a narrow gap between shops where no light could penetrate, leaving Neil and Daisy staring after them.

Carrie didn't make a sound. The moment they were out of sight, Amanda tore the girl's vocal chords out with her teeth - and when Amanda emerged from the alleyway sixty seconds later, she was carrying the wedding dress of her dreams.

Red, thought Amanda. *So glad it was red.*

No one would notice the bloodstains.

73
BITING MAN

Within the Eternal City, excitement was palpable; tonight was the climactic celebration that everyone looked forward to. Red and white lights twinkled everywhere in the halls and garlands of black bat flower - *tacca chantrieri,* the flower Julian used as his business logo - decorated hallways and booths, the dinner plate-sized black, purple-veined flowers hanging, their two-foot long whiskers tickling patrons' heads. Julian smiled, amused at the things that lingered from the old stories; someone was doing a thriving business manufacturing silk bat flowers. Originally, he had discovered the real flower on his travels in the far east and managed to bring a few specimens back. They were difficult to grow in all but moist, humid climates, but his greenhouse was as full of them as it was of the precious bloodberries. He smiled to himself. In the existing lore, Keliu was said to drape the memorial to his lost Euloan love in bat flowers and that when he left a place, bat flowers would spring up where he had stepped. It was almost all nonsense, of course.

Now, on the vendor-lined midway, he walked along behind Natasha and Michael with Chynna and Winter flanking him. Arnie and the new vampires brought up the rear. Beginning to feel rather claustrophobic, he stopped walking. "A moment, please."

The group gathered around him.

"Incendarius has not yet arrived and I would like a little time to myself."

"But–" began Natasha.

"I wish to visit the temple and speak with one of the priests there. I saw him yesterday and recognized him. I wish to pursue a reacquaintance."

"We're not going to leave you alone," Michael said.

"I appreciate that. I only ask for you to wait outside the temple. If you want, you may wait inside, but I need privacy. I assure you, I will be safe there."

∽

"I wonder where Crazy Daisy is," Lucy said to Ivy. They sat at a small table outside a plasma bar.

Ivy raised her shot glass. "I'm just glad she's not here."

"Good riddance to that twatsicle!" They clinked glasses and downed their shots. "Want another round?"

"Not yet," Ivy said. "Let's stay straight until after the Passion Play. For Julian's sake."

Lucy considered. Not only was Ivy sweet on Julian, but they'd promised Natasha they'd remain clear, in case that bitch Amanda tried anything. "Okay. For Julian." Lucy stood. "But the minute that play is over with, I want to get drunk."

"Me, too." Ivy slung her bag over her shoulder. "What should we do now?"

"You wanna go hear Plastic Taffy?" Lucy reapplied lipstick.

"Sure, why not?"

"I can't wait to see if they're better singers, since they changed," Lucy said as they headed toward the amphitheater.

"Doubt it."

Laughing, the girls entered the venue. The show was still half an hour off, but the crowd was hushed in anticipation as the guest of honor, Bela Lugosi, took center stage and bowed, the satin lining of his cape flashing crimson under the lights. Lucy and Ivy sat down near the exit.

"Good eve-en-ing," Lugosi said into the mic.

"Good eve-en-ing," called the crowd as if his words were a litany.

Lucy poked Ivy. "Half the vamps here are wearing Dracula capes."

"I know. It's crazy what a big deal he is. I wonder why."

"He set vampiric style for the twentieth century, dummy!" Lucy spoke as if it were gospel.

"I wish to thank you all for coming to the Biting Man Festival," Lugosi was saying. "Tonight, our show will begin with Plastic Taffy, a group who, though new to our world, has been playing together for a quarter of a century." Bela squinted at a teleprompter. "After Plastic Taffy, Ravensbite will perform." The audience cheered and hooted. "We will then adjourn before the witching hour so that you may attend the Passion Play." Bela smiled, showing fang, driving the audience crazy. "At one-thirty we will resume our concert. Corpsepussle, Medulazula, and many more will entertain you tonight! But now, here's Plastic Taffy!"

The cheering was deafening. Around them, vampires lit up bloodweed or pulled bottles of cheap blood from their bags, ready to party. Ivy would have indulged - so would her sister - but the promise to Natasha - *to Julian* - could not be broken. Seeing Plastic Taffy was no big whoop - the twins had seen them a million times in Candle Bay and being vampires hadn't improved their music. Ivy yawned and dug in her evening bag for a nail file.

74

THE GLOW OF LUNAE LUCEM

Julian entered the temple, thinking it wasn't nearly as grand as it had been in the days of the Treasure. His father had outfitted the vast chamber in the finest materials and back then, light came from thousands of lunae lucem - jarred "moonlight" derived from a rare fungus that grew in beautiful, glowing golden banks by Euloa's rivers, but had slowly died out when exported to other lands. In his father's days, this vast room - indeed, all the rooms - had shone with the light of lunae lucem.

Candles, then oil lamps, and finally, electricity had replaced the serene golden glow everywhere else in the Eternal City, but within the temple, a modicum of the old ways remained. It was not garishly lit. Soft golden lights illuminated statues and grottos and sometimes spot-lighted the waterfall beyond the throne. Candelabra holding beeswax candles stood near the podium and on either side of the throne. More candelabra, closer to the seating, held candles that glowed safely with electric light.

And the mosaic that spanned twenty feet of wall, with Keliu's image in the center, was now lit from above with tiny museum lights. The light was soft and white so that the colors shone true, even after two thousand years.

The high priest, Diego, stood before this image, his head tilted, hands folded behind his back. Julian had never liked the mosaic, nor did he like this place being called a temple. Many had insisted on worshipping the Prince of Blood, not just as Trueborn royalty, but as a god. It had been distasteful then, as it was now.

Julian approached Diego quietly, then stood behind him long moments, remembering the stance, and the character, of a young Incan priest from long ago.

"Diego." He said it so softly that the word was lost to ambient sound. "Tupa."

"I have not heard 'Tupa' in many centuries. Who calls me by this name?" The priest did not turn.

Julian came to stand beside him, his face not hidden this time. "Who do you think it might be?"

The priest turned slowly, his eyes at first downcast. "I dare not think it is true," he whispered. He looked up, caught Julian's gaze. "Keliu."

"It is good to see you, my old friend. I am known as Julian now."

Diego remained speechless, a slow smile gracing his face.

"We must speak in private."

The priest nodded. "Come with me."

Julian followed him deep into the cavern, passing the throne and then entering a passage behind the waterfall. Beyond that, a few more steps brought them to a steel door. It was the room where his father had kept his riches so long ago. Diego pulled a key from beneath his emerald robes and unlocked it.

Inside the small room, a vault was set into one wall. The others were lined with shelves and small cabinets, all trimmed in hammered gold, while a heavy table and six chairs took up the center of the room. The furniture was all dark wood, but for the small fountain set into the middle of the table where water burbled peacefully into the gold-edged tiled basin.

Diego locked the door behind them then clasped his hand. "It is good to see you, too, my friend. Julian. The last time you visited, you said you would not return - and you did not. Yesterday, a woman told me you would come. I did not believe her."

Julian shed the cape. "I had not intended to return to this place, but it became a necessity."

Diego went to a cabinet and withdrew a bottle and two goblets. "Please, sit. We will not be disturbed."

Glasses filled, they talked for a few moments, then Julian said, "I've much to tell you, and there is little time."

"I am ready." Diego folded his hands around his goblet.

"You have heard of Incendarius?" Julian sipped his blood.

"I have."

"Have you ever encountered one?"

"No. Are they not creatures of myth?"

"They are not." Julian paused. "And you *have* met one."

"The blond vampire ..."

"Indeed." Julian refilled his glass and proceeded to tell the priest the story of Amanda's incarnations. "On some level, I believe she always knew she was Incendarius. Talai and Paqari and others took their own lives to avoid the change, but Amanda, for reasons I've yet to understand, welcomed it. And now I am in great peril."

"Tell me what you wish me to do."

"If she manages to get close to me, I will lose my will, just as the stories tell. I shall need your help and that of my traveling companions, to evade her. You must understand that you may have to fight me if I fall under her spell again."

"I can't fight you—"

"You can." Julian's smile was blade-thin. "Just try not to destroy my physical form - that is, unless you must, in order to save yourself or any of the others." He drained his goblet in one long swallow. "She only desires my coronation because she wishes to be queen. That is her goal and it will guarantee my demise. Do not allow a marriage to take place." He rose. "My companions are waiting nearby. Perhaps it would be good for you to meet them."

Diego and Julian left the safe room, traversed the cavernous temple, and soon found Natasha, Michael, Winter, and Chynna just inside the entrance. Arnie and the new vampires, Erin and Norman, were further in, listening with fascination as Cornelius, the priest with a fondness for bloodweed, explained the history of a bank of statues carved into a vast pillar.

Diego and Julian led the four to the waterfall, where the noise would preclude eavesdropping. Introductions were made, and plans discussed.

"Would it be wise to tell the other priests what's going on?" Michael asked.

Diego shook his head. "My brothers are typical of younger priests and consider the Prince of Blood to be a religious figure rather than a philosophical one. They worship him; I think that they would be too smitten if they knew anything beforehand."

"They worship you?" Natasha asked. "You've been holding out on me, Julian."

"It's nothing." Julian didn't bother to disguise his distaste for the Dead Agains.

"Among our kind," the priest told them, "the Treasure demanded to be worshipped as a god-king. The people of the Eternal City were oppressed, and when the Prince of Blood came and freed them and imprisoned the Treasure - they naturally wanted to worship him in the same manner. But the prince refused and soon left. He wanted to be neither king nor god."

"This is true." Julian gazed at each in turn. "I wished only for peace, enlightenment, and privacy. It is all that I have ever wanted." *Almost all I ever wanted.*

"Yes," affirmed Diego. "When I met you at Machu Picchu more than five centuries past, you desired the same."

"As did you, my friend." Julian patted his arm. "And that is why I agreed to transform you. You have done great work since then, here and elsewhere, in trying to convince followers I am merely a Trueborn, not a god."

"It's nearly gotten me killed a few times. Nevertheless, it is a mission I cannot abandon." The priest looked toward his underlings as they made the temple ready for the Passion Play. "They do not understand why a Trueborn like you or a man like Gautama Buddha would refuse to be worshipped as a god."

"Gautama," said Julian, "taught me much about self-control and want and need. His was a transcendental soul and very wise."

"Indeed." Diego smiled. "You are fortunate to have known him."

"Now," Julian said. "I have no wish to roam the halls, so I am going to remain here in the temple. I will be safe - there are places within where Amanda cannot reach me and I will stay hidden until it is time to dispose of Incendarius."

His companions' faces continued to betray worry.

"But, you will need to act. If she cannot find me, she will not leave this place. She'll know I'm here and that will put Diego and his priests in grave danger. You will need to take control of her. And kill her. She is strong, but no stronger than I am - you four are enough to stop her long enough to kill her." Julian spoke with more confidence than he felt. He turned to Diego. "Do you have weapons for my friends?"

"Indeed. I will make sure you have everything you need."

75
SICKENING AND SUBLIME

Ordering them to stay put, his Mistress had left Neil and Daisy alone while she went into the ladies' lounge to change into her wedding gown. It was taking forever but that was okay - chicks always took forever.

To his surprise, Neil Trinsky was beginning to like being undead, and though a week ago he would have thought it the worst thing that could possibly have happened, it had grown on him. He was still himself for the most part - but better. Stronger. More intense. Everything was more intense, and as they'd made their way through the crowd at the Biting Man Festival, his finely-tuned senses took in the sights, sounds, and smells at a rate he was sure his human brain couldn't have processed.

But his brain was now vampire, and he was able to experience the details of things around him with quick, sharp clarity. It was like a perfectly arranged bouquet of flowers - an explosion of color and texture and aroma - and yet each blossom had the precise amount of room it needed to be enjoyed in its own right. It was everything, all at once, and yet each detail was its own, a solitary thing of beauty, the depths of which could be explored to as yet uncharted degrees.

Neil was keenly conscious of everything around him – the various food and skin scents, the almost touchable texture of the overlapping voices floating to the high cavern ceiling, each note of every instrument that the far-away band played – and it brought new layers of meaning to his existence, but Neil was still Neil; proof of that fact was everywhere.

For one thing, he was horny as hell. If the chronic fullness of his balls didn't ease, he'd need to find the nearest restroom and rub a good one out. He wanted to know what it was like to fuck as a vampire – and the thought of it made his already hard cock go stiffer – so stiff he worried it would rupture, leaving nothing but a gaping raw wound where his manhood had been.

"I'm back." Amanda wore a Dracula cape that hid her dress.

"What took you so long?" Daisy asked.

"I got us some backup. Plastic Taffy will help us with our enemies when the time comes."

Neil nodded, barely listening, staring at Amanda – she was his first choice to fuck, if only he could convince her.

Even in the shapeless Dracula cape he wanted to fuck her brains out, there was no question about that, but his emotions for the woman ran deep. He loved her. He needed her. He wanted to please her more than anything in the world. Yet, he hated her. Hated her for marrying someone else. Hated her for using him – and he was sure that's what she was doing. But most of all, he hated her for being able to control him. It would have been bad enough that *any* woman could sink her hooks so deeply into him, but a *vampire?* She was as sickening as she was sublime.

He and his female companions stopped at a kiosk for a glass of blood, and as they stood there, Neil's attention turned to Daisy. She and Amanda spoke animatedly about shit he didn't bother to follow. His eyes traveled down Daisy's backside to settle on her ass, which was small and firm beneath the taut fabric of her Vampira outfit.

When Amanda wasn't looking, he leaned close to Daisy's ear, took hold of one of those delectable back-end bubbles, and said, "Let's fuck."

Daisy whirled, her face a mask of fury, eyes blazing. She smacked him so hard it felt like his head toppled clean off his shoulders. Neil staggered back, colliding into a woman behind him, who said, "Watch it!" and promptly shoved him back toward Daisy, who slammed her elbow hard into his ribs, knocking the air out of him.

"You want to fuck," she said, "then go fuck yourself," and turned her back to him.

Neil rubbed his jaw, looking around, embarrassed. But if anyone - except the woman and her friends behind him - had seen anything, no one cared two squirts of piss about it.

That was when he saw Bat-Tat, who'd sworn up and down she was *not* a vampire. And yet, here she was, at the Biting Man Festival.

He caught only a brief glimpse of her as she made her way through the knots of people, but it was her, he had no doubt.

Dirty bloodsucker!

And he was going to fuck her. This time, he'd give her no say in the matter. He just needed to figure out how to get away from Amanda and Daisy. *Fuck them*, he thought. No way was he going to let either of these little bitches take his choices away.

Neil turned to head after Bat-Tat.

∽

"I ABSOLUTELY LOVE YOUR MAKEUP, and I can't wait to see your gown, Amanda!" Daisy smiled and licked her lips. "Can I have a sneak peek?" She giggled. "You could flash me!"

"No." Amanda was tired of Daisy. She talked incessantly in that simpering southern voice and it was beginning to sound like nails on a chalkboard. And the bubblegum … "You'll see it at the wedding."

"Neil, what time is it?"

But he was disappearing into the crowd.

"You little asshole," she breathed as she took off after him. A moment later she grabbed him by the ponytail and yanked him around. "Where the hell do you think you're going?"

"I-I saw her."

"Saw who?"

"The girl from the carnival. She ditched me, the bitch."

Daisy arrived. "What's going on?"

Amanda ignored her. "Who, you little toad? Show me." Her hand was an iron vice on Neil's elbow.

"They're going that way." Neil pointed and started walking. Seconds later, he stopped. "There. See her? The redhead. She disrespected me. She laughed at me." He pointed at a group of vampires standing near a connecting hall. "Come on." He tried to go forward but Amanda's grip halted him.

"You moron. What's so special about this girl?"

"She insulted me–"

"Oh, big whoop." Amanda kept a grip on Neil and watched the group the redhead was with. At first, all she could see were backs, but then one of the men moved and there was that fucking bitch, Natasha Darling, looking her way. Amanda seethed at the sight of her. She wanted to rip her arms off and shove them down her throat. *And I will. Later.*

She yanked Neil around. "Come on."

"But–"

"Not one word." She led Neil and Daisy to a stairwell. "Neil, those are the people I want you to kill. When I tell you to."

"Who are they?"

"My cousin, Natasha," said Daisy. "The others were from Crimson Cove. I met them all last night. We went to this great blood bar and–"

"Shut up, Daisy. Just shut up."

∼

"AMANDA IS HERE," Natasha told the others. "I just spotted her. And Daisy is with her."

"Where?" Michael scanned the midway.

"They beat it when they saw me."

"Should we go after them?" Winter asked.

"No." Natasha shook her head. "We must follow Julian's instructions to the letter."

"Seems reasonable." Chynna squinted into the distance, like a hunter watching a deer. "We knew she'd be here somewhere."

Natasha saw no trace of Amanda now. However, she did notice that the crowd was beginning to head toward the temple. "What time is it?"

Michael checked his antique pocket watch. "Nearly midnight."

"It's time. Let's go."

76

STAKES AND DAGGERS

The temple's seats were almost full when Natasha, Michael, and their friends filed in at twelve minutes before midnight. A priest stood by the door. Natasha approached him. "We have reserved seats."

He nodded. "Your name?"

"Darling."

"Yes, I remember. Father Diego told us only an hour ago. I am Father Milo. Please follow me."

He led them to the front rows of lyre-backed wood chairs with reserved signs on their red upholstered seats. They were on the center aisle, perhaps fifteen feet from the podium and twenty-five from the throne. Just to the right of the podium were the props for the Passion Play. The entire cella served as a stage. Beyond the props, tuxedoed musicians sat in a small group, tuning their instruments. "As you can see," the little priest said, "you have four chairs on the first row and three on the second. Will that suffice?"

Natasha looked around, scanning for the twins. "We're hoping that two more will join our party."

"I'm afraid that's all I could reserve."

"Thank you, yes, this will do then." It was just like the twins to be late - she could never count on them.

"I will tell Father Diego you are here." Milo hurried into the darkness behind the throne.

With a nod, Winter took the fourth seat in, Chynna beside him, then Michael, and Natasha on the aisle. Behind them, Norman and Erin flanked Arnie. Winter looked back at him. "Whatever happens, buddy, you stay safe. And don't move." He glanced at the others. "Same goes for you."

A moment later, Diego appeared. "It is good to see you again, my friends." He spoke so that he could be heard by those seated nearby as he slipped Natasha a small piece of paper. "We are glad you could attend." He gave them a meaningful look. "Everything is in order for the festivities tonight, so sit back and relax."

Natasha nodded. "Thank you, Father."

He bowed, turned, and disappeared into the crowd.

Natasha unfolded the note and shared it with Michael. *Stakes and daggers are hidden beneath the throne. I hope they are not necessary, but if they are, may they serve you well.*

Michael passed the note to Chynna and Winter, then squeezed Natasha's hand. She squeezed back. "We will prevail," he murmured.

Natasha nodded. "We will." Michael kissed her cheek, and they waited, scanning, always scanning, for any sign of Amanda.

∽

AMANDA HAD BACKED Daisy and Neil into the same alcove where Lucy had pummeled Daisy the night before. "Listen well, children-"

"I'm no child!" Daisy cried.

"Shut up, Daisy." She looked at Neil. "And you, you're going to do exactly as I say. You're not going to wander off or act on your own. Isn't that right?"

Neil's mean little eyes darkened. "That's right."

Amanda glared at him.

"That's right, *Mistress*," he amended.

"That's better. I'm glad we understand each other. Daisy, hand me the shopping bag."

Amanda dug past her clothes and extracted four syringes filled with clear fluid. "These contain holy water. You can squirt it if you have to, but you'll slow them down more if you inject it. Understand?"

Her pathetic minions nodded and pocketed the syringes, two apiece.

"Oh, and don't forget to take the cap off before you use it."

"What are they for?" Dumb Daisy asked.

Amanda rolled her eyes. "To make sure the Darlings and their friends don't interfere with my plans."

"Cool." Her gaze landed on the temple entrance. "I can't wait."

"Me, either." Neil patted his pocket.

"Then let's go." Amanda led them into the temple, then paused, scanning, trying to sense Natasha Darling. There were too many vampires to easily distinguish her scent, but she could tell, however faintly, that Julian, at least, was somewhere nearby.

Avoiding the priest at the door, she led her underlings toward the stage. Finally, she spotted Natasha and some of her people sitting front and center. While Amanda hadn't expected to see Julian with them, she was surprised the twins were missing. *Good.* She directed Neil and Daisy to take a pair of seats four rows back on the other side of the aisle. She didn't want them seen, but she wanted them seated close to her enemies.

"What about you?" Daisy asked, her eyes wide. "Aren't you going to sit with us?"

Amanda, the Dracula cape hiding her gown, smiled. "I have to get ready for my wedding. I must find my groom."

~

DIEGO RAPPED three times on the heavy door to the safe room – a signal to Julian – before entering.

"Have my friends arrived?" Julian watched as Diego closed and locked the door behind him.

"They have. I have spoken with them and they know where to find the weapons should it come to that."

"Excellent." Julian watched his old friend, noting the anxiety hidden behind his mask of serenity. He felt much the same. "Incendarius is here," he told Diego. "She is near and she is hungry." He glanced at the door. "Do you think it will hold?"

"I believe so." Diego studied him with great somberness. "But will *you* be able to resist her?"

"I intend to." Julian spoke with more certainty than he felt.

"Very well. I must leave you now; it is time to begin." Diego gazed at the table. Upon it lay weapons, from holy water to stakes to blades and a scythe. "Is there anything else you require?"

"Nothing."

"Good luck, Julian. I will be back soon."

77
PASSION PLAY

Amanda was grateful for the stupid Dracula cape. So many idiots were wearing them that she was able to move about freely as the orchestra tuned up. She'd even ordered the Plastic Taffy nitwits to wear capes on the off-chance they drew attention when they entered the temple to sit among the audience.

"May I help you?" A little priest smelling of bloodweed appeared from a dark corridor and smiled stupidly at her.

"The restroom?" She caught his eye and wet her lips.

"Oh, yes, yes." The man fluttered in her gaze. "Just go back that way and take the first corridor. It's on the right, you can't miss it."

"Thank you." Amanda turned and headed into the corridor, and waited until the priest looked away before she slipped back out to continue her search for Julian. She could feel his presence strongly now; there was no doubt he was in the temple.

As the narrator took the podium and the colorfully-garbed actors, the stage, Amanda concentrated, using the kind of stealth that could make her seem all but invisible. Quickly, she passed the mosaic and returned to the shadows cast by pillars and statues. No one noticed.

The orchestra played, the narrator spoke, and the actors began playing their parts. As she explored the darkened areas near the waterfall, she half-listened to the story of Keliu, the Prince of Blood, and snickered, realizing he was thought of as a god. *Some god. He refuses power. But now they will have a Goddess. A great Goddess who will rule with an iron hand and happily accept all the riches offered up.*

～

"Hurry!" Lucy pushed Ivy through the temple doors.

"I *am* hurrying!" They'd lingered, talking to a couple of cute guys after the concert and now the Passion Play was about to start and the temple was stuffed to the gills.

"Shh!" A green-robed temple priest approached, and put his finger to his lips. "The play is starting. Follow me," he whispered. As the musicians made ready to play, he guided them to a pair of seats halfway to the front and not too far from the center. They swiveled their way down the aisle, to the delight of the males and annoyance of most females.

"Where's Natasha?" Ivy sat.

"Down in front somewhere."

"Look! Plastic Taffy's over there!"

Lucy giggled. "They look so stupid in their little Dracula capes-"

Several neighbors shushed them as the narrator began the tale of the Prince of Blood and how he saved the vampires from the Treasure. Lucy and Ivy had heard it all before, but it never got old, especially because they knew the story was really about Julian.

～

Erin Woodhouse had never seen anything like it. At first, she'd been awed by the temple itself - the lush red aisle runners and ornate chairs with their plush scarlet seats - but once the Passion Play began, she'd found herself unable to pry her attention away.

As the story of the Prince of Blood unfolded, she felt a surreal sense of being a part of it. This was her history now, this was what ran through her veins, and as she watched, the truth of whom she'd become burned bright and deep within her - it fully *became* her, and for the first time since being turned, she completely understood and accepted, without fear or reservation, her new identity. *And I know the Prince of Blood!* It was awesome.

The feeling of belonging lay thickly over her. It was so strong that she wondered if the others felt it, too, and looking at Arnie - who'd instinctively reached for her hand as the plot thickened - Erin knew she wasn't the only one. It was cathartic, really, and glancing over at Norman Keeler on Arnie's other side, she felt a sudden fondness for the new vampire, for he too watched, enraptured, leaning stiffly forward, glittering tears standing in his eyes.

This is who Norman is now, too, she thought, and as if reading her thoughts, he glanced at her and smiled. Erin returned it and looked back to the play, giving Arnie's hand a gentle, reassuring squeeze. In that moment, she fully understood that Arnie was her family. Not just Arnie, but all of them - the Darlings and Julian, and Michael and Chynna and Winter, and even Norman Keeler.

It was the strongest sense of belonging that she'd ever felt in her life, and she knew that there was nothing under the sun - or the moon - that could ever tear her away from these people.

She'd die before she'd let that happen.

∽

NATASHA TRIED to enjoy the Passion Play but found it difficult to concentrate as she continually scanned for Amanda or any sign of the twins. As if sensing her worry, Michael squeezed her hand. She was grateful he was there.

But it wasn't all worry, not quite; certain revelations tugged at her. Julian had never told Natasha that he had been worshipped as a god. *And still is - that's who the Dead Agains worship!* In the years since he had first appeared in Candle Bay, her estimation of him had gone from rogue and scoundrel, to proper businessman, and now, if not sainted, then something akin to it.

He was, she realized, all these things and more, and they had to save him from Amanda. From Incendarius.

Out of the corner of her eye, she thought she caught movement near the waterfall, but it was gone in an instant.

78
WEDDING BELL BLUES

The safe room's walls and door were thick, but music and voices drifted through the air vents. The music was not of the era Keliu had spent in the mountain, but classical in nature. Julian thought he recognized Schubert. The voice of the narrator held its own rhythm in counterpoint to the orchestra's melody.

Julian had seen the Passion Play any number of times. Over the centuries it had become a sort of pastiche of the Catholic Easter pageant, evolving from the influence of Spanish missionaries on local natives as well as the influx of Spanish immigrants. Catholic influence had trickled into the vampiric community in Icehouse Mountain as new vampires were made and eventually, the original ritual was lost to history. A few centuries ago, a grail cup had even been added; it was said Keliu had spilled his own blood into it to heal vampires who were dying from his father's wrath. *Humans always love that which is most familiar.* He sighed. *As do we all.*

Someone tapped the door. Startled, Julian realized it was not Diego's knock and remained still and silent.

"Julie, I know you're in there. Let me in."

She's found me. Although Julian had known it would happen eventually, it shocked him. He turned his mind from her, even as she continued to wheedle and woo. *Do not listen!*

She talked, weaving spells with her words, and even as he tried not to listen to her vile suggestions, even as he reminded himself that she was his enemy, her sweet poison tried to insinuate itself into his system.

His blood began to burn. His mouth went dry and his heart thundered. *No! I will not let it happen. I am Trueborn. I will prevail.*

"Julie ..."

I am stronger than any hybrid.

"Julie, open the door, sweetie. I miss you. I want you."

I am stronger than Incendarius. But his fingertips trembled with the need to touch her.

"Don't you want me?" She pitched her voice lower, huskier. "I know you do. I can feel your want. Your need."

Julian felt it, too. His body rebelled against his better judgment and, consumed with desire, sick with fury, he watched himself reach for the door.

～

"OH, isn't this sweet? Look Julie, we're dressed the same." Amanda filled her voice and smile with seduction as she entered the room. "Are you wearing your royal robes under that cape?"

He stared, obviously trying to resist her. "I am not."

"Well, why not?" She unclasped her cape, revealing the diaphanous red gown. She'd removed the bodice lining so her nipples could jut against the chiffon. "I'm wearing my wedding dress." As she spoke she put a sheer red veil on her head and secured it with a cheap tiara. "Do you like it, Julie?"

Heat flared amber in Julian's eyes, giving her great satisfaction.

"You are wasting both your time and mine," he said. "I am not interested."

She heard the effort in his voice - he was fighting her with all he had.

"What a pathetic little worm you are, Julie."

Pausing, he turned and glanced briefly at her. "And you are as charming as always, Amanda." His condescension infuriated her.

Gritting her teeth, she felt rage course through her. "I always get what I want, Julie. You *will* submit to my wishes and we both know it."

Julian's chuckle was low, humorless. "Not this time, Amanda."

As his hand touched the door latch, Amanda saw the subtle tremble of his fingertips. She smiled and concentrated in that way that turned her eyes to midnight. "Look at me, Julie. Look at me."

He fought, trying not to turn, but slowly, slowly, he did, and when he faced her, she saw adoration in his eyes.

~

"You are Incendarius." Julian forced the words from his throat, more to remind himself than anything else. She stood there, her face painted in heavy, oddly sensual make-up, her confidence supreme.

"I'm *what*?"

"You are Incendarius."

"What the everloving fuck are you talking about?"

Say no more. That she still does not know is to my advantage.

"Julie? Answer me!"

Julian fought down the urge to confide in her, to tell her everything. "It means you are incendiary."

"What the hell does that mean?"

"You make me burn." Covering up, he spoke the words too quickly, but she didn't notice.

"You mean I turn you on?"

"You infuriate me." He watched as a slow smile slid over her mouth, then added, "And that is *not* a compliment."

"Oh, but it is. Don't you see? Your hatred is merely proof of your passion. If you felt nothing at all toward me, maybe then I would worry. But your hate is delicious." Her wide smile dripped with arrogance. "I'm going to make you wait till after we're married before I let you fuck me again, though. I'm nothing if not old-fashioned." She cackled at her own joke.

Julian's jaw flexed. His fists hardened and he wished he could will himself to punch her in the face.

Amanda giggled.

Julian could practically see her bathing in the rage that emanated from him - she luxuriated in it as if it were a hot bath on a cold winter night. He closed his eyes, steadied his breathing, tried to dim the low hum of his raw and buzzing nerves.

Then Amanda was right in front of him. "Just say yes, Julie." He could feel her breath brush across his face like soft warm fingertips. "You know it's the right thing to do. You can *feel* it, can't you?" She grazed his neck with a fang.

"Leave me alo-" but his voice snagged. He swallowed hard, fighting the urge to either hit her or kiss her; he wasn't sure - and didn't care - which.

"I'll never leave you alone, Julie." She rubbed against him, sending tiny thunderstorms up and down his body. The feel of her was so magnificent, so right.

No! She's bewitching me! But his body didn't care. It responded the way any man's body responds in such intimate proximity to a beautiful woman, and this, this horrible betrayal of his own physical being, was just what Amanda needed to take her efforts to the next level.

She cupped his manhood, stroked her graceful fingers softly along his contours, a suggestion of a touch.

"Please. Stop."

But Amanda did not stop. She leaned in closer, bringing her lips a razor's-breadth from his ear, breathing hotly, breathing, breathing, breathing as her fingertips ghosted along his hardened need.

"I'll never stop, Julie." And the gentle force of her breath nearly pushed him over the edge.

But Julian held himself together, standing there, rigid and unmoving, eyes closed, mouth and throat as dry as the dead; he did not crack, he did not crumble.

"I'll never stop and we both know it." Amanda gave him a firm squeeze; when the hot tip of her tongue touched the ridge of his ear, Julian's shaky resolve turned to dust, not slowly, not piece-by-piece, but all at once it shattered around him, so loud and sudden and hard that he thought he heard it crash to the floor around his feet as he fisted his hands in her hair, pulled her face to his, and kissed her as deeply and as meaningfully as he'd ever kissed anyone in all of his existence.

She seemed to dissolve in his arms, fitting into him perfectly, becoming one with him as she returned that kiss with equal passion.

79

LONG LIVE THE KING!

The Passion Play ended to wild applause and Father Diego took the podium. Natasha had seen no sign of Amanda and was feeling hopeful. It didn't hurt that Michael had taken her hand when the play began and had yet to let go.

Diego cleared his throat. "The Passion Play is a tradition in the vampiric community, a way for us to remember our roots with the legends of our beginnings. On behalf of the priesthood of Temple Vampirus and the Eternal City, I want to thank you all for attending." He smiled. "The night is still young, so I urge you all to go enjoy-"

"THE PASSION PLAY WAS ONLY THE BEGINNING!"

"Amanda!" Natasha gasped.

From the darkness, two figures emerged. The audience went silent, watching. As they approached the podium, their identities became clear.

Julian was caped, head down, hiding his face, but Amanda was dressed in a sheer red costume that showed off her body. Her makeup was theatrical - unnaturally pale, her face contoured in red, her eyes as painted as a Vegas showgirl's. Her hair was upswept and topped with a thin red veil held in place by a glittery tiara.

Michael bent to Natasha's ear. "She's dressed as Dracula's bride."

"That good-for-nothing bitch–" Natasha started to rise, but Michael stopped her. "Do nothing. We don't yet know Julian's state of mind."

Reluctantly, Natasha acquiesced.

Amanda grabbed Julian's hand and tugged him forward.

Natasha stared at Julian, willing him to look at her, but he would not. Amanda pulled him to the podium.

"Get out of the way, priest!" She backhanded Diego and he flew at least six feet. The audience gasped. "Loyal subjects, the Prince of Blood has returned to become your king!" She ripped the cape off Julian and he raised his head, looking proudly out over the audience. They gasped.

"I am Keliu and I return to you now." His words were firm but subdued.

Stunned silence filled the temple, then all four of the lesser priests approached the podium and fell to their knees in front of Julian. As one, the audience, bowed its head.

∽

SUCH BEHAVIOR WAS EXPECTED from the Dead Agains in the audience, but Diego was disappointed in his priests. He had hoped they would not participate in such behavior, let alone lead it, but he supposed it was inevitable. Vampires, after all, had been human and the majority of humans had always been prone to seeing gods in everything from the sun and moon to the forests and the sea. Humans were usually superstitious and becoming a vampire did not change that. It was as if they wanted – *no, needed* – a father figure to tell them what to do, to praise and punish them. *It is always the way of the world.* When he had been a priest of Inti at Machu Picchu, he had not dared admit he thought the sun god a symbol rather than a reality. He would have been killed for it.

"Why aren't you kneeling, priest?" The blond vampire – *Incendarius!* – glared at him.

He wanted to argue that Julian was a Trueborn, not a god, but he had not survived so many centuries by speaking his mind. He looked to his old friend, his Maker, trying to gain his eye, and when he finally did, he said, "I shall kneel if you wish it, Julian."

Julian stared at him, his face stern, his eyes uncertain and Diego sensed the power Incendarius held over the Trueborn.

"You *must* kneel before him!" she commanded. "See to it!" She ordered the other priests who, without hesitation, rose and shoved Diego roughly to his knees.

Incendarius stepped to the podium and Julian meekly moved aside as she leaned into the microphone. "Tonight is a special night. You are about to see the coronation of your new king. The Prince of Blood shall become the King of Blood!"

The audience, in various stages of subjugation, stood to roar approval.

"After the coronation," she continued, "There will be a royal wedding!"

The spectators went wild, clapping and cheering. Julian remained stationary, his face unreadable; only his eyes revealed his imprisonment in the woman's will.

Incendarius smiled cruelly and pointed at Diego. "You. You will perform both ceremonies."

Diego said nothing at first, then seeing the fury spark red in her eyes, he spoke. "I shall do as Julian wishes."

"You will do as *I* wish, priest." She started to step toward Diego, but Julian's hand shot out and grasped her wrist, hard.

"The priest will do as I command." Julian looked to Diego, his eyes dark and intense. "Retrieve the crown my father once wore. We shall have the coronation immediately." He glared at the other priests. "Release him!"

They obeyed and Diego rose, brushed off his robes and walked toward the safe room beyond the waterfall. He moved slowly, head high, a million thoughts colliding in his mind. When he entered the room he saw no weapons on the table. That was curious. He unlocked the safe and extracted the golden crown with its studding of emeralds and sapphires, and the myriad sprinkling of tiny rubies, like drops of blood, then set it on the table and began looking in the cabinets and drawers along the other walls. He soon found the weapons. Julian had hidden them in several places, no doubt knowing he might be taken by Incendarius. Diego slipped two daggers and a vial of holy water into his deep pockets, then tucked the short-handled scythe among the folds of his robes. At last, he retrieved the bejeweled crown and made his way back to the main temple.

Remembering that Julian had told him to go ahead with the coronation but to stop the wedding at all costs, Diego performed the first ceremony. The audience, knowing they were witnessing history that had been eons in the making, was silent as Julian took a knee and Diego spoke the rites. At last he set the crown upon the Trueborn's head, and the Prince of Blood became the King.

Julian rose and a cheer unlike anything Diego had ever heard filled the temple, echoing, echoing. It seemed to go on forever.

80

THE BRIDE WORE RED

Amanda could almost feel the power surge into her as the gallery cheered their new king. Julian's resistance was weaker now - she could feel that as well - but it wasn't entirely gone. He just stood there, accepting the cheers without acknowledgement. She joined him and whispered in his ear, "Wave at them, Julie. Smile at them. Show them what a great king you're going to be."

He ignored her.

"For Christ's sake, do *something!*" She put her hand on his chin and turned his face to hers then kissed him on the lips.

The audience loved it and she felt a certain desire within him return. She kissed him again, then stood back. At last, with the barest of nods, Julian acknowledged his admirers.

Diego stepped forward and spoke. "Thank you for attending tonight's Passion Play and coronation. Enjoy the rest of the festival. We will see you here again soon."

Amanda hissed at the priest as she grabbed his arm and yanked him away from the podium. Then she waved at the masses as she'd seen Princess Diana do. "My subjects," she cried out, her voice echoing throughout the vast chamber. "You are all invited to stay and help us celebrate the nuptials of the King of Blood and his consort." She paused to lick her lips. "Me!"

After a new round of applause died down, she announced, "The wedding will begin immediately."

She turned to the stupid high priest, who was rubbing his arm. "Prepare for the wedding!" Turning, she scanned the spectators. "As bride, I shall choose my bridesmaid now. Isn't that right, priest?"

"You may choose a paranymph to stand with you, yes."

Amanda stared out into the crowd. "Daisy Darling, come on down!"

The girl squealed in the silence then trotted up, all eagerness and wiggles, her breasts jiggling ridiculously in her Vampira costume. "Oh, Amanda, I'm so honored, thank you–"

"Shut up, Daisy."

∾

Diego, High Priest of the Eternal City, was at a loss. He could see Julian's friends in the audience, but not well enough to make out their reactions to what was going on. Julian did not wish the wedding to take place, they all knew that, but Diego, alone, could not stop it; the bride would merely kill him and substitute one of the lower priests. They were back on their knees, agog, Cornelius, Milo, Galen, and Lucius. Any one of them would conduct the ceremony in Diego's stead, he had no doubt. He glanced at the audience. He needed to remove them quickly; he feared that what might happen could cause a riot.

"King Keliu," he said, the words foreign in his mouth.

Julian looked at him without focus.

"Would you care to have an attendant as well?"

"He doesn't need one," Amanda cut in.

Julian ignored her, speaking with what seemed like great effort. "I choose Natasha Darling to attend me."

"You can't–" started Amanda.

"He is king," Diego said for all to hear, hope buoying him. "More importantly, he is the groom and he may choose any paranymph he wishes." He nodded toward the brash young woman standing beside

Amanda. "Just as you have." He looked toward Julian's friends. "Natasha Darling, please join us at the podium."

～

"There is hope he is not entirely bewitched," Natasha whispered to the others before she rose. "Julian is ensuring we can carry out our mission. Be ready." She leaned down and spoke quickly. "Michael, lead them when the time is right. Have someone try to get to the weapons, as well."

"Good luck, my love." Michael kissed her hand before she walked to the podium.

～

The twins squirmed in their seats. "What the hell is going on?" Ivy said.

"Got me. Look at those Plastic Taffy idiots." Lucy pointed. "They all look like they need to pee."

Ivy nodded. "They're thinking about getting up, for sure." She paused. "We need to, too. Get up, I mean, not pee. Should we?"

"Not yet. We don't know what's going on." Lucy stared at the caped musicians. Something wasn't right. Then she looked back up at Amanda and Julian. No, something wasn't right at all.

～

Neil wondered why Amanda had chosen Daisy instead of him. At first, he thought it was a chick thing, but Julian picked a girl, too, so Neil was a little annoyed, but he would gladly do as Mistress Amanda asked and kill for her. Maybe he could even kill Julian's attendant; she was a real little bitch. Restless, he tapped his foot, his knee jouncing until the old bloodsucking bitch next to him shot him a dirty look.

～

JULIAN WAS TRYING to resist Incendarius because he knew he was supposed to. But he did not want to. He was filled with a poison that made him want to serve her, to do her bidding and make her his queen. He wanted to rule with her by his side. He closed his eyes. *These are her thoughts, not my own.* She stood so close that he could smell the aroma of her skin, see the luster in her hair. He wanted to taste her lips and bed her.

He glanced at Natasha Darling, who stood at his side. *Why did I choose her? Do I not want this marriage?*

No, you do not! The voice held prisoner deep in his mind screamed at him, but he heard it as a bare whisper. *Natasha is your friend, Amanda is not.*

Talai. Amanda.

She is neither. She is Incendarius.

But he wasn't sure he cared.

Amanda's voice cut through his reverie, harsh and chill. "Begin the ceremony, priest."

~

NATASHA WATCHED the wedding unfold as if it were a play. She stood with Julian, biding her time, unsure of what to do as Diego spoke a few words in an ancient tongue. Julian inclined his head, listening. *He understands.* She wished she did as well.

Finally, Diego said, "And now, the vows. Amanda, repeat after me." He began the recitation, pausing to allow Amanda to speak each line.

"Eternal companion of mind and soul."
"I bond with you now and forever."
"Through eons of darkness and the death-sleep of days."
"I shall be one with your heart. Your mind. Your soul."
"And I shall drink deeply of dusk with you by my side."
"Forevermore, together shall we be as one."

THE SMUG LOOK on Amanda's face made Natasha want to rip it off and feed it to the wolves, but she kept her calm.

Then Diego turned to Julian. Once again, he spoke in the ancient tongue and, once again, it became obvious that Julian understood.

"What are you saying?" Amanda demanded.

"It is only a blessing."

"Don't I get a blessing?"

"No, it is for the groom only."

Amanda sniffed, avoiding Natasha's gaze, her eyes trained on Julian.

Natasha watched Daisy Darling. Her cousin had always been trouble and she wondered if the girl had hooked up with Amanda out of spite after the twins had rejected her.

Diego spoke again. "Repeat after me."

"Eternal companion of mind and soul."

Julian spoke the words, but they were stilted, slow.

He's resisting. Natasha felt hope as she gauged the proper moment to attack Incendarius. If Julian were able to resist Amanda, they could vanquish her, even if Julian couldn't actually fight with them.

Slowly, Julian repeated the rest of the vow, but it obviously held no meaning for him. And as he began the final line, he looked into Natasha's eyes, his own filled with fierce determination and something akin to terror. And she heard his voice, however faint, inside her mind: *Now!*

With a warrior's yell, Natasha launched herself at Amanda. She toppled her, held her to the ground as she heard Michael's yell, then Winter's and Chynna's.

As the audience stirred, Amanda threw Natasha, tossing her three feet in the air and ten feet away. Amanda was on her feet, her veil askew, looking like a deranged Baby Jane with her smeared makeup. She stepped toward Natasha. Winter rushed her. She shoved him aside easily. Natasha regrouped and dived in again, along with Winter, Chynna, and Michael.

Then Amanda grabbed Daisy by the arm, reeled her in close, closer, until she was pinned against her breast.

Diego's voice thundered through the temple. "Do not interfere," he commanded the audience. "Leave this place now!"

Amanda laughed and kept Daisy imprisoned with one arm. She pulled a glinting blade from a sheath and put it to Daisy's throat. Daisy whimpered and stared at Natasha with frightened doe eyes.

"Let her go." Michael's words were deep and commanding.

Amanda laughed again, pressing the knife harder against Daisy's neck. The girl whimpered as several ruby drops sprang and dripped down her throat.

"What's the point, Amanda?" Natasha stepped closer.

"This is the point!" The knife sank into Daisy's throat - her eyes bulged and her mouth gaped. Crimson fountained down her breast. She made wet gasping noises as blood burbled from her nose and mouth.

With a hard jerk, Amanda drew the knife across Daisy's tender white neck, drawing a gruesome smile that dripped, gushed, sprayed, and finally wept. Then, with a powerful twist, she snapped Daisy's neck. Bone cracked and splintered as she beheaded the girl with her bare hands. Daisy's body dropped like a sack of cement.

Amanda shrieked and swung the severed head by the glossy black locks, hurling it at Natasha.

~

NATASHA'S HANDS shot up and she caught the flying head just inches from her own face. Its blind eyes remained wide with terror as it stared at her, its blood-wet mouth screaming in silence.

The shock only lasted an instant.

Then came the rage.

81

SEEING RED

His father's crown heavy upon his head, Julian felt encased in stone, unable to move or speak. He saw Natasha barreling toward Amanda with Michael, Winter, and Chynna close behind. *How strong must Incendarius be to keep me from moving, from speaking, while fighting so many?* He had hoped her control over him would falter while under attack.

Incendarius was under a crush of bodies now and the audience, momentarily silenced by what they'd seen, came to life as Amanda sent Chynna, then Michael, tumbling. The two lunged back into the fray.

"Leave now!" Diego ordered again as spectators began protesting. But no one was listening.

Julian saw the flash of Winter's muscled arm as he pummeled Amanda's face. It lessened her focus, and Julian tried again to move. This time, he succeeded. The Trueborn pointed across the audience and commanded, "OUT! ALL OF YOU!" He looked at the still-groveling priests. "ESCORT THEM OUT, PRIESTS! YOUR KING COMMANDS IT!"

The priests rose and scattered to the aisles, driving the spectators out the doors as best they could. "LEAVE THE TEMPLE, ALL OF YOU!" Julian thundered.

He watched as Amanda once again gained her feet and knocked Natasha, Michael, Winter, and Chynna down in one massive roundhouse kick.

Amanda's control over him tightened once more. But then the quartet was back up and lunged as one. They drove Incendarius down under their combined weight. "Diego," Julian said as his self-control gained ground. "They will need the weapons you hid beneath the throne."

Diego sprinted.

Natasha screamed as she was hurled.

Winter tumbled behind her.

Amanda shrieked as she tossed Chynna, then Michael, toward the podium.

∾

DIEGO GRABBED the weapons from beneath the throne and looked up at Natasha. She pushed hair from her face and nodded at the knives. "Give me one!"

He handed her an onyx-hafted athame. She took it and lunged back into the fray.

∾

ARNIE WATCHED as Amanda kicked Papa Winter, knocking him down. "Papa Winter!"

"Don't!" Erin clutched Arnie's arm, as he hopped to his feet.

But Arnie pulled away from her and ran for the aisle. Erin followed, Norman right behind her.

∾

LUCY AND IVY pushed against the chaotic crowd leaving the temple, elbowing and kneeing their way toward the stage. They came to Plastic Taffy, huddled together in their Dracula capes, eyes wide, mouths gaping as they tried to block their way. "Our Mistress will prevail!" cried the lead singer.

Lucy kicked him in the nuts and punched another in his throat.

Ivy did the same to the other two and an instant later, the twins passed Arnie and the other two newbies in the aisle.

"Tasha, we're here!" Ivy called.

Their big sister was getting the crap kicked out of her. Amanda was kicking the crap out of everyone. Lucy looked at Ivy. "Amanda's strong!"

"Just like Julian said." Ivy spoke through gritted teeth. She saw Julian staring at the audience, looking glazed.

Lucy stepped back as Chynna tumbled across the marble floor.

The high priest rushed toward them. "You are Natasha's sisters?"

"We are."

The priest handed each a shining blade as Julian turned his tortured eyes upon them, his voice a whisper. "Kill Incendarius!"

The twins waded in, knives raised, fangs glistening, sidestepping Winter and Michael as both men skidded across the floor.

~

NEIL TRINSKY HID behind his chair as the priest passed. No way was he going to be herded out with the rest of the fucking sheep. Though exhausted from his recent trials, Neil had every intention of pleasing Mistress Amanda. As he entered the center aisle, he came face to face with Bat-Tat Girl and two men.

Pulling the syringe of holy water from his pocket, he uncapped it with his teeth. "Come on, you little bitches." He waved the syringe. "Come to Papa!"

"You're not my papa," said the big dumb-looking one. "You go away!" He was flanked by Bat-Tat and a guy who looked like he'd just got back from the beach.

"Come on, you *chicken shits!*" screamed Neil.

"You be nice!"

"Shut up, you retard!"

"I'm not retarded. Papa Winter says so!"

"'*Papa Winter says I'm not retarded,*' says the retarded retard!" Neil mocked in a sing-song voice.

The beach boy looked ready to lunge.

Bat-Tat's nostrils flared.

"And you," Neil said to her. "You're a little bitch liar! Liar, liar, *LIAR!*" If there was anything Neil couldn't abide, it was dishonesty. *And bigotry. And queers and retards. God is on my side!* He raised the syringe and charged Bat-Tat like a bull. She braced herself for impact.

But at the last second, the big dummy stepped in front of her. "Stop!"

Neil didn't stop. The needle sank into the man's chest. Neil hit the plunger, emptying the entire syringe into the dirty bloodsucker.

The effect was immediate.

The big dumb vampire screamed, dropped to his knees, writhing, rolling, and kicking, screaming as tears sprang from his eyes.

"Arnie! No!" Bat-Tat screamed.

The beach boy's eyes flashed red. "You're going to pay for that."

But Neil wasn't listening. He stared, fascinated, as thin ribbons of smoke rose from the vampire's chest. The smell of burning flesh hit like a brick wall.

Bat-Tat and the beach boy rounded on him.

"Drop the syringe." Bat-Tat's eyes glowed the color of blood and the beach boy's mouth yawned open, showing blade-sharp fangs.

"I'm going to kill you," said Bat-Tat.

"We both are," growled the beach boy.

Neil stepped back. Hot urine ran down his leg and the syringe clattered to the floor. "Please," he said. "Don't–"

But there was no mercy in their fire-red eyes.

82
HIGH STAKES

As the twins joined the fight, Diego looked to Julian. "My friend, I can stand here no longer." He withdrew two sharp ash stakes from his robes. "I must help." He gripped one stake and set the second on the podium.

"High priests are forbidden to fight."

"Rules are made for breaking." Diego unhooked something from his belt. "I believe you are ready to wield this." He handed Julian a gleaming short-handled scythe. "May it serve you well."

Julian accepted the weapon. "If you can keep Incendarius busy, it may. I feel more myself with every moment she is distracted."

"We will keep her busy." With those words, Diego, stake in hand, headed into the melee.

∼

D<small>IEGO SHOULD NOT HAVE GIVEN</small> *me this scythe.* Julian worried that if he got close to Incendarius, she would take him over and that would mean the end of everything.

Natasha, Chynna, Winter, Michael, and Diego were all mature hybrid vampires, and all were strong, excellent fighters. Now that the twins had joined them, it was seven to one. Yet Amanda was so strong that she continued to throw off her attackers.

Knives flashed, but so far, none had drawn blood.

∽

Natasha's broken ribs stabbed at her lungs. She gasped as she tried to pick herself off the floor, then felt helping hands from behind. "Michael."

"You are injured. You should not be fighting."

"I'm fine." She tried to turn, but he easily held her in place.

"You are weakened."

"I said I'm fine." Roughly, she tore away and headed back into the brawl.

∽

"Fuck you!" Bat-Tat clawed and punched Neil, pummeling hard, knocking the breath out of him as the beach boy drove his knee into Neil's lower back, dropping him.

Neil couldn't get to his feet. Each time he tried, he was battered back down.

"Fuck you! Fuck you! Fuck YOU!" Over and over, Bat-Tat and the beach boy drove him down. His ribs, his gut, his cock and balls, they spared no part of him.

Somehow, finally, Neil managed to get to his hands and knees, and that's when the beach boy kicked him square in the face. He flew back, wailing in agony, clutching the bloody mess that had been his nose. Bat-Tat lunged, driving her foot right into his balls, stomping and crunching and grinding her heel.

The pain was like cold liquid lead working through his insides, flooding his lower belly. He squirmed like a bug on a pin as the twisting agony made its way past his bowels and into his stomach.

Neil, gagging on his own bloody vomit, tried to crawl away.

∽

"You think you're such hot shit!" Amanda spat the words in Natasha's face as she wrested the athame from her grip. "You're not! You're nothing!"

Natasha grabbed for the knife. Incendarius held it out of reach with one hand and pinned her with the other. "Give it up. You can't win. The Darlings are done for. After I kill you and your stupid sisters, I'm going to Candle Bay to stake your brothers and uncle. Then I'll burn down your precious hotel!"

Amanda's fangs glinted as she brought the knife down and slammed it between Natasha's ribs, twisting, then throwing her as if she weighed nothing.

Chynna leapt at Amanda.

Winter charged.

Amanda yanked out a hank of Chynna's hair.

Winter slammed into Amanda. He bounced off, landing on his ass. She smiled down at him. The stories of Incendarius had exaggerated nothing except for the monstrous face. Amanda's face was not a monster's: only her soul was that.

Michael and Diego came at her now, and Winter got to his feet just as she knocked Michael flat with a raised elbow, then kicked Diego out of range as if he were a soccer ball. Winter seized the moment and rushed her, got his hands around her throat.

He squeezed hard, lifting her several inches off the ground.

She gagged, clawed at his hands.

Winter shook her like a rag doll. "Surrender, Incendarius! Surrender, or I will kill you here and now!"

She kneed him hard in the stomach.

Winter threw her. She sailed several feet before crashing to the ground. He thought he'd at least stunned her, but the bitch was quick; her strength remarkable.

In a single move, she was on her feet, eyes blazing, fangs dripping. "How *dare* you lay your hands on a woman!"

"You're no woman; you're a monster. Now get your ass over here so I can finish you off!"

His confidence surprised her. She only hesitated a moment, then came at him full-speed. She dropped, swept her leg out, and knocked

Winter's feet out from under him. He hit the ground and she leapt onto him, her fists beating like sledgehammers until ribs splintered and cracked.

She pounded, clawed, and shredded his flesh, intent on tearing his heart out of his chest.

83
RAGE

Natasha lay on the cold floor near the throne. Rarely had she felt such agony. Groaning, coughing painfully, she tried to sit up. She couldn't, not yet. Instead, she wiped away the blood bubbling from her mouth as Michael made his determined way toward her. His hair was loose and his eyes blazed as steadily as fire. She'd never seen him like this.

"Tasha!" He knelt beside her.

"I'm okay."

"No, you're not. Don't move. He took off his vest, folded it, pressed it against the wound. "Hold it there. Use pressure."

She obeyed.

"If you lose much more blood, you'll pass out."

She wanted to argue with him, to insist on getting back into the battle, but there was something different about him, something frightening, something that warned her not to defy him.

"I love you," he said. And then he was gone.

∼

THE OLD FURY raged inside Michael. He no longer reasoned; he was all instinct, all emotion - a killing machine.

As Amanda overpowered Winter, slashing at him, Michael caught sight - then scent - of the blood spilling over his friend's white shirt and pants, and the very thin thread that tethered Michael to his own humanity snapped.

Michael grabbed Amanda by the hair and jerked her off Winter. Slamming her to the floor, he drove his knee into her ribcage. Bones snapped beneath his weight. The blade spun out of her hand. Her eyes bulged as she gasped for air.

Michael slammed her head onto the floor over and over, starring the marble with bright crimson splats, and even as the back of her skull crunched and caved, he could feel her ribs reconstructing themselves.

Michael didn't care. His only interest was in bashing in the woman's head - bashing it and bashing it until nothing was left but blood and bone and brain and pulp.

It felt good to be alive again.

WINTER, Chynna, and Diego watched as Michael slammed Amanda's head so hard against the marble that Julian, another ten feet distant, could hear Incendarius' skull crunching.

Her hold on him was all but gone.

He lifted the scythe and stepped forward, the cruel curved blade glinting.

ERIN PUMMELED Neil with more force and strength than she would have believed possible. With each blow, she felt and heard the crack of bone until his ribs, his arms, his legs were ruined - and his face was nothing but splintered bones moving freely beneath his skin.

When he stopped moving entirely, Erin thought she'd killed him. *But that's not possible, is it? Can you beat a vampire to death?*

"Is he ...?"

"I don't know," said Norman.

Erin drew back, looking at the ruin in front of her. He lay covered in blood, arms and legs splayed, head turned to the side, mouth hanging open. Her fingertips began to tremble and a sick feeling swelled in the pit of her stomach.

She felt Norman's hand on her shoulder.

"Don't think about it," he said.

But it was all she could think about. *Murderer. I'm a murderer.*

From the stage came a series of sickening crunches.

Erin looked up and saw Michael slamming Amanda's head into the floor. He did not look like the same man - the wild, crazed eyes, the primal sneer. *He's a monster, too,* she thought. *We're all monsters.* She was suddenly aware of Neil's blood cooling and thickening on her hands.

Norman guided her away and when she looked back at the man she'd beaten, he was no longer there.

She hadn't killed him after all. Neil Trinsky had gotten away.

Erin was torn between relief and a blooming new terror.

84
DELIVERANCE

Julian, his fingers curled around the handle of the scythe, watched as Amanda shrieked and threw Michael a dozen feet. The others stood unmoving, shocked that she'd regained such strength in the fraction of a second that Michael had paused to wipe blood from his eyes.

Incendarius was on her feet before any of them could move. She screamed and doubled over as her broken, misshapen head resculpted itself into its original form.

Winter, Chynna, and the twins closed in around Amanda.

Then she whirled in another roundhouse, knocking them to the ground.

Natasha, propped against the throne, cursed, her clear voice ringing out in the vast chamber. "You are not welcome in our world, Incendarius. Your time here is ended."

Amanda's eyes riveted on Natasha and she stalked toward her, breathing hard, seemingly unstoppable. "You're wrong, Natasha. You're *so* wrong. *Your* time has ended." Amanda's voice rose in mad laughter, so loud and high that it made Julian's ears hurt.

Michael put himself between the two women. Amanda's laughter lowered into a growl as the others grabbed at her, trying to hold her back.

She knocked them off like flies, her eyes never leaving Natasha. "I'm going to twist your head off like I did your little cousin's, and then I'll do the same to your sisters and all your friends. You're going to watch. No one will stop me!" More laughter. "No one *can* stop me!"

Julian stalked toward Incendarius. Caught in her desire to kill, Amanda had forgotten him, and Julian's will grew ever stronger.

Amanda stood still and stiff, hands claws at her sides, as she faced off with Michael.

Julian was less than a dozen feet from her now and slowly raised the scythe, intending to behead her without warning.

But she turned, eyes flashing as they bored into his own.

Do not look at her. She will glamour you. He felt her will pressing at his consciousness. Sudden desire made him falter; he lowered the scythe a fraction of an inch.

The other vampires watched, silent and tense.

Amanda slowly straightened, composing herself. "Julie," she purred. "My king, my sweet Julie. Come to your queen."

"No." Paralyzed, he stood there as she neared, her eyes gleaming, her lips plump and appealing. *So beautiful. So ...*

Suddenly Michael leapt, knocking Amanda to the ground.

Julian's head cleared.

She was only down an instant before she leapt to her feet, growling and hissing at Michael. "How dare you! How *dare* you!" She lunged, moving so fast that Michael couldn't avoid her. She yanked him close, opened her mouth, showing fangs that belonged on a wolf, not a vampire.

"Amanda, my love ..." Julian said.

She turned, eyes on fire, fangs dripping long silvery ribbons of saliva. She shoved Michael away. "Julie ..."

Julian swung the scythe.

The blade sliced through the side of her neck, slashing flesh, snapping bone. Her head fell sideways, still attached by skin and tendon.

She staggered back, a grotesquerie, her head resting upside down on her shoulder as blood geysered from her neck. Her eyes never left his as her mouth moved wordlessly. He heard the message in his mind: *But you love me, Julie! Damn you! You love me!*

Everything moved in slow motion. Michael was up, his face feral with rage and bloodlust. He grabbed Amanda's head by the hair and tore it from her body. She fell, but the head was still alive, still staring at Julian. The blazing black eyes began to dull as the lips clearly formed the words, "You love me."

Slowly, her thoughts faded from Julian's awareness.

He stared at the head of the woman he had sought for eons. He had loved her lifetime after lifetime, and had not known why the attraction had never abated. Until now. *Incendarius.* He had been bewitched by the creature for millennia and had never even suspected.

Instead of buoying relief, deep sadness weighted him. He felt lost and wondered if there really was such a thing as love.

∽

DIEGO WATCHED Julian standing over the body, reading the slump of his shoulders, the cast of his face, and knew a certain magic had died for the Trueborn. Then Michael Ward approached, wearing a fearsome grin as he held the severed head of Incendarius up for all to see. There was a smattering of applause from the few who remained in the temple. It silenced as Julian - the new king - joined them.

Crowds mobbed the exits as they returned to the temple, cheering.

Diego watched Julian touch Michael's arm. The man looked at Julian, glanced back to the severed head, then at Julian once more. His face changed then, the maniacal grin fading, his eyes growing somber, the monster within him retreating. "I-" he looked at the head of Incendarius, then lowered his arm. Diego gently took the burden from him.

"I-" Michael began as their friends approached. Even Natasha was on her feet, supported by her sisters. Julian became aware of them all, yet looked as if he had lost his entire world.

"Michael," Julian murmured. "Thank you." He took Natasha's arm and she leaned against him, then he spoke to the warriors. "Thank you. Without you, all would have been lost."

Then Julian turned to face the returning spectators. "Incendarius is dead. This is a lesson you must all remember and continue to teach. Incendarius is no legend. It is real, and there may be more. Never forget." He nodded to Diego.

The priest lifted the severed head high, ignoring the blood dripping on his vestments.

Julian raised his voice. "The queen is dead!"

And before the crowd could cheer, Diego cried out, "Long live the King!"

The audience roared.

85
ENDINGS AND BEGINNINGS

When the temple emptied, Diego took the Darling girls as well as Julian, Michael, Winter, Chynna, Erin, Norman, and Arnie, to his inner chambers to shower and change into fresh clothing. Natasha was already able to move on her own, and Arnie, though still uncomfortable, was recovering quickly from the injection of holy water. The hybrids now sat together, talking, drinking blood, recuperating from the conflict. All seemed to be in a mild state of shock - just as Diego himself was.

But Julian ... Diego watched his Maker and old friend as he stood and stared at a painting of Machu Picchu he'd commissioned a few years ago. Silently, he joined him.

After a moment, Julian spoke. "The good old days?" He wore a faint sad smile.

"Were they?" Diego paused. "I have been happier as a vampire than I ever was in the human world."

Julian nodded. "Do you ever miss the sunlight?"

"On occasion."

"As a Trueborn, I am able to enjoy it as long as I am protected. Sunlight is beautiful, but like many beautiful things, it is also deadly."

"I am sorry," Diego said, laying his hand on Julian's arm.

"As am I." The Trueborn searched his eyes. "Do you know that, even though I have lived many millennia, I feel as though I lost my naiveté tonight? As if the last vestiges of childhood have been ripped from me?"

"How does that make you feel?"

"I'm not sure." Julian pondered. "I was devastated for all of a quarter of an hour, but already, I'm wondering what will come of it."

"You are king, now."

Julian eyed him. "Indeed. Your point being?"

"Will you rule?"

"No. I have no desire to rule." He laid his hand on Diego's shoulder. "Whether they call me king or prince, it makes no difference."

"True, but now that they know you are among us, our people will expect more."

Julian looked tired, his eyes old. "Then I shall name you regent to act in my stead. I will not be a ruler. I will not become-"

"Your father?"

Julian didn't reply.

"I understand, my friend, and will do as you ask as long as you are willing to advise me."

"That is acceptable." Julian's smile, though still faint, was real this time. "I should not care to lose touch with you again. You are my oldest friend."

Diego, honored, smiled back. "What will you do now?"

"I will go back to my veinery and my vineyards. I find peace there." He paused. "I hope you will visit. You are always welcome."

"I shall, but may I make a suggestion?"

"Of course."

"Stay on here for a bit, as my guest. There is plenty of room."

"I ..."

"If I am to act in your stead, I need your advice. There are things to be done, to be decided, and actions to put into place now that you are known. Your staying would help me tremendously."

Julian looked disinclined.

"There is history to be set down," Diego added, knowing what the

Trueborn loved most. "Modern history." He smiled. "Relatively speaking."

"Well." Julian's eyes gleamed. "Perhaps I could stay on a while. But I must return to the hotel now with my friends. We also have much to discuss. At sunset, I shall return and you and I will speak more."

"Thank you." Diego looked toward the other vampires. "You are a good friend to them."

"As they are to me."

"And they need you tonight. Especially that one." He nodded toward Michael Ward, who sat alone in a dark corner.

"Indeed."

86
AT THE INN

Back at the Icehouse Inn, Natasha reclined on the couch, drinking deeply of a rich and nourishing AB Neg. Lucy and Ivy hovered, keeping her glass topped off, acting like mother hens rather than troublemakers. Natasha smiled to herself, thinking that she almost missed their misbehaving ways. *Almost, but not quite.*

Michael and Julian, along with Winter, Chynna, and Arnie, plus the baby vamps Erin and Norman, sat across the room at a table, talking and drinking. Natasha saw Chynna put an arm around Erin's shoulders and hug her close. The girl lay her head against Chynna's shoulder the way the twins had done to Natasha when she'd read to them as children, long before their transformation. Watching Erin do the same with Chynna made her happy. The young girl was in great need of comfort and understanding because when her Maker was hurt, she had experienced a vampiric rage. It was a scary thing for any vampire, mature or baby, to find out what she or he was truly capable of when roused.

"More blood?" Ivy asked, bottle in hand. Lucy hovered beside her.

"I'm fine for now."

"Nonsense." Her sister refilled the half empty glass. "Drink up."

Lucy grinned. "Tasha, you are the baddest ass fighter I've ever seen! You're my hero!"

Ivy nodded, the familiar mischievous spark lighting in her eye. "Mine, too!"

∽

MICHAEL WAS EXHAUSTED and he could tell the others were as well. He glanced at Natasha and felt a stab of regret. *Getting involved again was a bad idea.* But being with her had been wonderful. Michael resented that double-edged sword, resented the way such great pleasure so quickly led to destruction.

He sensed eyes upon him and realized that Julian was watching him. There was something too inquisitive in the Trueborn's gaze as he rose fluidly from his chair and made his way to Michael.

"Would you care to join me for a drink on the balcony?"

"Of course."

The night air was cool and fresh and on it rode the scents of pine and fir. It was silent, and only a few lights glittered in the town below as Michael rested his arms on the railing and stared down.

"I am concerned for you, Michael." Julian's voice seemed to drift on the breeze and though he spoke gently, the words had jagged edges that made Michael wish he'd stayed in the room. He closed his eyes and sipped his blood.

"I have never seen one as ferocious as you were earlier."

Michael shrugged. "I did what needed to be done."

"Indeed." Julian was beside him now, his slender pale fingers grasping a goblet. The blood within it appeared black in the night.

"We were all ferocious tonight, Julian."

After a brief silence, Julian spoke. "I am not concerned by your deeds so much as the hunger, the lust, with which they were executed."

Michael looked at him, feeling his defenses beginning to rise.

Julian offered a thin smile. "I am not criticizing you, Michael. You saved us all tonight. I am merely pointing out what I saw."

Michael turned to face the room, watching the others through the glass doors. "And what did you see, Julian?"

"I saw a man gone mad with bloodlust." He paused. "Bloodlust that may have been reignited by his passion for a woman." He, too, stared at the others within the room, and Michael felt sure that Julian's eyes lit now on Natasha. "Indeed, if not for that hunger and lust, Incendarius may well have overcome us."

Michael sipped slowly.

"I have felt as you do and have fought my own desires to destroy. It is true that if you let yourself feel intense love, you may also feel other things with similar intensity. It is intrinsic to our vampiric nature. While one does not preclude the other, you can love without those other emotions running amok. You, Michael, have put yourself on a very strict path to enlightenment and understanding. I commend you for that, but know that there are other ways."

"Julian. You don't understand."

"Ah, but I do. You underestimate my history."

"Perhaps, but I am an addict - I always have been - and what I did with Natasha ... it cannot happen again."

"But that is what I am trying to tell you, Michael. You do not have to remain celibate for all eternity. With practice-"

"Practice? I have been practicing for decades, Julian."

"Decades are nothing."

Michael watched as Winter answered a phone call. "I am only interested now in reeling my urges back in, Julian. I cannot think beyond that."

Julian nodded. "When you are ready, I can help you."

Michael watched with growing concern as Winter hung up the phone. There was something in his friend's posture that told him the news hadn't been good. "Something is wrong," Michael told Julian. "I must go talk to-"

Just then, Winter headed to the door and stepped onto the balcony. "We've got a problem, Boss."

"What is it?"

Winter hesitated. "Gretchen VanTreese. There's reason to believe that she's returned to Crimson Cove."

Michael's stomach folded in on itself. "Impossible."

Winter's face was stony. "I hope so, Boss."

※

Natasha watched Michael, a pain in her heart. He was with Julian and she hoped the Trueborn was helping him cope with his rage. After she'd been injured, she had watched Michael's fury and it had frightened her; Erin's rage was simple in comparison. Michael had turned into a wild beast, growling and snarling.

I should not have tempted him. I should not have told him I could help him, either.

But he knew I couldn't. It was his decision. And my foolishness.

Guilt needled at her.

When Winter joined them on the balcony, Michael immediately began radiating authority instead of despair. Natasha admired that; he inspired her.

Something was going on. She sat forward, intending to stand, but gasped at the pain in her ribs. It had lessened, but it would take a day to heal.

"Tasha!" cried Lucy. "Stay still. I'll fix your pillow."

"No, I need to get up."

"No, you-"

"Yes, I do. I'm just going to talk to Michael."

Lucy and Ivy flanked her and she let them, but stopped them short at the door. Michael opened the slider and took her arm as Winter and Julian went inside.

"Michael, we have to talk."

"We do. I-"

"Me first."

He took her hands. "I'm listening."

"I know now I was wrong to encourage our reunion."

"No, I-"

She touched her finger to his lips. "Hush. Just listen. I understand now. I always want to be your friend, but we cannot, well ... I will respect your celibacy from now on. Never question that."

He kissed her forehead. "Thank you. Someday, perhaps, things will change." His smile was small, wistful. "Julian says it's possible. But until then, know that I value your friendship and that I do love you. Never question that."

She wanted to cry, but instead held her best friend's hand and stared out at the twinkling stars.

87
BEYOND THE CHAOS

From beyond the chaos, Neil Trinsky had watched the carnage, knowing how close he'd come to his own end. Though terrified and still in great pain, he was also aroused; there was something incredibly sexy about having come so close to death. All the blood was sexy, too. He knew he should've run when he'd gotten away from Bat-Tat, but he hadn't been able to resist sticking around - if only for a few minutes - to see what was going to happen next.

He was glad he had, but now, it was time to move on.

As he made his way through the darkened woods, he knew that although he himself was a vampire, his days of hunting the undead were far from over. If anything, his hatred for the dirty bloodsuckers had grown. He told himself it was because they'd beheaded his Maker, but avenging her was just an excuse. He knew she was no deity.

There are no deities.

The fact was this: Neil Trinsky was born to kill vampires - and even if he was one of the filthy fuckers himself, it was exactly what he was going to do.

He couldn't go back to Candle Bay, but there were plenty of other places that could use his extermination services. *Maybe I'll go check out Crimson Cove ...*

88

A TRAVELIN' MAN

Coastal Eddie slipped his shades on. Eternity's air was chill and bright this morning. He and Lois, Renny on a leash, stood on the sidewalk with Zach Tully and Harlan King. All four were nursing coffee.

"So there's been no sign of Neil?" Lois asked once more.

"Not so far," Tully said. "I'll let you know if we hear anything. Meanwhile, I'd advise you to be cautious and change your locks." He smiled. "Let me know if he turns up. He's wanted for murder. Rest assured, he'll be put away for a long time."

"Thanks, Sheriff," said Lois. "I hate to admit it, but that's a relief."

Eddie cleared his throat. "Anything happen last night?"

Tully glanced at Harlan, whose smile was his version of a poker face. The V-Sec team had called Harlan around one a.m. to warn him that something was going on in the Eternal City and to keep everything locked up tight. Tully had received the same call, ending up with a companion, V-Sec officer Matthew Moon, to patrol with last night. The pair had seen nothing unusual but they'd discovered a mutual interest in basketball. By the end of the shift, Tully was ready to drop and probably would have if Harlan hadn't brewed him up a Thermos of java so strong that it practically got up and danced.

"Sheriff?" Eddie asked.

"What?"

"Did anything happen last night?"

"Nothing that I know of - why do you ask?"

"Eh." Eddie shook his head. "I couldn't sleep. Nightmares." He sipped coffee. "Damned vampires are getting to me, I guess."

Tully chuckled. "They'll do that." He paused. "You two heading down the mountain today?"

"We are." Lois smiled.

"We figure we've earned a break so we'll be spending a couple nights in San Francisco. I want to go back out to Alcatraz and maybe show Lois the old Sutro Bath ruins." Eddie wagged his brows. "They're supposed to be haunted, you know."

"And I want to go to Haight Street," Lois added.

"She wants to check out my roots." Eddie laughed.

"Well, you two enjoy yourselves. Have a good drive. And be careful. I'll be in touch."

"Thanks, Sheriff." Lois smiled. "It was good to meet you both."

Tully stood with Harlan, watching until the unlikely couple disappeared toward Hotel Circle. "I'm damned glad that the vampires don't crown a new king every day," Harlan said.

"You and me, both. The vamps stayed out celebrating in the streets so late that I thought they'd end up frying in the sun." Tully grinned. "That'd be bad for business, right?"

Harlan chuckled. "They know better. Vampires are some of the canniest business people around."

Tully cleared his throat. "So ... who's this new king?"

"An old friend, actually. I'll introduce you some time. You'll like him."

"You don't say." Tully sipped coffee.

"Yep. I just baked some fresh jelly donuts. You in?"

Tully grinned. "Just try and keep me out."

ALSO BY TAMARA THORNE & ALISTAIR CROSS

Mother

A Girl's Worst Nightmare is Her Mother ...

Priscilla Martin. She's the diva of Morning Glory Circle and a driving force in the quaint California town of Snapdragon. Overseer of garage sales and neighborhood Christmas decorations, she is widely admired. But few people know the real woman behind the perfectly coiffed hair and Opium perfume.

Family is Forever. And Ever and Ever ...

No one escapes Prissy's watchful eye. No one that is, except her son, who committed suicide many years ago, and her daughter, Claire, who left home more than a decade past and hasn't spoken to her since. But now, Priscilla's daughter and son-in-law have fallen on hard times. Expecting their first child, the couple is forced to move back ... And Prissy is there to welcome them home with open arms ... and to reclaim her broken family.

The Past Isn't Always as Bad as You Remember. Sometimes it's Worse ...

Claire has terrible memories of her mother, but now it seems Priscilla has mended her ways. When a cache of vile family secrets is uncovered, Claire struggles to determine fact from fiction, and her husband, Jason, begins to wonder who the monster really is. Lives are in danger - and Claire and Jason must face a horrifying truth ... a truth that may destroy them ... and will forever change their definition of "Mother."

The Cliffhouse Haunting

When the Blue Lady Walks...

Since 1887, Cliffhouse Lodge has been famous for its luxurious accommodations, fine dining ... and its ghosts. Overlooking Blue Lady Lake, nestled among tall pines, Cliffhouse has just been renovated by its owners, Teddy and Adam Bellamy, and their daughter, Sara.

Cliffhouse has not always been a place of rest and respite, though. Over the years it has served many vices, from rum-running to prostitution - and although the cat houses have been replaced by a miniature golf course and carousel, Cliffhouse retains its dark history; darkest during the Roaring Twenties, when a serial killer called the Bodice Ripper terrorized the town, and a phantom, the Blue Lady, was said to walk when murder was imminent.

Death Walks With Her...

Now, there's a new killer on the loose, and the Blue Lady sightings have returned. The Bellamys are losing maids, and guests are being tormented by disembodied whispers, wet phantom footprints, and the blood-chilling shrieks of mad laughter that echo through the halls of Cliffhouse in the dead of night.

The little mountain town of Cliffside is the perfect hunting ground for a serial killer... and the Blue Lady. Police Chief Jackson Ballou has bodies piling up, and between the murders and the mysteries, he can hardly pursue his romance with Polly Owen. And Sara Bellamy may lose her true love before they even have their first kiss.

The Ghosts of Ravencrest

Book 1 in The Ravencrest Saga

Darkness Never Dies...

Ravencrest Manor has always been part of the family. The ancestral home of the Mannings, Ravencrest's walls have been witness to generations of unimaginable scandal, horror, and depravity. Imported stone by stone from England to northern California in the early 1800s, the manor now houses widower Eric Manning, his children, and his staff. Ravencrest stands alone, holding its memories and ghosts close to its dark heart, casting long, black shadows across its grand lawns, through the surrounding forests, and over the picturesque town of Devilswood, below.

Dare to Cross the Threshold...

Ravencrest Manor is the most beautiful thing new governess, Belinda Moorland, has ever seen, but as she learns more about its tangled past of romance and terror, she realizes that beauty has a dark side. Ravencrest is built on secrets, and its inhabitants seem to be keeping plenty of their own - from the handsome English butler, Grant Phister, to the power-mad administrator, Mrs. Heller, to Eric Manning himself, who watches her with dark, fathomless eyes. But Belinda soon realizes that the living who dwell in Ravencrest have nothing on the other inhabitants - the ones who walk the darkened halls by night ... the ones who enter her dreams ... the ones who are watching ... and waiting ...

Welcome to Ravencrest ...

Who is the man digging in the garden beyond Belinda's bedroom window? Who - or what - is watching her from the vents? From ghostly screams and the clutching bony fingers of death in the indoor pool, to the trio of gliding nuns in the east wing who come at Belinda with black blazing eyes, to the beckoning little girl in the red dress who died more than two centuries ago, Belinda is thrust into a world of waking nightmares where there is no distinction between the living and the dead, and there are no limits to the horrors that await. Witchcraft is afoot at Ravencrest and as unspeakable terrors begin to unfold, Belinda realizes that her beautiful new home is a keeper of tragedy, a collector of souls. And it wants to add her to its collection ...

The Witches of Ravencrest

Book 2 in the Ravencrest Saga

Dark and Unnatural Powers

In a remote part of California just above the coastal town of Devilswood, Ravencrest Manor, imported stone-by-stone from England more than two centuries ago, looms tall and terrifying, gathering its dark and unnatural powers, and drawing those it wants as its own.

Murder Lurks in the Shadows

Governess Belinda Moorland has settled into life at Ravencrest and, as summer gives way to autumn, romance is in the air. She and multi-millionaire Eric Manning are falling in love ... but powerful forces will stop at nothing to keep them apart. And as the annual Harvest Ball is set to begin, evil abounds at Ravencrest. Murder lurks in the shadows, evil spirits freely roam the halls, a phantom baby cries, signaling a death in the mansion, and in the notoriously haunted east wing, three blood-soaked nuns, Sisters Faith, Hope, and Charity, tend to the demented needs of a maid gone mad.

Vengeful Spirits

Ravencrest has come to life. In the gardens below, granite statues dance by moonlight, and a scarecrow goes on a killing rampage, collecting a gruesome assortment of body parts from unwilling donors ... But Belinda's greatest danger is the vengeful spirit of Rebecca Dane. Once the mistress of Ravencrest, Rebecca Dane has a centuries-old axe to grind with the powerful witch, Cordelia Heller - and Belinda becomes her weapon of choice.

Books by Alistair Cross

The Crimson Corset

Welcome to Crimson Cove

Sheltered by ancient redwoods, nestled in mountains overlooking the California coast, the cozy village of Crimson Cove has it all: sophisticated retreats, fine dining, a beautiful lake, and a notorious nightclub, The Crimson Corset. It seems like a perfect place to relax and get close to nature. But not everything in Crimson Cove is natural.

When Cade Colter moves to town to live with his older brother, he expects it to be peaceful to the point of boredom. But he quickly learns that after the sun sets and the fog rolls in, the little tourist town takes on a whole new kind of life - and death.

Darkness at the Edge of Town

Renowned for its wild parties and history of debauchery, The Crimson Corset looms on the edge of town, inviting patrons to sate their most depraved desires and slake their darkest thirsts. Proprietor Gretchen VanTreese has waited centuries to annihilate the Old World vampires on the other side of town and create a new race - a race that she alone will rule. When she realizes Cade Colter has the key that will unlock her plan, she begins laying an elaborate trap that will put everyone around him in mortal danger.

Blood Wars

The streets are running red with blood, and as violence and murder ravage the night, Cade must face the darkest forces inside himself, perhaps even abandon his own humanity, in order to protect what he loves.

Sleep, Savannah, Sleep

The Dead Don't Always Rest in Peace

Jason Crandall, recently widowed, is left to raise his young daughter and rebellious teenage son on his own - and the old Victorian in Shadow Springs seems like the perfect place for them to start over. But the cracks in Jason's new world begin to show when he meets Savannah Sturgess, a beautiful socialite who has half the men in town dancing on tangled strings.

Haunting Visions

When she goes missing, secrets begin to surface, and Jason becomes ensnared in a dangerous web that leads to murder - and he becomes a likely suspect. But who has the answers that will prove his innocence? The jealous husband who's hell-bent on destroying him? The local sheriff with an incriminating secret? The blind old woman in the house next door who seems to watch him from the windows? Or perhaps the answers lie in the haunting visions and dreams that have recently begun to consume him.

Secrets from Beyond

Or maybe, Savannah herself is trying to tell him that things aren't always as they seem - and that sometimes, the dead don't rest in peace.

The Angel Alejandro

Angel or Demon?

Naive and heart-stoppingly handsome, he calls himself Alejandro, and Madison O'Riley has no clue what to do with him. As they set out to recover his lost identity, Madison realizes the mysterious man who saved her life harbors deep, otherworldly secrets that will put her in grave danger.

The Devil is in the Details

Gremory Jones has something for everyone, and for a price, he's willing to make a deal. Walking the streets in top hat and trench coat, he tempts the citizens with mysterious wares from his shiny black briefcase. But buyer beware: All sales are final - and fatal.

A Scorching New Terror Has Come to Town

The townspeople are changing in appalling ways and it's up to Madison - with the help of a psychic, a local priest, and the new chief of police - to help Alejandro unlock his forgotten powers before an unspeakable evil tears apart the fabric of existence ... and costs them their very souls.

The Book of Strange Persuasions

In 2005, before the publication of his bestselling novels, Alistair Cross penned hundreds of poems which he sometimes shared on various social media platforms. His poetry has earned him appearances on radio talk shows around the world and attracted a large and loyal readership.

Passion and Seduction

Divided into four parts that are devoted to such subjects as love and loss, passion and seduction, and nightmares and horrors, The Book of Strange

Persuasions is a striking collection that features some of his most insightful, sensual, and poignant works.

Books by Tamara Thorne

Candle Bay

Shrouded in fog on a hillside high above an isolated California coastal town, The Candle Bay Hotel and Spa has been restored to its former glory after decades of neglect. Thanks to its new owners, the Darlings, the opulent inn is once again filled with prosperous guests. But its seemingly all-American hosts hide a chilling, age-old family secret.

Forever Undead

Lured to the picturesque spot, assistant concierge Amanda Pearce is mesmerized by her surroundings--and her seductive new boss, Stephen Darling. But her employers' eccentric ways and suspicious blood splatters in the hotel fill her with trepidation. Little does Amanda know that not only are the Darlings vampires, but that a murderous vampire vendetta is about to begin--and she will be caught in the middle. For as the feud unfolds and her feelings for Stephen deepen, Amanda must face the greatest decision of her life: to die, or join the forever undead.

Eternity

Welcome to Eternity

A little bit of Hell on Earth ...

When Zach Tully leaves Los Angeles to take over as sheriff of Eternity, a tiny mountain town in northern California, he's expecting to find peace and quiet in his own private Mayberry. But he's in for a surprise. Curmudgeonly Mayor Abbott is a ringer for long-missing writer Ambrose Bierce. There are two Elvises in town, a shirtless Jim Morrison, and a woman who has more than a passing resemblance to Amelia Earhart. And that's only the beginning.

Mysterious Legends

Eternity is the sort of charming spot tourists flock to every summer and leave every fall when the heavy snows render it an isolated ghost town. Tourists and New Agers all talk about the strange energy coming from Eternity's greatest attraction: a mountain called Icehouse, replete with legends of Bigfoot, UFOs, Ascended Masters, and more. But the locals talk about something else.

Grisly Murders

The seemingly quiet town is plagued by strange deaths, grisly murders, and unspeakable mutilations, all the work of a serial killer the locals insist is Jack the Ripper. And they want Zach Tully to stop him.

Undying Evil

Now, as the tourists leave and the first snow starts to fall, terror grips Eternity as an undying evil begins its hunt once again ...

Haunted

Murders and Madness

Its violent, sordid past is what draws bestselling author David Masters to the infamous Victorian mansion called Baudey House. Its shrouded history of madness and murder is just the inspiration he needs to write his ultimate masterpiece of horror. But what waits for David and his sixteen-year-old daughter, Amber, at Baudey House, is more terrifying than any legend...

Seduction

First comes the sultry hint of jasmine...followed by the foul stench of decay. It is the dead, seducing the living, in an age-old ritual of perverted desire and unholy blood lust. For David and Amber, an unspeakable possession has begun...

Moonfall

Moonfall, the picturesque town nestled in the mountains of southern California, is a quaint hamlet of antique stores, cider mills, and pie shops, and Apple Heaven, run by the dedicated nuns of St. Gertrude's Home for Girls, is the most popular destination of all. As autumn fills the air, the townspeople prepare for the Halloween Haunt, Moonfall's most popular tourist attraction. Even a series of unsolved deaths over the years hasn't dimmed Moonfall's enthusiasm for the holiday.

Horrible Death

Now, orphan Sara Hawthorne returns to teach in the hallowed halls of St. Gertrude's where, twelve years before, her best friend died a horrible death. In Sara's old room, distant voices echo in the dark and the tormented cries of children shatter the moon-kissed night.

Hellish Secret

But that's just the beginning. For Sara Hawthorne is about to uncover St.

Gertrude's hellish secret...a secret she may well carry with her to the grave.

Bad Things

The Piper clan emigrated from Scotland and founded the town of Santo Verde, California. The Gothic Victorian estate built there has housed the family for generations, and has also become home to an ancient evil forever linked to the Piper name...

Tiny Mischievous Demons

As a boy, Rick Piper discovered he had "the sight." It was supposed to be a family myth, but Rick could see the greenjacks--the tiny mischievous demons who taunted him throughout his childhood--and who stole the soul of his twin brother Robin one Halloween night.

Vicious Torment

Now a widower with two children of his own, Rick has returned home to build a new life. He wants to believe the greenjacks don't exist, that they were a figment of his own childish fears and the vicious torment he suffered at the hands of his brother. But he can still see and hear them, and they haven't forgotten that Rick escaped them so long ago. And this time, they don't just want Rick. This time they want his children ...

The Forgotten

The Past ...

Will Banning survived a childhood so rough, his mind has blocked it out almost entirely--especially the horrific day his brother Michael died, a memory that flickers on the edge of his consciousness as if from a dream.

Isn't Gone ...

Now, as a successful psychologist, Will helps others dispel the fears the past can conjure. But he has no explanation for the increasingly bizarre paranoia affecting the inhabitants of Caledonia, California, many of whom claim to see terrifying visions and hear ominous voices. . .voices that tell them to do unspeakable things ...

It's Deadly

As madness and murderous impulses grip the coastal town, Will is compelled to confront his greatest fear and unlock the terrifying secret of his own past in a place where evil isn't just a memory. . .it's alive and waiting to strike ...

Gertrude's hellish secret...a secret she may well carry with her to the grave.

Bad Things

The Piper clan emigrated from Scotland and founded the town of Santo Verde, California. The Gothic Victorian estate built there has housed the family for generations, and has also become home to an ancient evil forever linked to the Piper name...

Tiny Mischievous Demons

As a boy, Rick Piper discovered he had "the sight." It was supposed to be a family myth, but Rick could see the greenjacks--the tiny mischievous demons who taunted him throughout his childhood--and who stole the soul of his twin brother Robin one Halloween night.

Vicious Torment

Now a widower with two children of his own, Rick has returned home to build a new life. He wants to believe the greenjacks don't exist, that they were a figment of his own childish fears and the vicious torment he suffered at the hands of his brother. But he can still see and hear them, and they haven't forgotten that Rick escaped them so long ago. And this time, they don't just want Rick. This time they want his children ...

The Forgotten

The Past ...

Will Banning survived a childhood so rough, his mind has blocked it out almost entirely--especially the horrific day his brother Michael died, a memory that flickers on the edge of his consciousness as if from a dream.

Isn't Gone ...

Now, as a successful psychologist, Will helps others dispel the fears the past can conjure. But he has no explanation for the increasingly bizarre paranoia affecting the inhabitants of Caledonia, California, many of whom claim to see terrifying visions and hear ominous voices...voices that tell them to do unspeakable things ...

It's Deadly

As madness and murderous impulses grip the coastal town, Will is compelled to confront his greatest fear and unlock the terrifying secret of his own past in a place where evil isn't just a memory...it's alive and waiting to strike ...

The seemingly quiet town is plagued by strange deaths, grisly murders, and unspeakable mutilations, all the work of a serial killer the locals insist is Jack the Ripper. And they want Zach Tully to stop him.

Undying Evil

Now, as the tourists leave and the first snow starts to fall, terror grips Eternity as an undying evil begins its hunt once again ...

Haunted

Murders and Madness

Its violent, sordid past is what draws bestselling author David Masters to the infamous Victorian mansion called Baudey House. Its shrouded history of madness and murder is just the inspiration he needs to write his ultimate masterpiece of horror. But what waits for David and his sixteen-year-old daughter, Amber, at Baudey House, is more terrifying than any legend...

Seduction

First comes the sultry hint of jasmine...followed by the foul stench of decay. It is the dead, seducing the living, in an age-old ritual of perverted desire and unholy blood lust. For David and Amber, an unspeakable possession has begun...

Moonfall

Moonfall, the picturesque town nestled in the mountains of southern California, is a quaint hamlet of antique stores, cider mills, and pie shops, and Apple Heaven, run by the dedicated nuns of St. Gertrude's Home for Girls, is the most popular destination of all. As autumn fills the air, the townspeople prepare for the Halloween Haunt, Moonfall's most popular tourist attraction. Even a series of unsolved deaths over the years hasn't dimmed Moonfall's enthusiasm for the holiday.

Horrible Death

Now, orphan Sara Hawthorne returns to teach in the hallowed halls of St. Gertrude's where, twelve years before, her best friend died a horrible death. In Sara's old room, distant voices echo in the dark and the tormented cries of children shatter the moon-kissed night.

Hellish Secret

But that's just the beginning. For Sara Hawthorne is about to uncover St.

Thunder Road

The California desert town of Madelyn boasts all sorts of attractions for visitors. Join the audience at the El Dorado Ranch for a Wild West show. Take a ride through the haunted mine at Madland Amusement Park. Scan the horizon for UFOs. Find religion with the Prophet's Apostles--and be prepared for the coming apocalypse.

Violent Destiny

Because the apocalypse has arrived in Madelyn. People are disappearing. Strange shapes and lights dart across the night sky. And a young man embraces a violent destiny--inspired by a serial killer whose reign of terror was buried years ago.

Final Confrontation

But each of these events is merely setting the stage for the final confrontation. A horror of catastrophic proportions is slouching toward Madelyn in the form of four horsemen--and they're picking up speed.

The Sorority

They are the envy of every young woman--and the fantasy of every young man. An elite sisterhood of Greenbriar University's best and brightest, their members are the most powerful girls on campus--and the most feared ...

Eve

She's the perfect pledge. A sweet, innocent, golden-haired cheerleader, Eve has so much to gain by joining Gamma Eta Pi--almost anything she desires. But only a select few can enter the sorority's inner circle--or submit to its code of blood, sacrifice, and sexual magic. Is Eve willing to pay the price?

Merilynn

Ever since childhood, Merilynn has had a sixth sense about things to come. She's blessed with uncanny powers of perception--and cursed with unspeakable visions of unholy terror. Things that corrupt the souls of women, and crush the hearts of men. Things that can drive a girl to murder, suicide, or worse ...

Samantha

Journalism major Sam Penrose is tough, tenacious--and too curious for her own good. She's determined to unearth the truth about the sorority. But the only way to expose this twisted sisterhood is from within ...

ABOUT THE AUTHORS

Tamara Thorne's first novel was published in 1991, and since then she has written many more, including international bestsellers *Haunted, Bad Things, Moonfall, Eternity* and *The Sorority*. A lifelong lover of ghost stories, she is currently working on several collaborations with Alistair Cross as well as an upcoming solo novel. Learn more about her at TamaraThorne.com

Alistair Cross grew up on horror novels and scary movies, and by the age of eight, began writing his own stories. First published in 2012, he has since co-authored *The Cliffhouse Haunting* and *Mother* with Tamara Thorne and is working on several other projects. His debut solo novel, *The Crimson Corset*, was an Amazon bestseller. Find out more about him at AlistairCross.com

In collaboration, Thorne and Cross are currently writing several novels, including the next volume in the continuing gothic series, *The Ravencrest Saga: Exorcism*. Their first novel, *The Cliffhouse Haunting*, was an immediate bestseller. Together, they also host the horror-themed radio show Thorne & Cross: Haunted Nights LIVE! which has featured such guests as Anne Rice, Laurell K. Hamilton, Christopher Moore, Chelsea Quinn Yarbro, Charlaine Harris, V.C. Andrews, Preston & Child, and Christopher Rice.

For book deals, updates, specials, exclusives, and upcoming guests on Thorne & Cross: Haunted Nights LIVE!, join our newsletter by visiting either of our websites.

CPSIA information can be obtained
at www.ICGtesting.com
Printed in the USA
LVHW082029020321
680270LV00046B/319

9 781986 422963